LOSING KYLER

USA TODAY & WSJ BESTSELLING AUTHOR
SIOBHAN DAVIS

Original paperback published by CreateSpace April 2017

This paperback edition © October 2023

ISBN-13: 978-1-959285-47-2

Edited by Kelly Hartigan www.editing.xterraweb.com

Cover design and logo by Shannon Passmore

www.shanoffdesigns.com

Cover imagery © depositphotos.com

Interior graphics © Robin Harper www.wickedbydesigncovers.com

Formatted by Ciara Turley using Vellum

Condemned to repeat the sins of the past...

Faye thought losing her parents was the most devastating thing to happen to her, but she was wrong. Her uncle's scandalous revelation has sent her into a tailspin, leaving her questioning her entire existence.

Everything she believed is built on a lie.

And the one person she shares a passionate, soul-deep connection with can't be there for her.

Faye and Ky can't be together. It's forbidden. Though they are determined to avoid replicating their parents' mistakes, caving to their feelings is as tempting as the apple in the Garden of Eden.

Ky had sworn off girls until Faye bulldozed her way into his life. Now, she's his whole world, and their forced separation is crushing him. Once his manipulative ex resurfaces—hell-bent on ruining the Kennedys—he'll do whatever it takes to protect his loved ones including turning his back on the one person he can't live without.

Then tragedy strikes and all bets are off.

But is it too late?

When Faye needs him and he isn't there for her, guilt and hurt threaten to obliterate their love. As they start to rebuild their fractured hearts, another sordid family secret is uncovered, and Faye worries Ky may be lost to her forever.

But can you truly lose someone if they don't want to be found?

THE KENNEDY BOYS
FAMILY TREE

James Kennedy	Alex Kennedy
FATHER	MOTHER

Kaden Kennedy	Keven Kennedy
20	19

Kyler Kennedy	Kalvin Kennedy
17	16

Keanu Kennedy	Keaton Kennedy	Kent Kennedy
15	15	15

Glossary of Irish Words and Phrases

All her Sundays have come at once » Gotten her heart's desire.

Arse » Butt

Bill » Check

Bedside locker » Nightstand

Bleedin'/Bloody » Damn

Boot » Trunk

Chancing his arm » Taking a risk in order to get something you want

Cooker » Stove

Cop on » Realize/Get it together/Figure out

Compel me to up sticks » To go and live in a different place

Do a bunk » Make a hurried or furtive departure or escape

Doolally » Crazy/Insane

Duvet » Comforter

Garda/Guard » Cop

Gawp » Gape

Get out! » No way!

Getting pissed » Getting drunk

Gob » Mouth

Gobshite » Stupid, foolish, or incompetent person

Gobsmacked » Flabbergasted

Grand » Fine

Gutted » Heartbroken

Happy out » Happy/fine

Hoover » Vacuum cleaner

Kitted out » Provide with equipment/clothing to suit a purpose

Knackered » Very tired/exhausted

Knickers » Panties

Lick arse » Ass licker

Mobile/Mobile phone » Cell

Mum » Mom

Press » Cupboard

Ride » Hot/Gorgeous

Ripping the piss » To joke or lie about something in a humorous manner

Runners » Sneakers

Smart arse » Smart ass

Snog-fest » Make-out session

Sponger » Someone who accepts things from others without giving anything in return; a moocher/mooch

Tarmac » Asphalt

Trousers » Pants/Dress Pants

Wanker » Jerk/Asshole

Wrecked » Very tired/exhausted

LOSING KYLER

Chapter One

The room spins. Everything fades into the background as his words rebound in my mind. I sway on my feet, stumbling as I lose my balance. Ky steadies me, holding me around the waist, even though he's struggling to stay upright too. My lungs constrict, flattening like pancakes, and I can't breathe properly. My breath snakes in and out in panicked spurts as my lungs desperately suck in air.

This cannot be happening.

I pinch my arm hard, praying I'm dreaming. That I'm going to wake up in a world where James's words and an awful new reality don't exist. Where the last five minutes is just a figment of my sick, overactive imagination.

My traumatized gaze bounces from Kyler to James and back again. Ky looks as shell-shocked as I am. His arm is still wrapped around my waist, and I want to reach out to him, to cling onto him, to show him he's not alone in his horror and grief, but I appear to have lost control of my body. My arms hang loosely at my sides, and I'm numb all over.

James's confession reverberates in my mind like the lyrics

of a catchy song that refuse to go away. You know, the type of cheesy, corny song you wouldn't dream of ever singing in public —not if you wanted to hold onto any shred of dignity—but it latches onto your mind, replaying on a continual loop in your head until you feel you're going insane?

I'm stuck in that place.

"You're my daughter. I'm your father."

The words repeat over and over, taunting me cruelly.

"What?" Kyler's cracked voice is barely a whisper, as he finally breaks the strained silence. Hearing his gravelly tone snaps me out of my trance. "What kind of sick joke is this?" he demands.

James folds his arms across his torso. "I wouldn't joke about something like this."

"I can't be your daughter," I choke out. "Then that would mean you and my mum ..." I trail off as the many implications of his admission ricochet through my brain.

"We were like you two," he admits quietly. He, at least, has the decency to look ashamed.

Kyler releases his hold on me, and I'm instantly bereaved. Peering up at him, I spot the conflicting emotions tearing across his face, mirroring how I feel on the inside.

"No!" I shriek, staggering back, getting all tangled up in the sheet. I drop to the ground with a thud.

Is this why Mum kept James's identity a secret from me?

Because she had an incestuous relationship with her brother and then got pregnant with me?

I can't even ... I can't process. Emotions clutter my head, and I can't make sense of anything. Nausea builds quickly at the back of my throat, and my stomach lurches violently. I fight with the sheet, kicking out, my arms thrashing about. Sobs start in earnest as I try to yank it off me. Ky and James stare at me as if in a daze. Finally extracting myself from the tangled linen, I start crawling toward the bathroom. "I'm going to be sick."

The nauseated feeling surges forward, and vomit swims up my throat. Climbing awkwardly to my feet, uncaring that I'm in my underwear, I dart to the en suite bathroom, arriving just in the nick of time. I crouch over the toilet bowl, heaving up the contents of my stomach until I have nothing left to expel. Silent tears pour down my cheeks as I try to grasp the magnitude of what's been revealed.

My initial instincts were right. I should've stayed as far away from this house, and this dysfunctional family, as possible. Should have run away the first chance I got. I sink to my knees, cradling my head in my hands as tears continue to pump out of my eyes.

This can't be happening.

It's as if I've stumbled into my own version of soap opera hell.

After a few minutes, I stand up, flush the toilet, and wash my mouth out with water in zombie mode. Snatching my robe from the back of the door, I wrap it firmly around me, although it does nothing to quell the violent tremors rocking my entire body.

Raised voices coming from the bedroom barely register. I can scarcely hear over the thrumming of blood in my ears and the frantic pounding of my heart. Resting my hands on the counter, I stare at my ashen reflection in the mirror. I look like I've seen a ghost. My startled eyes are glossy and red-rimmed from crying, and my skin has a grayish quality to it, as if someone has drained all the blood from my veins. As if all the color has been sucked out of my life.

The arguing accelerates outside, and I force myself to get a grip. Taking deep breaths, I walk on shaky limbs back into my bedroom. All conversation ceases mid-flow. James hovers uncertainly in the center of the room. Ky is on the floor, leaning against the wall, with his knees pulled in tight to his chest. He has put his jeans on, but his upper body is naked, and my eyes feast on him with familiarity.

Until I remember.

I can't look at him like that anymore.

I clamp a hand over my mouth as the repercussions of the situation sink in. Averting my eyes, I look away from him, pain slicing a line straight through my heart.

The gravity of the situation hits me like a bolt of lightning.

I've been conducting an illicit, incestuous affair this whole time, and I never knew it.

I nearly had sex with my half-brother.

And that's not actually the worst of it.

I love him.

God, I do. I love Kyler.

I'm in love with my brother.

I don't know how long the three of us stay there, mute and frozen in the same position. All locked in our torturous thoughts. Gradually, the mist is clearing, and my shock is giving away to anger and frustration.

I need answers, and I need them now.

I walk over to the bed and perch on the corner. "When did you find out about me?" I gulp. "That I was your ... daughter, and why didn't you tell me?" My voice is low and shaky.

James walks tentatively toward me, resting on the other side of the bed. He wets his lips. "When our attorney, Dan, gave me your papers and I spotted your date of birth, I suspected I might be your father. I've always wondered why your mother chose that particular moment in time to run away." He looks at me sheepishly. "We had only started our ... romantic relation-ship four months previously."

A strangled sound emits from Ky's mouth. "I can't listen to this." He buries his face in his hands.

No matter how repulsed I am—and believe me, I am grossed out to the max—I need to hear the truth. "I need to hear this. Go on," I encourage James.

"I knew it was wrong," he whispers. "But we'd been growing closer and closer since our parent's death, and I didn't have many friends, so my whole world revolved around Saoirse. I'd given up school to get a job so that I could support her, and she became the singular most important thing in my life."

He pauses, looking down at his hands. "I don't know exactly when my feelings changed, but suddenly I was looking at her, thinking about her, in ways I shouldn't. I tried to fight it. Genuinely, I did." He drills me with an earnest expression. "I didn't want to have those feelings for my sister, but I couldn't stop thinking about her like that. She was so beautiful, and she had this light inside her, like a glow that emanated from her very soul, so warm and pure and good. I couldn't help being drawn to her." Out of the corner of my eye, I spy Kyler shaking his head in incredulous disgust.

James draws an exaggerated breath. "Keeping my hands off her became a daily battle, but I didn't touch her. I learned to tolerate the agony, accepted the pain as my punishment, and I hoped that my feelings would go away in time." He rubs the back of his neck as air whooshes out of his lungs. "I didn't make the first move. She did. She kissed me, and every shred of self-control I had evaporated."

Ky jumps to his feet. "I can't hear any more."

"Don't go!" My frantic eyes meet his, tears welling up again as I plead with him. "I can't do this on my own. Please, Ky. Don't leave."

His anguished gaze locks on mine, and I know he yearns to comfort me in the same way I long to comfort him.

But we can't.

Having him here in the room is as much as I can ask of him. He nods slowly, returning to his spot on the floor.

I refocus on James. "I don't want to know the specifics—I can't deal with that now. What I want to know is when you discovered I was your daughter and why you didn't tell me."

He presses his knuckles to his forehead and sighs. "I had my suspicions, but I needed more than that, so I hired a private investigator to check into your father's background, and when he reported his findings, I knew." He knots his hands anxiously in his lap. "Your father *can't* be your biological father, Faye." He pauses, grappling for the right words, and the look on his face sends shivers through me. "Were you aware he had Kartagener's syndrome?"

"You mean the genetic respiratory condition he had?" I whisper. Panic and fear almost choke me.

"Yeah. But it's a little more complex than that." He scratches the line of stubble on his chin, and my stomach does a funny twist. "Your dad was infertile, Faye. He couldn't father children." His words linger in the air as I wrap my arms around my waist, desperately trying to maintain a semblance of composure.

"Mum always said it was her," I mumble as my brain starts shutting down. "That the reason I had no siblings was because she couldn't carry any more children, but that was obviously another lie."

In this moment, I hate my mother, and I'm mad as all hell that she isn't here for me to yell at. To demand she tell me the Goddamned truth and explain why she thought it was such a good idea to lie about virtually every facet of my life. My hands ball into fists at my sides, and I'm barely holding it together.

"I also discovered that he was working for a firm in Belfast at the time your mother told you she met him. He wasn't working locally, Faye. There's no way Saoirse could've met him in the way she described to you."

Liar! How could she do this to me!

I don't even know who I am anymore, and every memory I have of my parents is tarnished by the knowledge that it was a fabrication. That I was being lied to every single day of my life.

Why? Were they ever planning on telling me the truth?

Hopping up, enraged and upset, and struggling with a million other emotions, I sweep the contents of my dresser clear across the floor. Picking up the stool, I fling it across the room, watching as it smashes against the wall, the sounds of splintering wood adding to James's shocked gasps. Tears erupt from my eyes, and my cries fill the room as I slump to the ground, sobbing uncontrollably into my hands.

Ky kneels down, gently enclosing me in his arms from behind. His limbs are tense, his arms a little stiff, and I feel it too—the lure of his warmth and the call of his body battling against what we've been told, forcing us to maintain a certain distance.

"Kyler." James's voice contains clear warning.

"Shut up, Dad. She needs me, and I'm only consoling her. You're the one who fucked up here, not us. And you're a damn hypocrite to criticize us after all you've done."

Ky's statement is paradoxical in part, because the truth is more complex than that. *Is James the hypocrite or are we?* I don't know what to think anymore. I massage my temples, digging my fingers into my skin with brutal intensity, welcoming the pressure. *What is right and what is wrong?* I'm not sure I know anymore, and my jumbled brain is incapable of constructing logical thought patterns.

"At least put a shirt on." James tosses Ky's shirt across the room, and I attempt to refocus my mind.

I wipe my sleeve across my moist cheeks, twisting around to face James. Ky puts his shirt on, and then his arms encircle me again. I lean back against his chest, siphoning slivers of his strength. "When did you get proof and how?" I sniffle. "Don't you need my permission to test my DNA?"

James looks down at his feet, and crunching pain rattles through my skull. Ky curses under his breath. "You *have* proof she's your daughter, right? Because you wouldn't have dropped that bomb without being one hundred percent certain. Even you wouldn't be that stupid."

I idly tuck my hair behind my ears, staring wide-eyed at James as I wait for his reply.

"I don't have proof, yet," he finally admits, lifting his chin and staring at me. A sudden darkness rushes me, and I don't know whether to laugh or cry.

"What!" Ky explodes, getting to his feet and stalking toward his father. He yanks him up by the shirt. "You could've caused all this heartache for nothing! She might not be my sister!" He shoves him, and I scramble to my feet. "I hate you! You destroy everything good!"

I loop my arm through Ky's, dragging him back from James before he does something he'll regret.

"I don't need proof to know she's mine. It's only a formality, one I will attend to immediately." James's pained eyes meet mine. "Don't you agree? It all makes complete sense. That's why Saoirse ran away. Why she never wanted to see me again. That one time I spoke to her, she told me she was ashamed of what we did. That it was wrong and she went to mass daily to beg for forgiveness, to try and atone for her sins."

My face crumples as his words floor me. She deplored what she'd done, and I was a constant reminder of her guilty sin.

She was ashamed of *me*.

I look up at Ky, feeling more lost and alone than I've ever felt before. If it were possible, I'd swear my heart is ripping apart in my chest, and the most unimaginable pain is twisting my insides into knots.

The person I thought of as my mother was a fraud. A stranger. Someone who doesn't deserve to hold that title because no mother should treat her daughter like this. I thought I knew her, but now I know better. And my dad isn't even my dad. My entire life has been one big, fat whopper of a lie, and my parents betrayed me in the worst possible way.

I don't care if they believed they were protecting me.

You don't lie to the people you profess to love, no matter how painful the truth is.

This whole time, I'm staring at Ky—the one person I thought I had by my side. The one person who truly understands me, who has the power to make everything okay just by his mere presence.

But I've lost him too.

He's been cruelly taken from me just as I felt he was finally mine.

I have no one.

And I've never felt more alone or more jaded with this life.

Cold and numb, inside and out, I stare blankly ahead as stress overtakes my body. Lying down on my side, I curl into a fetal position in a feeble attempt to ward off the intense trembling racking my body.

James drags his hands through his hair. "Faye, I'm s—"

"Shut the fuck up, Dad!" Kyler yells, dropping to the floor. Carefully, he pulls me to him, cradling me in his arms. "You cannot make statements like that unless you know the truth. And you don't know, for sure, that you are Faye's father!"

"I fucking know, Kyler! I was the only one having sex with Saoirse during that time. There's no one else it could be."

I'm far too numb to even feel repulsed at that admission.

The bedroom door swings open, and Alex walks into the room, surveying the scene with a wild, tearstained expression. I peer up at her through the filmy layer coating my eyes. She walks over to James, standing right in front of him, staring at him as if he's an alien specimen. No one speaks and the air is fraught with tension.

Slowly, her fists clench into balls at her side. A distressed whimper slips out of her mouth as she stares at her husband with fresh loathing. Tears roll down her cheeks as she slaps him. Once, twice, repeatedly, her slaps becoming more manic as she lashes out in rage. "You ... you're a monster! You make me sick! This whole time, I've been married to a pervert, and I never knew. Get out! You ruin everything! Just get out," she screeches, slapping and shaking him.

I'm horror-struck, staring at both of them as if I'm a mannequin.

James just sits there, taking her abuse without complaint.

Ky gets up, carrying me to the bed, and setting me tenderly on top of the duvet. He walks to his mum and tries to pull her off James. Her arms are thrashing about as tears coast down her cheeks. "Mom. Stop. This isn't helping. Please," Ky beseeches. Alex is weeping and yelling as James remains dazed and motionless on the bed.

All manner of thoughts flit in and out of my mind, and I genuinely worry that I'm going insane. I tug my legs into my chest, leaning my chin on my knees as a new thought occurs to me. A new layer of confusion starts to take root. Something about all this still doesn't add up. "Hang on here a sec," I mutter, speaking to no one in particular.

Alex's sobbing has petered out and she looks utterly

deflated. Ky keeps a firm grip on her as he watches me. Standing up, I pace the floor, my mind churning a hundred miles an hour. I flip scenarios in my head, and it doesn't compute.

I grip James's shoulders, forcing him to eyeball me. "Something isn't right, and I know you're holding back. I can't believe I didn't figure this out before. I'm a few months older than Kyler so that explains how you could be my dad as well as his." The words devastate me as they leave my mouth.

My gaze dances between Alex and James. A look of sheer terror washes over Alex's face and she turns a deathly shade of pale. I swallow the new lump in my throat as I crouch down in front of James. "But there is no way you can be Kaden and Keven's dad if what you are saying is true."

"Holy. Fucking. Shit." Kyler loosens his hold on Alex, pitching on his heels and stumbling awkwardly to the floor.

Alex leans into the wall, barely holding herself upright. Her panicked eyes dart around the room, and she doubles over as if she's winded.

James rises, finally emerging from his trancelike state. "Top marks, Faye. You've discovered Alex's big secret. Guess she's not so saint-like either."

Chapter Two

"**M**om?" Ky peers up at Alex from his spot on the floor. "Is it true? They have a different dad?" Alex's ashen face contorts in pain as she slowly nods. "And they know, right? That's what the big falling out was about?" His chest visibly heaves as Alex bobs her head in confirmation again. Shock is quickly replaced with anger on Ky's face, and I don't blame him. Pushing off the ground, he unfurls his long limbs, standing to his full height. "Were you ever planning on telling the rest of us?" His words are suffused with righteous anger.

"We were going to tell you on your eighteenth birthday," Alex whispers, desperately clinging onto the wall for support. Keaton's joking about Jacob and company in *Twilight* doesn't seem so far off the mark now. Minus the paranormal aspects, of course.

"Didn't you stop to think that we had a right to know at the same time our brothers found out? Or what?" He throws his hands into the air. "You thought we wouldn't notice the constant tension when Kaden and Keven show up or the fact there's this big gulf between you?"

"There's never a right time to divulge something like that," James supplies.

"Or the fact that you were sleeping with your sister, right?" Alex snipes.

James pins her with a sharp look. "You are in no position to cast stones. We've both kept secrets."

"And that, ladies and gentlemen, is the crux of the issues in this family." Ky's tone is acerbic and he's making no apologies.

"Your mother wasn't prepared to delve into her past until you boys were mature enough to handle it, and I supported her decision," James admits, his mouth pulling into a grim line. "Parenting isn't something that comes with a handy step-by-step manual. We try our best, but we don't always get it right."

Ky snorts. "I'll say. Your parenting skills suck." He shoots a glare at his mom. "Both of you."

No one says anything and you could cut the tension in the air with a knife. Alex has a dazed look on her face as she stares off into space. Ky doesn't hide his troubled expression, and James showcases a world-weary look of resignation that's hardly new.

"Where's Kal?" I ask, breaking the prickly silence. "What's happening?"

James rubs a hand across the back of his neck, as if he's only just remembering his younger son's current predicament. "He's being arraigned in the morning, and they insisted on keeping him in lockup overnight."

"Oh, God." I'm distraught at the thought of my cousin spending the night in a jail cell. "Couldn't you get the charges dropped?"

"There was nothing we could do. A rape charge is a very

serious charge, and no amount of money can buy his way out of this one."

"Lana's gone," Ky says, striding to my bedside locker. He retrieves the white envelope Lana's father gave him. "They're all gone. John asked me to give you this." He hands the envelope to his mother.

Alex opens it with trembling fingers. "It's their formal resignation." She tosses the handwritten page onto the floor.

"He didn't do it." I grind down hard on my teeth. "I know he didn't but something went down between them. Lana was in bits, and she was clearly hurting."

"You need to stay out of this, both of you," James says, looking between us. "I know you want to help but the best way we can help your brother is by stepping back and letting the experts do their jobs. We need to let Dan and his legal team handle this." An involuntary yawn escapes my mouth. "It's late," James adds, squinting at his watch. "Nothing will get resolved while we're all tired. Get some sleep and we'll pick this conversation up again in the morning."

"The others deserve to know about Kaden and Keven. You can't expect me to lie to my brothers. I won't do it." Ky crosses his arms over his chest.

James emits a frustrated sigh. "I know, son, but you have to understand how hard this is for your mother." Alex stares vacantly ahead and I'm not even sure if she's aware of the conversation going on around her.

Ky's face softens a smidgeon as he rakes in the broken shell of a woman clinging unnaturally to the wall. "I do," Ky confirms, "but they have to be told." He glances at me. "However, I don't think you should say anything about Faye or your ... relationship with her mother. Not until the tests have been done, and only if they prove your suspicions. That shit isn't easy to hear."

"What do you want, Faye?" James turns his attention to me.

"Although I hate the thought of more secrets, I agree with Ky. We shouldn't say anything to the others about me unless we know for sure. The revelations about Kaden and Keven are going to knock them for six, and there's no point heaping more stress onto the pile. Not until we know if it's true." I look down at my feet as a hideous fluttery sensation fills the empty space in my chest. "But I'd like the tests done as soon as possible." I peer up at him. "I'm sick of all the lies. I need the truth."

James nods. "For what it's worth, I am truly sorry for all you've had to endure, Faye. And whatever the outcome, it doesn't change anything about your position in this family. You will always be one of us. You will always have a home here with us."

Alex shifts away from the wall, averting her eyes as she smooths a hand down the front of her skirt. "I'm going to bed." She exits the room without another word.

Ky moves to go after her but James shakes his head. "She needs some space. We all do. It's been a long night. Get some sleep and we'll talk again in a few hours."

They walk silently to the door. Ky casts a final glance my way and his grief-stricken expression matches mine. His eyes convey all the things his mouth can't say, and I have to work hard to maintain my composure while my insides crumple into a sodden, emotional mess. He steps out into the corridor, closing the door gently behind him.

I crawl into bed, pulling the covers snugly under my chin as I curl into a ball, shivering profusely under the thick duvet.

At some point, I manage to fall asleep, but it isn't a peaceful sleep, and I toss and turn fitfully the rest of the night.

Daybreak slips into my room through a gap in the gossamer curtains, and I wake up yawning. The events of the early hours swamp my mind. The temptation to bury my head under the pillow and ignore reality is hugely appealing, but I'd only be delaying the inevitable. I'd rather get all the breaking over and done with at once so I haul my exhausted body out of the bed and head into the bathroom.

After I'm showered and dressed, I make my way down to the kitchen. When I step into the lobby, James calls out to me. "We're up here, Faye."

That hideous fluttery feeling returns to my chest, and I climb the stairs on heavy limbs, as if I'm walking toward my doom. I step cautiously into the study, wiping my now sweaty palms down the sides of my jeans. Alex is dressed in her usual office attire, sitting stiff and uncomfortable in one of the velvet-lined chairs. Ky is standing in front of the fire with his back to me. His muscles are bunched and tense under his tank top. Low-hanging sweats drape over his firm, toned ass, and I have to deliberately force my gaze away. The urge to enfold him in my arms is strong.

No part of my brain has gotten with the program yet, and I still crave his touch. I missed him in my bed last night.

I sink into the other chair, sitting on my hands in a feeble attempt to thwart my longing. Sharp stabbing pains lacerate my heart like someone's hacking at it with a penknife.

James clears his throat. "I have spoken with Kaden and Keven, and they are en route here as we speak. We'll hold a brief family meeting after breakfast to update everyone on the situation with Kalvin. Once he is back home, we'll tell everyone the truth."

"Which truth?" Ky asks, turning around to face us. One look at his sleep-deprived face has my resolve crumbling. He looks as miserable as I feel. I wish I could wrap my arms around him, squirrel into his warmth and his scent, and allow him to ease the frayed edges of my sanity while I do the same for him.

I press my hands into the chair beneath me, stabbing my nails into the velvety layer as I swallow the choking lump in my throat.

"I'm going to tell your brothers the truth about Kaden and Keven's parentage," Alex confirms in a steady, assured tone of voice. "You were correct last night. They have a right to know, and this has gone on long enough. I'm fed up with all of the deception, of how this family is falling apart before my eyes and I can't seem to do anything to fix it. The truth needs to come out."

Breakfast is a dreadfully awkward affair, and I can barely eat a thing. The triplets are distraught at Kalvin's absence, but James and Alex deflect their questions, imploring them to save them for the family meeting.

I hop up when the bell rings, grateful to have an excuse to leave the stifling atmosphere. I open the door wide, expecting to see Kaden and Keven, and I'm thrown for a loop when I see Addison perched on the top step, decked out in virginal white, looking as innocent as an angel. "What do you want?" I growl.

"What I always want." She smiles sweetly. "Kyler." Her eyes narrow to slits. "He's mine."

"You're delusional." I roll my eyes. "I think he made his feelings perfectly clear last week. He wants nothing more to do with you, so run along now." I move to close the door, but she wedges her foot in the doorjamb and darts into the lobby uninvited. Footsteps resound behind me. I glare at her. She's got balls showing her face around here again and a right nerve pulling a stunt like that. If I didn't dislike her so intensely, I might actually admire her.

"I'll deal with this," Ky says, materializing at my side. His arm brushes briefly against mine, eliciting the usual flurry of tingles. "Go back into the kitchen."

"Grand. You take the trash out." While I'm not happy to be

dismissed, I'm close to my drama-saturation point, so I leave him to deal with his troublesome ex on his own.

He returns to the kitchen five minutes later with a customary blank expression on his face. However, his shoulders are stiff as boulders and his fists are clenched so tight they blanch white with the effort.

I catch his eye. "What?" I mouth.

Subtly, he shakes his head, and some unnamed sentiment flows between us. His eyes lock on mine across the table, and I'm incapable of looking away. It's as if the room around us has disappeared and he is all I see. A few locks of his hair have blown across his forehead and my fingers itch to run through the silky strands. My eyes sweep over the face that I know so well. Memories surge to the forefront of my mind, and I recall brushing the tips of my fingers along his stubbly jaw, rubbing my cheek against the velvety fluff on his cheeks, inhaling his distinctly masculine smell, my tongue darting out to taste the throbbing pulse in his neck.

I don't even realize that I'm crying or that everyone else has stopped talking until Keanu shakes my arm, bringing me back into the present. Every pair of eyes is focused on me and a faint blush creeps over my neck. I stare at Ky but he looks away, gazing at the floor, the walls, at anything, as long as it isn't me. James coughs. "Faye. Do you need a minute? We were about to get started."

I tilt my head forward, letting my long hair fall around my face like a shield. "No. I'm fine. Sorry." I bite down hard on my lip, relishing the pain, although it in no way compensates for the agonizing ache in my heart.

"Let's talk in the living room," Alex says, sliding off the bench.

I take a seat on the long couch alongside Keanu and Kent as the doorbell clangs for a second time. James returns with a sullen Kaden and Keven. Once everyone is settled, we all sit patiently, waiting for things to kick off.

James rests his forearms on his upper thighs as he leans forward. "Your brother is being arraigned today. He is being formally charged with rape and sexual assault. Bail will be set at the district court, and we'll be able to bring him home then. Dan is going to find the best criminal attorney to fight this, but the weeks and months ahead will not be easy." He looks to Alex, sitting beside him on the smaller two-seater couch, but she resolutely refuses to return his gaze.

"Is he going to go to jail, Dad?" Keaton asks, the strain evident in his voice. He can still barely look at me, and that only adds to my misery. Keaton only recently discovered the truth about Ky and me, and he couldn't have made his abhorrence any clearer.

We disgust him.

He sits as far away from me as possible, casting surreptitious glances at Ky and me whenever he thinks no one is watching. Nothing gets past his shrewd eyes, so I doubt it has gone unnoticed that something is going on. My little episode at breakfast has seen to that.

"Not if I can help it," James replies through gritted teeth.

"I say we hire a hit man to take Lana out," Kent pipes up, shrugging his shoulders like it's commonplace to suggest murder as a means of dealing with issues. "Problem solved."

James sighs. "That is hardly helpful and the case doesn't solely rest on her testimony. Apparently, there's other evidence."

"What evidence?" Keven asks, suddenly alert.

"We aren't privy to that yet, but we should know more after the pre-trial hearing. We need to sit tight until Dan and his team find out exactly what's going on."

"Can we come to court too?" I ask. "To show our support? I

can only imagine what's going through Kal's mind. He needs to know we have his back. That we know he didn't do this."

"He knows, Faye. Kennedys always stick together in times of crisis." Looking around the room at the disjointed postures and fractured relationships, it's hard to trust in his statement. James's shoulders lift. "We want to keep this as low key as possible so only Alex and I will attend the arraignment, but I'll let him know you are all there in spirit. It seems unlikely that we'll be able to keep this out of the media for long, so we're in the process of hiring a security team to protect all of you and to man the property."

A chorus of groans breaks out in the room. "Ah, Dad. Do we have to go there again?" Keanu asks. "It was hellish last time."

"It's a necessary evil, son. I'll do whatever is required to protect my family."

Ky grunts, shaking his head in disbelief.

James's furious gaze slams into him. "Do you have something to add, Kyler?"

Ky folds his arms, glaring at his dad. "Nope."

"Well, then, your mother and I better get going. We don't want to be late." He stands up, extending his hand toward Alex. She examines it like it's germ ridden, rising to her feet unaided as she shoots another revolted look his way.

Keaton looks like he's on the verge of tears, and my heart breaks for him. He's always been a sensitive soul, and I can tell how devastated he is by everything that's going on. After Alex and James leave, I step toward him. "Are you okay?" Tentatively, I reach out and touch his arm, but he shoves me away.

"Oh, now you care about me? What, because you've had some tiff with lover boy? Quit using me. We're not friends anymore." He storms out of the room leaving me with my mouth hanging open and my heart lying in tatters on the floor.

Chapter Three

Warmth surrounds me from behind, and I spin on my heel, coming face to face with Kent. I step back to create some distance between us. He twirls a lock of my hair around his finger as he grins. "I didn't take you for a dirty girl, but looks can be deceiving." He smirks and a sour taste floods my mouth. "Don't keep us in suspense. Who's your secret fuck buddy?"

I take another step back. "You're disgusting and who I spend my time with is none of your business."

He gets all up in my face again, and this time I don't back down. I return his sleazy smirk with a glare. Large hands grip his upper arms, hauling him off to the side. "How dare you speak to Faye like that," Ky seethes. "Apologize."

"Screw you, asshole," Kent fumes, elbowing Ky in the ribs and freeing himself. "You two think you can stand on ceremony with me? Look down your nose at what I do in my private time when neither of you are any better?"

Okay, so I'm guessing he's still sore that we broke up his little foursome at the last party, and he clearly can't see how seriously out of control he is or that we're only trying to look out for him.

He jabs a finger in my direction. "She's only here a couple of months, and she's already whoring herself out, and you're back to slumming it with that slut Addison, so fuck off trying to tell me what to do." He shoves Ky as he stalks out of the room like a raging tempest.

I half-expect Ky to follow him, but I'm relieved when he doesn't. I rest my head in my hands, wondering what the hell I've done to deserve so much melodrama in my life.

"Now do you see?" Ky says, and I tilt my chin up. He's eyeballing Kaden. "You need to intervene because Mom and Dad can't or won't deal with him. Maybe he'll listen to you."

Kaden runs a hand around the back of his neck. "I'll talk to him but I'm not sure it's going to do any good." He rises, exiting the room with Keanu hot on his heels, leaving only Keven, Ky, and me behind.

"Man, this family is seriously fucked up." Keven shakes his head. "And we haven't even gotten to the good part yet." His look hardens as he glances between us. "Mom told you?"

"She had no choice," Ky replies. "Faye figured it out."

A deep furrow lines Keven's brow. "How the hell did you work it out? Neither Kaden or I had any clue when they dropped the bomb on our eighteenth birthdays. It came totally out of the blue."

"You should've told me. Why didn't you?" Ky jumps in, deflecting the question so I don't have to reply.

"It was so messed up, Ky. It took me months to come to terms with it, and then I was so damned mad at both of them for lying to us. Why do you think we've been arguing with them for so long? We've been pleading with them to tell you, but they were begging us for more time. They are already worried enough about all of you, and they were scared over what it'd do if you found out."

"And you bought that bullshit?" Ky's tone is incredulous.

Keven sighs, crossing one leg over the other. "Yes and no. At first I could scarcely see beyond my rage, but more recently, I've begun to see their point of view. This family can't cope with any more revelations."

If only he knew that the biggest bomb of all has yet to be dropped.

A dark cloud shrouds my brain as thoughts of James and my mum swim to the forefront of my mind. I'm purposely trying not to think about it because my emotions are fragile, and I'd rather focus on the current drama before confronting the more disturbing truths. Plus, I'm still hopping mad with Mum and terrified that what James believes will turn out to be my new truth. A teeny tiny part of me is desperately clinging onto the hope that he's mistaken. That Ky isn't my half-brother. That I won't have to give him up.

"I'm glad she's decided to tell everyone." Keven pulls me out of my head. "I think she needs to get this out in the open, and I don't want to avoid my brothers forever."

"That's why you haven't been around?" Ky asks.

"I'm sorry, Ky, but I couldn't face seeing you all the time knowing I was helping to keep something like this from you. It's better this way."

"Do you kn—"

Keven holds up a hand as he stands up. "Save it for the meeting later. I'm going to head outside for a game. You up for it?"

"Sure. Just give me a few minutes. I need to talk to Faye about something." Ky cocks his head to the side, and I get up and follow him silently out of the room.

"What did Addison want?" I ask the instant we step into my bedroom.

Ky closes the door behind me. "I don't want to talk about her." He moves directly in front of me. "How are you coping? Are you okay?" He raises his hand, angling it toward my face, and I peer up at him with longing. His hand falters, hovering in midair, mere millimeters from my cheek. Moisture pools in my eyes and my lip wobbles. The look of utter conflict on his face guts me.

My chest heaves as a wracking sob breaks free. "I'm trying to stay strong," I whisper, "but it's damn hard." My voice cracks.

"Come here," he says softly, opening his arms, and I fold into his embrace without hesitation.

My arms snake around his waist, and I ingest his scent, committing it to memory. Everything seems infinitely better locked in his embrace. I squeeze him tight, closing my eyes and uttering silent prayers, begging God to make this right. "I don't want to lose you. Not when I've only found you." I look up at him through blurry eyes.

"I know, baby. I feel the same."

He looks away but not before I see the look of sheer torment on his face. My heart damn near ruptures. "But?"

"But we have to stay away from one another until we have those test results. I'm not strong enough to resist you other- wise." He stares deep into my eyes, anguish and suffering reflected in his gaze. "You have no idea how badly I want to kiss you right now."

I rest my hand on his chest. "Believe me, I know."

He takes a step back, and my hands fall loose at my side. I'm instantly cold.

"Which is why we can't be alone until we know what we're dealing with."

"And what then?"

When he looks up again, I'm startled to see moisture building in his eyes. "I don't know, Faye. I can't even bear to think of the what ifs. I'm hanging on here by a thread, in case you hadn't noticed." He leans back, staring up at the ceiling. "Someone up there sure loves to fuck me around."

I half-snort, half-laugh. "Don't preach to the converted. My life is one big fuck-up after another."

"I want to be here for you, Faye, but I don't know how to do that and not be close to you, but I won't sink to his level. I'm not going to do what he did." A wave of revulsion washes over his face.

"I get that. I'm grossed out by it too."

He steps toward me, pulling me gently into his arms again. "Hopefully it won't come to that, but if it does we'll deal with it. Until then, let's just try and get through the next week. I'm sure Dad knows someone who can rush through the tests."

"Okay." I rest my head on his chest, listening to the rhythmic *thud, thud* of his heart. "I'll miss you," I whisper, as more tears spill out of my eyes.

"I'll miss you, too." His voice cracks at the end, and I can tell he's struggling to hold it together too. He strokes his hand down the length of my hair, and we cling to each other, both of us hesitant to let go.

After a bit, I ease out of his arms, wiping my tears away with the back of my sleeve. I sniff. "This is only short term. We can do this." I tilt my chin up and examine his beautiful face. So much emotion shines from his eyes, and it almost destroys my resolve. Every part of my being longs to reach out to him. To trail my fingers along his defined jaw. To pepper his mouth with long, explorative kisses. To run my nose along his neck, inhaling his unique smell. To circle my arms around him and take all the pain away.

I love you.

It's on the tip of my tongue, and I long to say it, to tell him his feelings are more than reciprocated, but I can't, because I may not be allowed to love him like that, and it's better he doesn't know. So, I lock that truth away in my heart, hoping that I'll get the chance to free it someday.

We are all huddled in the lobby, with the door wide open, as Max—the family chauffeur— pulls the car up to the front of the house. James and Alex exit first, swiftly followed by Kalvin. He hangs his head, his gaze fixated on the ground as he shuffles toward the house. Alex attempts to pull him into her side, but he shucks away from her gesture. Her eyes fill up and James sends her a sympathetic look which she ignores. My shoulders are knotted with tension, and the air is heavy with foreboding.

James and Alex step into the house, followed by a clearly reluctant Kalvin. He still hasn't lifted his chin or made eye contact with anyone. Frowning, Kaden takes a step toward Kal, unashamedly hauling him into his arms. "We're glad you're home, and we know you didn't do this. We have your back."

Slowly, Kalvin raises his face, eyeballing his brother. "Thanks, bro." His voice lacks the usual confidence, and a soulful pang hits me in the chest.

One by one, his brothers move forward, offering him a high-five or a slap on the back. His Adam's apple jumps in his throat, and whatever control Kal has over his emotions is weakening. Tears stream down Alex's face, and even James looks like he could blub. It seems he was right earlier—Kennedys *do* stick together in times of crisis.

Ky hugs Kal to him, whispering something in his ear. When

he moves aside, I step forward, enveloping Kalvin in my arms. "I don't know why she's done this, but we'll figure it out."

"Did you see her?" he asks, holding onto me. I nod slowly, worrying my lip between my teeth. "What did she say?"

"Kalvin, I don't think th—"

"Mom," Kal cuts in, turning to face Alex. "You can't protect me from this, and I want to know." He twists his face around to mine. "Well? Is she okay?"

I hate to be the one to tell him this, but he deserves honesty. "She was upset and crying. She ... she said she was in a bad place and that you hurt her..."

His eyes grow glassy as his stiff upper lip starts to waver. "I know I did, and I hate myself for that, but I still can't believe she's done this. I would never force her, or any girl, into sex. I ..." He steps out of my embrace, bending over and clutching his head in his hands. His chest heaves with audible sobs, and when he lifts his chin, tears are falling by the bucketload down his face. "Mom." His voice trickles out in an anguished plea as he pins forlorn eyes on Alex. If I thought my heart was breaking earlier, it's nothing on how I'm presently feeling. Tears glide down my cheeks, and my heart physically pains me, as I watch my cocky, confident cousin fall to pieces.

Alex races to his side, pulling him into her arms and holding him while he dissolves in front of us.

Chapter Four

The only sound in the room is Kal's anguished cries and Alex's placating words as she cradles her son in her arms. Tears continue to trickle down my cheeks, and there isn't a damn thing I can do to stop them. Ky catches my eye, concern and worry clearly evident in his gaze. He looks down at his feet, and I force myself to drop my eyes. There is so much turbulent emotion brewing inside me, and it feels like I'm on the verge of a massive blowout any second now. Stress has tied my shoulders into unyielding knots, and I wrap my arms around my waist, as if that will somehow hold me together.

An arm creeps around my back, and I'm towed into Keaton's side. I turn my gobsmacked expression on him, melting immediately when I notice the empathy in his eyes. Without hesitation, I circle my arm around his waist, leaning into him. Out of the corner of my eye, I spot James's frown, and my eyes narrow as I glare at him. *For flip's sake, what kind of girl does he think I am? Am I not allowed to care for any of my cousins-slash-could-be-brothers without it being construed as something else?* His features relax and he sends me an apologetic shrug. I rest my head on Keaton's shoulder, sniffling.

"Come through to the sitting room," James says, motioning us forward. "Let's give your brother some privacy."

I sit on the couch beside Keaton, looping my arm through his. "Does this mean I'm forgiven?" I whisper hopefully in his ear.

"There isn't anything to forgive," he whispers back, and it's the first thing to bring a smile to my face all day. "I'm sorry if I overreacted earlier. And the other day on Nantucket."

"What happened at court?" Kaden asks before I can respond to Keaton.

"Your brother was interviewed by a probation officer who recommended he be released on bail and upon condition that he doesn't leave the State," James confirms.

"Has he been charged?" Keven asks in a low tone of voice.

"Yes, and we're waiting for a pre-trial hearing date now. Dan is hoping we can get the case dismissed before it goes to a full trial, but it'll depend on the nature of the evidence, and so far, the prosecuting attorney is being very cagey."

Alex and Kalvin walk into the room and further conversation is halted. "I'm not sure now is the best time to do this," Alex offers up, her eyes skimming the room nervously.

"No way, Mom. This happens now." Kaden's tone is final.

"There will never be a good time to share this news," Ky adds. "Can we get on with it, please?" His expression is unrepentant.

Looking thoroughly petrified, Alex sinks onto the empty couch, keeping Kal glued to her side. She sits poker straight with her hands knotted in her lap. Her lip wobbles as she opens her mouth to speak, and there is no masking the sheer terror etched on her face. I can't help feeling for her even though she has gotten herself into this mess.

James reaches over, covering her hands with his. She levels him with a contemptuous look Addison would be proud of. James snatches his hands back, and a muscle clenches in his jaw as his entire face turns puce. Tension is palpable in the air, and I wish she would just get on with it.

Rip the Band-Aid off, Alex.

"There is something I need to tell you. Something I should've told you all at a much earlier time. Your father and I have always tried to do what we feel is right by you, but some-times we mess up. This is, arguably, one of those times."

Kent splutters, leaning back on the couch and crossing his ankles as if he's getting ready to watch a movie. "This should be good." He smirks.

Kaden swats the back of his head. "Can you stop being an asshole and let Mom speak?"

I'm surprised to see Kaden jumping to Alex's defense, espe-cially now I understand what's been driving the hostility toward his parents. Then again, I'd challenge anyone to look at Alex right now and not feel protective toward her. Her entire body is quaking in fright.

"This isn't easy to say, and I've been carrying it with me for a very long time." Her eyes glisten as she scans her son's faces. "I was in a relationship with another man before I met your ... before I met James. James isn't Kaden and Keven's biological father—they have a different dad." She averts her eyes as she lets her words settle in the room.

The triplets look shell-shocked, and Kent is speechless for once. Kal is blinking profusely, clearly struggling to take it in.

"Oh my God," Keaton breaks the awkward silence. "That's what she told you when you turned eighteen?" His gaze drifts from Kaden to Keven.

"Yeah," Kaden admits.

"How could you keep something like this a secret?" Keanu

looks distraught as he stares at his parents. "Fair enough if you didn't want to tell us, but how could you not tell them?" He stabs his finger in the direction of his half-brothers.

"When is a good time to tell your child that the man they believe is their father isn't their father?" Alex asks bluntly.

I smother my snort of disbelief. The irony isn't lost on me.

James winces, and Alex's face contorts. "I'm sorry," she whispers, looking James in the eye for what must be the first time today. "I didn't mean it like that." His eyes are downcast. "I know I haven't handled this well," she says, redirecting her attention to her sons, "but I don't regret the choices I made." Her eyes find Kaden and Keven. "James is your father in every way that counts. He loved you from the moment he met you, and he never treated you any differently to your brothers. The fact that none of you ever suspected anything is proof of that. He has loved you all equally."

"I've never disputed that," Kaden says quietly. "It's the manner in which you told us, and how you forced us to keep this from our brothers that I had issue with."

"I'm glad it's out in the open," Keven adds. "Maybe now we can all move on."

Silence engulfs the room as everyone absorbs the revelation.

"Who's *their* father?" Kent asks, a few minutes later. "Have you met him?" He looks to Kaden and Keven with inquisitive eyes.

"That's not important." Alex's words are urgent. "He was incapable of being a father to my children, and he abandoned me when I needed him the most. That's all you need to know."

Kaden and Keven share a loaded look, and Alex perceptibly stiffens. James narrows his eyes suspiciously. "What did you do?"

Keven squirms in his seat and Kaden draws an exaggerated

breath. They lock eyes and some unspoken communication filters between them. Kaden crosses his arms over his chest. "We met him."

Alex shrieks, clamping a hand over her mouth as her eyes widen in alarm.

"And Mom is right," Keven supplies. "Nothing good came from meeting that man."

James hops up and walks out of the room. Alex is in shocked submission, sitting rigidly still on the couch while a dazed Kalvin does his best to bolster her. No one makes a move to go after James. Call me soft, but I don't think that's right or fair, so I climb to my feet and follow him out of the room.

I find him in the games room, his forehead pressed to the wall, his body heaving as painful sobs rip through him. My emotions are skittering all over the place, and I've never felt so disconnected from myself and so unsure of how to act.

This man slept with my mother. *His sister.* He thinks he's my father. He's colluded with his wife to lie to his kids for years. He's had an affair with his wife's assistant. He's so caught up in the complicated mess he helped create that he's incapable of being there for his sons who need him so very much.

But, he took on another's man's children as if they were his own. Sacrificed his career ambitions to be a stay-at-home dad. He's acknowledged his mistakes and he's trying to face up to them. Inappropriate or not, he loved my mother fiercely, and he protected and cared for her after their parents died. He took me in without hesitation when I was orphaned, and he has made me feel part of his family.

He's not a bad man—he's simply made some bad decisions.

Looking at him now, so vulnerable and raw, it's hard to hold onto my hatred and my revulsion. James has no one in his corner and that doesn't sit right with me. I reach out and touch his elbow. "James."

He stops crying, lifting his head up to look at me. The expression on his face guts me. He is in agony, and I'd be a cold-hearted bitch not to react to that. I open my arms in silent invitation, and he stares at me with a myriad of different emotions flitting across his face. My heart pounds anxiously in my chest. He steps toward me, closing the gap as he accepts my hug. He holds me close, and his warmth is comforting. It's only now I realize that I need this as much as he does. We don't speak. We just hug. And it doesn't feel weird. It feels natural.

"Dad?" A quiet voice speaks out from behind me. I pull back, turning around to face Keaton. "I came to see if you were okay." James's face lights up momentarily. Keaton looks a little uncomfortable as he shoves his hands in his pockets, rocking back on his heels. "I, um, know this is a shock, but I haven't missed what's important in all this. I know things are terrible right now but it doesn't erase what's come before, or what you mean to us. I wouldn't want any other dad because you've always been the best."

I step aside, paving the way for James to envelop his son in his arms.

It's such a touching moment, and I could kiss Keaton right about now. He is the sweetest, kindest, most compassionate Kennedy of the lot, and I love him for it.

I'm lying on my bed a half hour later when my phone rings. It's Brad, so I pick up. "Hey."

"Hey, you. Just checking in 'cause you weren't at school and the rumors are rife. Is it true? About Kal?"

"Crap. I'd hoped the news hadn't broken yet but that was clearly wishful thinking."

"How is he? How's everyone?"

"I wish I knew how to answer that question, but the last twenty-four hours have been some of the most traumatic of my life." Considering what I went through a couple of months ago, that statement is very telling. I reach around, rubbing the tense spot between my shoulder blades. My brain feels like it's short-circuiting from the drama overload, and I wouldn't mind getting out of here for a while. "Are you busy?"

"Nope. You want to hang out?"

"Please. Can you come get me? I'll wait out front."

"I'm on my way."

Kaden and Keven are talking with Alex and James in the sitting room when I pop my head in. "I'm heading out with Brad for a while. I'll see you later."

"Wait a sec, Faye." James clambers out of the chair, striding toward me. He takes my elbow and steers me out into the lobby. "I haven't forgotten about the test."

"It's okay. I don't expect you to do that today, not with everything else that's going on."

He tucks a loose strand of my hair behind my ear. "It's equally as important to me." I stare at my feet, hugely uncomfortable with the look on his face. "I've already put in a call, and I'm waiting to hear back. Keep your cell close in case I need to contact you."

"Sure thing." I give him my best effort at a smile.

"And thank you for earlier. You've no idea how much that meant to me." My cheeks warm at his compliment. "I'm so sorry about all this. I know you're still grieving, and the last thing you need is to be dragged into more distressing situations, but these issues have been festering for some time."

"I'm not gonna lie—my head's a total mess, and I don't know what I feel anymore, but in a weird way, everything else that's going on actually helps. It's distracting me from my own crap, and I can't help thinking that's a really good thing."

A firm rap thumps against the door as James opens his mouth to reply. "That's my lift. I'll keep an eye on my phone. See ya."

I skip out of the house before there's any more of the heavy stuff.

"Let's get out of here," I say the instant my butt hits the passenger seat.

Brad puts his foot to the pedal and floors it. "Where to?" He keeps his gaze fixed on the road as he asks.

"Anywhere." I shrug, flipping my brunette locks over my shoulders. "I don't mind as long as it's quiet and I'm unlikely to bump into anyone from school." I have to psyche myself up for that. "Just distract me, please." I fiddle with the sound system, flicking through tracks until I find one I like.

"No problem. I can do that, and I know the perfect place." His eyes leave the road for a quick second. "You okay?"

"Not really," I answer truthfully.

"Wanna talk about it?"

"Yeah, but not here. Let's wait 'til we get wherever we're going. I need to chill for a while."

We drive in solitude for a half hour, and I close my eyes and listen to the music, deliberately trying to force all thoughts from my mind. It's pointless, of course, because no matter how hard I try not to think about everything going on in Chez Kennedy, it still creeps up on me, events replaying in my mind on a continual loop. There's no escaping the haunting shadows hanging over my life.

Brad kills the engine, and I open my eyes, scanning the decent-sized parking lot that is virtually empty except for two monster trucks. The site is bordered by gigantic trees that have obviously been around since the year dot. "What is this place?" I ask.

"My dad used to take me fishing here. There are tons of trails if you'd like to walk down to the lake?"

I stretch out my body as a yawn seeps out of my mouth. "Sounds good." I open the door and slide out of the car, zipping my coat up to my chin as a blast of cool air hits me full force in the face.

Brad retrieves his jacket and a scarf from the back seat, before locking the car. "Here." He snakes the scarf around my neck. "You look like you could use this."

"Thanks." I smile up at him as he zips his jacket, thrusting his hands in his pockets.

"This way." He offers a one-shouldered shrug and I follow his lead. We don't talk as we walk through the forest, but the silence isn't in any way unpleasant. Brad is so easy to be around. Intuitive and sensitive, he just gets me. Our feet crunch on debris as we saunter through the dusky, chilly forest, and the only sounds are the birds chirruping in the trees. After about twenty minutes, I detect the gentle lapping of water, and we emerge at the edge of a vast lake. A couple of men are across the way, sitting on deck chairs, with extended fishing rods snaking out into the water. Behind them, nestled in the dense forest, are fleeting glimpses of extravagant homes.

Brad guides me to a fallen log resting at the edge of the water and we sit down. He blows on his hands, rubbing them together. "I keep forgetting that the weather has turned. Probably should've suggested somewhere warmer."

"It's perfect here. Thanks for bringing me." I gaze out at the water, watching the gentle rise and fall of the supple waves, fascinated at the way the water creeps toward us like a silent thief and then rescinds with a barely detectable whoosh. Extending my hands behind me, I sigh as I tilt my face up toward the sky, wondering what, or if, there is anything beyond the clouds. Brad is quietly watching my every move, and I'm conscious of his singular devotion. "Sometimes I imagine God up there"—I jerk my chin skyward—"like an ominous puppet master, dangling the strings as he controls our lives. Does he laugh with glee as he throws curveball after curveball, or does he solemnly watch to see how well we'll cope?" I twist my face to Brad. "Or does he care? Is this merely a game to him?"

Brad bends over, picking up a stone and throwing it out into the lake. It skims elegantly across the top of the water before plunking into the hidden depths out of sight. "I know where you're coming from. I've thought of similar things these last few months." Brad shifts on the log, and our knees brush against one another. "I've often wondered why it is that some people seem to coast through life without any issues while others are dealt more than their fair share. It doesn't seem right, but I've come to the conclusion that God—if he exists—sends challenges to those he believes can handle it. Like an exercise in resilience." He picks up another stone and flings it out at the lake. "At least that's what I tell myself to get through every day."

I suck my lower lip into my mouth. "Hmm. That's an interesting theory, and I've no idea if you're right, but all I know is it sucks to be on the receiving end of it. Honestly, I've tried hard to get through the last two months, and without sounding conceited, I think I was doing okay, but now"—I emit a choked laugh—"now I'm well pissed because I've enough on my plate without all this new crap." I'm horrified when a tear sneaks out of the corner of my eye. I quickly wipe it away but not before he notices.

Reaching out, he takes my hands in his strong grip. "This is more than what's going on with Kal?"

"Yeah," I admit, opening up and telling him everything. About James's admission and what it seems to imply for my relationship with Ky and how it's altered my perception of my parents. How awful the tension is back at the house due to Alex's revelation about Kaden and Keven's dad, James's affair with Courtney and the fractured state of his relationship with his wife, and Kalvin's situation which sounds grim. He listens without interruption, rubbing soothing circles on the back of my hand the whole time. I don't hold back, and when I've let it all out, I feel heaps better. I needed to offload that.

"Shit, Faye." Brad exclaims when I've finished talking. "I thought I had issues but that's totally messed up."

I massage my temples. "I know. It's bad when you've so many problems you don't know which one to tackle first."

"No wonder Ky hasn't returned any of my calls today."

"Don't take it personally. He's trying his best to be strong. We all are." I kick the stones at the base of my foot.

"I'm so sorry." I arch a brow, wondering why he feels the need to apologize. "For how I reacted over your relationship with him and the fact that you're hurting now. I don't like to see you so upset." It's true that Brad had been weirded out when he first discovered Ky and I were together. It's majorly frowned on in these parts to date your cousin, even if it isn't illegal. Although, I'd like to think he was coming around to the idea.

I clutch his hands tightly. "What am I going to do, Brad? If he's my brother ..." I trail off as an iron grip squeezes my heart inflicting the worst pain imaginable. I hang my head, fighting a fresh bout of tears, and I hate that too—that this nightmare has turned me into an emotional wreck when normally I pride myself on being the last girl to break down and cry.

"Hey." Tentatively, he hauls me into his arms. "You're one of the most resourceful people I know. You'll figure it out."

As I rest my head on his chest, I wish I had the same faith in me.

Chapter Five

On the walk back, I make him faithfully promise not to breathe a word of what I've said to anyone. I've never been the type to parade my private business around town but it's even more pertinent with this shameful secret. The less people that know the better. It's the first occasion in my life where I've felt embarrassed and ashamed of my mother, and while I hate that it's come to this, there isn't anything I can do to change how I feel. I still don't understand it; perhaps I never will.

What if I had grown up around Ky? Would I still love him in a totally inappropriate way? Is it hypocritical to be ashamed and disgusted of my mother and James when we could be in the same position? Would I have been strong enough to resist acting on my feelings, or would we have ended up in the exact same place? And is it wrong when it feels so right? Did my mum ask herself these questions or did she go with the flow? My brain unhelpfully flips these questions over and over as I walk alongside Brad, but there are no answers, and the dull pounding in my skull is all I've got to show for my inner analysis.

It's only when we're safely back in the car that I realize how brutally selfish I've been. Brad has plenty of his own crap to deal with, and I've monopolized the last hour with my "woe is me" tirade. "What's the latest with you, anyway? Any update?" I ask.

He wrinkles his nose as he cranks the car into gear. "Nothing that can't wait." I may be imagining it, but his shoulders appear to stiffen. I've always had good observation skills, and I can tell when someone isn't being one hundred percent straight with me.

I twist in my seat so I'm facing him. "I spilled my guts. Now you're up. What's happening?"

"It's not important. Honestly." He gives me a quick once over. "You have enough stuff to be worrying about."

"I swear to God, Brad, if you don't tell me what's going on right now, I'm going to kick you in the nuts. I don't care that you're driving."

His lips curve up into a smile as one hand cups his junk. "No touching these bad boys," he teases.

"Well?" I fold my arms sternly over my chest, deliberately ignoring his attempt at humor.

He sighs in resignation. "I got an eviction notice this weekend."

I bolt upright. Brad had only recently confided in me about the embezzlement charges his dad is facing and how he refused to escape the country with the rest of his family, preferring to graduate and enroll in college as he'd always intended. He's been living in the family home all alone these past few months, although he understood it was only a matter of time before the authorities seized the property. "Damn. When do you have to be out by?"

"End of the week." His fingers clasp the steering wheel fiercely.

"What are your plans?"

He barks out a laugh. "That backseat is looking mighty cozy."

"Absolutely not. I'll talk to Alex when I get back."

He turns ferocious eyes on me. "The hell you will. She has enough troubles without adding to it. Besides, she's done enough for me already. I'll sort this out by myself."

"You're being ridiculous. You're practically family, and they have tons of room. I know she won't mind."

"No." There's a finality to his tone. "I knew I shouldn't have told you."

That totally raises my hackles. "Now you're being an ass. Friends confide in each other." I gesture between us with my hands. "And if this is about your pride, there's nothing wrong with admitting you need help."

"I said no," he grits out.

"You are so Goddamned stubborn!"

"I said I'll sort it!" he yells back and everything locks up inside me.

"Fine. Be a stubborn jerk. See if I care."

A layer of tension fills the empty space between us, and neither of us speaks for the remaining duration of the journey. I nibble on my lower lip as I stare out the window.

When we turn the corner toward the house, I jerk forward in my seat, my eyes out on stalks as I scan the crowd in front of the Kennedy gates. Five TV vans and a plethora of cars are parked off the side of the road, and hordes of journalists block the entrance like hungry vultures in desperate need of a feed. "You've got to be kidding me." I slink down in my seat, hurriedly covering my face with my hair.

"Damned parasites!" Brad seethes, honking the horn in an attempt to clear a path in front of the gate. He whips out his cell, punching in some numbers quickly. "Hey, man. It's me.

I'm with Faye at the gate, but I don't want to input the code as this place is swarming with reporters. Cool, thanks."

"I noticed a black SUV trailing us about ten miles out," he admits, pocketing his phone. "Now I know why."

"What?" I spin in my seat. "Why didn't you say anything?"

"You weren't exactly talking to me, and I didn't want to concern you."

I scowl at him. "I'd have thought you know me better by now."

"Please, Faye. I don't want to fight with you."

"Grand." I huff, slinking farther in my seat as I notice the prying lens of a camera pointing into the car. Brad sticks his middle finger up, and I can't stop the laugh from bubbling out of my mouth.

"Put your head down between your knees," he instructs, and I obey without argument. The last thing I want is my face projected across TV screens. I like my anonymity, and I have plenty of reasons for not wanting the press to know who I am or where I come from.

A few minutes, and several blasts of the horn later, Brad eases the car through the gates and up the driveway. "You can come up for air now."

I take a fleeting look over my shoulder, watching the baying crowds back at the gate. "That was insane."

"Get used to it. Word is obviously out."

Ky is waiting at the front entrance when we pull up. Butterflies flood my stomach at the sight of him, and blood thunders through my veins. A piercing ache stabs me clear through the heart. Simply seeing him hurts so much.

My fingers are curled around the door handle when Brad places his hand on my elbow. "Wait a sec." I turn around. "I don't want to leave things like this between us. I know you want to help, and I love you for that, but I need to do this on my own."

"I'm worried about you."

His face softens. "Thank you, but let me sort this myself. Please."

I hate lying to him, because there's no way I'm letting him sleep in his car, but I can tell he isn't going to back down so I've no choice. I bob my head, convincing myself it's not so bad because I haven't lied out loud.

"Will you be in school tomorrow? Do you want me to pick you up?" he asks.

"Yes, and I'm not sure. James said something about body-guards earlier, so I'll need to check with him. Plus, I don't like the thoughts of you navigating that mob out front."

"I've handled worse." He grins.

Ky is watching us with inquisitive eyes, a concentrated frown creasing his brow.

"I'd better go." I dart forward and press a light kiss to his cheek. "Thanks for today. I needed that."

His smile expands. "Glad to help." He tucks a stray strand of hair behind my ear. "I know it seems like your world has turned upside down, but you'll get through this. I can relate and, with time and perspective, it does get easier."

"I hope so." I offer him a weak smile as I climb out of his car, purposely avoiding Ky's penetrating gaze as he stalks toward Brad's side.

I slip into the house quietly and head toward my room. Silence surrounds me and I briefly wonder where everyone is. Throwing myself onto my bed, I bury my head in the duvet. My phone pings in my pocket and I fumble for it. It's Rach and Jill calling, my two best friends from back home. I hold the vibrating phone in my hand, staring at it like it's some alien object. Even though the girls are basically my surrogate sisters,

I can't summon the courage to answer. Because I won't be able to conceal my distress and I'll have to tell them everything, and I'm not ready for that. I needed to get all the crap off my chest earlier, and I knew Brad was a safe bet—that he wouldn't judge me or betray my trust, but it's different with my Irish friends. Jill and Rach practically lived in my house, and they were super fond of my parents, of Mum, in particular. I don't want them to know what she did and not solely because I know it will tarnish their memory of her.

It's also because I'm so ashamed.

My mum willingly slept with her brother, and that knowledge makes me so sick.

But what's even worse is the thought that I could be a chip off the old block.

Like mother, like daughter.

Because if Ky turns out to be my brother, how the hell can I stay away from him when I already love him so much?

I must've nodded off because the next thing I'm aware of is a persistent knocking on my door. "Faye," James calls out. "Can I come in?"

"Sure," I reply in a sleep-drenched voice, sitting up and pushing clumps of knotty hair out of my eyes.

James steps into the room. "Sorry for disturbing you, but I wanted to let you know that a specialist medical team is on the way. We thought it best to conduct the DNA testing here."

"Oh. Okay."

"They'll arrive in twenty minutes if you want to freshen up."

I recall episodes of crime shows I've watched on TV. "Are they just going to swab my mouth or something?"

"I think they'll probably take blood samples from both of us too."

I absentmindedly scratch my head. "Fine. Come get me when they're here."

I brush my teeth and drag a comb through my hair. Once I've pulled on a fresh pair of jeans and a sweater, I set out for Ky's room. Brad said he didn't want me to talk to Alex, but he said nothing about Ky. Okay, I'm splitting hairs but hopefully he'll get over it. Ky isn't in his room, so I try the second most likely place.

The whirring noise of equipment greets me as I push open the door to the gym. Predictably, Ky is standing up on the bike, his feet working a hundred miles an hour. His workout shirt is in a discarded heap on the floor, and his muscular back glistens with sweat. My core pulses with need, and an indulgent moan escapes my lips as I close my eyes and pray for strength I'm terrified I don't have.

When I reopen my eyes, Ky is peering at me over his shoulder. Beads of sweat dot his forehead, and his cheeks are flushed red with exertion. The bike slows down and he jumps off, grabbing a towel from the handlebars and wiping it across his slick brow. He walks toward me but I hold out a palm to stop him. "Stay right there." I step back, flattening my body to the wall. My knees have turned to jelly, and the firm concrete against my spine is the only thing keeping me upright.

My attraction to Ky has always been off the charts, and it's taking every morsel of self-control not to fling myself into his arms. I rub the sore spot over my chest as I force my eyes to the floor. "I need to talk to you about Brad. He's being evicted from his house on Friday, and he has nowhere to go. I told him I'd speak to your mom, but he went apeshit on me."

I sense Ky's presence in front of me before his shadow

darkens the floor, alerting me to his proximity. "Faye." His voice is barely more than a whisper.

Despite my better judgment, I look up. My eyes follow a line from the defined ridges of his perfect abs, over his broad chest and shoulders, up to his stunning face. His mouth parts ever so slightly and visions of sucking his lower lip between my teeth resurrect to taunt me. I stare at his mouth, remembering how amazing he tastes, how silky smooth his lips feel moving against mine, and how luxuriant his tongue is when it caresses mine. I almost choke on the anguished lump in my throat.

Then I make a fatal mistake.

I immerse myself in his eyes.

Everything I'm feeling is perfectly mirrored in his gaze, and my heart thumps wildly in my chest. My fingers twitch with potent need, and my chest visibly inflates as my breath rushes out in transparent need. Every molecule of my being craves the boy in front of me, and the fact that I can't act on that urge is killing me.

Holy crap. I am totally losing the plot.

My errant emotions have complete control over me, and I hate feeling so disconnected from myself and from him. Ky is the only person who understands me. Who completes me. The first time we met, we saw inside one another in a way that is inexplicable. There's a dark, empty void in both of us that calls out to one another. An unspoken, undefined connection that irrevocably links us. *We belong together.* There's no other truth that resonates more fully.

Uncertainty and pain is written all over his face, and I know he longs to touch me. It's the same for me with him. He takes another step forward, until we are toe to toe, and my breath hitches. We stare at one another—deep, addictive, hankering stares—and I can scarcely breathe over the burning longing infusing every cell, every nerve ending, every nook and cranny. This is awful and I don't know how much I can take before I crack. Having to revert to where we were a few weeks ago is almost unbearable. Anticipation wafts through the air, interlaced with an undercurrent of danger that is alluring and intoxicating. Ky and I have always fed off that dangerous vibe we share, and it's never been more precarious than right now.

He lowers his face toward mine, and I shutter my eyes. I'm terrified and excited and disgusted and turned-on all at the same time. He presses his forehead to mine, and that tiny touch ignites the fire inside me. His seductive breath oozes over my skin, tempting and taunting me, and I almost cry out in frustration. My heart pounds frantically, and we're only a hairsbreadth from one another.

It would take nothing to close the tiny gap between us.

To press my body against his. To place my palm over his chest and feel the pulsing of his heart against my hand. To tilt my head up and claim a kiss. To bury my tongue in his mouth and allow his taste to overpower me. To make me forget everything. To help him forget everything.

Yes, it would take nothing to do that, to take that, but I can't.

Instead, I thrust my hands in my pockets to stop myself from reaching for him. "This is the worst form of torture," I whisper, still refusing to open my eyes. If I do that, I know I won't be able to resist.

"This is going to be much harder than I thought," he rasps, threading his fingers in my hair. "I miss you so much already."

"Stop, Ky. Please. Don't touch me." I don't mean it. I don't want him to stop, but my self-control is floundering, and one of us has to halt this before it goes any further.

I love you so much.

The words hang on my tongue, and I want to tell him so badly but I can't. I'm seconds away from losing it as it is.

"I love you," he whispers in that hypnotic voice I adore. "It can't be wrong. It just can't be. Not when it feels like this."

My resolve crumbles and I bury my head in his chest with an audible whimper.

"I'm sorry, baby," he whispers, rubbing his hands up and down my spine. "I'm sorry I'm weak, but I want to be here for you, and it's killing me that I can't."

My arms lock around his waist, and I practically mold my body to his, wanting our embrace to never end.

He could be your brother.

I freeze the instant that thought lodges in my mind. Summoning the last vestiges of my strength, I let go, pushing him gently away. Finally, I open my eyes, and I'm startled to see his eyes soaked in such naked emotion. Ky doesn't let many people see the real him, and I'm still awed whenever he shows himself to me. But his vulnerability on this occasion is so visceral, so raw, and coming straight from his heart, it guts me. I hate that he's suffering as much as I am. I hate this situation, but we have to find strength from somewhere. We need to do the right thing. "You don't want to be like him, remember? We are stronger than this."

Ky's face contorts and for one horrendous, breath-stealing moment, I think he's going to break down. I'm not sure I'm resilient enough to deal with that. At the last second, he pulls himself together. Stepping back, he creates some much-needed distance between us. "I'm sorry," he whispers. "I'm so fucking weak."

"You're not, and I'm struggling too. You're definitely not in this alone." I pinch the bridge of my nose. "You were right earlier. We have to stay away from one another because we can't give into our feelings."

His mournful eyes pierce mine. "I know." He laughs dryly. "You've brought everything to the surface again, Faye. After months of feeling dead inside, I feel *everything*. And that's both wonderful and fucking awful at the same time." Determination replaces the previous look on his face. "But I can do better and I will because that's what you need. This won't happen again."

"You'll talk to your mom about Brad?"

"Of course, and then I'll speak to him. I'll smooth things over, so don't worry about that, okay."

I shoot him a small smile. "Thank you." I turn to leave, but at the last second, I spin back around to face him. To hell with it. I may regret this, but I think I'll regret it worse if I don't say it now. "For the record, I love you too." Then I race out of the room before he can acknowledge or respond to my statement in any way.

As I sit in a chair in James's study ten minutes later, with a strap around my arm and a needle in my vein, I'm not sorry that I told Ky I loved him. I know we may both pay for it later, but he needed to hear that from me. The doc has said it will take two weeks to receive the test results—even with James paying for a rush job—and I hope my profession of love helps him get through the period of separation. I'm going to cling to his love like a lifeboat, because it feels like the only thing that can keep me afloat in the difficult days ahead.

Chapter Six

James shows up at the house bright and early the next morning. Alex has already left for work. He introduces us to our personal bodyguards and gives us a lengthy lecture on the dangers of foregoing our protective detail. The mob at the gates has apparently doubled in size overnight, and James has warned us to expect tails. As if it isn't bad enough that I have to be chauffeur-driven to the school door, now I'll have a shadow too. Great.

"I've spoken with Principal Carter," James tells me, planting a large hand on my shoulder as he ushers me toward the front door. "She has approved the installation of additional security at the front gates which will keep the media off school grounds. Lenny here"—he motions toward the broad-shouldered man with the crew cut and sharp black suit waiting outside—"will escort you to and from the school property. I'd advise minimal excursions outside of school, and you should reconsider your job."

I swing a defiant look his way. "No way! I'm not giving up

my job. Not if you expect me to hold onto my sanity. Lenny can stand guard outside Legends if it makes you feel any better."

James rolls his eyes. "I'd a feeling you might say that." I scowl, and he raises his hands in a conciliatory gesture. "Fine, fine! But if there are any issues, we *will* be discussing this more seriously, young lady."

All the small hairs lift on the back of my neck at the fatherly tone he's adopting. I'm nowhere near ready to contemplate the implications of that. My face drops and James's expression softens. He presses a kiss to my forehead. "Try not to worry and come to me if you have difficulty with anything. I'm here for you."

The others hover in the background, watching the scene unfolding in front of them, and that makes me hugely self-conscious. Kent slants a vicious glance my way, and I sigh. As if he needs any other reason to hate me. He is still giving me the cold shoulder for breaking up his little sex party last week.

I step toward Kal and enclose my arms around his stiff body. I'd called into his room last night to see how he was, but he was either asleep or avoiding me, and I didn't want to push it. I'm so worried about him—he didn't utter a word during breakfast, and he barely managed to eat either. "Good luck today." I kiss his cheek. "Don't forget we love you and we believe you. Ignore the assholes in school. Nothing they say matters, okay?"

His arms tighten around my waist, and that's the only type of response I get. As I shuck out of his embrace, I share a concerned look with Ky.

"I'll watch out for him," he mouths.

I'm lost in my head the entire journey to school, and I'm working hard to maintain a serene inner peace because I'm going to need it to get through this day. I don't need an overactive imagination to visualize what's lying in store for me. My fingers drum off the seat as my foot taps anxiously off the floor. Every so often, I spot Lenny looking at me from the passenger seat. If my fidgety behavior bothers him, he can screw off. He's being paid enough, I'm sure.

As Max eases the Merc around the bend and Wellesley Memorial High School appears in my line of vision, my stomach churns sourly, and I fear the contents of my breakfast may be about to make an unwelcome reappearance. I tap out a quick message to Brad to let him know I'm here as Max glides the car past three reporters lingering on the pavement outside the school. I duck my head down in time, grateful that I seem to have escaped the interest of the main news outlets. That doesn't bode well for my cousins, though. I can only imagine the vultures awaiting them at Old Colonial.

The front entrance is thronged with students hurrying into the building, and I cringe as Max brings the car to a halt directly in front of the steps. *Could he be any more obvious?* My innards twist into knots, and I genuinely think I'm going to be sick. This reminds me too much of those months when I used to dread going to school, contemplating what hideous torture Daniel and Vera were waiting to inflict on me.

I can't go back to that.

I won't go back to that.

I'm stronger than this.

With renewed determination, I slide out of the car and walk with my shoulders back and my head up toward Brad, ignoring the hushed whispers and pointed fingers. Brad is leaning against a pillar, smiling at my approach.

"Hey, beautiful." He slings his arm around my shoulders and smacks a loud kiss against my cheek. I lean back, staring at him in confusion. "Fake boyfriend, remember?" he whispers.

I'd forgotten all about our little arrangement. Ky and Brad both felt it was a good idea for Brad to pretend to be my boyfriend to deflect some of the heat from Peyton and her cronies. I figure I need that insulation now more than ever, so I stretch up, snaking my arms around his neck as I press my mouth to his ear. "I do now. We should probably set some ground rules at lunch." Noticing tons of inquisitive eyes, I grip his neck tighter with one hand and run my fingers through his hair with the other.

He goes still. "Yeah, that's a good idea."

He takes my hand and leads me into the corridor waiting by my locker as I gather the books I need.

Brad plays the part of dutiful boyfriend to a T. Except I doubt there's much performing involved. Brad is a natural—perfect boyfriend material—if only I swung that way.

The morning flies by quite fast and rather uneventfully, apart from the odd snide comment hurled at me in the corridor in between classes. Lunchtime, however, is a whole other ballgame.

Brad and I take our usual seats in the cafeteria, avoiding the hostile glares from the girls at the end of the table. "How's it hanging, girlfriend?" Rose asks, giving me a quick one-armed hug as she claims a seat across from us.

"It's hanging," I deadpan, playing with the food on my plate. My appetite is effectively slaughtered as I try not to cower under the weight of so many stares. "Is it my imagination or is everyone looking at me?" Rose sends me a sympathetic look. "Not my imagination?"

"'Fraid not." She scoops up a mouthful of pasta. "Ignore them and they'll go away."

Brad snakes his arm around my waist and draws me in close to his side, kissing the top of my head. "We've got your back, babe."

Rose's fork clangs off the table as her mouth hangs open.

"What the heck did I miss the last couple of days?" Her gaze bounces between us.

"I'll tell you later." I wink conspiratorially.

Zoe plops into the empty chair beside Rose and I visibly stiffen. Zoe is Lana's best friend and the last person I expected to sit with me. Silence engulfs the room, and everyone waits with bated breath to see how I'll react. "What are you doing?" I hiss.

"Eating lunch." In typical Zoe fashion, she looks at me with her "duh" face on.

I lean forward on the table. "Have you heard from her?"

"Nope." She grimaces. "Not sure I want to either."

I frown. "What do you mean by that?"

Zoe looks around, before leaning across the table. "Look, I'm not your cousin's biggest fan," she whispers, and I snort. That's putting it mildly. She and Kal are like two hangry grizzly bears whenever they meet. Butting heads is par for the course with those two. "But what Lana's doing is wrong."

Icy chills rip up and down my spine. "What do you know?"

Zoe looks around her again. "Not here. Can you meet me after school? I've got an hour before the vigil. I'll explain then."

"Okay." Our heads are almost touching and we're in our own little bubble which is why I don't see or hear Peyton approaching until she's on top of me.

Something wet and cold slides down my back, and I jump up, knocking my chair over in the process. "What the hell?" I peek over my shoulder, spotting the rivulets of brown liquid sluicing down my back, staining my white sweater.

"Oops. My soda spilled. My bad." Her smirking grin is nothing new, and I'm tempted to dump my glass of OJ in her face, but then all hell will break loose, and I'm really not in the mood for dealing with Addison's trashy cousin today.

"Grow up, you idiot." I tug my wet sweater up and over my

head. My white vest is technically lingerie but it can easily pass as outerwear until I reach my locker where I now have a stash of clothes for occasions like this.

"Wear this, babe." Brad hands me his hastily removed sweater, gesturing sideways with a subtle nudge of his head. My gaze lands on the table where most of his football teammates sit with drool on their faces. "Best not to give them another show," Brad murmurs in my ear.

"Going for sloppy seconds again, Brad, hmm?" Peyton asks with a conniving sneer as panic climbs up my throat. *What the hell does she mean by that? She can't know about Ky and me? Can she?*

"I'd watch that nasty mouth of yours, if I was you, Peyton," Brad replies coolly. "It's liable to get you in a lot of trouble one of these days. And you should be careful before you start slinging mud. Not unless you're prepared to have it thrown back at you."

"What's going on, McConaughey?" Lance, Peyton's boyfriend and Memorial's quarterback wanders over to our table. Peyton nestles under his arm, sending me another smug look.

"You need to ask your girlfriend that question, Fielding, and while you're at it, tell her to lay off my girl."

"Your girl?" Lance quirks a brow as his greedy gaze fixates on my chest.

"Put that on," Brad says through gritted teeth, thrusting his sweater at me again. "Yeah, my girl." He moves in front of me, shielding me with his impressive body. "Eyes up, Lance, unless you're happy for me to eye fuck your girl's tits in return." I shuck Brad's sweater on and stand beside him, threading my fingers in his. Brad's mouth lifts in a half sneer as his eyes roam briefly over Peyton's chest. "Second thoughts, I'd rather keep my lunch down."

A muscle pulses in Lance's jaw, and I squeeze Brad's hand in caution. I don't want to cause any issues for him with the football team.

"I'll let you have this one time, man, but don't push it with me. Either of you." Lance's gaze alternates between us.

"Keep your woman away from mine, and we'll have no problem." Brad doesn't back down, and I respect him so much for that.

"Consider it sorted, bro." They high-five, and I somehow resist the urge to roll my eyes.

Peyton is biting her lip, clearly furious this didn't go her way. It pleases me no end. Already this fake boyfriend scenario is paying dividends. "You shouldn't scowl. It'll give you wrinkles," I tell her, shouldering my bag.

"Faye," Brad mutters a warning under his breath.

I smile sweetly at him, in a great mood all of a sudden. Keeping a hold of my hand, he leads me out of the cafeteria. "I do not understand what Lance sees in that spiteful bitch." Brad shakes his head, guiding me toward my locker.

"I bet she fucks like a porn star," I joke. "She's had plenty of practice, no doubt."

Brad barks out a laugh. "Meow. You certainly don't need those claws sharpened."

"I've dealt with my fair share of Peytons. I know the type and how to deal with them." I rifle through my locker until I find a spare hoodie. My vest lifts as I tug Brad's sweater up over my head. My hair flies around my face, blocking my vision. I'm untangling the mess when I feel a surge of warmth against my belly. Brad's fingers linger on my skin as he slowly pulls the hem of my vest down. An undercurrent zips through the air making me uncomfortable. "I got it." I remove his hand from my stomach, thrusting his sweater at him.

He shuffles nervously from foot to foot. "Um, sorry."

I zip my hoodie halfway up my body so the lacy edge of my vest is showing. "Thanks for standing up for me back there," I say, choosing to ignore whatever just happened.

"No problem." He makes eye contact with me, looking a little sheepish. His piercing blue eyes probe mine with intensity. "Do you want to head outside?"

I scrunch my nose. "Not particularly." I'm afraid to even poke my head outside for fear the vultures will have expanded exponentially. "I'm going to try and wash out some of the sticky shit in my hair."

Brad walks with me, and I'm just pushing the bathroom door open when the sounds of approaching footfalls tickle my eardrums. "There you are!" Rose sprints toward us. "Wanted to check you were okay."

"I'm grand." Brad and Rose both grin. "I'm *fine.*" I enunciate the word, rolling my eyes as I do. "I just need to clean up."

"I'll wait here," Brad confirms, and I step into the bathroom with Rose hot on my heels.

I stick my head in the sink and turn on the taps, running my fingers through the icky soda mess in my hair.

"Here." Rose hands me a towel from her bag. "I always keep a spare in case I can fit in a few lengths in the pool."

"Thanks." I wrap my head in the towel and straighten up. "So what have people been saying all day?"

"You sure you want to hear?"

"Yep." I rub the towel over and back across my head. "I'd rather know so I can prepare myself. So far it's been low key, but I'm sure that won't last."

She props her butt against the counter. "If I didn't know any better, I'd say this town was waiting for something like this to happen. I swear I've never seen such a swift turnaround in opinion. All I've heard all morning is how the Kennedys had it coming to them and that Kalvin clearly takes after his womanizing father. Sympathy for Lana is huge." I sigh, rubbing my head more vigorously. "Is it true that James cheated on Alex?" she asks, and my hands stop moving.

"*That's* out in the open?"

Rose extracts a crumpled paper from her bag. "My parents still insist on a real paper. Thought you might like to see it." I take a glimpse over my shoulder. "No one is here but us," she assures me. "I checked when we came in, and I locked the door."

The headline stares mockingly at me. THE KENNEDY CURSE STRIKES AGAIN. I skim the article which focuses on James's alleged affair with an employee of Kennedy Apparel —thankfully, Courtney's name isn't mentioned, although I'm sure it won't take long for them to identify his mistress—and references Kal's arrest for rape and sexual assault.

"How do they get their hands on this stuff so fast?" I shake my head in frustration as I hand the paper back to Rose. "You can burn that."

Her tongue darts out and she wets her lips. "Is it true? About Kal and Lana?" she asks quietly.

"No. Kal is a lot of things but he's no rapist."

"Yeah. That's what I thought." She folds her arms over her chest. "What was Zoe saying back there?"

"She implied that she knows something is fishy, but she didn't want to say anything in front of a packed cafeteria. I'm meeting her after school to find out more."

"I don't get it. Lana never struck me as the dishonest type. Why would she make up such an allegation if it weren't true?"

"I don't know, Rose." I fold up the towel and hand it back to her. "But I fully intend to find out."

Chapter Seven

"**K**ennedy scum!" A boy with grungy shoulder-length hair shouts at me as I close my locker door at the end of the day.

"Is that the best you can do?" I shout back at him, flipping my middle finger up.

A muscular arm snakes around my waist from behind, and I flinch. "Relax," Brad says. His warm breath leaks over my skin, and I shiver involuntarily. "It's only me."

"We need to discuss boundaries," I murmur, unnerved by the level of touchy-feely stuff going on already.

"Peyton and Lance are watching," he whispers, nuzzling my hair with his nose.

I turn in his arms, locking my hands around his neck as he presses me back against the locker. "Alrighty then. Let's give 'em a show but no kissing on the mouth," I whisper back.

Brad dips his head to my neck and starts planting a trail of feathery-soft kisses across my skin. I throw my head back, moaning, as I lift my leg up to his waist. His hand grips my thigh, holding my leg in place, as his lips continue to worship my neck. Shivery tingles flood my body, and bile swirls in my mouth.

Faking it is one thing, but actually enjoying it is another matter entirely. I need to shut this down before it escalates.

Looking behind Brad, I spot Lance's and Peyton's attentive gazes. "That's enough," I rasp, lightly pressing on Brad's shoulders. "They're buying it."

He straightens up, snatching my bag and swinging it over his shoulder. Gripping my hand, he urges me forward. "Let's ditch this place."

He doesn't need to say it twice.

Zoe is waiting for me outside, just in front of the entrance. "Where do you want to talk?"

Max steps out of the waiting car, opening the door for me. My eyes flit to the gates, and I notice the growing media swarm outside. "Let's talk in the car," I suggest, walking toward it with my hand still in Brad's. Once we are all seated inside, I ask Max to park around the back of the school, and he raises the privacy screen without complaint.

"Right." I swivel around to face Zoe. "What do you know?"

"Lana's lying."

Tell me something I hadn't already figured out. "Why? And what exactly happened with her and Kal because I know something was going on between them."

Zoe crosses one knee over the other. "Lana has been in love with Kalvin since they were little kids. Honestly, it was borderline obsession at times. She has gone on dates over the years, but even if she liked the boy, she always stopped it before it could become serious. She always said she was saving herself for Kal."

"And he knew this?"

"Not at first, but I'm pretty sure she told him that lately."

She looks absently out the window. "I knew, with his rep, she was going to get hurt, but she wouldn't listen to reason."

"That's why you don't like him."

She gives me her undivided attention. "As far as I'm concerned, he's been stringing her along these past few months, and she didn't deserve that."

"What exactly went down?"

"She plucked up the courage a few months ago to tell him how she felt. At first, he brushed her off, but then he said he had feelings for her too, but he didn't know if he could commit to one girl." A dour expression wafts over her face. "Spoken like a true player," she snarls. "Anyway, they kissed a bunch of times, even though there were no labels or exclusivity or anything, but Lana kept on hoping. A month ago, she told me he'd said he loved her and he wanted to give them a try, but he wanted to keep their relationship secret because his mom wouldn't approve." Zoe scoffs again, and the more she talks, the angrier she's getting. "I can't believe I'm actually helping him because thinking about all the shit he put her through is almost enough to convince me he deserves to be locked up." She scowls.

"Go on," I implore, deliberately ignoring her little anti-Kal outburst.

"So, Lana was all 'heads in the cloud' in love, and she gave him her virginity because he promised her there was no one else for him, that he was done messing about with other girls." Zoe pierces me with hateful eyes. "Then Addison told her that Kal had come on to her and she'd slept with him. It broke Lana's heart, and she was inconsolable. She told me he was going to pay for playing her like a fool, and I guess she came up with the perfect revenge."

"I bloody knew it! I knew that bitch had a hand in this somewhere." I'm seething.

"I told Lana not to trust Addison, but she fell for it completely. I mean, I don't even know if it's true!" My face betrays me, and Zoe's eyes flare with liquid hatred. "Your cousin is a fucking asshole." Her skin turns puce.

"There's more to it than you think. Addison is playing some angle to get Ky back, and she set Kal up, pounced on him when he was drunk. He hates himself for it."

"Oh, boohoo! Drunk or not, he should've kept it in his pants!"

"I know, and he's an idiot, but he's not a rapist, and no matter how much you hate him, it isn't right that he's being accused of something he didn't do. Unless Lana said he did?"

Zoe trails a hand through her hair as she sighs. "Nope, she never said that. Things were pretty strained between us after she told me what Addison had said, and I was pissed that she wouldn't listen to me. I've been her friend for years, and that bitch blows in, spouting crap, and Lana believes her in a heartbeat. I was so freaking mad."

"That's understandable, and ordinarily, I don't think Lana would've been swayed by Addison, but she was clearly broken-hearted and vulnerable, and Addison used that to her advantage," I surmise.

"That's her usual MO, but I don't know how you're going to prove anything." Brad cuts in for the first time.

"Can you try talking Lana around?" I suggest.

Zoe shakes her head. "I have no way of contacting her. Her cell is disconnected, and she's shut down all her social media accounts. It's as if she's disappeared off the face of the earth."

"Would you testify? Would you tell the court what you told us?"

Her face contorts unpleasantly. "I'd really rather not, but ... if the case goes ahead and I'm needed, then I'll do it." She looks down at her lap. "I can't stand your cousin, but he doesn't deserve to go to jail just 'cause he's a jerk. Besides, I will always be on the side of justice."

"Thank you." I take her hands in mine. "I appreciate it."

Brad leans forward in his seat. "Is this about Jessie, too?"

I'm startled when moisture starts to form in Zoe's eyes. "A little."

"Who's Jessie?" I ask with a frown.

"She was my cousin." Zoe sniffs, and I shoot a curious look at Brad.

"Jessie was kidnapped and found a week later, buried in the woods. Today is the one-year anniversary," Brad quietly explains.

"I'm so sorry, Zoe. I didn't know."

She stares at me as she speaks but it's like she's looking right through me. "Another girl went missing around the same time, two years previously. The police are clueless. They still have no leads, and no one has been arrested for their murders. It isn't right!" Her voice raises an octave. "How can someone get away with that?"

We don't respond because there are no words. There is absolutely nothing either one of us could say that would make her feel better.

She creaks her neck. "I better go. The vigil is starting soon." She wipes under her eyes. "Let me know if you need me to talk to the police or your cousin's attorney."

She has one foot out the door when I clasp her elbow. "Wait. Can we come? To the vigil?"

She shrugs. "Free country. Do what you like." *Aaannnd* the familiar Zoe is back in her body. She walks away without another word or look.

After checking in with James, and okaying it with Lenny and Max, Brad and I attend the vigil which is being held in a little hall at the back of the school building. Jessie was a student here, and according to Brad, she was a sweet girl who never harmed a fly. News of her murder was a massive shock.

A framed picture of a pretty girl with dark hair and blue eyes rests on an elevated stand at the top of the room. A bunch of assorted flower arrangements surround the photo, along with some personal affects including a Wellesley Memorial sweater, a worn-looking teddy bear, a One Direction poster, and a sketch pad. My heart aches for the sweet girl whose life was ended before it had properly begun.

I hunt Ky down the minute I return to the house, determined that I can talk to him without losing the run of myself. He needs to hear what Zoe confided in us. "Come in," he calls out in that rich, hypnotic voice of his when I knock on his bedroom door. All my lady bits rejoice, and I silently caution myself to get with the program. Drawing a long breath, I open the door and step into his domain.

Ky is sprawled across his disheveled bed, hurriedly pulling a shirt on over his bare chest. But he wasn't fast enough, and I've witnessed enough to stir the usual longing inside me. His tantalizing flesh glistens invitingly, and I bite down hard on my lower lip, almost drawing blood. I close the door, purely because I don't want anyone else to hear what I have to say, but being in his room, alone with him, is far too intimate, and already my resolve is wavering.

Focus, Faye. Mind out of the gutter!

"How did today go?" He scoots to the edge of the bed, swinging his bare feet to the floor.

"Fine, apart from Peyton drenching me in Coke, but that had nothing to do with Kal and everything to do with me."

Ky's eyes narrow. "I might need to have a word with Fielding again."

I slump to the ground where I stand, leaning my back against the door, with my knees pulled up to my chest. "No need. Brad sorted it."

A glimmer of annoyance and something else flashes across Ky's face. Before he can get mad or jealous or release whatever it is he's feeling, I jump in with a question of my own. "How bad was it in Old Colonial today?"

Ky rests his chin in his hand. "Pure hell." I wince. "I spent the entire day trying to keep Kent out of fights and the rest of the time I was glued to Kal's side. The whole school has gone insane, and we're public enemy number one. Not that I can blame them. Getting in and out of the school grounds was akin to fighting your way across an open battlefield. Reporters swarmed the car when we were trying to leave." He shakes his head. "Fun and games." Air whooshes out of his mouth.

"How is he?"

"Not good, Faye. I could barely get two words out of him all day. I've never seen him like this and it's scaring me."

"I'll try talking to him. See if I can get him to open up."

"Thanks."

An uneasy silence fills the air. I clear my throat. "I had an interesting conversation with Zoe today."

His head tips up and his eyes spark to life. "Yeah?"

"She knows Lana is lying." I proceed to tell him everything Zoe imparted. When I get to Addison's involvement, Ky's whole face and demeanor changes. He holds himself rigidly still, and a muscle snaps in his taut jaw. If looks could kill, Addison would be stone-cold dead by now. "I don't know what you did to that girl, but she sure as shit is out to ruin this family."

Ky hops up. "I didn't do anything except fall for the bitch!"

He starts pacing the room, and steam is practically billowing out of his ears.

"I know. I'm sorry. I shouldn't have voiced that." I climb to my feet, fighting the almost irresistible urge to rush to his side and reassure him. "I should go."

"Forget it. I'm overly sensitive right now." He scrubs his stubbly jaw. "I'd prefer if you kept this conversation between us. I'll tell Dad so he can pass it on to Kal's legal team, but I don't want you to tell Kal. I don't want to get his hopes up for nothing. At the end of the day, it will be Zoe's word against Lana's, so I'm not sure how helpful it will be."

"Surely, it's got to count for something? She's Lana's oldest friend and she's never been a supporter of Kal so the fact she's willing to speak out on his behalf says a lot."

He shrugs. "Maybe. It all depends on the evidence the prosecution presents."

Having said what I came in here to say, I reach for the door. "I suppose so. Anyway, I'd better go." Before the craving to kiss him hits me full whack in the face.

"Wait." Ky rushes toward me, and I instinctively shrink back. A pained look crosses his face.

"It's not like that," I rush to reassure him. "It's only th—"

"I know." He sighs wearily. "Look, leave Addison to me, okay? I'll handle her." My cheeks pucker sourly. "I mean it, Faye. I don't know what she's up to now, but I don't want you involved. Promise me."

I want to, but I don't trust Addison around him. She knows how to push all his buttons, and I want to protect *him*. "I can't make that promise, Ky."

He lets loose a string of colorful curses as he invades my personal space. "Goddammit, Faye. For once, can you please just do something I ask." His tone is frustrated, and that rubs me wrong.

"Why can't I protect *you* from her?"

He exhales loudly. "Because I know how her mind works, and this is all tied up with me."

"And that's exactly why you should steer clear of her. She'll suck you in and trap you again."

His face relaxes. "That's what you're worried about?" He leans in, pressing his forehead against mine. My heart skyrockets, slamming against my ribcage. "I've told you I love you. You're the only one for me, so if that's what you're worried about, stop it. You have no reason to be concerned in that regard."

His warm breath snakes over my skin, clouding my senses. "But what if we're ... if you're my ..."

"If that's our reality, it's not going to change how I feel even if I'm forced to ignore those feelings. And I won't magically love Addison again. She's dead to me, and she has been for a long time."

I cup his face, ogling his lips with a craving so intense I think I could expire from it. "You really mean that?" I ask, shuttering my eyes to avoid temptation.

"Yes. Now stop worrying, and leave Addison to me."

Chapter Eight

Famous last words. That's what I'm thinking as I walk on auto-pilot to the kitchen. *Does it make me a bad person that I keep wishing for something life threatening to happen to Addison?* Like she's run over by a car or hit by lightning or someone she's pissed off beats her up so badly that she gets amnesia and she can't remember who Ky is? It's not that I want her dead, per se—even I'm not that cruel—but I'd like her solidly out of the way.

Keaton slams the fridge door in a temper as I step into the kitchen. "What did the fridge ever do to you?" I joke.

"Gobbled all the food and left nothing to eat, that's what," he retorts with a glum face.

I open a few of the presses, and Keaton is right. The cupboards are bare too, and without Greta around, we'll most likely starve if we're relying on any of my cousins to shop or cook. I take a quick peek at my watch. I still have a couple of hours before my shift at the diner starts. I was planning on speaking to Kalvin, but feeding the horde of hungry men in the house seems like more of a priority at present. "I'll make you a deal. If you come to the supermarket with me, I'll cook you whatever you want when we get back."

"Where do I sign up?" His eyes twinkle.

"Come on." I loop my arm in his and drag him out of the room. "Let's go grab some grub."

"Can you quit moaning for five seconds or we'll be here half the night?" I ask Keaton after his latest bout of grumping. His patience for grocery shopping is nonexistent as I've discovered to my peril the last half hour. I've never been to a store as mammoth as this one, and it's taking me forever to find the things I need. Plus, I've never shopped for so many people before, and I'm not sure if I'm adding too much or too little to the cart. A frustrated sigh slips out of my mouth. At this rate, I won't make it to work on time. "If you stopped complaining and actually started helping, then we'd be done that much quicker."

"Fine. You're the boss." He lets go of the trolley and walks to my side, nudging me in front of it. "You drive while I fetch. Tell me what we need."

Our new system works much more effectively, and a half hour later Lenny, Max, and Keaton load the grocery bags in the boot of the Merc and we are en route back home. "How was school?" I ask once we're settled in the backseat.

"Don't mention the war," Keaton deadpans. "Hopefully some other scandal will crop up soon and people will forget about ours." He stares out the window. "The timing sucks."

"In what way?" I'm thinking no time is a good time for stuff like this to blow up in the public domain. He messes with a loose thread on the hem of his shirt, and he's uncharacteristically quiet. "Is there some other big secret I don't know about?"

I'm only half-joking, because, honestly, if there is more stuff waiting to come out of the closet, I'm going to freak the hell out.

"I have a girlfriend," he blurts out a few minutes later, his cheeks flushing red.

"Cool! When do I get to meet her?"

"If she's still my girlfriend by the end of the week, I'll bring her over to the house this weekend."

"You think she's going to dump you because of everything that's going on with the fam?" My brows nudge up.

He shrugs. "I know I probably would."

I poke his ribs with my elbow. "Give the girl some credit. If she didn't dump you today, I'd say you're fine on that score."

Lines crease his forehead as he thinks about that. "Hmm. Maybe you're right." He looks at me strangely.

"What?"

"I, uh, I owe you an apology." He looks embarrassed.

"For what?"

"For the way I behaved in Nantucket."

Understanding washes over me. When Keaton had discovered Ky and I kissing, he hadn't taken the news of our relationship well. He'd been distinctly frosty in the following days. "You already apologized. Besides, you were perfectly entitled to react as you did."

"That's the thing," he says, turning into me so our knees brush. "I shouldn't have reacted all judgy like that. I'm ashamed that I was so closed off. I didn't think that was the kind of person I am. I don't want to be like that."

Not that it matters, at the moment, because Ky and I may be over before we've even begun, but my natural curiosity is piqued. "Why *did* you react like that?"

He tilts his chin up until he's eyeballing me. "This is going to sound so immature but ... I was jealous." My eyes pop wide. "Hells, not like that!! That didn't come out right." He laughs nervously. "I thought we were friends, and I liked that we'd bonded in a way you hadn't with my brothers." His cheeks stain a darker shade of red. "Then you started spending more time with Ky, and I was already annoyed over that because I wasn't seeing as much of you. When I realized why, and what was going on between you, I ... I was hurt and upset. I thought it meant that you wouldn't have time to hang with me anymore."

He drops his head, clearly ashamed, but I'm glad he got that off his chest. I close the gap between us and pull him into my arms, hugging him to death. "Oh, Keaton. You little idiot." I muss up his hair. "I'll always make time for you, and I won't ever forget how much you helped me settle in. You will always have a very special place in my heart." I kiss the top of his head before pulling back. His blushing is out of control, and it's so sweet. I love that he still has this fresh-faced innocence about him and a heart brimming with goodness. It's a vast contrast to Kent who is completely the other side of the spectrum and Keanu who is still a total enigma—I haven't sussed out his personality yet. They may be triplets, but they couldn't be any more different if they purposely tried.

I smile at him. "When I was growing up, I hated that I didn't have any siblings or any other family to call my own. I had my parents driven demented asking for a baby brother or sister until my mum sat me down and explained she couldn't have any more children." An icy layer grabs a hold of my heart as the pleasantness of my memory is tainted with the knowledge of her deceit. But I force it aside, because this is about making Keaton feel better; this isn't about me.

"When I imagined having a little brother, this is what I imagined it would be like." I gesture between us. "You're like the brother I always wished for, Keaton, and nothing or no one will ever change that." My voice chokes as the words register in my brain. Keaton looks like he might burst with happiness.

Keaton isn't just *like* my brother; he very well may *be* my brother.

Blinding lights go off in my mind. *Wow.* I hadn't thought of it like that before. I've been so consumed at the prospect of losing Kyler, and sick over what mum and James did, that I hadn't even considered what I'd be gaining in this situation. It doesn't lessen the blow, or ease the heartfelt pain, but it does help put certain things in perspective.

Mum may have given me my siblings after all—just not in the way she envisaged.

"What's all this?" Ky strides into the kitchen like he owns it. Keaton is unloading the groceries while I've made a start on dinner.

"What's it look like, ass face?" Keaton playfully shoves his brother. "Faye and I went shopping because there was nothing to eat in the house."

"How did you pay for it?" Ky asks, leaning back against the counter.

I stir fresh basil into my homemade tomato sauce. "I put it on the card your mom gave me."

He pulls a wad of notes out of his pocket, offering it to me. "Here. Does that cover it?"

I swat his hand away. "I don't want your money. I covered it." It's not as if it's my money I used anyway, so there's no need to big-deal it.

He frowns again. "I'll get another bankcard off Mom for groceries so you don't have to use your own money in future." I don't bother arguing as I don't have time, but it's blatantly obvious that my views on money differ greatly from my cousins.

"About that." I scoop the meatballs onto the tray and place

them into the oven. "I don't mind helping out short term, but I'm going to have swim practice most days after school from next week, and with my shifts in the diner and homework, it doesn't leave much time for housework." I stretch my stiff back as I straighten up. "I don't mind helping out as much as I can, but I'm not going to be able to look after this entire house singlehandedly."

"Of course, and no one expects you to. I'll talk to Mom and see if she's done anything to find a new housekeeper, and in the meantime, everyone can help out with chores."

"Sounds good, thanks." I busy myself removing a saucepan from the press and filling it with water. Anything to avoid looking at him. Not that it makes much of a difference because the usual tingly charge electrifies the space between us. You could lead me blindfolded into a room, and I'd be able to detect Ky's presence in a heartbeat. So far, our plan to stay out of one another's way isn't working so smoothly. In a house this size, it should be doable, but his presence looms large, and there doesn't seem to be any getting away from that.

"Where should I put this, sis?" Keaton asks, holding up a bag of rice. I almost choke on a cough, and Ky's eyes dart wide in alarm.

"Over there." I point at a cupboard on the left, and he scurries off to stow it away.

"He doesn't know," I mouth at Ky, and his shoulders visibly relax even as he sends me a perplexed expression.

Keaton whistles under his breath as he unloads the last of the shopping bags.

"Can I help with anything?" Ky asks, looking around.

"Nope. Keaton and I have this." I don't make eye contact this time, and I catch Keaton looking curiously between us.

"Okay. I'll leave you to it." An edge of unhappiness creeps

into Ky's tone, and I'm waylaid by guilt, but separation is for the best. "Oh, one other thing," he supplies a minute later.

I risk a quick glance at him. He's standing in the doorframe with a half-smirk on his face. "You might want to avoid Brad for a little while. At least until he calms down."

"You agreed it with Alex?"

"Yep, and she's cool with it, but Brad doesn't want to be seen as a charity case, so he might take a few days to come around."

"Thanks for the heads up." I offer him a small smile, and his sad eyes meet mine in shared understanding.

"What's that all about?" Keaton asks.

"Brad's coming to live here, or, hopefully, he is, if he can get over himself."

"Sweet." Keaton plucks an apple from the bowl and sinks his teeth into the juicy flesh. I grab some cutlery from the drawer and move to set the table. "But that's not what I meant. What's up with you and Ky? I've seen strangers more comfortable with one another."

"Don't ask," I plead, praying he'll let it drop.

"Have you guys broken up already?"

His words strike fear into my heart. "Things are a little complicated." Inside, I'm begging him to let it slide, because I can't tell him what's going on yet, and I really don't want to lie to him, especially when things are back on track with us. I almost collapse with relief when he does.

I have no choice but to grab mouthfuls of my dinner in my bedroom as I get ready for work because at this rate I'm not going to make my shift on time. I fly outside like I'm being chased by a gun-toting madman, flinging myself into the back-seat of the car while cramming the last morsels of pasta in my mouth.

I make it through the front door of the diner with seconds to spare.

"Cutting it close, girlfriend," Rose teases, looking up from the till.

"Tell me about it. It's been all go today."

I reckon I'd make it into the *Guinness Book of Records* for the speed with which I get changed into my uniform. I exit the locker room a couple of minutes later, tying my apron around my waist. Rose thrusts a pad and pen in my hand as our boss, David, emerges from his office. "We don't want to give any customers a side of hair," he semi-jokes, reaching up to tuck a few escaped strands into my hat.

"Sorry," I mumble under my breath, shooting Rose a side look.

David's eyes latch on the creature with the boulders for shoulders standing guard outside the door, and I cringe. "Who the hell is that guy?" he asks, his gaze landing instantly on mine.

I cringe again. "Um, that's Lenny. My new bodyguard."

"He can't stand there—he'll scare away all my customers!" His tone is bordering on coronary-inducing territory.

"Give me two minutes and I'll sort it." My feet are already moving in the direction of the door.

Ten minutes and two arguments later, Lenny is ensconced in the passenger seat of the Merc, scowling at me as he closes the door with unnecessary force. I have an almost over-whelming urge to stick my tongue out at him, but I manage to refrain from indulging in such childish behavior.

David makes it clear that Lenny is not welcome anywhere near the premises, and I have to promise faithfully that he'll never darken the door again. I'm hoping after a few shifts when James sees there is no need for him to be here, he'll allow me go to work without the Hulk watching over me.

I'm dead on my feet after the first couple of hours, but I plow through. Ignoring the harsh glares and whispered gossip is harder than I thought it'd be, but I do my best. After a while, Rose takes pity on me. "I'll take your station, and you can man the counter for the rest of the shift if you like?"

"You're an angel. Thanks." I gratefully accept her offer, and it's a welcome relief to be away from the gossipy bunch out on the floor.

"You seem to have your hands full tonight," a smooth male voice says, and I look up from the register, meeting twinkling blue eyes and a firm smile. I'm not sure how long he's been sitting at the counter, but judging from the menu still in his hands, it can't be more than a few minutes if he hasn't ordered yet. He's in his late thirties or early forties, if I had to hazard a guess, and very attractive for an older dude. He runs a hand through his short, dark hair as his eyes invade mine.

"It's always busy in here." I regard him warily even if my tone is polite. I'm suspicious of every stranger right now. "What can I get you?"

"What would you recommend?"

"The Works Burger is good if you're super hungry. All the salads are tasty, but my favorite is the fish and chips. It reminds me of home." I don't know why I said that. There's something about his warm smile that encourages me to drop my guard. I wipe down the counter and set a fresh placemat and cutlery in front of him.

"And home is Ireland?"

I put my hands on my hips. "What gave me away?"

"I know an Irish accent when I hear one." He smiles more expansively even though it doesn't quite meet his eyes.

"No doubt, the longer I'm here, the less I'll sound like myself," I muse, thinking of James's warped half-Irish, half-American twang. I hope I don't end up sounding like that.

Somehow, it seems vitally important that I continue to sound like myself. I catch myself before I fall back into that introspective well, before I admit something I shouldn't. I've never seen this guy in here before and my spidey senses are on high alert. "And now I'm babbling." I laugh to disguise my suspicion, although, in his snazzy designer suit and with what looks like an expensive watch strapped to his wrist, he seems more like a businessman than a nosy journalist. However, one can never be too careful, and James's recent lecture is still ringing in my ears. He pretty much put the fear of God into me when it comes to the hacks hanging around town looking for more juicy tidbits. I won't be the one to deliver the goods.

"What can I get you, or do you need more time?" I ask, putting this convo clearly back on a professional footing.

He closes the menu over, handing it to me with a sad look in his eyes. "I'll go with the fish and chips. Thanks."

The rest of the night is a blur, and I don't know how I'm still standing on my weary feet. When David tells me I can go home early, I almost cry in relief. I'm supposed to be on lockup tonight, but he obviously sees how exhausted I am.

Despite the fact I can scarcely keep my eyes open, once I'm back in the house, I quickly get ready for bed and then pad to Kal's room. I knock lightly on the door, expecting to be turned away like last night, so I'm pleasantly surprised when he answers. "Who is it?" he calls out.

"It's Faye. Can I come in?"

I'm greeted by initial silence, and then the door swings open a minute later. Kal is wearing sweats and nothing else, and it's refreshing to see he's at least dressed like his usual self. Bruising shadows darken the skin under his dull eyes, and his skin has lost some of its radiance. He steps aside, wordlessly, leaving space for me to enter. Picking over the trail of dirty clothes on the floor, I flop into the chair by his messy bed as he crawls back under the covers.

"On a scale of one to ten, how shitty was today?" I ask.

His lips curve slightly up at the corners. "As shitty as you can imagine." His voice is low and serious with no hint of humor.

Ky had asked me not to tell Kal about my chat with Zoe, and I understand where he's coming from, but keeping secrets has done this family no favors, and I deliberately made him no promises in that regard. "I spoke with Zoe today." His dead eyes latch on mine, but he says nothing so I persist. "She knows the sex was consensual, and she's willing to testify to that."

He props his head up with one hand as he stares off into space. "Has she heard from Lana?" I shake my head. "Does she know where she is?"

"No. She's gone into hiding."

Kal lies flat on his back, resting one arm across his face. "What did Lana say when you talked to her?"

"Not much. I was hoping to get the truth out of her, but Greta caught me and went ballistic before I had a chance to properly talk to her."

He removes the hand from his face, piercing me with anguished eyes. "How badly was she hurting?"

"She wasn't good, Kal. She was crying her eyes out and really upset."

"I messed up real bad this time, Faye," he whispers.

He looks so sad, and I wish I could take his pain away. I don't hesitate. I get up and lie down beside him, resting my head on his shoulder.

"One part of me thinks this is karma and that I deserve it. Is this my punishment for how I've behaved with girls? How I've treated Lana?"

"Did you rape her?"

He props up on one elbow. "No! You know that!"

"Then you don't deserve this. We all make bad choices, and no one deserves to be punished unfairly. I can't believe she's doing this to you. It's as if the girl I was getting to know was someone else. While I'm sorry she's hurting, I'm furious with her for doing this to you. She has no right to lie about something this serious. It's girls like Lana who scare genuine rape victims out of reporting it."

"She isn't herself, Faye, because the Lana you were getting to know *is* the real Lana. She's a sweetheart."

I sit up, an incredulous expression on my face. "I can't believe you're defending her."

"I haven't forgotten who she is. She may have, but I haven't." He sighs. "I never meant to hurt her. I care about her so much, and I tried to stay away because I knew I was no good for her, but she wouldn't take no for an answer." A strangled sound rips from the base of his throat. "She must be in unbelievable pain because the real Lana wouldn't ever do something like this."

His words settle like sour milk in my gut. I want to tell him that Addison has manipulated this situation, and I know I swore I'd tell him the truth, but I'm afraid of making a bad situation even worse if I disclose that information. *I've been plotting creative deaths for the bitch all day, so who knows how Kalvin would react?*

The last thing he needs is a murder charge added to the existing rape charge.

So, although I feel horribly guilty for hiding this part of the truth, I keep my lips sealed and hope it doesn't come back to haunt me.

Chapter Nine

Kal gives me a delicate kiss on the cheek the next morning, but he hasn't said anything else since last night, and he's retreated back into his shell. I want to help but I don't want to push him before he's ready to confront everything. *If this is his way of coping, who am I to tell him he's wrong?* He knows I'm here for him, and I'd like to think that I helped in some small way. It devastates me to witness his transformation from cocky, confident, playboy to such a sullen, silent shadow of himself. I know he must be scared shitless—I would be—and I wish I could erase his pain.

Alex and James are nowhere to be seen this morning, so I help Ky organize the others, and then I race out the door and into the waiting Merc before I'm late for school.

Strong arms cage me in from behind while I'm sorting out my locker and I go rigidly still. "You're in my bad books, beautiful," Brad confirms, brushing my hair to one side and planting a soft kiss to the back of my neck. I visibly shudder as a flurry of tingles whip up and down my spine.

I push him back a little and turn around with an unapologetic expression plastered on my face. "Get over it."

He cranks out a laugh, unable to contain his smile. "And here I was expecting lots of groveling."

"I don't grovel, and I only apologize when I'm genuinely in the wrong," I retort, stuffing the last book into my bag and shutting my locker. "And I've done nothing wrong. This is me being a good friend, and you'll be thanking me any day now."

He smirks. "It's impossible to stay mad at you."

I give him my best sugary-sweet smile. "I know. I'm far too adorable." I tweak his nose and start walking in the direction of my class.

He falls into place alongside me. "You shouldn't have interfered, Faye. I specifically asked you not to."

"Ugh!" I swing around, grabbing hold of his sweater and yanking him off to the side of the corridor. "You are so infuriating! I was only trying to help. Seriously, Brad, put your head on right. You say you want to secure a scholarship and go to college, and you let your family leave without you so you could stick to your life plan. Tell me how you can achieve that if you are living out of your car and surviving on fresh air?"

His lips thin. "That's only temporary until I sort something out! I'm a resourceful guy, and I *will* figure things out. I *will* get that scholarship and go to college. You watch!" He storms off, brandishing his bruised pride like a weapon, and I take a deep breath.

"Don't tell me there's trouble in paradise already," Lance says, materializing at my side.

"Is he always so stubborn?" I ask, and he laughs.

"Stubborn is every footballer's middle name, sweetheart." He gives me a saucy wink as he walks off.

I drift through my morning classes like an aimless cloud. Cluttered thoughts crowd my mind, making concentration virtually impossible. It's far too easy to get lost in my head. To think about it all—Mum, James, the test results, Ky, Kal, Brad—and my head feels like it could explode. No matter how hard I try to dispel all such thoughts, they refuse to leave me alone. The one positive is that the growing mountain of insults and taunts leveled my way barely register.

I'm working out a groveling speech in my head when Brad accosts me outside the cafeteria at lunchtime. Clutching my hand, without a word, he leads the way to the empty auditorium and ushers me inside. I open my mouth to speak, but he silences me with a finger to my lips. "I'm the one who needs to apologize. I shouldn't have snapped at you earlier, and I'm sorry. I know you're only trying to help."

I can't smother my grin, and he sends me a funny look. "I was preparing to grovel for the first time in my life, and now you've saved me from lowering my standards." I loop my arm in his. "Apology accepted."

"Someone's looking mighty pleased," Rose says as we settle into seats for the last class of the day.

"I managed to convince Brad to move into our house, and it took minimal persuasive skills to pull it off, so, yes, I am feeling pretty pleased with myself." I smirk, dropping my textbook on the desk.

Rose leans in, speaking close to my ear. "What is the dealio with you two?"

"He's pretending to be my boyfriend to take some of the heat off me," I explain.

"Pretending, huh?" Her brows lift.

I slap her arm. "Stoppit! It's not like that between us. You know I'm crazy about Ky." I avert my eyes before she can read anything in my expression. I haven't confided in Rose because the fewer people who know about the incestuous background in my family, the better. Makes me feel like a shitty friend though.

"Does Brad know that?"

"Of course, he does, and he came up with this idea together with Ky, so stop planting awful thoughts in my head."

"I hope you know what you're getting yourself into is all. I can't see this ending well."

"You are overthinking it. Brad's my friend, and that's all he'll ever be. He knows that."

"If you say so." Her lips purse as she flicks open her book to the allocated page. The teacher starts the lesson, and I'm grateful that it's put an end to that particular convo.

Rose pulls me aside after class. "I'm sorry if I freaked you out earlier. I happen to think Brad has feelings for you, and I'm worried you might both get hurt is all."

I inwardly cringe. "I'm sorry for being so defensive. If I'm being honest, I think you could be right. Maybe I should put an end to this fake boyfriend lark without delay."

"If it was me, I'd just be completely blunt with him so he doesn't harbor any false hope."

The diner is crazy busy tonight, but I have less to do than most nights thanks to David and his overeager planning. He scheduled additional staff onto the rota, and now there are way too many of us. I mentally fist-pump the air when David lets both Rose and me leave an hour earlier than expected. An idea has been taking root in my head all day, and this feels like too good of an opportunity to pass up. I fill Rose in as we get changed in the locker room, and her eyes light up at my suggestion. Not only that, she has some great intel which aids our planning, and I'm so glad I decided to confide in her about this now. We plot our best plan of action, and I'm giddy with anticipation. Even though what we're planning is technically illegal, and if we get caught we'll be in a whole world of trouble, I think the risk is worth it.

Taking decisive action is a great distraction, and it'll feel good to be physically doing something to help. Ditching Lenny is imperative but problematic, so we mull over some ideas before the perfect escape plan comes to mind.

I head home in the Merc—purely to keep up appearances— and I have a small window to get changed before I need to meet up with Rose. Raised voices greet me the second I enter the kitchen from the garage. Ky and Kent are going at it full throt- tle. "You're not going out at this time of night. You've got school in the morning."

"Get lost, Ky," Kent says, shoving his brother. "You're not my dad, and you don't get to tell me what to do."

"Listen, here, you little shit." Ky jabs a long finger in Kent's chest. "This family has enough to deal with currently without you adding to it. So you can forget whatever whoring or stealing you have in mind for tonight and get your ass in bed. If I have to call Dad, I will."

"Call him! I won't be here to care!" Kent yells, backing away.

Ky's hands curl into taut balls until the skin on his knuckles bleach white. "Get back here, Kent. I mean it."

Kent flips him the bird and a taunting smile before spin- ning on his heel and sauntering out the door.

"Aagh!" Ky slams his balled fist down hard on the counter, and I wince. His head jerks up and he notices me for the first time. "You heard that?" I nod. "He's going to get himself arrested too, and I wouldn't put it past the little shit to do it on purpose." He locks his hands behind his neck. "I better call Dad." Pulling his phone from the back pocket of his jeans, he emits a frustrated sigh as he punches the buttons.

A commotion at the front door startles both of us, and we start running to the lobby.

"Mom! You're scaring me!" Kent is holding Alex's shoulders, lightly shaking her. Tears are streaming down Alex's face as she holds herself at the waist, swaying precariously on her dangerously high heels.

"Mom. What is it?" Ky steps forward, circling his arm around Alex's back to steady her.

"I've lost. I've lost everything," she babbles. "Why?" She turns pleading eyes on us, her harried expression jumping from me to Ky to Kent. "Why me? What have I done to deserve this? I have worked myself to the bone for years, for this? I can't even ..." Pushing the boys away, she kicks off her shoes, sending them flying in different directions. I duck down, narrowly avoiding a stiletto in the face as she storms into the living area like a woman on a mission. She reappears a minute later carrying a bottle of white wine and a large wine glass. "I'm going to my room, and I don't want to be disturbed."

A muscle ticks in Ky's jaw and Kent has a "little lost boy" expression on his face that guts me.

"Mom, please, this isn't the way to deal with it." Ky steps toward her, appealing with his eyes.

Alex is halfway up the mezzanine stairs when she turns around. "Don't you dare attempt to lecture me! You know nothing! Just leave me alone, all of you." She stomps up the stairs, leaving us all flabbergasted in her wake.

Ky is trying hard to keep his reactions neutral but Alex's words have cut deep.

"I hate my life," Kent says matter-of-factly. "I hate this dysfunctional family. I wish I was dead."

"Kent." I step toward him, and he harrumphs.

"Don't even bother, Faye. You're wasting your energy on a lost cause." Shaking his head, he turns in the direction of the bedrooms and walks off.

Ky laughs bitterly. "At least he's not going out anymore." He looks over at me, a mix of longing, anguish, and torment etched on his face. "He's right though. You should get as far away from us as you can. I can't see how we're going to end up in a good place, and you're too good to be brought down with us."

I walk to him until we're face to face and lace my fingers in his. "I'm going nowhere. Irrespective of what the tests reveal, I'm already part of this family. And family stick together."

Ky releases another bitter laugh. "Pity my parents didn't get that memo."

"I want to comfort you, but I don't know how." I give his hand a gentle squeeze which is about the extent of what I can offer.

Ky extracts his hand from mine, pinching the bridge of his nose as he looks to the floor. "Just go, Faye, please. I know you mean well, but you're only making it worse."

His words pick at invisible wounds, hurting more than they should. I know where he's coming from and that he wants the same things I do, but his statement still cuts me to the bone.

Without looking at him, I walk away, and my aching heart feels like deadweight in my chest.

I'm dressed all in black as I slip out my window the second the guard patrolling this side of the house rounds the next bend. I race across the lawn, keeping to the right-hand side to avoid triggering the spotlight as I approach the woods at the rear of our garden. I'm panting, and out of breath, by the time I push through the creaky wooden gate behind the guesthouse my cousins normally use as party central. I doubt it'll be seeing much action in the coming weeks.

Rose is lounging against the side of her car, tapping her foot impatiently off the ground while she waits for me. "Psst!" I hiss and she jumps about ten feet in the air. I snigger. She whacks me in the arm. "Ow! You pack a mean punch!"

"You all but gave me a coronary!" She slaps a hand over her chest. "Dammit, Faye! Don't creep up on me like that."

"Sorry," I say, sniggering again as I jump in the passenger seat.

She starts up the engine. "We still doing this?"

"Hell to the yes. I need to know what that cow is up to. Ky warned me to leave Addison to him, but I don't trust her not to manipulate him. My instinct tells me she's at the root of everything that's going on, and I won't sit around any longer twiddling my thumbs while she plots other ways to ruin my cousins. We're going to shut her down."

"Alrighty then, let's get this show on the road."

Rose parks the car in a dark, spooky lane around the corner from Addison's house. "Come on," she whispers once she's locked the car. "This way." She nudges me with her shoulder.

"Why are we whispering?" I whisper.

She shrugs. "I'm being careful in case anyone is around."

My eyes survey the blank canvas surrounding us and I grin. "Stop being a nervous Nancy. There's no one here."

We traipse through empty fields, wading through long, muddy grass, for about fifteen minutes until Rose holds up a hand to caution me. "We are at the back of her house now," she whispers. "See there." She points to a row of tall trees bordering a succession of high fencing. I nod. "We'll follow that line up the side of her house, and then we'll have to climb over. I'm not sure where her bedroom is, but let's get on the property and check things out."

"That's fine by me. Today is only a scouting mission anyway. We'll have to plan a return when no one is here so we can do some snooping in her room."

"Well, look at you, Nancy Drew!" she whisper-teases, and I have to stifle my snort.

"I loved those books! My mum had read them as a child, and she kept them for me. I lost count of the number of times I reread them. I so wanted to be a detective when I grew up!" A soulful pang hits me in the chest. It's the first time in days that I've thought happy thoughts about Mum.

"I was talking about the TV show."

"That was pants. You've gotta read the books." Light is minimal, and our vision is restricted, but I don't need to see her to know she's rolling her eyes. "Are you rolling your eyes at me?"

"Are you planning on spying on Addison anytime this century, or did you want to resume discussing amateur sleuths?"

"Antsy today, aren't you?" I snark back, but there's no heat behind my words.

"That was me giving you the middle finger, in case you didn't sense that one."

I laugh quietly. "Okay, serious hat back on. Are you sure there's no operational security system? I'd rather not get arrested tonight." James would throw a hissy fit.

"I told you my uncle installed the security system, and he said all the cameras are for show. Addison's dad is a real penny pincher despite the fact he's loaded. Rumor is his wife splashes the cash with abandon, and he won't part with a dime."

"Well, I don't see Addison wanting for much."

"Oh, Mrs. Sinclair always makes sure her princess has everything she needs."

"Did you just roll your eyes again?"

This time it's Rose's turn to laugh. "Totally." She tugs on my elbow. "Come on. The longer this takes the more we risk being discovered. Let's scout the place out and then get the hell away from here."

Keeping close to the perimeter of the Sinclair property, we run quickly and quietly until we've reached the farthest point of the fence. I prop Rose up with my hands, and she swings her petite body over the top of the fence with ease. Pushing off the panels on the fence, I hoist myself up and over, landing quietly on the other side. My eyes scan the vast garden before raking over the two-story mansion to my left. It's clear the Sinclairs have plenty of money even if the house is smaller than I was expecting. Then again, the majority of houses seem small when compared with the Kennedy estate. Most of the house is in darkness, which is not unexpected at eleven p.m. at night, but buttery light streams out of one lower level window, attracting our interest. "They won't operate the alarm until they go to bed, and I can see lights on downstairs, so someone is definitely still up," Rose whispers. "It's safe. Come on."

Crouching down, and keeping our bodies flush to the wall, we creep slowly toward the only sign of life. My heart is pounding in my chest, and an influx of adrenaline floods my system. My palms are sweaty, and the nervous-excited sensation bouncing around my veins has me wired and edgy. I gulp back my panic as we inch closer. The large bay window is ajar, and as we draw nearer, the sounds of an argument waft through the air.

"Haven't you ruined my life enough already?" Addison's familiar whiny voice greets me.

"Darling," a posh female voice says. "That was never the inten—"

"Stop it, Mother!" Addison's voice is cutting. "I'm sick of hearing the same lies over and over."

"Addy," another woman says. "We did what was best for you." Her voice is rough, coarse, like she's had a twenty-a-day-cigarette habit since she was in nappies. "If you'd just lemme explain."

"You shut your mouth!" Addison yells, sounding more and more like a fishwife. "I have nothing to say to you. Not now. Not ever. And this is the last time I'll tell you both—stop ambushing me like this, or the next time I'll disappear. I mean it."

Oh, please mean it. Please disappear. I'm already planning the celebratory party in my head.

Sounds of stomping feet are accompanied by loud, exasperated sighs in the room. As Addison's footsteps recede, the conversation resumes. "This is hopeless," the woman with the distinctive, crude, gravelly voice says.

"You should never have forced me to tell her. You reneged on our deal!"

"Bullshit, Veronica!"

"Do not use that foul language in this house!" Addison's mother sounds like she's on the verge of self-combustion, and I can imagine her sitting stiffly in her seat with her chest puffed out and her cheeks turning red. I clamp a hand over my mouth to smother my giggle.

A light flickers on upstairs, emitting a rainbow of golden brightness, which illuminates our position, scaring the heck out of me. I jump in fright and my foot meets something solid on the patio beneath me. My breath hitches as I look down at the ground, just in time to watch the brown plant pot topple over with a loud thud. Rose's eyes widen in terror.

"What was that?" Addison's mum declares from inside the room. I grab Rose's arm and start running, so grateful that we had the foresight to wear soft-cushioned sneakers. We fling ourselves around the bend of the house as a wide spotlight illuminates the outdoor space and the tappity-tap of heels lands on the stone patio floor. My heart is racing erratically in my chest, and I'm working hard to recalibrate my panicked breathing. A line of sweat coasts down my spine even though I feel frozen all over. Rose clutches my hand in a death grip as we listen with bated breath.

"The cat knocked over one of my plants," Mrs. Sinclair says. "Stupid animal. I've no idea why Addison adores that cat so much." We wait for another couple of minutes—which feel like years—until the light and the sound of voices dies out before scrambling back over the fence and running across the fields as if our lives depend on it.

We don't even talk when we are back in the car. Rose drives us a few miles from Addison's house, before pulling over and slumping over the steering wheel. "Ohmigawd, I think I died about ten times."

"Holy shitballs for dinner," I croak. "That was way too close." I bark out an adrenaline-fueled laugh. "We are crappy spies."

Rose lifts her head, laughing with me. "We aren't completely clueless. We still gathered some intel, and I think it's safe to say we now know which bedroom is Addison's."

"I'm not sure I have the guts to return," I admit, holding out my trembling arm as evidence. "I haven't stopped shaking since we left."

"What do you think all that was about?" She looks contemplative.

"I don't know, but I'd love to find out." I wrack my brains, going over my previous conversations with Ky. "Ky said something was going on with her at home and she changed. Whatever they were discussing back there is obviously connected. I wonder what is going on with her. If that's when all this stuff with Ky started, maybe that's where we need to look first." I tap a finger off my lips as I muse out loud.

"How the heck do we do that?"

"Haven't a clue," I admit, salivating at the notion that Addison has buried secrets she wants to keep hidden. This could be the exact weapon we need to play her at her own game.

All I need is to figure out a way of uncovering the truth.

Chapter Ten

I wake at the butt crack of dawn the next morning, the noise of a very loud drill penetrating my brain. I'm unsure if I'm dreaming, if the noise is real, or if someone is boring an actual hole in my skull. I lift my head up and listen. Definitely real. Ugh. Glancing briefly at the time on my phone, I groan as I bury my head under the pillow, cursing whoever has woken me up two hours before I need to get ready for school.

The next time I'm woken up, it's to the sound of a loud ruckus in the corridor outside. Yawning, I haul my weary ass out of the bed and tie my dressing gown around my waist. I open my door and enter the corridor the same time Keaton emerges from his room. "What's going on?" I ask, as arguing voices tickle my eardrums.

I lift my eyes to the ceiling. *Here we go again.*

I'm half-thinking of phoning one of the TV production companies to see if anyone is in the market for a new family soap opera. The Kennedys would definitely give the Kardashians a run for their money.

The rest of the family is in the lobby when Keaton and I arrive. Alex's hair is sticking up all over the place, and she hasn't a scrap of makeup on her face. She is wearing baggy sweats and a wrinkled T-shirt, and I have to blink a few times to make sure it's the same woman. The press would have a field day if they saw the state of the Kennedy Apparel CEO right now. Bloodshot eyes watch me examining the glass of half-drunk wine in her hand, her fingers clutching the stem like a lifeline. "Don't judge. You have no idea what I'm going through." Her eyes plead for understanding.

Ky shoots me a worried look. Persistent thumping rattles the front door as James hollers at his wife. "Alex. This is ridiculous. Let me in!"

"Mom, you can't lock him out forever," Ky ventures.

Alex puts her glass on one of the steps before standing up with her arms folded in a matronly fashion across her chest. "Want to bet?"

"You changed the locks?" Keaton peeks up at his mother with big, sad eyes. "You're kicking him out permanently?"

"Yes, and he'll have to get used to it."

"But he's my dad. Our dad. I don't want him to go." Tears glisten in Keaton's eyes, and I slip my hand in his.

Alex's face yields a smidgeon as she steps off the stairs, approaching her son. "I'm sorry, honey. I didn't want this, but he's left me no choice."

Kent's face is wound tight as he rushes past me, returning to his bedroom without uttering a single word. All my cousins have their issues, but, out of all of them, Kent is the one most likely to do something completely reckless. Ky and I exchange more troubled looks. Alex rakes a hand through her hair, her resolve wavering in the face of her children's distress. She wets her lips, looking at all of us, unsure of what to say.

Ky pushes off the wall and walks toward her. "At least let

him in to get the rest of his stuff. I know he's hurt you, and he probably deserves what's coming to him, but you can't leave him outside like this. The media is still at the front gates, and if they figure out what's going on, they'll most likely send in a chopper. Do you want any more of our personal business splashed over TV screens?"

Alex pats Ky's arm, while James maintains his assault on the front door. "Okay." She folds him in her arms. "I'm sorry for what I said last night, sweetheart. I didn't mean to take it out on you or your brother. I'm sorry if my words hurt you."

Ky looks at me over his mother's shoulder. "It's okay, Mom. I understand and I'm here for you."

She presses a kiss to his forehead. "I love you. No matter what happens in the future, know I've always loved you."

Alex is sporting some serious mood swings lately, and I don't know about the others, but I've a bad case of whiplash from the aftereffects. I can never predict exactly what she's going to say or do next. Grief and heartache impacts everyone differently, I guess, and I'm not unsympathetic, but she needs to get a grip, and quickly. She isn't the only one hurting around here.

She opens the door with a flourish, glaring at her husband. James is furious. His cheeks are bright red, and his eyes glimmer with raw anger. "You have no right to change the locks. This is my home too. My name is on the deed."

He pushes past her into the lobby, stalling when he sees all of us watching.

"That's something else I'll be rectifying soon," Alex replies in a cold voice.

"Over my dead body you will!"

"That can also be arranged," she retorts, pinning her hands on her slim hips. "Don't fucking tempt me, James."

Keaton has an ice-grip on my hand, almost constricting the blood flow.

"Please don't do this, Alex. I've told you I'm fixing it."

She cranks out a laugh, throwing her head back in an exaggerated fashion. "This is your idea of fixing things!" she shrieks. "I'm losing everything I've worked for and you have the nerve to say that to me!"

"You need to give me a chance to make this right!" The desperate quality to James's voice doesn't go unnoticed by any of us. Every one of my cousins looks like their insides are being wrung tight, and my heart aches for them. James and Alex should be handling things in private instead of airing all their dirty laundry in front of their kids, but it's obvious both of them are in bits over their deteriorating marriage and are incapable of acting in a calm, mature fashion.

My parents rarely argued, but I recall some humdinger rows behind closed doors. It's only now I appreciate their attempts to conduct them in private even if that was a virtual impossibility within the confines of our small house and thin walls.

"I don't *need* to do anything." Alex straightens her spine and glares at her husband. "I don't owe you a thing." She jabs a slender finger in his chest. "This is all your fault. You just had to get mixed up with her because you're like every other weak man who can't keep it in his pants. I thought you were different, but I was wrong."

"It was one mistake, Alex!"

"You think that makes it all right?!" She shoves him hard, and Ky moves into position beside her, planting a cautionary hand on her lower back. "I stand to lose everything because of your *one mistake*. The only chance I have of protecting myself and my boys is to distance myself completely from you. I have no other options."

Tension filters through the air, and James goes rigidly still. "What do you mean by that?"

Alex's shoulders sag in defeat. "I'm divorcing you, James. You can expect paperwork from my attorney later today."

"No, Mom." Keaton cries out, yanking his hand out of mine as he moves toward his mother. He clings to her. "Please don't do this. Don't break up our family." His anguished pleas rip fresh strips off my already shredded heart.

Tears glean in Alex's eyes. "Baby," she purrs affectionately, caressing his cheek. "I'm sorry you're hurting, but I'm not the one who broke up this family. You can blame your father for that."

I chew on the inside of my cheek as I peruse James. He looks distraught, like someone has hacked at his insides with a chainsaw. His dazed eyes meet mine, and I feel for him, even if he has been the creator of his own doom. "You should probably come live with me, Faye."

Dread lodges like a boulder in the pit of my stomach. Technically, he's right. Either way, I've no blood ties to Alex.

"She's not leaving," Ky grits out.

"Faye is always welcome here," Alex tells James. She turns to me. "This is your home for as long as you want, but it's your decision, sweetheart, and if you want to live with James, that's your call."

Ky opens his mouth to speak, but Keaton beats him to it. "Don't go, Faye. Please. We can't lose you too."

I shuffle awkwardly on my feet. I know what I want to do. I want to stay here, but James has no one, and he's blood.

"Leaving might be for the best," James says, subtly gesturing toward Ky.

Ky growls under his breath. "Quit with the blackmail, Dad."

James straightens his shirt and heads toward the stairs. "I'm going to pack the rest of my things." He faces me. "Take a few minutes to think about it." He kisses the top of my head.

When I look up, five pairs of eyes are focused on me. "I'd better get ready for school." I scurry back to my room, weighted down with expectation and uncertainty.

As the scalding hot water cascades down my back, I mull over my options and try to figure out this new mess in my head. I should go with James. I can keep him company, and it's the perfect way to maintain distance from Ky. That's what I *should* do, but I can't. I can't leave Ky to deal with the fallout on his own. My cousins need me, and I like feeling needed. And Brad is moving in tonight. I can't convince him to do something he wasn't one hundred percent on and then ditch him at the last second. But the real clincher is the fact that I don't know the status of James's relationship with Courtney, and the thoughts of being around her make my skin crawl.

I pull on my snug-fitting jeans and a black lace-trimmed vest underneath a pink off-the-shoulder sweater. Toeing on my flat, black pumps, I fluff out my damp hair and leave my bedroom with my bag flung over my shoulder.

I'm walking down the corridor when I'm yanked sideways and dragged into Ky's room. A tiny shriek skips out of my mouth as my bag drops to the floor with a thud. Ky envelops me in an all-consuming embrace, and I melt into his arms. He buries his head in my hair, inhaling sharply. "Don't leave. Please."

I rest my head on his chest, listening to the steady beat of his heart. "I'm not going anywhere," I whisper.

He lets out a shuddering breath. "I was so scared you were going to go because it's the easier route."

He kisses the top of my head, and I close my eyes, savoring his touch. "There's that, but I can't bear the thought of leaving you any more than you can."

He holds the back of my head in both his hands and tilts my chin up. "When everything else is shattering, you feel like the one true constant."

"You can't rely on that, Ky, because I mightn't be that forever."

He presses a kiss to my forehead and I feel it all the way to my toes. "I know, babe." His lips linger there a little longer and my arms grip his waist a little tighter. "For the first time in years, I'm praying every night," he admits, leaning back to look at me. "I'm praying so hard that I don't lose you." I try to gulp over the messy ball of emotion in my throat. "You're mine, Faye. *Mine.*" His gaze drops to my mouth, and a shot of electricity charges the teeny space between us.

It's only been three and a half days since we last kissed, but it seems like an eternity has passed since I tasted him on my lips. I want to taste him again, to hell with the consequences. I lift my hand and brush my thumb across his lower lip. He shivers in my arms, and that gives me an inordinate thrill. He lowers his head, and I watch his mouth slowly descending with the intensity of a hunter stalking its prey. My chest heaves in anticipation, and blood thrums through my eager veins. Gripping my hips, he pulls me closer, his mouth now a hairsbreadth from mine. He stops, poised in midair, and we share breaths as the ever-present dangerous vibe bleeds into the miniscule gap between our mouths. Jumbled thoughts and emotions battle inside me. I've never needed a kiss as badly as I currently need his. Ever so softly, his lips brush mine, sending lusty tingles ricocheting all over my body. That feather-light touch has ignited every dormant part of me, and that's a serious talent. I moan into his mouth as my fingers dig into his hips.

"What the hell is going on in here?" James's reprimanding voice startles me, and I scream as a mixture of shock and fright whittles through me.

Ky pulls away from me instantly, his jaw taut with stress as he glares at his dad, transferring all his pent-up frustration in that direction. "Nothing that concerns you," he warns.

"Don't take that line with me, Kyler. My patience is hanging on by a thread, so don't push me."

"You've made your bed." Ky crosses his arms.

"I got that message from your mother, thank you very much." His features turn more pliable as he faces me. "Are you ready?"

I straighten up. "I'm not coming with you, James. I'm needed more here."

"The hell you aren't, young lady. Especially after what I walked in on. You two can't be trusted alone."

"I take great offense to that, James. This whole situation is a nightmare, but we're doing the best we can, and we *can* be trusted. This was a moment of weakness. It won't happen again." I can't even look at Ky.

"You're coming with me and that's final." He takes my elbow.

"Get your hands off her. It's Faye's decision, not yours." Ky faces off with his dad, sending him a threatening glare.

"Please, James. Go. If anything changes or I think I can't control myself, then I'll call you to come get me, but for now, my cousins need me here. You wouldn't leave them to starve and rot in their own filth, now would you?" My feeble attempt at humor dies an immediate death.

"If this is about a replacement housekeeper, I'll prioritize that straightaway."

"It's not, but it'd be great if you could do that sooner rather than later."

His shoulders deflate, and that's when I know I've won this round. "Okay, fine—for now." He tenderly kisses me on the cheek. "Call me if you need anything." He stands unsurely in front of Ky. "I don't want to leave things on bad terms with you, son."

"Perhaps you should've thought of that before you cheated on my mother and almost destroyed her. Before you had sex with your own sister." The repugnant look is blatantly obvious on Ky's face. "You make me sick."

"I can't win," James mutters sadly under his breath, shaking his head. "Call my cell if you need me. I'm not abandoning this family, and I'm not going to stop fighting for your mother either. I'm giving her some space, and I'm hoping she'll come around."

Ky grunts. "I wouldn't hold my breath if I was you."

"So, you'd prefer us to divorce?" There's an icy undercurrent in his voice.

Ky's smirk disappears. "I didn't say that."

"For what it's worth, son, I'm sorry. I wish I could go back and undo everything I've done." Giving me one last small smile, he exits the room, leaving a layer of stale tension in his wake.

"I don't want them to divorce," Ky quietly admits. "But it seems inevitable."

I want to reassure him, but no words spring to mind, because his statement is too hard to refute.

I ride with Brad after school to his house with Lenny and Max trailing us in the Merc. It took almost twenty minutes to convince Lenny that it was safe to travel with Brad, and considering my patience is in limited supply these days, he's lucky he didn't get a punch in the face.

Brad has most of his stuff boxed up already, so I'm merely helping him pack the last few bits, and then we'll be on our way. "Will you miss it?" I ask, while loading some of his football paraphernalia into a brown cardboard box.

He stops what he's doing, staring off into space. "Yeah. It's the only home I've ever known." He walks to the large window and surveys the vast back garden. The grass is overgrown, and weeds litter a lawn that was once no doubt pristine. The cover enclosing the rectangular-shaped swimming pool is laden down with leaves and other earthy debris. "Can you see the tree house at the very back of the garden?" He waggles his fingers, gesturing me over.

I join him at the window, straining my eyes in the direction he's pointing. "I see it."

"My dad built that for me when I was eight." A surge of pride infiltrates his tone. "He could've easily hired someone to do it, but I really wanted us to build it together, and I'll never forget how happy I was that weekend. He even stayed out with me the Saturday night. We slept in sleeping bags and had a midnight feast that we'd managed to sneak out past Mom." He twists sideways, leaning against the glass, a nostalgic look on his face. I mirror his position, listening avidly. "I have hundreds more memories all tied to this house, and that's all I have left of my family at this stage." His eyes shutter momentarily. When he reopens them, there's a wealth of pain in his glossy eyes. "I'll miss this house, but I miss my family more."

His voice is thick with emotion, and I don't hesitate—I lace my fingers in his. He pulls me a little closer, resting his chin atop my head. "I don't even know where they are or if they're all right."

"They haven't contacted you?" I tip my head up to meet his eyes.

He shakes his head. "They can't risk it in case they're caught."

When Brad had explained how his father had embezzled

funds from some of his stockbroking clients and was now on the run from the law, I hadn't fully considered the implications of same. "That's awful, Brad. You must feel so lonely." Our circumstances are different, but we're both effectively parentless, and I can relate. A rush of similar sentiments bubble to the surface, and a slicing pain spears me through the chest.

That's the thing with grief—it jumps out and waylays you when you least expect it.

"I do," he whispers.

"Why didn't you say anything?"

He shrugs. "Mostly I'm fine, but I have my moments."

"I get those too."

His fingers weave through my hair. "This is the part where I eat my own words." I frown, thoroughly confused, and he throws back his head, laughing. "Prepare yourself," he teases. "I'm going to thank you."

"Oh, lordy," I exclaim. "And so soon too!"

"I'm too much of a softy."

"You won't hear me disagreeing, but that's a good thing."

He staggers back, clutching his heart in dramatic fashion. "Did you just ... compliment me?" He fakes surprise.

"Knock it off jerkface"—I elbow him playfully in the ribs —"or I'll take it back."

He grins. "You're good people, Faye."

"You're good people, too, Brad."

We smile at each other, and for one millisecond, everything seems right with the world.

Chapter Eleven

I notice the frown building on Brad's brow as he steers his SUV up the Kennedy drive. "What's wrong?" I ask.

Lines furrow his brow, and his eyes are dead set ahead. I twist in my seat to see what's distracted him. A shiny, white open-top Porsche convertible is parked in front of the door. Now it's my turn to frown. "Whose car is that?"

"What?"

I look over at him. "What has gotten into you? Why are you acting so weird?"

His face contorts. "I just realized I left a box in the garage back at the house. We'll have to turn around."

I collapse in my seat. "That's all? Jeez, I thought someone had died by the look on your face." He's looking at me strangely, and my eyes narrow suspiciously. "Are you sure that's all it is?"

He spins the car around, retracing the path we've recently traveled. The Merc skids to avoid us. Lenny is gesturing wildly with his hands, but I pretend not to notice. He rubs the back of his head. "Yeah. I just hate putting you out."

I scoff. "Don't be ridic. It's not like I've anything else to do today. Besides, it's nice to get out of the house for a while." I don't elaborate because I'm afraid if he realizes exactly what kind of cesspool he's walking into that he'll change his mind, even if living in the midst of all the Kennedy drama is better than sleeping in his car.

"In that case, I'm taking you for something to eat after. My treat."

"You don't have to do that," I say in a muffled voice as I force my head through my knees. We've approached the gate and the cameras are already flashing in my face. It's funny how commonplace it's almost become.

I wait outside the car for Brad while he takes the steps two at a time and disappears into his former house.

The Merc slows down as it pulls up alongside Brad's SUV. I start a mental countdown in my head, and I'm only up to six when Lenny jumps out and starts tearing me a new one. Apparently, spontaneity is banned, and I'm required to give him *advance notice* when my plan changes. I'm tempted to let him talk to my middle finger, but I let him vent it all out of his system before I respond. "Chill out. Brad forgot something and we had to come back. It's not that big of a deal."

"I doubt your uncle will see it that way when I report back to him."

I shrug. "Report away, Lenny. Your threats don't scare me." I really don't like this dude, and he needs a serious attitude adjustment. Brad pulls the front door shut and strides toward me with a small black box in his arms. "By the way, Brad is taking me for something to eat before we head back to the house. I've given you advance notice. Happy now?"

Lenny glares at me. Out of the corner of my eye, I spot Max fighting a smile, and I send him a conspiratorial wink.

"Everything okay?" Brad asks, kick-starting the engine into gear.

"Lenny was getting his knickers in a twist, but he'll survive."

Brad bursts out laughing. "Aw, Faye. You crack me up!"

I grin. "It's my life's mission to entertain you."

"Never a dull moment, babe!"

Brad pulls up in front of Legends diner, and I groan. "Seriously? This is where you're bringing me?"

He frowns. "It's the best place in town. I didn't think you'd mind." He starts the engine up again. "But it's cool. There's a little Italian place over the other side of town that isn't bad either."

I place my hand over his. "It's fine. We can eat here. That was a total overreaction." The prices in the diner are reasonable, and I don't want to make assumptions about Brad's financial status which I know can't be the healthiest. He said his parents left him some money, but I imagine he has to be careful with his spending habits.

"I don't mind, honestly."

He's looking at me like I'm a little crazy. He's probably not wrong. "Nope. Let's head in."

Leanne and Jenn are working shifts tonight, and Jenn escorts Brad and me to a booth at the back. Unfortunately, a whole host of our classmates are seated at the front of the diner, and we pick up our fair share of surreptitious looks as we pass. Brad high-fives a few of his football teammates while I mumble a surly hello.

We both order salads, and after our drinks have been delivered, I decide to broach a subject I've been purposely avoiding. "So." I lean forward on my elbows. "I think we need to establish some ground rules." Brad's brows knit together. "For the fake relationship," I whisper-add.

"Ah, right." He takes a long slurp of his drink. "What did you have in mind?"

Cripes. Why is this so difficult to articulate? I look down at the Formica top, tapping my foot nervously off the floor. "You're a little too hands-on at times, so I'd like to keep that to a minimum, if possible."

· I glance up and feel instantly guilty. His cheeks flush red, and there's a hurt look in his eyes.

"Shit. I didn't mean to offend you, Brad, it's, just, it makes me a little uncomfortable."

He stretches across the table, speaking in a quiet voice. "Because you like it or don't like it?"

"What the heck does that have to do with anything?" I don't like the direction this conversation is taking.

"Humor me." His eyes penetrate mine. "If Ky wasn't on the scene, would you have any interest in dating me?"

Oh, ground, please open up and swallow me.

"I'm not answering that. It's irrelevant to this discussion." I totally chicken out.

"I beg to differ. This goes to the heart of the issue, does it not?" He takes another greedy glug of his drink.

"Maybe this was a bad idea. Maybe we should stage a public breakup."

He shrugs. "If that's what you want. I won't force you to do anything that makes you so uncomfortable. How awful this last week must've been for you." The sarcasm and hurt in his tone is evident.

What in the actual hell is going on here? How did me wanting to discuss some boundaries end up bringing us to this point?

I reach over for his hand but he snatches it away. "Quit with the mixed signals, Faye."

"Hang on here a second," I hiss, anger starting to fuel my veins. "I have never given you any reason to believe I was interested in more than friendship. Have I not specifically said on more than one occasion that that's all I was interested in?"

"If I remember correctly, you said you had no time for a relationship," he snaps back. "But my bad, I should have realized you just meant with me."

I spy Leanne approaching with our food, so I seal my mouth shut until after she has departed. "Why are we even having this argument?" I stab a piece of salad with my fork. "Weren't you the one who said you wouldn't ever betray Ky again, or do you have an exclusive short-term memory?"

He flinches, carefully placing his fork down on his plate. "Maybe I'm not the one doing the betraying this time."

An icy hand squeezes my heart and my face pales. "What are you insinuating?"

Superfast, he reaches over the table and takes my hand before I can object. "Fuck. I shouldn't have said that, and I'm not insinuating anything. I'm being a total ass. I'm so sorry, Faye."

I pull my hand out of his. "I'm struggling to understand what's going on here, Brad, and, quite frankly, I wished I hadn't broached the subject at all. I was having fun until we came here. Now, I don't even feel like eating." I push my plate away.

He looks contrite. "This is all my fault. Forget I said anything. We're friends, and I'm really glad about that fact. I'll tone down the PDAs, it's no problem."

I stare out the window, feeling hurt, confused, and vulnerable. Brad is clearly backtracking, and I'd like to know why.

The atmosphere is still strained in the car on the journey

back to the house. Day has given way to night, and I look up at the eerie, empty sky, wondering if it's some form of warning. Brad parks in a vacant spot in the garage, and I move to get out, but he stops me, holding my elbow in his strong grip. "Wait up, please."

I twist around in my seat. "I hurt you, and I'm sorry about that. I'm in a weird mood today is all. It's been an emotional day, and some of that subconsciously transferred over. Please say you forgive me. I value your friendship, and I don't want to lose it, or you."

I'm not quite sure if I'm buying that excuse. Rose is right—it's best to be upfront about this, so I say what I need to say. "Do you have feelings for me? Because if you do, then we need to call the whole fake boyfriend thing off."

He lifts his eyes to the ceiling, and his chest heaves. The air is suddenly frigid with tension. Sighing, he lowers his eyes and focuses on me. "I think I got a little carried away with the role playing, and I could imagine us together, but it wasn't real. You're Ky's girl. I get that." He looks down at his lap. "I don't have those kinds of feelings for you."

"Oh. Okay. Good." *And this is a good thing, so why do I feel a little disappointed? Am I that shallow?* I shake it off before I give myself emotional whiplash, offering him my best smile. "How about we agree that if the arrangement isn't working for one of us, we'll be honest with the other and immediately call it off?"

He gives me a tentative smile in return. "Sounds like a plan."

"So, we're good?"

"We're good."

We remove some of the boxes from the boot, and I show Brad the way to his new room. On our way back, I knock on Ky's door. "Brad's here!" I call out. "And we could use a hand with these boxes."

The door slowly opens, but my smile withers up and dies when I catch one look at Ky's cold, impassive face. It's a look I'm well familiar with but one I haven't seen in a while. "What's gotten into you?" Anxiety explodes in my gut.

"I don't know what you mean." He speaks to me while staring at Brad over my shoulder. I flit around, startled to see a cold glare on Brad's face. "What is going on?"

"Nothing." Ky purses his lips as he pulls the door shut. "What do you need help with?"

We walk in absolute silence back to the garage and unload the rest of Brad's things. My level of anxiety is off the charts. Something is up with him, and I don't understand what's happened between this morning and now to cause him to withdraw behind his protective mask. I stop abruptly as a thought occurs to me. "Who was here earlier?"

"No one." Ky is too quick to reply. Brad sends him a dirty look, and that tells me all I need to know. Nausea swims up my throat.

I drop my box on the floor. "I saw her car, Ky. What did she want?"

"Nothing."

I stalk toward him, getting right up in his face. "Don't lie to me. What did she say this time?"

"I told you, it's nothing," he says through gritted teeth, taking a step back from me.

"You're lying." Brad's furious tone spears him.

"Don't pretend like you know me, because you don't," he snarls, and I shrink back from the venom in his voice.

"Why are you acting like this?" I reach for him, but he steps sideways, out of my grasp.

"I don't know what you're talking about." He shrugs, feigning indifference. "And you need to get yourself in check. I don't have time for this bullshit."

My stomach drops with fear and loathing. He is not going to treat me like this. "I don't know what's going on, but I'm not letting you do this to me again."

He looks through me, as if I'm invisible. *How can he say what he said to me this morning and now turn into the mean, moody version of himself from before?* I scrunch handfuls of my hair. "Oh my God. She's gotten to you, hasn't she? What is the crazy bitch saying now? What's her game plan this time?"

He shakes his head, as if I'm insane. "Faye. You're the one acting crazy right now."

"Don't. Don't do that. You can try and shut me out all you like, but I'll still know who's behind it." Frustration and anger are not a good combination. It's on the tip of my tongue to tell him what Rose and I observed last night at Addison's house, but I'm afraid to own up to it because with the weird mood he's in, who knows how he'll react. I don't want to add further fuel on the fire.

"Why do women make a big deal of everything? Like seriously!" He rolls his eyes at Brad in a deliberate move. "You have the right idea staying single. Trust me, life is far less complicated."

He sneers, and I see red. If I don't get out of here now, I'm liable to do or say something I'll regret. I face Brad. "I'm going to turn in for the night, unless you need a hand with unpacking?"

"No, I'm good. Thanks for everything today." His eyes are kind and I'm glad at least one of them is acting normal again.

"No problem. I'll see you in the morning."

I ignore Ky as I slip around them, storming toward my room as fast as my legs will carry me.

I lie awake in bed until way past midnight, fervently hoping Ky is going make an appearance at any moment to explain his behavior. But as the clock chimes two, I have no choice but to face facts.

He isn't coming.

And it feels ominous.

Like the winds are changing, and destiny is altering.

His absence is more than telling.

It has a finality to it that scares me half to death.

Chapter Twelve

If I managed to snatch two solid hours of sleep last night, I'd say I was lucky. It took considerable effort to haul myself out of bed this morning, and now I'm running late. It doesn't bode well for the rest of the day. At least it's Friday.

Brad and Ky are engaged in a heated argument when I reach the kitchen, and it doesn't take much imagination to figure out what or whom they are arguing about. They cease talking the minute they spot me. "Don't stop on my account," I snark, reaching down to remove a bowl from the press.

"Here." Keaton says, getting up from the table with a plate in hand. "I made pancakes earlier. Saved you some." He slides the plate across the island to me.

"Hmm," I say, eyeing the mess littered across the sink, the stove, and the countertop. "I can see that. Were you planning on fixing that"—I point in the general direction of the massacre —"or leaving it for the cleaning fairy to take care of?"

His face drops and I feel like the biggest bitch on the planet. "Ignore me. I didn't get much sleep last night, and I'm cranky as hell. Thanks for making breakfast, and don't worry about that. I'll tidy it after school." His face brightens. Thank fuck. "And thanks for saving me some. I'm starved." I take a big bite and groan. "God, that's good. We might make a chef out of you yet!" He beams at me and all is right with the world again. I squint at the clock. "You better make a move unless you want to be late." I shove him with my hip. "Go on, get your ass in gear!"

He musses up my hair as he races past me, laughing. Sensing eyes on me, I look up. Brad and Ky are both staring at me as if I've grown two horns out the top of my head. Ignoring them, I take my plate to the table and sit down across from Kent. He's toying with the remnants of his breakfast, looking bored, as usual. "Shouldn't you be getting ready too?" I ask, in between mouthfuls.

"Mind your own business," he snipes, glaring at me. If I didn't know him, I'd think he hated me. But Kent hates everyone and everything so I'm nothing special.

"Watch your mouth," Ky growls. "And Faye is right. Get out of here. The last thing Mom needs is tardy reports from O.C."

Kent, typically, flips him the bird. "Watch that."

Ky flies across the room, yanking Kent off the bench by his shoulders. "Listen up, you little shit. You are going to school, and you are going right now if I have to drag you there myself." Kent shoves Ky with force. "Don't push me, Kent. I'm warning you." Kent clearly has a death wish because he charges at Ky, mouthing a stream of obscenities as he tries to grab his brother in a headlock. Brad wades in, and between them, they manage to hold Kent's arms behind his back. He thrashes about, cursing his head off and shouting in frustration.

"What is going on in here? I could hear you all the way from my bedroom." Alex saunters into the room in her new favorite outfit—sweats and a disheveled shirt—with the obligatory glass of wine in hand. She obviously isn't planning on going into the office again today.

"Kent is refusing to go to school," Ky confirms.

Alex walks toward her son with a sigh. "You don't want to go to school, sweetie?" She reaches out, touching his face.

Kent slaps her hand away. "No, and stop touching me."

Alex waves her hands flippantly in the air. "Leave him be. If he doesn't want to go to school, he doesn't have to." Her words are slightly slurred, and wine sloshes out of the glass onto the floor.

"Mom, I don't think that's a good idea. Kent needs the discipline of school," Ky says.

Kent scoffs. "Would you listen to yourself? You sound like you're fucking middle-aged. I'll kill myself if I end up like you."

"I'm not going to school either," Kal says, and we all turn around to look at him. He is stretched lengthways along the bench with his socked feet crossed at the ankles.

Alex waggles her finger at him as she walks toward him. "Yes, you are."

He sits bolt upright. "What? Why is Kent allowed to stay home for *no* reason when I have a really good reason to never step foot in that building again?"

"Sweetie." Alex cocks her head to the side. "That's exactly why you need to go. You need to show this town that you've done nothing wrong. That you are falsely accused. You need to go about your business as you always have done. Show them nothing has changed and you are not going to bow down to lies and idle gossip. You're a Kennedy, for God's sake! Act like one! You are better than all of them!" Her voice elevates until she's practically screaming that last part.

"It's not fair and you are seriously losing your mind!" Kal seethes, brushing past his mother with an unhappy pout on his face.

I peek at Brad and he looks like he wishes he was anywhere but here. I can relate. I have zero tolerance for the drama-rama this morning, and I want out of here. "We should make tracks before we're late," I say, offering Brad an out.

He latches onto it with both hands. "Definitely. Let's go."

"Have a lovely day, sweetie," Alex purrs, kissing the top of my head. "And you too, darling. Sorry I wasn't around to greet you last night, but you are most welcome. You're practically family, Brad, so make yourself at home." She yanks him into an embrace so fast that he stumbles, landing face first in her chest. It's almost comical except that it's far too sad to be in any way remotely funny.

Ky pulls Brad back, pinning him with an apologetic look. "Go. Get Faye out of here."

We walk in silence to the lobby, grabbing our bags and coats and heading out the back door to the garage.

"So," I say, securing my seat belt around my waist. "Happy you moved in?"

"Glad you didn't sugarcoat anything on my behalf," he drawls in a sarcastic tone.

I scan the backseat. "Is there room for two back there?" It's only after the words have slipped out that I realize how they could be misconstrued. I attempt to backpedal furiously. "Shit! Didn't mean that to come out how it sounded."

A wry smile tugs up the corners of his mouth. "I know what you meant, and I heard your message loud and clear last night."

All semblance of lightness evaporates, and I curse myself for putting my big fat mouth in it. That's what happens with minimal sleep. My brain plays rooky and I end up spouting the most ridiculous crap.

"Can we not mention last night ever again?" I plead.

He takes a quick sideways look at me. "Which part?"

"All of it?"

"Sure."

As Brad maneuvers us out of the garage, Max glides behind us in the Merc with the ever-faithful Lenny riding shotgun.

"You knew, didn't you?" I ask Brad without facing him. I stare glumly out the front window, lifting my feet up onto the dash. "You saw her car, and you knew she was here."

He sighs. "Yeah. Sorry I wasn't honest about that, but I didn't want to see you upset."

"It's okay. I'm not mad at *you*." I chew on the tip of one fingernail. "Did he tell you why she was here?"

He huffs out a laugh. "You're kidding, right? As if he'd tell me anything about Addison."

"Is that what you two were arguing about?"

"Partly." He vigorously rubs his temple.

I'm tempted to probe further, but what's the point? Ky has always gone into lockdown mode when it's anything to do with Addison, and I doubt he's confided in Brad, of all people, even if they are besties. A painful ache radiates in my chest, and I can't dispel the sense of futility I feel. "She's playing some new game."

"Most likely," Brad agrees.

"And Ky is incapable of beating her at it, so that means we need to intervene." I duck my head as we approach the gate and wait for Brad to navigate past the media pests and head out onto the open road before resuming our conversation. "I have a few ideas. Are you in or out?"

"Is this legal?" He quirks a brow.

"Mostly."

He rolls his eyes. "Okay. Let's hear it."

I fill him in on the events of Wednesday night and what Rose and I overheard at Addison's house. "If we discover her secret, we can use that to get her to lay off Ky. I bet Keven can dig into her background for us. He's already investigating the email Ky received, and I'd like to find out if he has an update. Are you up for a road trip to Harvard tomorrow?"

"I only had loose plans to go to the track with Ky. Count me in. Let's do this."

I have a few almost run-ins with Peyton during the school day, and I'm in no mood to tolerate Her Highness. Brad runs intervention, and I know I must be testing his patience to the limit, but I'm in a real foul mood today, and woe betide anyone who crosses me.

Alex is passed out on the couch when we get back home after school is out, an empty wine bottle and glass tossed on the floor at her feet. Brad shakes his head sadly as he takes a blanket off the other couch and fits it over her. I remove the empty bottle and glass and bring it into the kitchen. Together, we clean up the mess left from breakfast before I go to my room to change into my swimsuit. I haven't swum any day this week, and I need to rectify that. Practice sessions start after school on Monday, and I don't want to fall behind.

It's too cold to use the outdoor pool, so I head to the indoor one and dive in. I've only swum ten lengths when the door creaks open and Brad steps into the room. I swim up to the edge of the pool, draping my arms over the tiled floor.

"Do you mind if I join you?" he asks.

"Of course not. There's more than enough room."

He tugs his T-shirt up over his head and dumps it and a towel on a bench in the corner. Muscles flex and roll in his chiseled abs as he strides toward the pool, and I try not to ogle, but it's damn hard. Brad is well fit, easily in Ky's league, and he'd definitely give him a run for his money in the semi-naked hotness stakes. Pulling my goggles on, I start into a butterfly stroke as Brad dives into the pool in one flawless move. We soar up and down the lanes in unspoken competition, and my muscles burn with the effort involved in keeping up with him.

Brad's an expert swimmer, not that I'm altogether surprised. He grew up with a pool in his backyard and the beach close enough at hand.

A large yawn escapes my mouth, and I slow to a gentle crawl, swimming to the edge of the pool and leaning back. "Can't hack the pace, beautiful?" Brad teases, swimming up alongside me.

"I'm knackered." He chuckles. "And I have to be at work soon, so I think I'll grab a power nap before then." I hoist my weary body out of the pool and clamber to my feet. Brad follows behind me.

"Here." He thrusts a towel at me. "I grabbed an extra one."

"Thanks." I flick my hair over and scrub it with the towel before straightening up. Brad is bent at the waist, drying his legs, and I take the opportunity to study him on the sly. His wide shoulders are broad, tapering down to a well-defined back, slim hips, and toned, muscular legs. He has the same sporty physique as Ky, and he's equally as nice to look at.

He straightens up, catching me watching him, and he smiles as my cheeks flare up. I drag my towel back and forth across my back, arching my chest in the process. Brad's eyes latch onto my bust, and my nipples pebble under his keen attention. Lightning-fast, I secure the towel across my front, wrapping it around my back and tucking it in under my arms before he notices. When Brad's gaze meets mine, there's no denying the interest there. Something indecipherable wafts through the air, and my skin prickles with uneasiness. Lines are starting to blur, and I don't know which side of the fence I'm on. I'm becoming far too aware of him, and I don't want that.

A loud throat clearing snaps me out of my haze. Ky is glaring at Brad from the open doorway. I hurry toward the exit, brushing past Ky without even acknowledging him.

I flop down on my bed, groaning into my pillow. *Why is*

everything so complicated? Is it too much to wish for boring and normal? As I strip off my suit and step into the shower, I reluctantly acknowledge the fact that I'd hate boring and normal, but some happy medium would be nice.

I've just shoved the lasagna into the oven when Alex wanders into the kitchen, yawning. "Something smells delicious."

"I hope you like lasagna?" I ask, putting the finishing touches on the accompanying salad.

"I do." She hovers uncertainly while I set the table and fill the water jug. "Thank you, Faye. I appreciate all you're doing to help." She flops down onto a stool. "I'm finding it so difficult to function at present."

I'll say. I lean my elbows on the island unit. "I understand, and I'm happy to help out where I can." I pause, contemplating my next words carefully. "Is Courtney still at Kennedy Apparel? Is that why you're reluctant to return to the office?" A pained expression appears on her face as she nods. I frown. "Why don't you fire her skanky ass?"

That raises a small smile. "I wish I could." She sighs heavily. "I can't stand to be around that calculating bitch, but unfortunately, having an affair with your boss's husband isn't grounds for dismissal. Her employment contract is watertight." She jumps up too quickly from the stool, stumbling and almost losing her balance. I rush to her side, but she has righted herself by the time I reach her. She puts out a hand. "I'm okay. I feel a headache coming on, and I think I'll just go lie down."

The diner is packed as it is most Friday nights, and I'm rushed off my feet from the second I step foot in the place. I'm typing an order into the system when Rose approaches. "The guy at table seven is asking for you to serve him."

"Fine," I reply, not even looking up. Taking long strides toward the table, I extract my pad and pen from my pocket as I make my approach. "What can I get you?" I ask, lifting my head up. Curious blue eyes meet mine as his lips pull into a smile. "Oh, hello again." My guard is instantly up as I recognize the man from his previous visit.

"Hello, Faye." He scans my name badge as he hurriedly tidies up a bunch of photos and papers in front of him.

My eyes flit subconsciously to the table, and he quickly flips the documents over. My cheeks stain with my embarrassment. "Have you decided what you'd like to order?"

"I was going to have the fish and chips again, but I thought I should try something different this time, so I'll have the Works Burger with all the trimmings and ice water, please."

I quickly jot it down. "I'll place the order. Thanks." I turn to leave.

"Wait, Faye, ah"—he runs a hand through his dark hair—"I was hoping you might have time to talk for a few minutes."

My eyes narrow suspiciously. "About what?"

"The other waitress said you are new to town. I'm considering moving here, and I was, ah, wondering if you had any insight to offer? Is it a nice place to live?"

I shrug. "I guess."

"So, you're happy here?"

I purse my lips as I ponder his question. On the surface, it appears straightforward, but it's way more complicated than a simple yes or no reply. "Mostly." I aim for honesty.

His intelligent eyes probe mine and all the tiny hairs on the back of my neck lift. There is something about this guy that isn't on the level. I think my initial instincts were correct. He must be a hack and he's trying to befriend me in the hope I'll divulge Kennedy family secrets. Well, he can think again. I plant my best sweet and innocent smile on my face. "I'd love to chat with you ..." I let my words die off as I quirk a brow.

"Mark!" he blurts out, looking a little flustered. "The name's Mark." He holds out his hand, and I reluctantly shake it.

"Well, Mark. It was nice talking to you, but I've got to get back to work. It's crazy busy, as you can see, and I don't want to give my boss any excuse to fire me. I'll input your order, and then I'll be back with your drink."

"What was all that about?" Rose asks when I return to the counter.

"I think he's a reporter fishing for dirt on the Kennedys."

"Get out!"

"I could be wrong, but there's something about that guy." My brow wrinkles as I tap in his order. "Would you serve him? I'd rather steer clear."

"No sweat."

David calls me into his office a little while later. Being summoned by the boss never fails to spark a burst of anxiety, and I'm the first to assume it's because I've done something wrong. "Have a seat." He waves at the two chairs in front of his desk, and I sit down stiffly in one.

"Relax, Faye." He gives me a yellow-toothed grin. "Nothing is wrong. I just wanted to check in with you and see how you're doing. I know you've had a lot of stress this week, and it can't be easy with reporters breathing down your neck all the time."

"Is this about my bodyguard, Lenny? Because he stays out in the car, and I'm confident I can get my uncle to renege on the need for his presence soon."

David flaps his hands in the air. "Breathe, Faye. There's no need to get all worked up. I won't deny that it'd be nice not to see his face at all, but I can't complain. Trade is brisk. In fact"—

he sends me a semi-apologetic look—"business is up by twenty-five percent thanks to the influx of visitors to the town."

"Oh, well, that's good." At least someone is benefitting. My knee jerks up and down as I wait for him to get to the point.

He taps his pen slowly off the top of his desk. He leans back in his chair, and his gray shirt is stretched over his protruding gut, the buttons looking like they're about to pop. His eyes roam my face in a way that makes me ill at ease. He offers up another toothy grin, and I squirm in my seat. "If there is ever anything I can do to help, you know you can come to me?" he says, and I nod weakly. "And if you ever need to switch or cancel shifts because of external factors, then please speak to me. I know this must be difficult for you, being so new to town and all, and if I can help in any way, I'd be happy to."

His eyes are kind, and my trepidation ebbs. I'm not sure why I'm edgy around him, and I think I've misjudged him, because this isn't the first time that he's extended an olive branch, and he seems to genuinely care about his staff, which is damned rare to find. The manager of the restaurant I worked in back home in Dublin was a right cow, and she never made concessions for anyone, no matter what was going on at home. "Thank you, David. I appreciate you saying that, and I'll bear it in mind."

He beams at me like a proud father. "Very well, Faye. I'll let you get back. It's a busy one tonight."

The rest of the shift passes uneventfully and I don't see or speak to Mark the rest of the night.

When I arrive back at the house later, I make a quick call to James letting him know that someone was asking questions at the diner. He made me promise to tell him if anything like this happened, and I'm happy for him to deal with the situation. Hopefully, that's the last I'll see of Mark.

I'm woken early the next morning by a continuous pelting of rain against my window. Scrubbing the sleep from my eyes, I lift the curtain and groan. Heavy sheets of rain are tumbling in angry waves from the sky, slapping noisily off the ground outside. Rolls of dull, smoky, gray clouds crowd the sky, casting a layer of drabness over the land below. It perfectly matches my mood. I tap out a short message to Brad, wondering if he's awake yet. He responds mere seconds later, and we agree to meet in the kitchen.

I grab a quick shower and dress warmly in my favorite pair of jeans, combat boots, and a gray and pink hoodie. Brad is whistling to himself as he stirs eggs on the stove. "Morning," I say in an overly exuberant tone of voice that is clearly fake.

Brad chuckles. "That bad, huh?" I stick my tongue out at him, and he laughs again. "I made enough for two." He gestures at the pan.

"Great, thanks." I drop some bread in the toaster and busy myself making coffee while he plates up our food. I carry the mugs to the table, sliding onto the bench as Brad places a steaming plate of scrambled eggs and toast in front of me. We tuck in, eating silently and amicably.

"What's the plan?" he asks, when he's finished eating.

"I got the address of Kaden and Keven's apartment on campus from Keaton last night, so we'll head there and hope they're in." I take a sip of my coffee. "And if they're not, I'll ring them and find out when they'll be back, and we can find some-place to hang out until then."

"Cool. You wanna make tracks soon?"

I catch sight of Ky approaching out of the corner of my eye. "Yeah, and if *he* asks, I'm going shopping and you're keeping me company," I whisper urgently.

Brad swivels on the bench. "Hey, man. You heading to the track?" Ky's routine is pretty regimented so it's a safe bet he's heading to the Middleborough motocross training facility this morning.

"Yep." He moves about the kitchen, opening and shutting presses. With a bowl in one hand and a mug of coffee in the other, he sits down beside Brad, completely ignoring me as he starts eating.

"Will you let May and Rick know I'm living here now and tell them I'll drop in during the week."

"Sure." He looks at his bowl as he eats, still refusing to meet my eyes.

"How are the renovations coming along?" Brad asks, trying his best to alleviate the awkward tension in the room.

"Good."

Ky has mastered the art of one-word replies. Trying to have a conversation with him when he's in a mood is like spending a continuous twenty-four hours in the dentist chair. Air flees my lungs and I can scarcely breathe. This reminds me so much of the early days, when Ky acted like I didn't even exist. *How can things have gone so awry in only one day?*

I don't need anyone else to answer that question.

I already know the reason.

Addison.

This stinks of her in spades.

Ky may be content to let her walk all over him again but I'm done being a doormat.

I'm going to play her at her own game, and I'm going to thoroughly enjoy it too.

Chapter Thirteen

With renewed determination, I swing my legs over the bench and snatch Brad's dirty dishes up along with mine. I walk to the dishwasher and stack our things before cleaning the pan and wiping the counter clean. Brad and Ky are whispering with their heads bent, and I hate the fact that I'm excluded from the conversation.

"I'll meet you in the lobby in fifteen, Brad," I shout, and he gives me a swift thumbs-up. I exit the room without any acknowledgment of Ky. I'm not speaking to him until he apologizes for the way he treated me yesterday.

"Okay, so, here's the plan," I tell Brad when he enters the lobby a little while later. "We need to ditch Lenny 'cause I don't want anyone knowing what we're up to. You don't have a tail, so you can drive out the front gate and meet me at the old side entrance. I'll wait for the guard to finish his rounds of the back garden, and then I'll slip out my window and escape through the forest."

Brad high-fives me. "Sneaky. I approve." He winks and I give him a playful shove. "Go. I'll see you in a bit."

The plan works beautifully, and twenty minutes later, we are free as birds on the open road. I flick through the list of music on Brad's phone until I find something I like. He groans when the rhythmic beats pump out and I tap my fingers in time to the music. "Your taste in music is *diabolical.*"

"If you hate Katy Perry so much, why'd you have her on your playlist?"

His lips tug down, and his teasing expression fades. "My sister put it on there."

"Oh, sorry. Do you want me to turn it off?"

He wiggles his nose. "Nah, leave it. It reminds me of her, and that's not a bad thing."

I sing along, uncaring that I'm completely tuneless, and his shoulders shake with laughter. I stick my tongue out at him in between crooning, and that makes him crack up even more. By the time we reach the campus, he's doubled over as if winded, with tears streaming down his face.

"I'm not that bad!" I poke him in the ribs.

"A dying cat would sound better than you!" He shakes with laughter as he swings the car into a parking space.

"You. Are. Mean." I mock pout, as he kills the engine and pivots in his seat to face me.

"Ah, you know I love you." He playfully messes up my hair. "And I love that you don't care. Your confidence is very attractive."

"Whatever!" I roll my eyes and open my door, suddenly very anxious to end this convo before it veers into treacherous territory. "Come on! Let's go find my cousins."

We stroll past beautiful, stately red-bricked buildings and manicured lawns that look glorious even swathed in a heavy sheet of rain. There's something magical in the air around here, and it's clear the campus is steeped in history. My mouth hangs open as I drink it all in. Trees with varying autumnal-colored leaves line the pristine paths as we walk through the college grounds. There is barely a sinner around at this early hour on the weekend, and it only adds to the enchanting quality of the place.

We stop in front of a well-preserved building that looks like it dates back to the eighteenth century. Brad holds the door open for me, and I step into the lobby of a clean, well-maintained building. We sign in, retrieving directions, and after a few wrong turns, we eventually end up in front of my cousins' door. I rap decisively a couple of times and step back, shuffling anxiously from foot to foot. I'm not sure what kind of reaction I'll receive. I'm not close with either Kaden or Keven, and I don't know what they'll think when they see me on their doorstep.

Sounds of muted voices confirm someone is inside, but the longer we stare at the closed door, the less confident I am that they're planning on opening it.

Brad twists his cap to the back of his head, slanting an amused look my way. "Maybe our timing sucks," he suggests with a knowing wink.

"Oh, shoot!" I exclaim, instantly catching his drift. It's early on a Saturday morning, and it's not inconceivable to think one or both of my cousins have female company. "Maybe we should come back later?"

Brad takes my hand. "Good idea, come on."

We have only taken three steps when the door swings open and Kaden pokes his head out. "Faye?" His voice can't conceal his curiosity.

I turn around. "Surprise!"

"What are you doing here?" he asks. An older woman with

smoldering brown eyes appears at his back, clutching a brief-case and a stack of files to her chest.

"I need to speak to Keven about something, but if this is a bad time ..." I smile over his head at the woman.

"No. It's fine. Professor Garcia was just leaving." He moves aside to allow the woman to pass through. Her heels click noisily on the polished hardwood floors.

"Same time next Saturday, Mr. Kennedy," she says in a clipped tone of voice, flicking her thick, dark hair over her shoulder. With her voluptuous mouth, sallow skin, and curvy figure, she reminds me of a younger Sophia Vergara. She even has that sexy, sensual quality to her voice.

"Thank you. I'll see you then." Kaden avoids looking at her as he ushers us into the room. I take a quick wander around. The suite is larger than I expected, incorporating two separate double bedrooms and a shared bath. The common room is spacious and expensively furnished with two wide reclining leather couches and a massive wall-mounted flat screen TV. A top-of-the-range gaming system is hooked up to the TV, and the glossy coffee table is cluttered with a multitude of games and related paraphernalia. It's a bona fide man cave.

"Scored some private lessons?" Brad teases.

"She's one of my professors, asshat! And she's married." He closes the door with a bang.

"She's clearly *very* dedicated to turn up so early on a Saturday." Brad plops down on one of the couches, stretching the length of it as he folds his hands underneath his head.

"Make yourself at home, Brad," Kaden drawls sarcastically, "and drop the insinuation. I don't appreciate it."

"Jeez, man, when'd you get so serious? I was only messing around."

Kaden ignores him, leaning over the back of the couch as he

pins that intense gaze of his on me. "Keven isn't here, Faye, but he's due back shortly. Anything I can help with?"

I push Brad's feet out of the way and sit down on the end of the couch. "I wanted his help with some computer stuff, so, not really, although, we could use your help back at the house."

Kaden sighs. "What's the latest?"

I proceed to fill him in on Alex's drinking and lackadaisical attitude, especially when it comes to her work and Kent's school, the showdown with James the other morning, and the threatened divorce—which, apparently, he was aware of because Ky had called him straight after—and Kal's understandable melancholy mood. "Goddammit." He exhales in frustration. "This entire situation is a clusterfuck of epic proportions."

"I'm not going to argue with you on that front."

"And what about the revelation about us, about our ..." He stops mid-sentence, casting a furtive glance at Brad.

"Brad knows," I confirm. "I told him." Kaden scowls. "He's not going to say anything, so take a chill pill." His scowl grows darker. "And to answer your question, none of your brothers have said anything else to me or around me about your real dad. To be fair, it's kinda minor in the context of everything else."

"True," Kaden agrees, letting go of his evil Eddie expression.

"You're still their brother. Who your dad is doesn't change that." I twirl a lock of my hair around my finger as the door swings inward and Keven strolls into the room. He halts on the spot when he sees me and Brad, his eyes widening in surprise.

"To what do we owe this honor?" he deadpans, unzipping his jacket and flinging it over a chair in the corner of the room. Muscles bulge and flex in his arms as he lounges against the desk.

"I need your help."

His brows inch up. "Go on."

"Firstly, have you made any progress tracing that email Ky received?"

He shakes his head. "Not yet. Whoever they are, they knew what they were doing or hired someone who knew what they were doing. Every time I think I've gotten to the source, I'm rerouted again." My brow puckers unhappily. "Don't worry, sweetheart." He pats my knee. "This is my forte, and I'm damned good at it. I'll crack it eventually."

"Modest much, Keven?" Brad teases.

"That's enough out of you, pipsqueak."

"Pipsqueak?" I alternate my gaze from Brad to Keven and back again.

"It's the nickname he gave me when I was growing up because I was so small. I was a late starter," Brad explains for my benefit.

My eyes trail up and down his strong, muscular, tall body. "Well, you sure as shit made up for it."

Brad's gaze lands on my mouth as he shoots me a cocky wink. "Yep. Sure did."

Kaden coughs purposely. "Enough with the flirting. Keven and I have stuff to do, so can we wrap this up."

My good mood evaporates on the spot. It seems Kaden can't get me out of here fast enough. Brad pushes up off the couch, glaring at Kaden. "Hey, man, she's your cousin, and you can't give her ten minutes of your time?"

Kaden cricks his neck from side to side. "I didn't mean that how it sounded, Faye. I'm cranky from lack of sleep, and I've got a shit ton of stuff to do today is all. Don't take it personally. You're welcome to visit anytime. Maybe, just call first next time?"

"Of course, yeah." I look down at my lap, embarrassed and a little hurt.

"What do you need help with?" Keven asks, making a deliberate effort to temper his tone.

I'm feeling a little nervous about saying this out loud, fearful for how it's going to come across, but there's no backing out now. I lift my chin up, piercing Keven with a confident expression. "I need you to spy on Addison."

His eyes open wide. "Okaayy. Wasn't expecting that. What exactly are you looking for?"

"She's twisting the screws on Ky again, and we know she's playing some angle, but he seems unwilling to contemplate that," Brad adds.

"Shit!" Kaden curses. "Don't tell me he's mixed up with her again?"

"Looks that way," I supply.

Brad leans forward, jabbing his elbows in his knees. "But he's not admitting to anything so we're blind. Faye overheard some stuff last week and we know Addison's hiding a secret. We were hoping you could do some digging into her background and see what you can come up with."

"Consider it done. I hate that lying whore."

"That's not all," I add, proceeding to tell them about Addison's involvement in the whole Kal-Lana saga.

"Why does she have such a hard-on for our family?" Kaden asks. I shrug. "Does Dad know about this?"

"Ky said he was going to speak to him although he wasn't overly confident that it'd help Kal's case much," I explain.

"I presume Ky knows nothing about this request, and that's the way you'd prefer to keep it?" Kaden asks, stretching his arms out over his head as a loud yawn escapes from his mouth.

"Yes. If you're okay with that." I look from one to the other.

"She's a poisonous little bitch," Keven says, "and she did a number on my brother last time. I still don't think he's over it, so

I'm happy to help. If we can dig up some dirt and use it to get her to leave Ky alone, then I'm all in."

I stand up. "Great. We're all on the same page, and this stays strictly between us."

We return to the house a few hours later, and the place looks like a bomb hit it. Unwashed dishes are heaped in the sink in the kitchen, food remnants from lunch and breakfast clutter the countertops, and various items of clothing and personal belongings are dotted all over the sitting room. Alex is fast asleep on the couch, snoring softly. Out in the utility room, piles of dirty washing are heaped in a giant mountain in the center of the floor.

"My cousins are such slobs," I mutter, and Brad chuckles.

"Guess I know what I'm doing this afternoon." I kneel down, starting to sort the clothes into darks and lights. Without complaint, Brad sits down beside me and we set about catching up on laundry.

After I make us a bite to eat, we wander to the games room. Keaton and Keanu are arguing over some stupid game on Xbox when we walk in. "What's up, assholes?" Brad asks, dropping lengthways on the couch.

"I'm going crazy cooped up in here," Keaton retorts, tossing the Xbox controller across the room.

"I thought you were bringing your girlfriend over today?"

"Eh." His cheeks flush bright red. "Would you bring anyone new into this house? She'd run a mile."

"Valid point," I acknowledge.

Keanu swivels in his chair, pinning his brother with an incredulous look. "Shut the fuck up. You have a girl?"

Oops. Didn't realize I'd let the cat out of the bag.

"Don't sound so surprised." Keaton is immediately on the defense.

"How much you paying her?" Keanu teases, and Keaton grabs him into a headlock.

"There is far too much testosterone around this place," I murmur to myself, flopping back on the couch.

"Let's grab a movie," Brad suggests. "That new *Star Wars* one is showing and I'm dying to see it."

I perk up. "I'm game. I love *Star Wars*."

"You're such a nerd," Keaton teases.

"Get your girlfriend to meet us there. I need to put her through her paces to see if she's worthy of you." I wink, and he groans. His eyes spark alive. "I'll bring Melissa if Keanu brings *Selena*." Her name rolls slowly on his tongue.

Selena models for Kennedy Apparel, and if the shots I've seen of her and Keanu are any indication, they have serious chemistry. But my cousin is remarkably reticent on the status of his relationship with her, and he gets all prickly the minute her name is mentioned.

"Yeah, nice try." Keanu gives him the middle finger.

I leave the boys arguing among themselves as I pad to Kalvin's room. I knock tentatively on the door. "Kal? You in there?"

"Where else would I be?" he asks sourly, opening the door with a savage swing.

"We're going to catch a movie. Why don't you come?"

He's shaking his head before I've even finished speaking. "Thanks, but no thanks." I open my mouth to argue my point, but he beats me to it. "Besides, someone has to stay with Mom, and Ky and Kent are both still out."

I admit defeat. "Okay. Maybe another time?"

He shrugs nonchalantly. "Maybe."

The movie is awesome and I indulge my sci-fi geekiness to

my heart's content. Neither of my cousins' girlfriends makes an appearance, but I'm glad it's only the four of us. We grab takeout on the way home, so it's late by the time we return to the house.

Alex is sniffling in front of the TV when I walk into the living room, and my shoulders instantly cord into knots. I've huge sympathy for Alex, but it's like walking on eggshells around here all the time. It's not as if *I* don't have serious issues occupying my mind. My mum had an incestuous affair with my uncle, and he may or may not be my dad, but you don't see me wallowing in it. I know I seem harsh, but I didn't peg Alex for the type to lie down and let some conniving cow trample all over her. There are still things she can control, and she has responsibilities to her business and this family, and she needs to focus on those instead of drinking herself into oblivion. I'm disappointed that the high-powered ballsy no-nonsense woman I first met seems to have evaporated into thin air.

But I'm not totally coldhearted, and I hate to see anyone hurting, even if they are perpetuating the situation themselves. I drop into place beside her on the couch, resting my head on her shoulder. She leans her head against me. The screen is frozen on an image of Alex and James on their wedding day. She's the classic golden beauty wearing an elegant figure-hugging white silk and lace dress. A simple veil frames her radiant face. James is peering into her eyes, and they are both laughing like they haven't a care in the world. The love shining between them is obvious.

I place my arm around her back. "It's true what they say, you know?" She lifts her head up as she speaks. Her sad eyes search mine. "Your wedding day is one of the best days of your life. At least, mine was. It was magical." An errant sob breaks free. "I thought he was my knight in shining armor." More choked sobs filter through the air. "And he was for a long time."

"Is it genuinely over between you?" I risk asking.

"Yes," she whispers, tears gliding down her face like an avalanche.

"I'm sorry."

"I am too." A pregnant pause fills the air, weighted with grief and loss, but at least her crying has stopped. Her chest heaves painfully up and down, and the look on her face is heart wrenching. She hits the stop button on the remote and stands up. "I think I'll call it a night."

I help her into bed, fixing her some sweet hot tea and propping the pillows up behind her back.

"Thank you, Faye." She kisses my cheek. "I know I've been absent this week but I needed to take some time for me. I'll be back on top of things next week."

It's as if she's read my mind and I'm instantly swamped with guilt for my previous uncharitable thoughts. "It's okay. I understand." I start backing out of the room. "Sweet dreams."

I meet Brad at the bottom of the steps. "Is she okay?" he whispers.

"She will be." My faith has somewhat been restored.

He takes my hand and pulls me into the corridor. "Chase is having another party. Do you want to go?"

The one and only time I attended Chase's party was the night Ky and Brad got into a fist fight and I felt like clawing Addison's eyes out. I'm not sure I'm up for a repeat. Before I can respond, Keaton approaches from the direction of the games room. "Kal's up for it, too. You in, Faye?"

"I don't think Kal going is such a good idea."

"Mom said I shouldn't hide," Kal responds, stepping out from his room dressed in a black shirt and jeans. "And this is the best way of making a statement, so I figure I should go. I'd appreciate the backup." He gives me his best puppy-dog-eye impression and my heart melts. It's not difficult to understand how girls swoon at his feet.

I cross my hands over my chest. "I can hardly refuse now, can I?"

"Yay!" Keaton high-fives me, before a fleeting concerned look glimmers in his eyes. "Ky will probably be pissed, but he'll just have to deal."

I frown, asking, "What?" the same time Brad does.

"Yeah, about that." Keaton winces and his eyes scrunch up. "Ky left me a note saying he was heading to the party and to make sure you didn't attend."

I shiver as an intense chill snakes its way through my veins. "Why would he say that?" A queasy sensation lodges in the pit of my stomach while I contemplate his reasons for making such a request. I don't need to be a brain surgeon to figure it out.

Keaton shrugs, while Brad and I exchange suspicious expressions. "There's only one surefire way of finding out," Brad murmurs.

"Yep." I toss my hair over my shoulder. Even though I may not like what I discover, wild horses wouldn't keep me away now. "We're going to that party, and I'm going to find out exactly why Ky doesn't want me there."

Chapter Fourteen

Brad drives off in his SUV and Kal, Keaton, and I sneak out through the garden, across the woods, and out beyond the guesthouse. When we slip out through the dilapidated old gate, Brad is already waiting.

"You little minx," Keaton says, sliding in beside me in the back seat. "How long have you been sneaking out?"

"Just a couple times." I shrug.

"You're most definitely a Kennedy," Kal says from the passenger seat, offering a rare smile.

"I'll accept that as a compliment."

"It was meant as one." He stares out the side window, contributing nothing further to the conversation for the rest of the journey.

Rows of vehicles line up in front of Chase's magnificent mansion, and it looks like a full house. The rhythmic pounding of beats pulsates in the otherwise silent night air as we tumble out of the car. Brad takes my hand and leads me around the side of the house to the back garden, like last time. I cling to him for support, tottering on my high heels, as I stumble over the stoned pathway. Before we round the corner, I remove my silk bomber jacket, tying it firmly around my waist. My fitted black leggings are practically welded to my legs, and the body-hugging black lace corset-style dress-slash-top accentuates my ample chest while slimming my waist. Stretching to my thighs, it barely covers my ass. I know I've probably gone slightly overboard, but I needed to at least feel confident and in control on the outside. Inside, all my organs have turned to mush, and there's a vile taste in my mouth.

I have a strong premonition that nothing is going to be the same after tonight.

I'm praying I'm wrong, but I'm also petrified that I'm right.

Brad's eyes are out on stalks as his gaze slowly rakes over me. Keaton whistles. "Wow, cuz. You look sexy as hell."

I'm almost speechless under the intensity of Brad's heated stare, and all I manage is a raspy "Thanks."

Brad leans down, pressing his mouth to my ear. His warm breath swirls over my skin, raising tiny goose bumps everywhere it touches. "You look absolutely stunning." His eyes drill into mine. "Don't leave my side."

The house is packed to capacity when we ease our way inside. I'm instantly hit by a searing wall of humidity. Sweat and perfume mix in the air to create a sweet and sour combo that's part intoxicating and part puke-inducing. Other noxious smells cause my nose to wrinkle in distaste. Writhing bodies throng the cleared-out living space, as boys and girls dance enthusiastically to the tunes the DJ is spinning. Buckets of beer and wine coolers cover numerous surfaces, and half-eaten bowls of chips and dips are littered throughout the room.

Brad guides us over to an empty space in the corner of the room. I drop my bag on the table behind us. My eyes instantly scan my surroundings with laser focus. I do a few laps of the room while Brad goes to grab us some beers, but I can't see Ky anywhere. That isn't in any way reassuring, especially considering I can't spot Addison either. My stomach lurches to my toes.

"Ho. Lee. Fuck!" A sonorous voice swoons in my ear. "Look at you."

I peer up into Jeremy's hungry eyes, watching as his gaze feasts on my chest. Suddenly, dressing so provocatively doesn't seem like such a smart move.

"Stand down, man. She's with me," Brad states, rejoining us with perfect timing. I take the offered beer and lean into him. He wastes no time staking his claim, clamping a firm hand to my hip and towing me into his warm body.

Jeremy raises his hands in surrender even though he looks like he's just sucked on a lemon. "Wasn't aware, bro. That's cool." He leans into my ear. "If you ever want to test drive a real man, give me a call." With one final sleazy wink, he slinks away, and I release the breath I'd been holding.

"What'd he say?" Brad asks, scowling.

"Nothing worth repeating." I take a swig of my beer, relishing the taste of the cool liquid.

"Steer clear of him, Faye," Kal warns. "He's totally sketch." Harsh glares spear him like daggers from all corners of the room, and a familiar ache takes up residence in my chest. Surrounded by blatant hostility instead of the usual harem of fawning girls, Kal couldn't have fallen any lower on the popularity ladder if he tried. Not that he gives two shits about that, I'm sure, but it's an acute reminder of how altered his reality is.

"I don't need convincing. I know Jeremy's a jerk." I send him a reassuring smile as my eyes continue to explore the room. I'm growing antsier with every passing second.

"You want to go look for him?" Brad asks with a solemn expression. I nod. "You sure about this?"

Brad is clearly drawing the same assumptions I am. The

beer settles in my stomach like rotten milk, and a layer of slime coats my tongue, but I nod again. This is no time for backing down.

We leave Kal and Keaton in the living room, squeezing past sweaty bodies as we maneuver a path through to the kitchen. There's no sign of Ky in here or outside, so Brad guides me out through the back of the kitchen into a long wide corridor with a myriad of closed doors on either side. Moans and groans filter through the air, twisting my insides into knots. I grind to a halt, smoothing a hand across my belly, unsure if I have the gumption to go through with this. "You want me to check?" Brad asks, intuitively knowing what I'm thinking. It's cowardly but I bob my head in acquiescence.

I keep my eyes trained on my gold-tipped black stilettos as Brad checks one door after another, apologizing profusely as a multitude of colorful language is leveled his way. Someone even throws a shoe at him, but he ducks in time, narrowly avoiding impact. "He's not in any of the bedrooms," Brad confirms, sidling up alongside me a few minutes later.

"What about the upstairs bedrooms?" I inquire.

"Upstairs is sealed off so all partygoers are restricted to the lower level. These are the only bedrooms down here."

I slump against him as sweet relief washes over me. "Maybe he decided not to come after all." I hate how pitiful my voice sounds. Tellingly, Brad doesn't reply.

I push off the wall and straighten up. "Come on, let's check out the front of the house."

Heat pumps off Brad as he follows behind me. Butterflies are having a field day in my chest, and I'm still on the verge of chucking as we exit the corridor and head around the front part of the house. It's quieter here, sounds of the music muffled by the thick floor-to-ceiling solid stone walls. The only lights are from a few carefully positioned lamps casting fleeting rays of illumination over the couples making out on all available surfaces. Every couch and chair in sight is occupied with boys and girls kissing, straddling, and dry humping one another. Lustful whimpers and cries suggest some are taking things further, and I hurry through the room, only glancing fleetingly at every couple, my heart pumping with much-needed hope when I fail to identify Ky.

Perhaps I've been jumping to wrongful conclusions. A calmness starts to soothe my insides as I reach the top of the room, passing by the alcove under the stairs to my right. A breathy moan stops my progress in a nanosecond, and my heart starts slamming around my ribcage in clear panic.

"Don't look," Brad whispers, slinging a firm arm around my waist from behind and attempting to shelter me with his body. All that does is crank my curiosity to the max.

Summoning courage, I turn my gaze to the hidden space under the stairs and the two bodies meshed together in the dark shadows. I'd know Ky's body anywhere, and my heart rate spikes to coronary-inducing levels while I watch him grinding his hips against Addison as he claims her mouth in a searing kiss. Addison's back is to the wall, and she has one of her legs hitched up to his thigh level. Her hands clutch at his back through his shirt. His lips leave her mouth to fit to her neck, and she emits another needy moan. "Oh, yes, Ky. Like that, baby."

A strangled cry escapes my lips before I can stop it. Brad's arm curves around my waist as Addison turns calculating eyes in my direction. When she recognizes me, her lips flick up into a wide smile. Reaching down, she grabs Ky's ass and pulls him even closer to her. Every muscle in Ky's body has gone stiff, and he's frozen in place.

"Don't do this here," Brad pleads in my ear, attempting to tug me back.

"Stop." My voice is loud and commanding, like ice and steel.

Addison cups the back of Ky's head. "Ignore her."

Ky reaches up and removes her hands and her leg, setting her carefully on the ground. Slowly, he turns around and faces me with a carefully constructed mask in place. "I need a minute," he says over his shoulder, not giving Addison any time to object before he stalks toward me.

He pulls me away from Brad, keeping a firm grip on my elbow. "Leave us." Brad opens his mouth to object but thinks better of it when Ky pierces him with a venomous glare. Ky lugs me back the way I walked and out through the front door. "You shouldn't have come here! I left explicit instructions!" He drags his hands through his hair, conspicuously avoiding looking at me.

"I'm glad I came. I needed to see it with my own two eyes, or I'd never have believed it." As I stare at his beautiful face, I swear I hear my heart split in two. "I know it's not real, that she's behind this," I whisper, appealing to him to throw me a lifeline. I'd rather accept that than the alternative. "What's she blackmailing you with this time?"

A sad, pitiful look appears on his face as he finally looks me straight in the eye. "She's not blackmailing me, Faye." His voice is quiet and firm.

I put my hands on my hips while my heart tries to take flight out of my chest. "Don't try and tell me you genuinely want to be with her?" I snort.

He nods without hesitation, his pale blue eyes betraying no hint of emotion, and something inherent dies inside me. "I don't believe you." It isn't true. I know it isn't. I hate how my voice trembles, how my resolve starts to weaken. "She's doing this. I know she is."

A brief flicker of emotion skates over his face, but it's gone before I can fathom it. "I know the truth is hard to accept, but you'll have to find a way. You and I are finished. I'm back together with Addison." He absentmindedly kicks at the dirt under his shoe as my heart shatters into a million pieces.

"No! Why?"

"You come with too many complications, Faye."

His words gut me, all twisty and hurtful, but I still can't give up the fight. "You don't know that! It's only a little over a week until we have the test results—would it have killed you to wait? To do that for me? For us?"

He sends me a simpering sympathy look. "Even if you're not my sister, you're still my cousin, and people will never accept that. This is for the best, and if you thought about this rationally, you'd see that too."

Ignoring his cruel barb, I step right in front of him, putting my face in his. "So, you're settling for her for an easy life?"

"I didn't say that." He is quick to disagree. "She understands me, and we have too much history to throw away."

"This is complete and utter bullshit." I glare at him. "And what about what she's done to Kal? She is as much responsible for his situation as Lana is!"

"You aren't apprised of all the facts." He grinds down on his teeth.

I plant my hands on my hips. "So, enlighten me."

He shakes his head, exhaling deeply. "It doesn't matter. It won't change a thing. Get a grip of yourself, Faye. I'm with Addison, and the sooner you accept that, the sooner you can move on."

"What about everything you said? You told me you loved me. I ..." I stop talking before I say something else I'll regret. I've already made a big enough fool of myself. I'm shivering profusely, and the frosty night air isn't responsible.

He doesn't reply either way, pointedly averting his eyes,

and I hate how that fills me with hope. "Are you saying everything we shared was a lie?" I reach out and touch his arm. "Tell me you didn't mean any of it, and I'll walk away without a fight. Without further argument."

His eyes caress mine as he stares at me and through me. My heart is thudding in my chest as a million different emotions, thoughts, and sensations fill the gap between us. His eyes touch every part of my face in turn, and it's torture being this close to him and not being able to touch him. The silence is deafening, but every second that he doesn't reply increases my fragile hope. I'm clinging on by a thread, silently praying to hear the words I need to hear.

He meant everything he told me.

I'd stake my life on it.

This is all part of some manipulation on Addison's part and nothing more.

That's all this is.

I shiver some more, closing my eyes briefly as I beg him to speak. Anxious adrenaline swamps my system and my legs turn to jelly. I clamp my hands against the wall at my back to steady myself.

"It wasn't real," he says, his voice gruff. "Those feelings were fleeting." His detached tone spins my insides into a raw, sodden mess. "My feelings for you don't compare to how I feel about Addison."

Unshed tears fill my eyes, and I can't open my mouth to speak. I'm afraid to. In case the whole dam bursts and I make an even bigger show of myself. I'm a complete mess. It's as if my entire world is collapsing around me again. Grief and heartache surround me like a suffocating blanket.

I need to get out of here.

With my mouth set in a displeased line, I acknowledge him with a terse jerk of my head. With great effort, I walk away from the house in measured strides, holding my head up high even though inside I'm in complete bits. I keep walking, my head churning, my heart pounding, and my limbs aching, but I don't stop. I have sole-minded focus—to put as much distance between me and him as I can.

I hear my name called, but I don't stop, I can't stop. I pick up my pace, jogging now, pushing my legs as fast as they will carry me in these heels. I'm pounding the pavement along the side of the driveway, about halfway to the front gates, when a car pulls up, tires screeching and rubber burning. I stop, bunching over and pressing my palms to my knees as I attempt to recalibrate my breathing.

"Get in," Brad says, flinging the door open. Ignoring him, I straighten up and start walking again. Shrouded in a cloud of denial, I'm walking on auto-pilot, hurt lancing me on all sides. Suddenly, I'm lifted off my feet and carried to the car. I stare numbly ahead, incapable of putting up any kind of resistance. Brad locks my seat belt in place and runs around the front of the SUV, sliding into his seat. The engine roars as he steps on the pedal.

"Stop," I say, when we reach the gates. "Turn around." *What the hell am I doing? Running off and letting him win? Letting* her *win?* I can still see her smug, condescending face in my memory, and I latch onto it, letting rage and anger replace the heartache and pain.

Brad slams on the brake, and turns to face me. "What?"

"I don't want to leave. Bring me back."

His brow furrows. "Why?"

I pull my knees up to my chest and stare straight ahead as I talk. "He's chosen her over me, because, apparently, I'm too 'complicated.'" I make air quotes with my fingers. "If I leave like this, he'll think I care. *She'll* think I care, and I'm fecked if I'm leaving that impression."

"You *do* care." Brad's tone is sincere and without pity. He's merely stating a fact.

"I do, but I'm not going to forever, because if he doesn't care about me, then I'm not going to care about him either."

I tilt my face up to Brad's. "I'm not giving either of them the satisfaction of knowing how much they've hurt me. I don't run. *I'm not running.* So, please, turn the car around, and take me back."

Chapter Fifteen

"What's the plan?" Brad asks, parking in the same spot outside the mansion.

I smooth my hands down the front of my dress, fluff up my hair, and apply a fresh coat of lip gloss before replying. "I'm going to party." A devilish glint glistens in my eye. "I'm going to get drunk and kiss a boy." I shrug nonchalantly. "I'm just going to cut loose and see what happens."

"Em, Faye." He worries his lower lip between his teeth. "You can't. Do the kissing another boy part." He looks at me knowingly. "I'm your fake boyfriend, remember?"

I drill him with a look full of intent as I open my door. "How exactly is that a problem?"

I slam my door and stalk toward the house, flicking my hair confidently over my shoulder as Brad hurriedly locks the car and chases after me.

I storm through the room like a tornado, swanning past the alcove where I last saw Ky and Addison without a glance, charging into the kitchen and helping myself to two beers. Brad takes my elbow and steers me out into the main room, weaving across the floor as he looks for my other cousins. Keaton and Kal aren't where we left them, so I figure they're in the midst of the crowd moshing on the makeshift dance floor. I chug my beer, draining half of it in one go. I offer the second bottle to Brad, but he shakes his head. "Designated driver, remember?"

"Oh, goody. More for me." I proceed to finish my beer and waste no time getting stuck into the second one. I can tell Brad isn't down with this plan, but I appreciate he doesn't try to stop me.

I swipe another bottle of beer right out of a boy's hand as he walks past. "Hey!" he protests, before turning his interested gaze on me, his eyes latching on my chest.

"Like what you see?" I give him a half-wink as I raise the bottle to my mouth. My lips slide up and down the neck of the bottle and his eyes glaze over.

"Get lost." Brad sends him a death-glare. "She's with me."

"Good luck taming that one!" He chuckles, daringly slapping my ass before walking away.

Brad curses under his breath, and I throw back my head and laugh. I like this new plan far better than my old one. I haven't felt this out of control in a long time—like I want to peel off my skin and adopt a new persona or bleach my brain and free it of all the things reminding me of Ky. The image of him rubbing up against Addison surges to the forefront of my mind, cleaving a line straight through my heart.

I drain my third beer without stopping, and my hips start swaying to the alluring beat of the music. I stretch my arms up over my head and wiggle my hips, doing a sexy little shimmy to the floor. I'm well aware of the heated stares I'm picking up from several corners of the room, and that spurs me on. I'm buzzing and loving the feeling. Sure beats feeling rejected and heart sore. With an upsurge of confidence, I press against Brad, circling my hands around his neck as I pull him closer. "Kiss me."

I lower one hand, trailing it slowly up and down his back. "Come on, Brad. I know you want to." I lick my lips, and his conflicted eyes follow the movement wantonly. Leaning in, I dart my tongue out and run a line from the bottom of his neck to his jaw, scratching the line of stubble with my cheek. "You want to kiss me so kiss me." I slap a hand against his firm ass and groan.

"Dammit, Faye." He closes his eyes, shaking his head. "Can't believe I'm going to do this," he mumbles. Removing my hands from his body, he steps back, creating some distance between us. "This isn't going to happen."

Rejection hits me hard and I switch to defensive mode. Narrowing my eyes, I plant my hands on my hips. "You're rejecting me?"

"No!" His knuckles are pressed against his brow.

"Then you'll kiss me?" I bridge the newly formed gap, sliding my hands up his chest.

He sighs in exasperation. "Will you stop touching me. Please."

I remove my hands in a flash as a fresh wave of pain assaults me. "If you won't kiss me, then I'll find someone who will." I spin on my heel, but before I can move, Brad has hauled me back to his side.

"You don't know what you're doing, and you're going to regret this in the morning."

I laugh. "I know exactly what I'm doing, and if you don't want this, I'm sure there are plenty of boys who'd be happy to take me up on my offer."

"Undoubtedly there are plenty of guys in this room happy

to take advantage of you, Faye, but I'm not one of them, and I'm not going to let that happen. You'll thank me tomorrow."

I prod him in the chest, snarling. "When did you become such a bore? And you don't have any claim over me. You're not even my real boyfriend, and I don't need you. I don't need anyone. Now, get out of my way or I'll make you."

Veins protrude in his neck, at odds with his calm expression. Gently, he takes my wrist. "Please, Faye. I know you're hurting, but this isn't going to make you feel better. Let me take you home."

I push him away, smoothing my hands down the front of my dress. "I'm going to dance. Alone." I pierce him with another scathing look. "Until I'm not." I straighten my shoulders and walk toward the dance floor, snatching another beer from one of the buckets on my way.

The dance floor is teaming with sweaty, writhing bodies, and I thrust myself into the middle of the crowd, shaking my hips and letting the music take over, eradicating the confusion in my mind and blanking everything out. All I'm aware of is the euphoric thrumming of blood in my veins, the blissful sway of my limbs, and the enhanced buzz as the alcohol races through my system helping me to blot everything out. Heat waylays me as a warm body presses into me from behind. "Hey, gorgeous," a sultry voice croons in my ear. "You want some company?"

I turn slowly around, peering into the grayish-green eyes of the guy looming over me. His broad shoulders and strong physique give his footballer status away. He looks vaguely familiar, but I can't remember if he's on Brad's old football team or his new one. Not that it matters. Judging by the way his hot gaze is roaming my curves, I'm figuring it won't take much to seduce him. "Do I know you?" Tossing my beer aside, I slide my fingers up over the planes of his ripped chest. With his strong jawline, dark hair, and mischievous eyes, he is darkly attractive, and he'll more than meet my immediate needs. I don't feel guilty that I'm using him to avoid reality because I know his type. He's never going to be boyfriend material, and that suits me just fine. I'm only interested in one night, and this guy fits the bill perfectly.

His hands land loosely on my back. "Do you want to?" he asks in a husky voice.

"Maybe." I play coy, running the tip of my tongue over my lips.

"What about your boyfriend?" His eyes flit over my head, and I follow his gaze. Brad is standing with his arms folded, looking directly at me with a furious look on his face. "I don't want to invade Brad's territory. Bro code and all that."

Ignoring his blatant sexist remark, I lean in closer, inhaling his woodsy all-male smell. "He's not my boyfriend anymore."

He grins. "It looked like you were arguing, but I wasn't sure." His hands hold me closer at the waist.

"You were watching me?" I flutter my eyelashes in a deliberate provocative gesture. I don't quite know what's gotten into me tonight, but I'm going to indulge this new persona and throw caution to the wind.

"Baby"—he caresses my cheek—"every guy in this room is watching you."

"Well, then"—I run my thumb across his lower lip, smiling when his body thrusts against mine—"I guess this is your lucky night." I eye his full lips with obvious intent. "I need to be kissed. Right. Now."

He barks out an amused laugh. "I like a girl who knows what she wants and isn't afraid to ask for it."

"So?" I tilt my head to the side. "What are you waiting for?"

He chuckles as his large hand slides to the back of my neck. He pulls me flush to his body, grinding his arousal against me. When he smashes his lips to mine, he devours my mouth without apology. He plunders my mouth greedily, groaning as our tongues mesh together. He tastes like beer and smoke, and while his technique could use some work, I'm not going to complain because he's making me forget, and that's exactly what I signed up for. His muscular arms wrap firmly around me, and he lifts me clear off the floor, which is no easy feat, but he holds me aloft as if I weigh nothing. Angling his head, he extends the kiss, and I move my mouth against his, enjoying the hard thrusting of our mouths and our bodies.

"Get your filthy hands off her, Edwards," Brad demands as a second pair of hands lands on my waist.

"Get lost, McConaughey." He removes his lips from mine and places my feet back on the floor. "She's a free agent." He hasn't relinquished hold of me, and I'm hemmed in on both sides.

"Faye." Brad's voice contains clear concern. "Come on, please."

I shuck out of Edwards embrace and turn to face Brad. "Have you changed your mind?"

He reaches his hand out to me. "Please, come home with me now."

"That's a no, then." I slide my arm around Edwards' waist as a shout echoes around the room.

"Fight!"

Our attention is instantly diverted. The crowd surges forward, and there's a mass exodus from the room. Keaton appears at our side. His cheeks are flushed, and there's a worried expression on his face. "Brad, Ky needs your help to break up a fight. Kal and some asshole are kicking the shit out of one another."

Brad lets loose a string of colorful obscenities. "Okay." Brad eyeballs me. "Stay right here. We're leaving when I come back and that's final." He jabs a finger in Edwards' chest. "Don't try anything or you'll have me and the entire Kennedy clan on your ass."

Edwards shows him the middle finger.

"Wait. I'm coming too." I grab hold of Brad's arm. "He's my cousin." And I had promised I'd support him, but instead, I got lost in my own drama and left him to his own devices. I'm a pathetic excuse for a cousin.

"No." Brad shakes his head sternly. "I don't want you getting caught up in the middle of this. It could get messy. Stay here and I'll be back."

He races off behind Keaton. Edwards winks at me, running his finger along the edge of my mouth. "You sure you and him are done? Didn't much sound like it."

"I'm not with Brad, and he doesn't dictate what I do or don't do."

Edwards fuses his mouth to mine without warning. "Prove it," he whispers against my lips, straightening up and taking my hand. I let him lead me out through the kitchen and into the back corridor where the bedrooms are. One part of me knows this is a bad idea, but another part of me, that illusive alien part of me, propels my legs forward in encouragement.

He opens a door and steps aside to let me enter. The room is bathed in complete darkness, but I can make out the wrinkled double bed resting alongside a heavily curtained window. Edwards stalks toward me, pulling my body against his. His eyes smolder with a lustful gleam that is unmistakable. "You want to have some fun, babe?"

He rocks his hips into mine so there's no misconstruing the intent. I shouldn't do this. It's not my usual M.O., but I can think of no better way to scrub Ky from my body and my mind. I run my hands up his impressive chest. "I'm game."

He sends me a devilish smile, and then his mouth is crashing against mine as he walks us back to the bed. I fall back on the downy mattress and his body covers mine. His hands entangle in my hair, and he moans when I roll my hips up to meet the bulge in his jeans. His teeth graze the skin on my neck, and he nips and bites his way down to my chest. I writhe underneath him, deliberately blocking all conscious thought. I want to lose myself in the moment, in the feel of this stranger's lips and body moving against mine. His hand slips under the band of my corset top. As he roughly kneads my breast, I moan out loud.

"That is so fucking sexy," he murmurs. "No wonder McConaughey was trying to keep you all to himself." He slides down my body, pulling my shoes and leggings off in a few swift well-practiced moves. Cool air washes over my exposed skin, and before I have time to reconsider, his calloused hands are creeping up my legs. His eyes shimmer with potent need as he cups my sensitive place. Heat rushes through me, and my back bows off the bed. His mouth seals to mine again, and his tongue is frantically exploring my mouth while his hand slips into my knickers. I claw at his back, trying to drown out the noisy protests in my head and the sudden unease trickling through me. I should just stick with the program, see this through, but I can't. This isn't who I am, and no matter how badly I wish to replace the memory of Ky's touch, all this is doing is highlighting how much I miss him. Edwards isn't Ky. Isn't even close to him, and now I want to get as far away from him as I can. *What the heck am I doing? What was I thinking?*

My head is a jumbled mess, and the alcoholic buzz isn't helping either.

His finger slides inside me, and I shudder in disgust. This is wrong. I don't want to do this with him or anyone who isn't the boy I love. Sleeping with someone else won't repair the hole in my heart or make me forget everything that Ky means to me. This will only make me feel even more used.

Just as I've decided to call a halt to this, a hulking form drifts out of the shadows in the corner of the room, and I scream in fright. Edwards clamps a hand over my mouth. "Chill, sweetheart. It's okay."

My entire body trembles as adrenaline surges through my veins. My eyes blink furiously as light drenches the room in a sudden burst of luminosity. "That's much better," a familiar masculine voice says. "I want to see every inch of your glorious body as he fucks you."

Bile floods my mouth as I open my eyes and glower at Jeremy. "Excuse me?" I remove Edwards' hand from my knickers and shove him away.

"Don't go all shy now, Faye." Jeremy grips my chin, pulling my face up so I've no choice but to look him in the eye. "I've been watching you, dirty girl. You want him inside you. You're practically begging for it." He reaches into his pocket, pulling out a bunch of foil packets and tosses them on the bed. "I'll show you if you like?" he smirks, waving his cell at me. "You've already given me quite the show." He presses a few buttons on his phone and holds it out to me.

My eyes dart wide in panic as I realize what he's done. A rush of nausea assaults me as I watch myself moaning and writhing on the recording. *No! This isn't happening to me again!* "Give me that!" I make a grab for the phone, but he holds it out of reach.

"I'll make you a deal." He licks his lips as his eyes zone in on my chest. "Let us both do you, and we'll give you back the recording, and we can all walk away having had a good time. What do you say, Ireland? You up for a threesome?"

I stand up, unfurling to my full height. I may be only at chin-level with him, but he's not going to intimidate me or blackmail me. "In your dreams, asshole." My heart is slamming against my ribcage as I hold out my hand. "Give me your phone. Now."

He shakes his head, sending me an amused look. "No." My hand quivers with almost uncontrollable rage. "My cell. My property. My content, and I'll do whatever the hell I want with it. The guys on the team are gonna go crazy for this."

I push him. "Listen, jerkface. If you do anything with that recording, I'll sue your sleazy blackmailing ass."

This time it's Edwards who laughs. Approaching from behind, he wraps his strong arm around my waist, pressing his mouth to my neck. "You're getting all worked up for the wrong reasons. The three of us can have a good time, and then you can watch while we delete the recording."

"How stupid do you think I am? And get off me!" I try to wrestle out of his arms, but his hold doesn't budge.

"Come on, Faye. We were having a good time. Loosen up and go with the flow."

"I said GET. OFF. ME!" I yell, shoving my elbow into his ribs. He jerks back and I reach around, digging my nails into his groin. Edwards emits a guttural roar, clutching himself between the legs as he stumbles backward with tears leaking out of his eyes. He crashes into a dresser, knocking it on its side with an almighty thud.

"You really shouldn't have done that," Jeremy warns, dangling his phone in front of me like a predator luring a child with chocolate.

I make a lunge for him. I bring my leg up to kick him in the junk, but he intercepts my move, grabbing my foot, and I lose my balance. I fall to the ground on my back, pulling him down with me. His large body flattens me to the floor, and his face thwacks against mine. The phone flies out of his hand, skating along the floor and under the bed. Edwards is shouting obscenities at me, and Jeremy is moaning on top of me. Stars distort my vision, and an instantaneous throbbing pain takes up residence in my skull. A fluid substance trickles over my face, and the room spins as the door flies open.

The weight pressing down on me is gone as Jeremy is lifted off me. "Oh my God, Faye." Ky's tone and look is horrified as he takes in the sight of me. The left strap of my dress has snapped, exposing the upper half of my breast, and blood is leaching out of my nose. Bending down, he swoops me up into his arms. "Are you hurt anywhere else?" he asks in an almost whisper. "What did they do to you?"

I clutch my head in my hands, groaning as I try to focus my vision. "The phone," I mumble. Ky steps out into the corridor and places me gently on the ground.

"What?" He peers into my eyes as I lift my head up noticing Brad for the first time. He's standing in the doorway, fury seeping out of his pores like fog spreading soundlessly and swiftly across the land. He removes his shirt, leaving him in only a white tank top, and hands it to me. "Put this on." His kind tone is at odds with his fierce expression. Ky helps me into the shirt, buttoning it all the way up to my chin. There's a look of absolute terror and rage etched on his face.

"I warned you, Edwards. I fucking told you to leave her alone," Brad yells. "You're fucking dead!" With that, he charges into the room with a roar.

"Wait!" I try to get up, but a burst of dizziness keeps me rooted to the spot.

"Don't move," Ky says. "Stay right here. We'll deal with them."

I open my mouth to explain, but Ky has already raced into the room with his fists raised. Oh crap. Things are about to turn to utter shite.

I have a front row seat from where I'm positioned, and I watch as Ky throws himself into the fight alongside Brad with gusto. I know I should get in there and tell them that they have the wrong idea, but my legs won't work, and every time I try to climb to my feet, I end up collapsing onto the floor. Ky yanks Jeremy off Brad's back, pummeling him repeatedly in the face. Jeremy doesn't stand a chance. Ky has him pinned to the floor as he rains savage blows on his face and upper torso. Brad has a similar advantage on Edwards until more rallying cries ring out, and a surge of bodies hurtles down the corridor and into the room.

It's a virtual blood bath. There's got to be at least twenty boys crowded into the bedroom, exchanging punches. Bodies move like lightning, darting up and down, heads thrusting back, and spatters of blood soaring through the air. Furniture screeches and slides across the floor as bodies are flung around the space. Roars and shouts are commonplace as I stare numbly at the chaos in front of me. Tucking my bare legs up to my chest, I tremble underneath Brad's shirt, hyperconscious of my half-naked state. Someone comes flying out of the room, and I have to scoot sideways to avoid being trampled.

The shrill sound of steel-toed heels approaching captures my attention. I turn and watch Addison stalking toward me with venom in her eyes. Her nostrils flare up in a most unattractive fashion. She stalls in front of me, observing the scene in the room before turning around to face me. With considerable effort, I hoist myself to my feet, clinging to the wall for support. Her eyes scan me from head to toe with a look of utter disdain. "Slut," she hisses.

"Takes one to know one," I bite back.

She takes a step toward me. "I will only say this one more time. Kyler is mine. Do not stand in my way or you'll be sorry."

I glare at her. "I know you're blackmailing him into this. There's no way he's with you of his own free will."

Her lips turn into a snarl. "You've hit your head, and you're delusional. It's time you faced facts, *Ireland*." She prods a bony finger in my chest, and I thrust it away. "He is *my* boyfriend, and that's not going to change anytime soon. Or ever." She straightens up and a sly smile creeps over her mouth. "Why do you care who your cousin dates anyway?" Her eyes narrow to slits as a loud crash from inside the room reminds me the fight it still ongoing.

Even with what I suspect is a minor concussion, I know not to fall into a trap when I hear one. "Because Kyler deserves to be with someone decent. Not some cheating tramp who has worked her way through the entire football team!" I yell.

Grabbing my wrist, she twists it hard, and I cry out. "Careful now. You're playing in the big league, and you're completely out of your depth." She drops my hand, smirking as she takes a step back. "You know, you sound almost jealous. You wouldn't be crushing on your cousin, now would you?" Her eyes glisten with malice. "Because that would make you a total sicko." She glances over her shoulder as another loud thud emanates from the room. When she turns around again, there's a calculating expression on her face. "I can ruin you. Just like that!" She clicks her fingers. "Stay out of my way. I won't warn you again." I flip her the bird as she walks away, and her gleeful cackles are still piercing my ear drums when the sounds of sirens ring out in proximity.

There's a crazed stampede in the main room outside if the shrieks, shouts, and urgent trumping of feet is any indication. "Cops!" someone yells into the corridor, and it's almost comical how speedily the fight breaks up.

Boys stream out of the room, covered in cuts and bruises, and I watch as a couple of others jump out the bedroom window. Brad reaches down, scooping me up in his arms as Ky hurtles out of the room. "Fuck! We need to find my brothers and get the hell out of here!"

I cling to Brad's neck, burying my face in his shoulder as he races down the corridor and out into the main room, the heavy thread of pounding footsteps following behind us.

"Stop right there!" a gruff voice commands. "You are all under arrest."

Chapter Sixteen

I shiver profusely in the cold, stark cell. The blanket the kind police lady gave me is threadbare, and although it covers my exposed legs and feet, it doesn't provide any warmth. My teeth chatter relentlessly as icy tremors rock my body.

"Jeez, Faye, you're freezing," Keaton confirms, dropping onto the bench alongside me. He hauls me into his side, and I cling to him, desperate to siphon some of his body heat.

"You should try keeping your clothes on next time," Jeremy snipes from the holding cell next door. I have zero energy to enter into a battle of wills at this Godforsaken hour, so I count to ten in my head and bite back my snarky retort.

"You're lucky there's a steel bar separating us, Roberts," Ky snaps. He's sitting on the opposite side of our cell alongside Brad and a few other boys from the party. Edwards and Jeremy are in the cell behind us with the rest of the boys who were arrested. To borrow Kaden's phrase, it's a clusterfuck of epic proportions.

We were all interviewed separately, and I've already given my statement so I don't know why I'm still locked up. I wasn't engaged in the fighting, and as far as I'm aware, they have no grounds to detain me. None of us have seen Kal since we were brought in, and I can only imagine the world of trouble he's in.

The sound of approaching footfalls halt the flow of conversation and everyone perks up. The surly looking male police officer from earlier appears with James and Kaden at his rear. Some of my pent-up stress releases at the sight of my uncle and cousin.

"Kennedys, Donovan, and McConaughey," the police officer shouts. "Come with me." He unlocks the cell, stepping aside to allow us to pass.

"What about us?" Edwards demands. The sound of his voice twists and turns in my gut. I can't believe I was so idiotic. I let stupid pride and alcohol override common sense, in a feeble attempt to ignore my aching heart. I nearly slept with that douche because I was doing everything to avoid actually feeling the pain of Ky's rejection, and if I'm being brutally honest, because I wanted to hurt Kyler like he hurt me.

I'm thoroughly disgusted with myself.

I swore I'd never place myself in a vulnerable position again, and now, it's as if I've regressed five years, and I'm stuck in the same spot with an intimate recording of me hanging over my head. I cringe as I recall exactly what's on that footage. I'll never be able to show my face around town if that gets leaked.

"Get used to your new home," Ky hisses at Edwards. "You're not going anywhere anytime soon." He's still operating under the illusion that the guys attacked me or something. It isn't difficult to see how both he and Brad jumped to that conclusion, and I should've set them straight, but I didn't want to open up that conversation with Jeremy and Edwards in the adjoining cell. Although, I can't delay telling them much longer

—not when I'll need their help getting that recording. Goose bumps the size of golf balls sprout on my arms at the mere thought of that video in the public domain.

"Shut your mouth," the cop says, glowering at Ky. "Or I'll put you back in there."

"Kyler. Let me handle this." James slants a warning look at his son.

We follow the policeman out of the holding cells, through the main office, and into a large room with white painted walls. An older man with salt and pepper hair is waiting for us, seated on one side of the table with a grim expression on his face. Kal is seated across from him, and although his head is down, I can still identify the numerous injuries on his face. His hands are cuffed and resting on the table in front of him, his knuckles shredded and bloody.

I race to his side, losing the blanket in the process.

"Where the hell are your pants and shoes?" James is aghast as he runs his gaze from my naked feet to my bare legs. I'm still wearing Brad's shirt over my dress, but it scarcely covers my ass, and I may have just flashed the room. Carefully, I dip down, securing the blanket around my waist before I take a seat beside Kal.

"They're back at Chase's house. The officers who arrested us wouldn't let me get them," I explain.

"It's not *her* fault." Ky's tone and look suggests he's on the verge of a complete meltdown, and I know that's my cue to come clean, but Brad interjects before I can speak up.

"No, it's not," Brad grits through clenched teeth, speaking decisively after remaining mute the whole time we were in the cell. "It's your fucking fault!" He rushes Ky, shoving him hard. "Faye wouldn't have been in that position if you hadn't upset her earlier."

"She was with you!" Ky yells back, shoving him equally

hard. "If it's anyone's fault, it's yours for letting her go off with them!"

"Shut. Up." James' tone is curt. "And sit down. Right now. All of you." He glares at everyone.

Brad slams into the seat beside me, his body rigid with stress. Ky claims the chair on the end, sending daggers in Brad's direction. Keaton sits in between them while James sits beside the stranger, who I'm assuming is our solicitor. Kaden leans against the wall with his arms folded, his features a smoldering hotbed of intensity as he scans our faces.

You could light a match with the hormone-infused tension in the air.

"Where do you want to start?" the man asks James.

James locks his hands behind his head as he exhales. His eyes look tired. I flip my gaze to the clock mounted on the back wall, surprised to see it's only four a.m. It felt like we were in that cell for eternity.

"Faye, are you up to explaining what happened tonight?"

I sit up straighter in my chair. "Sure."

"I'm Dan Evans," the stranger says, reaching across the table to shake my hand. "I'm the Kennedy family attorney, and I'm also representing you and Mr. McConaughey in this matter."

I lean forward, pressing against the edge of the table. "I don't understand. Am *I* under arrest?"

"Mr. Edwards and Mr. Roberts are alleging you assaulted them causing actual bodily harm."

I snort, throwing my head back. "You've got to be kidding me?" I send an incredulous look across the table. "They were recording me without my knowledge, and I was trying to get my hands on Jeremy's cell so I could delete it. It turned a bit messy, and we all ended up on the floor." I point at my face. "I got injured too."

James curses, leaning his elbows on the table and cradling his head in his hands.

"What?" Ky roars, jumping up out of his seat. He starts pacing the room. "They were going to rape you *and* record it?" I open my mouth to explain, but his pacing picks up in earnest. "I'm going to kill those sick fucks!" he yells.

Brad settles his hand on top of my clenched fists, squeezing lightly as he misinterprets my expression. Keaton looks like he might cry, while Kal still has his head bent, and I'm not entirely convinced he isn't asleep sitting up. I slump a little in my chair, terrified to confirm how the fight is actually all my fault. That it was a misunderstanding and if I'd only explained that then maybe we wouldn't be here right now.

Dan is astutely watching me. "Several witnesses have said they saw you willingly enter the room with Mr. Edwards. Can you please explain how you came to be in that room and what exactly happened?"

I shift uncomfortably in my seat. "I did go willingly with him," I admit, lowering my eyes. I can't say this while looking any of them in the face. "And, eh, what we were doing was consensual." I slink a little lower in my chair, and Ky stops pacing. I daren't look up at him. "But I didn't know that Jeremy was hiding in the corner recording everything."

A chorus of expletives emit in the room. "He's dead," Ky snarls. "That fucking son of a bitch is so dead!"

"Mr. Kennedy!" Dan shouts. "Sit back down and zip your lips. Do I need to remind you we are in a meeting room in a police station? Although we are supposed to have client-attorney privilege, I have no doubt there are people listening in. You cannot make idle threats like that, even if they are all talk."

Dan slams his fist down on top of the table. "No one is to speak unless spoken to. I am asking questions to determine what happened tonight so I can extract you all from this mess.

Your father is paying me by the hour, so I suggest you shut up and let me do my job. Is that clear?"

Several reluctant heads nod, and he's got a new fan in me. I admire his no-bullshit attitude.

"What happened after you discovered Mr. Roberts was in the room?" Dan asks, returning to his mild-mannered tone.

My brow furrows as my alcohol-addled brain struggles to remember the exact course of events. "Jeremy flipped on the light and said he wanted to see every inch of me while Edwards … you know …" There's no way I'm repeating what Jeremy said verbatim. Not in front of my uncle and the solicitor. "And then he taunted me with his phone and said he'd delete the recording if I got behind a threesome." I slip farther in my chair as I practically whisper the last word.

The table rattles as Brad's entire body jerks in his seat. Ky curses, and they exchange a long drawn-out look. Dan nods at me to carry on.

I tuck my hair behind my ears. "Edwards was trying to convince me, and when he wouldn't take his hands off me, I reacted instinctively. I elbowed him and he went flying back into the dresser. Then I tried to kick Jeremy in the junk while I made a grab for his phone, but he grabbed my foot, and we both fell to the ground. We butted heads as he landed on top of me."

The surprising sound of quiet chuckling reverberates in the room, and I look over at Kaden. His entire body is shaking with laughter. "Remind me to never get on your bad side."

"This isn't a laughing matter," James roars. "That douche has an intimate video of your cousin, and need I remind everyone of how serious this situation is for your brother." All eyes swivel to Kal who still hasn't lifted his face up.

Dan frowns, pulling his glasses on as he thumbs through the file in front of him. "I see no mention of any recording in your statement." He looks at me over the rim of his spectacles.

"Yeah, um, about that." I grimace. "I didn't mention it because I was hoping to use it as a negotiation tool."

"Come again?" He stares at me in confusion.

"She didn't want the video in circulation." Ky speaks up for me. "She was going to use it as leverage. The video in exchange for not ratting them out to the cops. It's an infringement of her privacy, and they can get in trouble for that, right?" My mouth hangs open at his accurate assessment. He knows me almost as well as I know myself.

"Is that true?" Dan asks.

I look down the table at Ky. "Yeah." He stares back at me with a mixture of anger, regret, and understanding in his expression. That one look conveys so much. Addison has him by the balls—she's forcing him to be with her, I'm convinced of it.

"Faye, sweetheart." James reaches over the table. "I know what you were trying to do but you have to revise your statement. The police need to find that recording ASAP. The last thing you need is that turning up in the hands of the media. We've enough heat on us as it stands."

"I understand. I'll amend my statement." I turn pleading eyes on Dan. "Just get that recording before he can do anything with it. The last I remember, his phone flew across the floor and under the bed. I doubt he'd time to retrieve it before the fighting broke out and then the police were on the scene."

Dan stands up. "I'll sort it. Give me a moment, please." He leaves the room and silence ensues.

I lean my head on Kal's shoulder, and I'm surprised when he rests his head on mine. He has yet to contribute to the conversation, and he hasn't uttered a word since we stepped foot in the room. I'm worried about him.

Dan steps back into the room a minute later. "The sergeant

will re-interview you after we're done here, Faye. They are getting a warrant for Jeremy's cell as we speak."

He looks between Brad, Keaton, and Ky. "All charges are being dropped against you. There were too many involved in the initial fight and the ensuing one to determine who is ultimately at fault."

James breathes a sigh of relief.

"Right. Moving on." Dan opens up a new file. "Who wants to tell me about the earlier fight?" He looks to Kal first. "Kalvin? Can you explain how that came about?"

Kal slowly lifts his head, and I gasp as I get a proper look at his face. The left side is awash with purplish bruising, his nose is severely swollen—it might actually be broken—and there's a deep gash in his forehead and numerous cuts slash his dried lips. He looks like he's done a few rounds with Conor McGregor and definitely come out the worst for it.

"Ben called me a rapist in front of the whole room, and I lost it."

"Jesus, Kalvin." James shakes his head in consternation. "What were you thinking going to a party?"

"Mom said I should go about my life as normal otherwise I'd make myself look guilty." His sulky expression drills into James.

"Your mother isn't in the right frame of mind to be making those kinds of decisions. You should've talked to me." His shoulders sag. "But there's no point discussing that now. The damage is done. You are on house arrest until the trial, and you have to wear a monitoring device."

"Dad, that's totally unfair." Ky's shoulders are stiff with stress. "You haven't heard the abuse he's had to put up with all week at school. I'm not surprised he snapped tonight." He fixes Dan with an imploring look. "Can't you appeal for leniency?"

"This is leniency, Kyler." He looks over at Kalvin. "It was this or jail. You were told to keep your nose clean. That's all the police and the court care about. I've spoken with the D.A., and they've made their point very clearly. This is the best I could do."

"I know you've done your best, Dan. Thank you," James acknowledges.

Dan asks a few more questions, and then everyone troops out as the sergeant steps into the room. Kalvin leaves with the nice female cop to have his anklet fitted while Dan stays with me. I revise my statement, accepting a stern lecture from the sergeant in the process, and then we meet the family in the main walk-in area. All our personal possessions are returned, and I'm grateful Keaton had the foresight to keep a hold of my bag. I rummage through it, checking everything is intact.

We are preparing to leave when a large man, wearing a long black woolen coat, bustles into the station, rubbing his hands and making immediate demands. His nostrils flare when he notices us. "If you think I'm letting this go, Kennedy, you can think again."

"Jack." James steps forward, straightening his shoulders as he goes toe to toe with the other man. "Ben started a fight with Kalvin, while Jeremy was recording my niece without her permission. What a fine job you've done raising your sons." I clamp a hand over my mouth to smother my snort of disbelief. James couldn't be any more ironic if he tried. "You can bet your bottom dollar that I'm not letting this go, either."

The man's face turns an unflattering shade of red, and steam is practically billowing out of his ears. "Does anyone work in this Godforsaken place?" he roars, turning from James without further argument.

James ushers us out of the building, and we leave Jeremy's

dad stewing in his own venom. The frosty night air whips around my bare legs and feet, and my teeth start chattering again. Kaden removes his long coat and places it around my shoulders, tucking me in under his arm. I smile up at him, and he winks conspiratorially.

"Kaden will take you home," James says, gesturing to Keaton, Kal, Ky, and Brad. James walks to Kalvin and pulls him into a fierce hug. "It's going to be all right, son." He sighs. "I'm sorry I can't go back to the house with you, but until the legal stuff is sorted out with your mother, I can't step foot on the property."

"Take care of your brother and your mother." James looks over Kal's head, speaking directly to Keaton and Ky.

"Dad." Kal eyeballs James with unfettered emotion. "I don't want you and Mom to divorce."

"I know, son," James replies quietly. "I don't want that either."

"I love you, Dad." Kal says it with real feeling, and my trodden heart jumpstarts in my chest.

James looks adoringly at his son. "I love you, too, Kalvin." He holds him even fiercer. "I love you all, and I'm going to fix everything, I promise. Hang in there."

I pull Kaden's coat around me as a blast of ice-cold wind whistles around me, lifting my hair and blowing it across my face.

"We need to get going, Dad," Ky says. "Faye is shivering."

James releases Kal with a final squeeze of his shoulders and moves over beside me, piercing me with those keen blue eyes. "I think it's best if you come and stay with me, Faye."

Ky rolls his eyes. "Not this again."

"I'll go with you," I confirm instantly.

"What?" Keaton's hurt look is like a knife to the gut. "You promised!"

"I know, and I'm sorry, but things have changed, and I think it's for the best."

Brad glares at Ky, understanding my motives in a flash. Ky beseeches me with his eyes but I look away.

I peer into James's face. "I want to live with you. Let's go."

Chapter Seventeen

"Are you okay, sweetheart?" James asks from behind the wheel. My knees are pulled into my chest, with Kaden's warm coat still encasing me. He insisted I take it, assuring me he had plenty of others.

"I'm tired, but apart from that, I'm fine," I lie. Getting away from Ky was all I was thinking of back there when I agreed to come and live with him, but now, I'm not so sure. At least in the house there is plenty to occupy my mind. Having too much time on my hands is the invisible enemy. The mute threat to my sanity. This could end up being my worst decision yet.

"What happened to change your mind?" James asks without removing his eyes from the dimly lit road. "I know there was other stuff going on before all the fighting broke out."

"It's nothing I wish to talk about." The image of Ky and Addison is forever branded in my subconscious mind, and I'm sick to my stomach every time I recall it. I wish there was a way to self-lobotomize because I desperately want to scrub the memory from my brain. At least it's deflecting attention from what almost happened tonight. *I can't believe I was so stupid. I* made a faithful promise all those years ago that I'd never expose myself again, and I did it in a heartbeat tonight. It'd be easy to blame Ky. To say he drove me to the breaking point, but he didn't force me to kiss Edwards or go voluntarily with him to the bedroom. I almost choke on my startled laugh—I don't even know the scumbag's first name.

And that's beyond idiotic.

No, this isn't Ky's fault.

This one is all on me.

James parks the car along the road outside the Wellesley Beechwood Hotel. I inwardly groan. Talk about returning to the scene of your crime. A sour taste floods my mouth as I recall that night after work when Ky came to collect me and we discovered James outside this very hotel kissing Courtney up against his car.

"Courtney isn't staying with you, is she?"

James grasps the steering wheel with a death grip. "No." His tone is clipped, and I want to call him out on it because it's a reasonable question, but I'm too exhausted to pursue this topic at six a.m. I'm surviving on zero sleep, and I know it'll be lights out the second my head hits the pillow. "I would hardly ask you to come and live with me if she was here."

I bob my head and get out of the car. James carries me up the steps, placing my sore feet on the plush carpet of the lobby. He acknowledges the porter with a subtle nod and smile, slipping him a twenty before we take the lift upstairs. I lean my head against the side of the lift, closing my eyes as I yawn. I can't wait to crawl into bed.

James turns the key in the lock and steps into the penthouse suite.

"Get naked, baby," a slurred voice says, and I instantly perk up.

I walk in beside James, my eyes blinking ninety to the dozen when I cop a load of Courtney. She is naked—as in completely and utterly starkers—with a string of pearls curving around her neck and dangling in between the gap of her exposed breasts. She totters on ridiculously high heels with a glass of champagne in one hand. Spotting me, she smirks.

"Ditch the bitch and let's get our nasty on." She licks her lips as she starts sliding a hand down over her flat stomach.

"I'm out of here!" I spin around and race out the door before I have any more hideous images to add to the collection of horrors in my head. All I'm thinking in this moment is how I need to put as much distance between me and that slut as possible.

"Faye! Wait!" James runs after me, and I press the button on the lift repeatedly, willing it to hurry up.

"I'll get rid of her!" he says in a frantic tone. "I didn't know she was here, I swear."

As I watch the lift ascending, I turn and face my uncle. I believe him when he says he didn't know she was waiting in his room, but that's the extent of my trust. "Answer me one thing. Have you ended your affair with her? Is this Courtney being delusional or normal?"

He massages his temples as he pins me with a beseeching look. The lift pings and I shove his hand off, stepping inside. "Yeah. That's pretty much what I thought." I shake my head. "What you said to your sons back there was complete bullshit, wasn't it?" I shake my head again.

"No." James moves his hand to the gap between the doors, stopping the lift from closing. "I meant every word I said. I *am* fixing things, and I still love Alex. I want to return to my family."

"Baby! Come back here and fuck me!" Courtney hollers down the corridor, and I cringe.

She's certainly showing her true colors now. I push James's hand out of the way as he exhales noisily, closing his eyes and shaking his head. "Yeah. It sure sounds like it."

The door closes and I sag against the wall, numb more than anything else.

I hurry outside, ignoring the pain underfoot when I run down the road and around the bend so that I'm out of sight of the hotel. I hold my pace steady until I'm around the next two corners, and only then do I stop running. My feet are throbbing with stinging pain, and I hobble up the road like a cripple. I sincerely hope there are no reporters milling about at this early hour. They'd surely hit pay dirt if they saw me like this. Swathed in an ill-fitting man's coat with no shoes, bare legs, and my blood-caked face, I look more like a hooker than a relative of the wealthy Kennedys.

I climb onto the bench a few meters down from the diner, wincing as I lift my sore feet to inspect them. Both soles are black and filthy, and one foot is bleeding. I snuggle into Kaden's coat, grateful for it. With cold, trembling fingers, I pluck my phone from my bag, flipping it over and almost crying when I spot the blank screen. I press the power button but nothing happens. It's completely out of charge, and I'm officially screwed. I should probably go back to the hotel and use their phone to ring Brad, but exhaustion has done a right number on me, and I'm incapable of lifting my little finger let alone hobbling back through the streets. I lie down on my side on the bench, as a tortured sob starts building in the base of my throat.

How ironic that I feel like a homeless person when that's effectively what I am.

I don't fit in anywhere.

The one place I had begun to think of as home is now the

last place I wish to be.

My eyes are shuttering, and I welcome the incoming unconsciousness.

I don't care who finds me or how I'm found.

All I care about at present is blocking it out.

I'm seconds away from sleep when something or someone brushes against my feet, and I jerk up, immediately alert and on guard.

A man is sitting at the end of the bench, slouched against the side, hiding his face in his arm. A strong smell of alcohol and urine tickles my nose, causing my nostrils to wrinkle in disgust. I get up, prepared to make a hasty getaway, when his head lifts and my eyes widen in surprise.

"David?" I peer at the man with the five o'clock shadow and the haunted eyes, wondering if it's actually my boss or someone who looks remarkably like him.

"Faye?" he slurs in an unmistakable voice.

Cautiously, I sit back down. "What's wrong?"

His eyes fill up and the wounded look on his face tells its own story. Leaning toward me, he grabs my hands, holding them firmly in his sweaty grip. All the tiny hairs on the back of my neck stand up. "She's gun. Dead ash dead can be." His eyes roll in his head even as tears trickle down his face. He digs his fingers into my flesh, and I try to wrest my hands away, but he has me in an iron grip. "I mizz her. So much. It wazn't ri." His whole body sways from side to side as tears plop onto our conjoined hands. "Iz I culd go bash, I ... Aggh." He releases my hands, curling into a ball as he starts rocking back and forth, mumbling to himself. I stand up, jerking my head around, looking for any sign of life close by. I don't have any medical training, but he's clearly in need of intervention. If I had to bet on it, I'd say he's taken something else besides alcohol, and I'm concerned for him.

My eyes narrow as I zone in on the blurry shape in the distance. Squinting in the faint light, I watch as an SUV approaches, and I step out into the middle of the road, waving it down.

Brad hops out of the car, running toward me. "Are you okay? What's happened?"

I gesture at David. He's rambling to himself, talking gibberish as he continues to sway from side to side. "Call an ambulance, quick."

We wait with him in silence until the ambulance arrives, and I give some details to the EMT staff before they take him away. Without a word, Brad bundles me into his arms and carries me to the car.

"How did you know where to find me?" I ask as he drives away from the town.

"James called Ky. In a place like Wellesley, I knew you couldn't have gotten far, but Keven logged into the tracking app on your phone, and he told me exactly where to find you."

Even though I'm barely keeping my eyes open, I still jerk forward in my seat. "They're *tracking* me?"

"Hey." His eyes rake briefly over me. "Don't shoot the messenger."

I rest my head against the window, sighing. I shouldn't be all that surprised. What with Keven's mad IT skills and James's penchant for security, it makes sense. And, on this occasion, it came in handy.

Brad parks the car in front of the house and cuts the engine. "I know you're tired, but can we talk before we go in?" Unbuckling his seat belt, he twists around to face me. The leather protests with a loud squelch.

I lead with "I owe you an apology."

He pins me with incredulous eyes. "How on earth do you figure that?"

"I was horrible to you last night, and you were only trying to look out for me. I should've listened to you."

Reaching out, he threads his fingers in mine. "I was so scared when you staggered out of that room. I'm sorry, Faye. I should never have left you with him."

"It's not your fault." I pinch the bridge of my nose. "And our apologies cancel each other out so we're square."

"No." He shakes his head vehemently. "I owe you another one." His clear blue eyes pierce mine. "I hurt you when I rejected you and I'm sorry for that." He holds up a hand when he sees my mouth open to speak. "Let me say this." I clamp my mouth shut. "I want to kiss you so badly—all the time—but not like that. Not when you didn't know what you wanted. I won't ever take advantage of you or the situation. When you kiss me again, it will be because you want to kiss me, not because you're upset and trying to make him jealous." He lifts our conjoined hands to his lips. "I know you need time. I can wait."

I almost topple out of the car when my door is abruptly opened from the outside. Ky doesn't speak, but his expression speaks a thousand words. Reaching in, he releases my seat belt and slides me into his arms, carrying me into the house. Perhaps I should be grateful that he rescued me from what would surely have been a very awkward conversation, but that's the last thing I'm feeling.

I want to slap him.

Curse him.

Scream at him.

Slap him some more.

I want to reach a hand into his chest and squeeze that life-sustaining organ until he collapses from the lack of blood flow and the agonizing pain pummeling his heart until it's scarcely beating.

I want him to hurt so badly that he can barely breathe while strips tear from his heart.

I want him to feel everything I'm feeling.

To hurt as much as I do.

I want all that.

But I can't convince myself it's the truth.

Because I love him too much.

I don't want him to hurt like that.

Because I'm so bloody weak.

Instead, I curl my arms around his neck, inhaling his scent and absorbing the feel of his skin under my fingertips, pretending he's still mine. Brad stays behind us, his disappointed gaze locked on mine as we walk to my bedroom. We stare at one another, and my emotions veer all over the place.

"Put me down." I attempt to wriggle out of Ky's arms, but his hold only tightens. Uncurling my arms from around his neck, I shove at his chest. "I said let me go."

"Stop being ridiculous," he scoffs, instantly raising my hackles. "You're too injured to walk."

He strides forward with purpose, and my anger returns in spades. "Put me down or I'll scream blue murder. I mean it."

He slants dark, determined eyes on me. "Work away, sweetheart. See if I care."

"Aagh! You're the most frustrating person ever! And don't call me sweetheart. I'm not your anything."

"Stop it!" he hisses as I attempt a new bout of wriggling. "I'm not putting you down, and we're not going there."

My eyes flit to Brad, beseeching him for help. I can almost see the little wheels turning in his head. "Please," I mouth, and he picks up his pace.

"I'll carry her," Brad says. It's less of an offer and more of a demand and we all know it.

"The hell you will!" Ky fumes. "I left her in your care tonight and look what happened."

"You're one to talk!" he retorts. "If she's upset with anyone tonight, it's you, and you damned well know it."

I count to ten in my head, relieved when we reach my room. Ky kicks my door open with his booted foot and lays me down gently on the bed. Brad stops at the end of the bed, glaring at his best friend. "Can you fetch a bowl of warm water, some cotton pads, and a towel from the bathroom." Ky makes the request without looking at his friend, and Brad responds without acknowledgment, pushing off the door and heading into the en suite. Ky disappears into my walk-in-wardrobe, returning a minute later with some clean pajamas. Sounds of running water greet my ears as Ky removes Kaden's coat from around me before fingering the hem of my dress.

I slap his hands away. "What the hell are you doing?"

"Don't be difficult, Faye." He folds his arm over his chest. "You're injured, and you're exhausted, and I'm only helping."

"Who said I want your help?" I snap rather childishly.

He emits an exaggerated sigh, unfolding his arms and sitting on the edge of my bed. "Just let me take care of you. I need to do this for you. Okay?"

I want to tell him to get stuffed.

Not to touch me.

But I don't.

I can't hold onto my anger, and I'm not really sure why.

Only that I hate myself for it.

Wordlessly, I let him help me out of my clothes and into the pajamas. Brad reenters the room a couple of minutes later holding a small bowl, some cotton wool, and a white towel. Ky props pillows behind my head, and one underneath my feet. "This might hurt a little."

He starts dabbing at my feet, and I instinctively jerk my

foot back, wincing. "That stings like fuck."

With his lips twitching, he tenderly clasps my ankle, easing my foot back to the pillow. "Take deep breaths and before you know it, I'll be done." His gentle voice and soft touch send delicious little tingles ripping up and down my leg and I want to slap myself in the face when a little whimper flees my mouth involuntarily. *Could my humiliation be any more complete?* I drape an arm across my face so I don't have to look at Brad's dejected face or Ky's smug one. The urge to scream my lungs out is riding me hard.

"Try to hold still and I'll clean it up as quick as I can. There's a lot of debris in your foot, and you have a few cuts that are bleeding." I nibble on my arm, relishing the sting as my teeth sink into my flesh, clinging to it as a vital distraction tool. Ky cleans my feet, while I do my best to ignore the pleasure-pain. "I'll be back in a bit," he says a few minutes later, and I lift my arm off my face, watching the two boys exchange thunderous looks. I only release the breath I'd been holding when Ky exits the room.

Brad sits down beside me. "May I?" he asks, holding up some cotton wool. "You have some dried blood on your face."

"Sure. Thanks."

He begins cleaning me with infinite tenderness, as if I'm a delicate, precious flower. My nose is sore to the touch, and I flinch when his fingers carefully prod it. He gets up, bringing the bowl and the rest of the supplies into the bathroom. When he returns, he drops down onto the bed again, this time with his back to me. Tension has corded his muscles into knots, and he sits hunched over, inspecting his nails, sealing his lips, and bottling everything up.

"Brad."

Slowly, he looks over his shoulder, and I pat the space beside me. He stares at me for a few seconds before lying down on his side. "You should know I'm a total mess," I tell him. "I scarcely know who I am anymore let alone what I want. I'm so confused." It's the truth. My emotions are as unreliable as the weather. One minute I'm all sore and hurt, the next I'm desperately clinging to every second with Ky, devouring each crumb he throws my way as if it'll be the last. Add Brad to the mix, and my emotions become a hodge-podge of epic proportions. My feelings for him aren't cut and dried, and that's only exacerbating the turmoil inside my head and my heart. I gulp, placing my hand over his. "You mean so much to me, and I don't want things to be strained between us." He stares into my eyes, and I hold his gaze. "Please." I gulp again. "I need you," I add in a whisper, hoping he understands the meaning behind my statement and that he isn't reading too much into it.

With great affection, he cups my face. "I want you to need me but not half as much as I want you to want me."

"You don't waste any time." Ky sneers, scowling at his best friend from the doorway. "Not that I'm all that surprised."

"You're with Addison," Brad retorts harshly, and that familiar surge of bitterness twists my insides into knots. "What do you care?"

"I care about Faye and she's been through a lot tonight, in case you'd forgotten, so give her a break. She doesn't need any more of the heavy."

Brad hops up, stalking toward Ky. "We all know whose fault that is." If looks could kill, Ky would be ten feet under by now. "And if that's all this was, then I'd totally accept it, but it's bull and you know it. You've pushed her away, but no one else is allowed to go near her? Have I got that right?"

They are squaring up to one another, and a fresh surge of frustration is growing in my chest. The urge to open my mouth and scream from the pit of my lungs is hugely tempting.

"I'm not having this conversation with you. Get out, and let me look after my cousin."

"I don't know what's happened to you, man, although I can guess," he jeers. "I don't much like this new version of you."

"I don't care what you think." Ky brushes past him, moving toward me with the first aid kit in one hand and a steaming mug in the other.

A furious look dances over Brad's face, like he wants to pummel Ky into next week. Not sure I'd blame him. Ky is way out of line.

"Please don't fall out because of me." My eyes implore the pair of them. "We're all exhausted and taking it out on each other. Let's get some sleep and talk later."

Brad bravely walks back to the bed, bending down and kissing my cheek. "I'm glad you're okay. Get some rest. I'll see you later." He ignores Ky as he exits the room, and the temp turns from icy cold to a few degrees above chilly.

Ky attends to my feet without speaking, applying some sort of salve and then bandaging each foot. I sip on the hot sweet tea he brought, and each mouthful warms the frozen inner parts of me. When he's done, he helps me into the bed, tucking the covers up to my chest. "You feel any better?"

"Yes. Thanks."

He rubs the back of his neck and kneels down in front of the bed. "I'm sorry this happened to you, and for what it's worth, I hate myself for the part I played. I'm sorry I hurt you. I've never wanted to hurt you."

"Yet you keep doing it."

He grimaces, before hanging his head. "I know. I'm sorry."

Silence descends, and I finish my drink, placing the mug on my locker as I sink into the nurturing warmth of the bed. It's hard to see Ky in here and not remember the many nights he spent sleeping beside me, holding me in his arms, loving me with his words, his lips, his touch. Tears prick my eyes, and I'm glad I'm too exhausted to cry. "Did you care about me at all?" I whisper-ask because I must love torturing myself.

His chin kicks up. "Of course, I cared. I still do. I'll never not care about you."

"You just don't love me."

Yep. Kill. Me. Now.

He looks away, and air leaves his mouth in a panicky rush. "You really want to do this again?" His eyes beg me to drop it.

"No." A crafty tear slips out of the corner of my eye. "It hurt enough the first time." I purse my lips, willing myself to hold it together as a tornado rips through my insides, wreaking havoc. I want to believe that my earlier assumption was right—that this is all Addison's doing, but he's not giving me much to work with. He cares for me—I know that much—but that appears to be the extent of it. Perhaps he *has* written us off in favor of a less "complicated" life, though, how anyone could refer to Addison as less complicated is beyond me. But they share a past, which is something we don't. Maybe I never really knew him at all.

My mind is in agony, veering from one scenario to another. I want to believe he's doing this because he's being blackmailed, but I know I'm most likely clutching at straws. I'm barely clinging onto my sanity, and I'm on the verge of a meltdown, and I'd rather do all my breaking in private. "I'd like you to leave now." My voice is shaky, betraying some of what I feel. I don't look up as he leans down and kisses my cheek.

"I'm so sorry, Faye."

His words are cheap.

He closes the door quietly, and I stave off the storm for a couple of minutes before it breaches the wall and sobs burst free of my soul.

Burying my head in the pillow, desperately trying to muffle my heartache, I fall asleep drowning in a sea of tears.

Chapter Eighteen

Isleep like the dead and I've no idea what time it is when I hear a light tap on my door. "Come in," I croak, hastily sitting up as I scrub the sleep from my eyes.

Ky pokes his head around the door. "I thought you might like something to eat."

"What time is it?" I ask, yawning.

He steals into the room, closing the door behind him. Tantalizing smells tickle my taste buds as he carries a tray toward me, setting it down on my lap. The plate is heaped with eggs, bacon, and pancakes, and he's added a glass of OJ and a mug of coffee. Saliva pools in my mouth, and my eyes devour the plate with longing.

He hands me a knife and fork, smiling softly. "It's after three."

"Shut up! Someone should've woken me earlier!" I attack my food like it's been years, rather than hours, since I last ate.

"You needed your sleep, and I wouldn't let anyone disturb you."

"Thanks." Bile floods my mouth as remembered heartache

resurrects to the forefront of my mind. The fact he made me breakfast changes nothing. I pause with my forkful of food in midair. "It's okay. You can leave now."

His forehead creases. "I want to make sure you're okay."

"That's not your place anymore." My eyes bore into his, willing him to challenge me. To say it isn't so.

He averts his eyes. "You're right. I'll leave you to eat in peace." He turns to walk away.

"Wait a sec." I put the fork down on the plate. "I need to talk to you about something that's been playing on my mind."

He folds his arms across his broad chest. "Okay. Let's hear it."

"What if Jeremy is the one who sent you the recording of Brad and Addison?"

Ky holds his chin between his thumb and forefinger as he contemplates my question. "You could be on to something. His family is close to Addison's, and they've hung out together since they were kids. I always got jealous vibes off him."

I lean back against my pillows. "So maybe that was his way of breaking you two up." I worry my upper lip between my teeth, frowning. "Except he wasn't with her." It doesn't add up.

"Maybe it wasn't about him hooking up with her."

"He only wanted to make sure she wasn't with you," I concur, filling in the gaps.

"That figures. He's never liked me, and he knows the feeling is mutual." He stands. "I'll talk to Keven. See if he can do some digging on Jeremy."

"Good idea." I practically bury my face in my breakfast—anything to avoid showcasing my expression. I'm not sure I won't give the game away especially when he reads me all too easily.

"Okay." He shoots me a perplexed look before exiting the room without another word. The now-familiar ache in my heart starts pulsing out of control as he quietly closes the door. I don't know if this will ever become manageable or if I'm destined to live with this soul-crushing pain for the rest of my life. Trying to resurrect my appetite, I force food into my mouth and down over the traumatized lump in my throat.

I check in on Kal a few times during the afternoon but he's always sleeping.

My phone chimes, and I gnaw anxiously on the inside of my mouth when I spot Jill's goofy profile picture blinking up at me.

I've been avoiding talking to my friends.

Avoiding confronting the reality of what my mum did with my uncle.

Avoiding the possibility that my uncle could be my dad.

Avoiding acknowledging my broken heart.

Ugh. I break out in goose bumps as I shiver all over.

I'm drowning.

Adrift with all these errant thoughts and feelings surrounding me, suffocating me, closing in.

Scared that I won't ever find solid ground.

I exhale deeply, dropping down onto my bed and holding my phone delicately, as if it's a grenade resting in the palm of my hand.

I need my best friends almost as much as I need air, and it's ridiculous to be ignoring them. They won't judge. They'll be on my side. So, I force my shame aside and accept the call. The instant I see Rachel and Jill's familiar faces across my screen, some of the churning anxiety in my gut settles down.

I waste no time filling them in on what's been going on with me, and they listen patiently while I relay it all. The shocked look on their faces when I tell them about Mum and James, and the fact that the man I thought was my dad isn't my dad, says it all, but they remain quiet, allowing me to vent until it's all off my chest.

I'm instantly relieved.

There are a couple of seconds of utter silence when I finish my sordid tale.

"Strewth, mate," Rach says in her best Aussie accent—it's her go-to persona when she's out of her comfort zone, and she has a whole host of humorous sayings to draw from thanks to a visit from her Australian rellies a couple of years ago.

"I can't believe you've been dealing with all this on your own." Jill smiles sadly. "I wish you could come home."

"Me, too," I admit, although the truth is that I don't feel like I fit in anywhere anymore. "I miss you guys so much."

A sound at the door alerts me to his presence. "Sorry to interrupt," Ky says, looking a little embarrassed. "I have dinner ready, and I wanted to know if you intend to join us in the kitchen or would you like me to bring you a tray?"

"I'll be there in a minute," I reply curtly, pointing at my phone. With a quick nod, he shuts the door quietly.

"You should take his dinner and dump it over his cheating head," Rach suggests, her nostrils flaring.

I've come clean about everything with Ky, and they know he's back with Addison now after slumming it with me for a while. "He didn't actually cheat on me. Nothing was ever official, and we aren't together anymore." I'm not sure why I'm defending him per se or why it even matters. What's done is done.

"You're far too nice, Faye," Jill supplies. "I'd totally give him the cold shoulder."

I shrug. "It is what it is. I can't force him to feel things he doesn't feel, and I can't shut him out. Whatever his status, he's still family." Maybe if I say it enough times, the truth will sink in. That's all Ky can and will be to me in future, and I need to find some way of accepting that.

I join Keaton, Keanu, and Ky in the kitchen. "Where are the others?" I ask, accepting a piping hot bowl of pasta from Ky.

"Kal and Mom are eating in their rooms. Kent's out somewhere, *as usual*, and Brad took off this morning, and I haven't seen him since."

We eat in silence, everyone locked in their own thoughts. Rose texts in the middle of dinner to say the diner is closed tonight, and I wonder how David is doing. After we've eaten, I get up and clear away the dishes.

Keaton is sullen again, pissed this time that I chose to leave with James at the police station. I remind myself that he's only fifteen and still a little immature at times. I remember how hormonal I was at that age and how every little thing was embellished to the nth degree. "Wanna watch a movie?" I ask him after I've finished putting another load of laundry in the machine. He's lounging on the couch, halfheartedly watching a program about endangered species on Netflix.

He shrugs dejectedly and I decide to bring matters to a head. I throw myself on top of him, tickling him until he squirms and he can't fight the smile on his face. "You can't stay mad at me forever."

"Want to put money on that?"

I snort. "Hells, no! Your stubbornness knows no bounds!"

"Okay. Stop." He holds his palms up. "I surrender."

I pull him up from the couch. "Let's watch a movie in my room. I have something I want to tell you that should help." I feel considerably lighter after having unburdened to my friends, and I figure I owe Keaton an explanation and that it'll do me good to clear the air between us once and for all.

Keaton makes the popcorn while I grab a bag of cookies and

some drinks, and we retreat to my room. I fill him in on the situation with me and Kyler, leaving out any mention of incestuous relationships and potential half-sibling status because I promised James we wouldn't mention anything until the test results were back.

"Okay, now I understand why you wanted to go with Dad," he admits a little sheepishly. "But it was still dumb. You can't avoid Ky forever, and you can't let him drive you out of your home."

"I know. It was a spur of the moment thing, and I'm part-blaming lack of sleep for the lapse in my decision-making ability." I plonk myself down on the bed and kick off my sneakers, grateful he hasn't asked *why* I ran out on James. I still have to update Ky on that particular development, and I'm not looking forward to that convo.

"Ky is an idiot." Keaton shakes his head as he lines up the movie. "But Addison's always had this unnatural hold over him. I don't get it."

"Me, either, but I'll have to live with it. Now, enough talking about your brother and she-who-shall-not-be-named. Press play."

He taps two fingers off his forehead. "You're the boss."

James phones at the end of the movie, begging me to come to the hotel to meet him. He's desperate to explain, and he insists he wants to talk face to face. Once he reassures me that Courtney most definitely won't be there, I grab my coat and meet Max out the front of the house.

James is waiting in the hotel lobby for me. "Thanks for coming." I shrug casually. "I reserved a table in the corner of the bar. It's nice and sheltered so we can talk in private."

"'Kay." I follow him into the half-empty bar, and a waiter

escorts us to a small table tucked into a cozy little alcove at the back. James orders a whiskey for himself and a sparkling water for me while I take off my jacket. I sit with my hands folded in my lap, waiting for him to start.

"I apologize for last night, Faye. I swear I didn't know Courtney was here. She charmed the front desk into letting her into my suite. I doubt that man has a job after my conversation with the general manager this morning." He stops talking while the waiter places our drinks on the table. James hands him a fifty telling him to keep the change. I take a sip of my water, as James takes a healthy glug of his whiskey. "I'm trying to end things, but she's extremely persistent, and she refuses to believe I want nothing more to do with her." He scrunches his shoulders against his neck. "I want my wife back. I want my family back. That's all I care about."

I take another sip of my drink, not sure how to respond to that or if he even expects me to. "It's none of my business. I just don't want to be around her; I hate everything she represents."

"I respect that, and I promise that if you move in here, I'll ensure nothing like that happens again."

I put my drink down and eyeball him. "I want to stay at the house. I was upset last night when I agreed to move in with you, but I would rather live with my cousins, if that's okay." I only tack that last part on to try to alleviate any hurt feelings.

"Are you very sure?"

"Yeah."

"Fair enough, but if you change your mind, there's always room for you here."

I run my hands down the front of my jeans. "Thanks. I appreciate that."

He knocks back some more of his drink, reclining in the seat. "Can I say something?"

I twist slightly in my seat. "Sure."

"Kyler cares about you a lot. I can tell. My son is guarded but he loves fiercely. Intensely. For him to say what he said in front of me last week speaks volumes." He pats my hand. "For both your sakes, I hope I'm wrong, but for mine I hope I'm right."

"Why?" My question comes out in a half-whisper. "Why is it so important that I'm your daughter?"

He drains his drink, motioning at the waiter with a click of his fingers. "Another round, please."

He leans forward on his elbows. "Besides the fact that any man would be proud to call you his daughter, Faye, it will reconfirm my belief that what your mom and I shared was special."

My eyes go out on stalks. "How can you say that? It was wrong on so many levels."

He sighs. "I've spent years going over everything in my head, all the different ways it could've played out, and I regret it because I lost the most important person in my life, but I've never really believed it was wrong." My mouth hangs open. "I've had moments where I've felt it was wrong, but, deep down, I can't criticize what we did because I loved Saoirse so much." His voice cracks, and the waiter chooses that moment to return with our new drinks, affording him time to pull himself together.

"I'm trying to understand," I admit, "but I'm struggling. And that feels hypocritical, even though the situation with Ky and me is different."

"It is different, but it could end up being the same."

"I know, and that's what I'm terrified of."

There's a lull in our conversation as we both mull things over.

"I don't understand how it could happen with you two because you grew up together. How did you go from siblings to"—I deliberately lower my voice—"lovers? How the hell did that feel right? I just can't fathom it."

"I don't blame you. I find it hard to explain it myself, but you've got to understand what it was like for us growing up. Our parents were both alcoholics, and they were neglectful and sometimes abusive."

"What? Mum never told me that!"

"She was never on the receiving end of it, don't worry, I made sure of that." He drains his whiskey in one go. "Honestly, when they died, I actually felt like I was only properly breathing for the first time. For as long as I can remember, I was looking out for Saoirse and acting as the man in the house. I don't know how my father managed to hold down a full-time job with such a severe alcohol addiction, but he did. My mother slept the day away, and as soon as Dad came home from work, they were gone out drinking with their cronies. I had to make dinner, keep the house tidy, do all our laundry from a very young age. I was determined to protect Saoirse from that, to give her as normal a childhood as I could manage."

I'm hooked on his words, lost in the past with him, emotional at the picture he's painting. His whole life, James has been looking after others. *Who has ever looked after him?*

"She was my whole world. With our parents gone, the insurance paid for the house, and we had a roof over our head but no money for anything else, so I got a job in the local factory and left school. And we were happy, Faye. For the first time in my life, I could say I was truly happy." He shrugs. "Our roles gradually shifted, and it became more like a husband and wife setup. Your mom was home from school before my shift ended, and she always had the dinner on the table. I provided for her, and we spent our evenings and whatever free time I had at weekends together. Things changed. My feelings transformed, and when she made a move on me, I realized she felt it too."

He takes my hands in his. "I don't expect you to approve, but I'd like to think that one day you might understand." I peer into his eyes. "It was always me and Saoirse against the world. I thought she was all I'd ever need. Ever want. But I was wrong, because then I fell head over heels in love with Alex, and I was able to appreciate the difference. To put things in perspective. It didn't mean I stopped loving your mom, but I was able to look back on it as a certain moment in time. It was something we both needed back then, but I've no doubt had Saoirse stuck around that we would have moved on with our lives; would've built our futures with different people. And that is why I can't ever consider it was wrong."

He clicks his fingers at the waiter, and we sit in silence long after he brings a fresh round of drinks. After James's heartfelt confession, it's easier to find some understanding although I'm not sure I'll ever properly comprehend it. "I should get going," I say a little while later when I notice the time.

"I'll walk you out to the car."

I turn to say goodbye to him on the pavement. "Thank you for sharing that with me."

"Thank you for listening." I offer him a smile, and he pulls me into a gentle hug. "And I meant what I said before that. I'm here for you. Now and always."

Chapter Nineteen

I'm woken at three a.m. by the sounds of scuffling in the corridor outside. I get up to investigate, groaning as I approach my bedroom door when I hear Brad and Ky's elevated voices. Ky has Brad in a headlock when I step into the corridor. "Are you two ever going to grow up?" I rest my hands on my hips.

"A little help?" Ky motions at Brad just as he opens his mouth and hurls all over the floor.

"Crap." I pinch my nostrils shut to avoid gagging.

"He's smashed. Help me get him to his room."

Ky slings one of Brad's arms over his shoulder while I prop him up on the other side, and together we move him to his bedroom. Ky places him, chest up, onto the bed and starts removing his shoes while I head to the bathroom to grab a wet facecloth. When I return, Ky has managed to get his shoes and jeans off, but he's struggling to remove his shirt. We take an arm each and pull it up over his head. Brad moans, curling into a fetal position and clutching his abs. "I'll get a bowl," I suggest, already backing out of the room.

I jump over the pool of vomit in the corridor and race to the kitchen, opening cupboards until I find what I need. I grab a couple bottles of water and tuck them into the band of my sleep shorts. Tearing off a few sheets of kitchen paper on my way out, I toss them loosely on top of the revolting mess in the corridor. I'm so nominating Ky for cleaning duty. I don't think I'll be able to stomach it without hurling myself.

I shove the bowl under Brad's face in the nick of time. He heaves repeatedly, and I look away, feeling nauseated just looking at him. I trace my hand up and down his back in what I hope is a soothing manner. When he's done, I hold a bottle of water to his lips. "Drink this. You'll feel better."

He rinses out his mouth, spitting the liquid into the bowl, and I get up, quickly flushing the contents down the toilet. I wash out the bowl and return it to the locker beside Brad's bed. Brad is sitting up, with his back against the frame of the bed, sipping from his water. Muscles ripple across his toned abdomen, and I can no longer deny the uber-hotness he's got going on. I look away, feeling like a creeper for ogling him when he's sick.

"I feel like crap," he moans, throwing his head back.

"No shit, Sherlock." I place my palm to his hot, sticky forehead. "I think you'll live."

He takes my hand, cupping it around his cheek. "Thanks," he whispers.

"Do I want to know why you got in such a state?" I'm almost afraid to ask, but I'm on an unscheduled quest for the truth today.

"Got a call from a reporter today. My dad's story will be front page news tomorrow."

"Shit." Ky starts pacing the room, wearing his carefully constructed impassive face.

"You knew it was going to happen eventually." My tone is sympathetic.

Bloodshot eyes meet mine. "I know, but I don't feel ready to deal."

"No one ever is," Ky says. "Once word gets out about the party, it'll be old news."

That isn't in any way reassuring, and I don't entirely agree, but I wisely keep those thoughts to myself. I reach out and take Brad's hand. "I'm here for you."

"I know, and that's the only thing that's keeping me going."

"You should sleep. School's going to be hell on earth tomorrow." I try to extract my hand, but he keeps a hold of it. An unspoken question rests at the back of his eyes, and sudden unease trickles down my spine. I want to console Brad because he's been there for me on several occasions, but this is all too much, too fast, and I'm conscious that everything could very well blow up in my face. The thought of crawling in his bed and sleeping in his arms is tempting but not enough to follow through on it. I should do it to see if it garners any reaction from Ky, but I can't manipulate Brad like that. Not when he's harboring some kind of hope where we're concerned.

I can't use him to make Ky jealous. It's not fair, and I doubt it would work anyway.

Brad appears to read it all on my face, and there's no need for words. He releases my hand, looking swiftly away, but not before I notice the hurt in his eyes. A pang of guilt slaps me in the face, but I won't back down. I know I'm doing the right thing. I pull the covers up over him, fitting them around his shivering body. Pressing my mouth to his ear, I whisper, "I just need time." I kiss his forehead and walk briskly out of the room, ignoring Ky and whatever expression or non-expression he's currently sporting.

I was wrong. School is worse than hell on earth the next day. The rumor mill is thriving, and Brad and I are virtual pariahs, but at least we're in it together. Gossip about the party is rife, and I spend the day ignoring all the new slurs and taunts leveled my way.

Rose and Zoe are the only two brave enough to sit with us at lunch. I'd already filled Rose in on the events of the weekend in between classes, and Zoe operates a strict need-to-know policy. When I tried to explain, she told me it was none of her business and that was that. "You know you'll be shunned now, too," I admit, biting an angry chunk out of my apple.

"It'll blow over," Rose says with a casual shrug.

"And I've never been bothered about popularity," Zoe says, even though there's no need. Everyone knows Zoe marches to her own beat. She puts her fork down and looks across the table at us. "I didn't have an opportunity last week to say thanks for coming to Jessie's memorial."

"It was no problem. We wanted to be there, and I should be the one thanking you. My uncle told me you gave a statement to the police and that you've agreed to speak at the trial if necessary. We're grateful." She waves off my gratitude in typical Zoe fashion.

"I still can't believe it's been a year since Jessie died," Brad says in a quiet, reverent tone.

"It's been three for David's daughter," Rose confirms.

I stop mid-chew. "What?"

"That's why the diner was closed last night. David's wife told me he's been hospitalized again. Apparently, it was the same the last two years and when his daughter's murdered body was first discovered."

I push my lunch away, appetite destroyed. "That's what he

was mumbling about," I mutter to myself. How awful. No wonder the man was in bits.

"What do you mean?" Rose asks.

"I met him early Sunday morning, and he wasn't in the best shape. I couldn't understand a word he was saying, but I knew he wasn't well. Brad called the ambulance, and we waited with him, although, I'm not sure if he was even aware."

"Poor man." Sympathy shimmers in Rose's eyes.

"Why didn't you ever mention his daughter was murdered or the fact he has a wife?" I ask. Come to think of it, I don't recall ever seeing a wedding ring on his finger.

"It's not something you just slide into a conversation, and he's separated from his wife. If the rumors are to be believed, she couldn't handle his depression after their daughter died."

"That's a bit harsh." I lean back in my chair. "What about the in sickness and health part of her vows?"

"The same person did it. Killed both of them," Zoe blurts out, uncaring that she's interrupting us mid-convo. She picks at the label on her bottle. "I'm convinced of it."

Brad shares a look with Rose. "Don't look like that!" Zoe snaps. She hunches forward, talking in a hushed tone of voice. "They both had a similar look, and they went missing around the same time of year."

"But it was two years apart," Rose says sympathetically.

"And, according to the reports I read, the modus operandi was different," Brad says.

She rips the label off the bottle, and her face inflames. "I know all that! You sound like the cops last week, but I don't agree with them or you. You can't tell me it's a coincidence that two girls go missing and are murdered from the same small town and it's two separate killers? I'm not buying that at all."

"I've got to agree with Zoe. That does seem very suspicious," I supply.

"Thank you." She offers me a snarky face to match her biting gratitude.

"Do the police have any new leads?" I ask.

"Nope, and from what I can tell, it's at the bottom of the priority pile." She sighs and pushes back her chair. "I can't talk about this anymore. I get so incensed. I'll catch you later." She files out of the cafeteria before any of us have even had a chance to say goodbye.

"I pity whoever ends up with her," Brad says rather uncharitably. It's most unlike him to be cruel unless it's warranted. "She makes Addison look like a walk in the park in comparison."

I elbow him in the ribs, hard. "Take that back. Zoe may be all prickly on the outside, but she's not a vindictive bitch like Addison. That was a low blow, and I can't believe you said it." Brad must totally be out of sorts today.

He has the decency to look ashamed. "You're right. I'm sorry. She's just tough going at times."

"I know, but I happen to like her. At least you always know where you stand. I can't say that for a lot of the people I've met in Wellesley."

Chapter Twenty

Afternoon classes seem to drag on forever, and when the final bell eventually rings, it's like music to my ears. I push my body to breaking point during swim practice, and my limbs actually hurt by the time the coach blows the whistle. I throw on my clothes after the quickest shower in history and bolt out of the locker room. I can't get out of this building quick enough.

Alex and James are locked in a vicious row at the front door when Brad and I drive up. "Park in the garage," I request, and he duly obliges. We enter the kitchen via the utility room, and I try to ignore the shouting as I fix us a snack.

Kal ambles into the room with a scowl on his face. He's wearing an unbuttoned shirt and a pair of gray gym shorts. The black monitoring device is conspicuous around his left ankle—a constant reminder he's on house arrest. A small, matronly woman follows behind him. Her gray hair is pulled back off her forehead in a severe bun which does her no favors. Her lips are pinched tight, and her eyes have a feral look about them. She looks close to blowing a gasket.

"We are done for the day, Master Kennedy, when I say we are done for the day."

Kal waves his hands in our direction. "If I have to be home-schooled, then I'm keeping regular school hours." He glares at the woman. "My cousin is already home so that means school is out, and so am I."

"Hey!" I protest wholeheartedly when he swipes my sandwich off my plate, instantly sinking his teeth into it.

He gives me a grin, and it warms my heart to see it. "I'm not used to using so many brain cells, and it's given me one hell of an appetite."

The woman stomps her foot—for real! I thought they only did that in the movies.

"Throw a temper tantrum. See if I care," Kal tells her in between mouthfuls. "You can't force me to study."

Steam practically billows out of her ears, and I'm struggling to contain my burst of laughter. She finally gives up, spinning on her heel and stomping out of the room. Brad and I convulse with laughter, and Kal watches us in amusement. When I've managed to control myself, I go over and hug my cousin. "You seem in better form."

"I am, but don't ask me how. That woman would drive the sanest person to pitch themselves off a cliff. Trust Dad to worry about my schooling with all the other shit we have going down."

He finishes *my* sandwich in two more bites, and I swat the back of his head. "You can make me another one."

"Deal." He jumps up, smacking a wet kiss on my cheek. I'm not sure how or why he's reverted to norm, but I'm glad to see it. He was so down the last week, and it's been difficult to watch.

The shouting at the front door accelerates, and I can hear every hurtful word my aunt and uncle are spewing at one another. I inwardly cringe. They are going at one another hell for leather, and it's not pleasant to hear. "How long have they been arguing?" I ask, propping my elbows on the counter as I watch Kal fixing my sandwich.

"Feels like forever," he dryly replies.

The rest of the week passes by in slo-mo, not helped by the fact that the diner is still closed. Even though I attend swim practice every night after school, I still have far too much time on my hands, and I can't stop my brain from starting a mental count-down. By Friday, I've all but chewed my fingernails to the bone. Monday is D-Day—test results day, and the closer it draws, the more anxious I get.

At least the media hounds are all but gone, distracted initially by the McConaughey fraud revelation and now by some scandal in Washington involving a leading politician and a slew of hookers. James eventually relented, and we can go around town without a bodyguard in tow. They still patrol the grounds, and if we travel farther afield, we have to take someone with us, but apart from that, we're emancipated, and it's great. I didn't realize exactly how uncomfortable I was until Lenny is no longer breathing down my neck and sending me condemning glares.

We are walking to my locker at the end of lunch, when Brad asks me out. "Want to do something after school today? Just the two of us?" I'd almost swear he has a hotline to my brain. I've never needed distracting as much as I presently do.

"What do you have in mind?"

He arches a brow, and his lips curve up as a naughty glint appears in his eye. I sense his mind has wandered to the gutter, and another layer of anxiety heaps atop the existing pile.

There's been no more of the heavy this week, but an unspoken tension still lingers between us which I hate.

I've barely seen Ky all week, and I'm presuming he's purposely staying out of my way.

Not that it's helping much.

He's like my own personal kryptonite.

I know I need to stay away, but I can't help craving him. I'm only resisting his allure because he isn't in front of me, tempting me with his dark good looks and his dangerous, sexy vibes. If he was, I don't know that I'd be able to ignore my longing, so I'm glad he's maintaining his distance. I've already humiliated myself enough. There's no reason to go back for seconds.

No matter how much I beg my heart to reject him, I can't evict Ky when he's already set up camp there. I'm trying to prepare myself for the worst-case scenario, to accept that he's my sibling, to coach my heart to get over him because I can't have those feelings about my brother, and especially now that he's reattached himself to Addison, but it's no use. I can't get him out of my mind.

Logic and rationality don't come into it where the heart is concerned.

Once the heart has laid claim there is no going back.

And I'm locked in a world of pain because of it.

I love him, and I'm missing him like crazy, and I wish there was some cure for that.

"You're thinking about *him*, aren't you?" Brad asks with an exasperated sigh, drawing me back into the moment.

I frown, grabbing the books I need and stowing them in my bag. "Why do you say that?"

"You get this look on your face. All swoony and wistful." He sighs again, this time with resignation.

"I didn't realize." I hope to God Ky hasn't copped on either.

"What I wouldn't give to have you daydream about me like

that." Brad pierces me with serious eyes, and it's impossible to get mad that he's gone there, not in the face of such daring honesty.

"Would you believe me if I said I wish for that too?" One part of me does. Brad's a great guy, and I wish I felt like that about him.

"I don't know whether to feel complimented or insulted." He slings my bag over his shoulder and takes my hand, automatically steering us in the direction of my next class. I swear he knows my schedule better than I know it myself.

"It's a compliment," I insist.

"We're not finished with this conversation," he says when we reach the door of my classroom. "Will you come out with me later?" He reaches out, twirling a lock of my hair.

"Of course. I'll see you out front."

I find it hard to focus on my classes all afternoon. Brad consumes my thoughts, and I know we're going to have "the conversation" later. He's getting braver, and I don't know if I like it or not. One part of me thinks me plus Brad equals a match made in heaven, and that it'd be the best way to move on, but that other more sensible part of my brain knows it's wishful thinking. I can't force myself to feel things I don't. Brad is amazing in so many ways, and if I invested time in it, I think it could lead somewhere, but I don't want to start something I may not be ready for, and I don't want to hurt Brad or cause further issues between him and Ky. Things are already strained enough as it is.

Like every other part of my life right now, my love life is one big complicated mess.

Brad takes me back to the lake and we take a seat on the same log as last time. We are facing the lake, and my eyes skim across the beautiful surroundings while he unfolds a blanket and removes some sandwiches from the small basket he brought. The place is completely deserted today and the only sounds are the quiet chirruping of birds and the gentle swish of the leaves blowing pleasantly in the cool autumn breeze.

Brad pours soup from a flask into two paper cups, handing me one, along with a sandwich.

"Thanks." I wrap my hands around the cup, allowing the warmth to infuse my cold, numb fingers.

"I love it here," he says, sipping his soup. "I've spent a lot of time here the last few months. It's one of the few places where I can organize my thoughts into some kind of order."

"Is that why you brought me here?"

He looks straight into my eyes. "I know you've got to be worried. You get the results on Monday, but you haven't said one word to me since the last time we were here. I thought you might need an ear to bend."

I groan. "Why'd you have to be so bloody perfect?"

His brows shoot up his forehead. "Let's imagine, hypothetically, that that's true," he says, holding up a hand to halt my protests. "Why is it a problem?"

A grimace appears on my face. *Why'd I have to open my stupid gob?* "It makes it harder."

He frowns. "I don't understand."

I groan again, putting down my soup to rub my hands over my frozen face. "Do I have to spell it out?"

He twists around, his knee bumping mine, taking my cold hands in his slightly warmer ones. "A gentleman never makes the lady go first." He smiles, but it doesn't quite meet his eyes. "I'm falling for you, Faye, but you already know that."

Maintaining eye contact takes considerable effort, especially when he's looking at me like he's looking at me presently. Like the universe starts and ends with me.

"And we'd be so good together, I know we would."

"I know that too," I whisper. "In a lot of ways, we are so alike. We're dealing with similar situations; we both have no parents around, and I know you feel lonely and disconnected like I do. I know we could be good for one another. I know all these things."

"But?" His eyes roam my face. "I know there's one coming, and I'm fairly confident I know what it is."

My admiration for Brad elevates a few notches. He came here today to have this conversation with me, prepared to lay his heart on the line, even though he suspects I will always love Ky. But he hasn't let that hold him back, and I only respect him more for it. I reach out and cup his face. "You're hot, and sweet, and funny, intelligent, and so thoughtful, and I could list a hundred other ways you are endearing." I press my forehead to his, whispering as I continue. "I wish I was falling for you, too. I wish that more than anything, but I can't force myself to feel a certain way."

God, how I wish I could love Brad instead of Ky.

Why is the universe doing this to me?

Loving Brad could be as simple as breathing, but I don't love him. I love Ky.

I pull back, maintaining eye contact even though it hurts to see the pain in his eyes. "I'm sorry, Brad. Maybe in the future, my feelings will change, but I still love him. I love Ky."

"He's with Addison." His voice is devoid of emotion.

"I know that." I kick the stones at my foot violently, frustration stealing into my pores. "Unfortunately, it doesn't help. I know I could be fooling myself, but I still think she's forcing him into it some way."

Brad shakes his head. "Faye, I'm not saying this to hurt you, but you've got to open your eyes. You saw them at the party, and I've asked him repeatedly if there's something going on we're not aware of, and he insists there isn't."

I stand up, and my entire body feels like a block of wood. "And did he tell you that with his real face on or the mask he hides behind?" Brad purses his lips, bending down to retrieve a stone. He says nothing. "Exactly my point." He skims the stone out across the lake.

"If he's your brother, it's a moot point," he adds quietly, and all my internal organs curl up into painful knots.

I slump back down on the log. "I know."

Brad takes my hands again. "I'm sorry. I know I shouldn't be hitting you with this when you're dealing with something so difficult. I'm just frustrated because I like you, and I know you like me, and I wish it was enough, but I'm being selfish. I'm sorry."

I squeeze his hands. "Don't apologize. There's no need. I feel the same way, and this might not last forever. I don't know how I'm going to feel next week if the tests confirm James is my dad and my cousins are my half-brothers. Instead of using this time to get used to the idea, I've buried my head in the sand, and now I'll have to face the consequences of my actions."

"You're hoping James is wrong."

I bob my head. "So much, and not purely because of Ky." I look away. "I can't wrap my head around the fact that my mum slept with her brother and that she lied to me about everything that was important. What kind of person does that?"

"I don't know, Faye. I've spent months wondering how my dad could steal from his clients and his friends, querying whether I actually know him at all."

"Yes!" I hiss. "That's how I feel, too. It's like the person I grew up respecting and admiring and loving was a fraud."

"And it makes you question your own identity and your

judgment and the things you value," he adds, clasping my hands tighter. "Or at least it has for me."

"Me, too. Even more so because my identity is now entangled with another families, and it's like I don't belong anywhere."

"I can relate to that, too." Brad tilts my chin up, and we stare at one another as the weight of our words settle.

Locks of his blond hair fall into his probing eyes, and as I examine his gorgeous face, my gaze fixes on his lush mouth, remembering what his lips felt like on mine that one time we kissed. I want to like Brad in that way. I do. It would make my complicated life that much simpler. As if he can read my thoughts, his gaze drops to my mouth, and his chest inflates. His eyes seek permission, and I'm conflicted. Maybe, I'm overthinking this. Perhaps I should let this happen and see where the chips land. Acting on impulse, I lean in closer, and he moves toward me, his lips tugging up into a slight smile. My heart starts pounding in my chest. The devil in my ear urges me to go with it, but the angel on my shoulder screams—hollering at me to see sense, reiterating this will only make a complicated situation even more complicated.

Decisions, decisions.

The warring voices continue their heckling as Brad waits for a sign that tells him he can bridge that final distance and take what he wants.

But the voice of the angel wins out, and I scoot back on the log, creating a gap between us. "I'm sorry, Brad. Can we head back, please. I'm cold."

Chapter Twenty-One

"Do you mind if we stop for coffee?" I ask when we reenter Wellesley. I'm not ready to go back to the house yet.

"No problem," Brad says in the same affable, polite voice he's used the entire journey.

I know I've hurt him, but he hasn't taken it out on me. That's not who he is. My eyes catch something in the mirror, and I glance over my shoulder, frowning as I spot the large SUV with the blacked-out windows following in the distance. "Hey, was that the same car that was following us the last time?"

Brad peers through the front mirror, and his eyes narrow suspiciously. "Seems to be."

"Crap. I thought we'd seen the last of the media."

"Or maybe it's one of your uncle's vans. We did break the rules by leaving Wellesley."

Brad pulls up in front of a small café, and I jump out of the car as the black SUV soars past us without any interest. Maybe I'm paranoid and it was nothing to do with us after all. My eyes narrow as I notice the familiar-looking motorbike parked outside the shop across the road. "Is that Ky's bike?" I lift my arm and point it out.

Brad locks the car and steps onto the footpath beside me to take a look. "Could be, but he's not the only one with that make and model in town."

I rub my hands together as we wait in line, trying to loosen the cricks from my stiff fingers. There are no seats available, so we take our coffee to go, choosing to sit on the bench outside. We sip our drinks in silence, and I wonder if his head is as addled as mine. Brad coughs. "Faye?"

"Hmm." I peer up at him.

"I know you wanted to kiss me back there as much as I wanted it. Why'd you stop?"

"Because it will only make things more complicated," I answer truthfully.

"Or it could have the opposite effect." His arm slides around my shoulder, and he toys with my hair.

I know what he means, and it mirrors my own thought process back at the lake, but my head is still a jumbled mess, and it could go either way. "Maybe." I shrug.

He scoots down the bench until his leg brushes mine. The hand in my hair tenses as he tilts my face toward his. "If you kiss me, we'll both know either way."

My blood pressure skyrockets as his warm breath oozes over my face. His eyes are a heady mix of pleading and wanton lust, and it's doing strange things to my insides. "I don't want to ruin our friendship."

"How about this," he says, pulling me into his arms. "One kiss. One *meaningful* kiss"—he enunciates the word so there can be no misinterpretation—"no strings attached. If you're feeling it, you agree to go on a date with me and see where it goes. If you don't feel anything, then I'll walk away. I swear I won't bring it up again, and I promise I will not let it affect our friendship." I bite on my lower lip and his eyes trek the movement greedily. "Your call."

My foot taps restlessly off the ground as my stomach does a full flip. My heart is thudding in my chest, and my mind is grappling with all the pros and cons. *A kiss shouldn't be such hard work, should it?*

"Jeez, throw a guy a bone here." Brad's tone is teasing, but I hear the fear of rejection lingering underneath, and that seals the deal.

I'm totally overanalyzing this. It's only one kiss. *What harm can that do?*

I circle my arms around his neck. "Okay. One kiss." I plant a finger over his mouth as he starts to speak. "One *meaningful* kiss." His tongue darts out, and he licks my finger, before sucking it quickly into his warm mouth. He can't contain his grin as I huff out a sharp gasp.

Slowly, he reaches up and removes my finger, drawing me in flush to his chest. He rubs his thumb along my bottom lip as he lowers his head. He plants a delicate kiss below my ear, and a tiny shiver spreads over my limbs. His mouth leaves a hot trail from my ear, across my jaw, and over my cheek, before hovering over my lips. "Last chance to back out," he rasps, and I lift my head and fuse my mouth with his.

I kiss him softly at first, but he clamps his arm confidently around my waist, slanting his head so he can deepen the kiss. His lips worship mine, reverentially, in long, languid strokes. My hands grip the back of his neck, my fingers winding naturally in his hair. He moans into my mouth, and the kiss intensifies as his lips move more frantically against mine. Our tongues mesh, tangling and dancing, and tentacles of desire sweep through my system. I tug on his hair, sliding into his lap as I allow myself to get lost in the moment, to think of nothing but the hot boy kissing me as if his life depended on it.

We only break apart when breathing becomes difficult and my jaw aches from such ardent kissing. He cradles me in his arms, kissing my temple as the persistent roar of an engine distracts me across the road.

I already know what I'll see before I look over.

Ky is sitting atop his bike; his ice-cold glare locked on Brad and me. I shuck out of Brad's embrace as he curses, and I step out onto the road without even looking for traffic. Ky glares at us as he slams his helmet down over his head. "Wait!" I call out, quickly looking left and right before I race across the road.

But I'm too late.

The motorbike shoots forward with an angry roar, coasting the bend before I can reach it.

Brad is already in the car by the time I cross the road and haul ass into the passenger seat. From the strained look on his face, I can tell he's wound tight. The car kicks into life with an almighty growl, and Brad thrusts it into gear, zipping up the road like the speed limit is only a fictional notion. "Slow down or you'll kill us both, please."

Common sense prevails, and he eases his foot off the pedal. I look out the window as I try to figure out how to make this right.

"Don't tell me you didn't enjoy that because I can tell you did," he grits out.

"I'm not going to deny that," I admit, quietly, turning to look at him. His hands have a death grip on the steering wheel.

"But let me guess." His nostrils flare. "It's still not enough."

And that's the truth. I most certainly enjoyed kissing Brad, and he made me feel good, but it doesn't come close to kissing Ky. That electrifying spark, that all-consuming craving for one another, doesn't exist between Brad and me. At least not on my part. I can't speak for him.

"I'm sorry."

He says nothing else until we pull into the garage at the side of the house. He turns off the engine, and we sit there in silence. His breath snakes out in audible spurts as he turns to face me. "Okay. You kept your side of the bargain and I'll keep mine."

"I hope you mean that because you're important to me." The thought of losing Brad as a friend is akin to losing a limb. He means so much to me, and I hope he can tell, because I know this isn't what he wants, and I understand how much the sour taste of rejection can truly hurt.

"You're way too important to cut out of my life. I'll get over it." He lifts my hand to his lips, planting a delicate kiss on my skin. "Friends?"

I smile through blurry eyes. "Friends."

The diner is still closed and I'm at a loss as to what to do. I think it's wise to give Brad some breathing space, and I'm going nowhere near Ky until he's calmed down. A party is a big no-no after how the last one ended up, and I'm not in the mood for company. I'm in a right funk after how things went down with Brad, and I'm drowning in a sea of guilt and self-revulsion. I should've stuck to my guns, refused to kiss him, and now neither of us would be feeling like a pile of shite. I decide to hide out in the cinema room, caving to self-indulgence.

Tears are streaming down my face as I watch the tragedy unfold on the screen. Rose, a.k.a. Kate Winslet, is kissing Jack's, Leonardo DiCaprio's, hands as she releases his frozen corpse into the sea, telling him she'll never let go. A loud sob travels up my throat. No matter how many times I watch *Titanic*, it still kills me, like a knife plunging straight through my heart. It was Mum's favorite movie, and I never got the fascination until they brought out a 3D version a few years back and I went to the cinema with her to watch it. It hooked me, and now I'm a lifetime addict, even if it conjures up more memories of my mother. I'm hoping that one day I'll be able to recall the happy times without the bitter edge chipping away at me.

The door swings open, and footsteps invade my private sanctuary. "Could you be any more cliché?" Keaton gestures toward the screen, depositing his lanky frame in the seat in front of me.

"I don't care. It's my pity party and I'll cry if I want to." I stick my tongue out at him.

"Can anyone join this party or is it a solitary affair?" He smirks, swinging his legs over the side of the chair and leaning back on his folded arms.

"I'll grant you entry if you abide by the rules. One, no calling me out on the obnoxious amount of crap I'm stuffing into my body. Two, what's discussed at said pity party stays within these four walls. Three, no trash-talking *Titanic*. It's sacrilegious. Four"—he holds up a hand to halt me, but I ignore him—"*Four*. I can cry my heart out, and you're not allowed to call me pathetic or tell me to snap out of it. Five"—Moaning, he buries his head in the crook of his elbow, mumbling under his breath—"You're permitted to call me an idiot as many times as you like because maybe if someone else says it, it might sink in."

I cram a handful of popcorn in my mouth as I slouch lower in my chair. Rose is blowing the whistle now and the rescue boat is turning around. My sobs transform to sniffs as I take a loud slurp of my soda. Reaching out, I snap another square of chocolate and stuff it in my mouth. Keaton stares at me like I'm the world's biggest slob. "Wha?" I say in between chomping.

"You're going to make yourself sick."

"Don't care," I mumble, loading more chocolate in my gob.

"And you're going to get stupendously fat and gross," he adds, getting into the spirit of it now.

"With a bit of luck," I deadpan.

He moves rows, snatching up my goodies and moving them to the other side so he can sit down. I scowl at him, and he chuckles. "You want to be gross and fat?"

"Yep." I stretch my legs out, planting my feet in his lap. "I want to be so ugly and gross that no boys will even look sideways at me. No boys equals no heartache equals happiness. I'm committing to spinsterhood or maybe the convent though I doubt Sister Mary will let me step foot anywhere near the place, but one can hope."

"You've got it all planned out, huh?"

"Yep." I rest my head on the armchair of the seat, making myself comfy. "And I'm deadly serious too."

"Uh-huh." His eyes twinkle mischievously and my gaze narrows. Superfast, he grabs a bunch of popcorn and starts stuffing it in my mouth. "What kind of a cousin would I be if I didn't help with your life's mission? Huh?" I try swatting his hands away but it's impossible. Next, he smears chocolate over my mouth, and I'm laughing so hard I'm practically choking. I slide off the seat, falling flat on my bum, as Keaton crawls after me, waving the bucket at me like the Popcorn Monster. I shriek, climbing to my feet and running away from him. He comes after me— naturally—and we chase each other around the movie room, hopping over seats, sliding under rows, and I'm doing everything to avoid him until laughter gets the better of me, and I drop to my knees, keeling over as tears roll down my face.

"Enough." I hold up a hand as he advances. "You win. I'm

not serious. I love boys too much to ever give them up." I flatten out on the floor, bending my legs at the knees.

Keaton drops down beside me, nudging me playfully. "Good choice, oh wise one," he teases. "Now tell me what this is about."

"Promise you won't tell a soul." I twist my head so I'm facing him.

"Scouts honor." He grins, showcasing his beautiful white teeth. His face is starting to fill out, and he's losing that baby-faced look. He's growing his hair longer on top, and that artfully messy style works for him. "You're staring."

"You're really beautiful, Keaton."

His eyes go wide in alarm, and I can't contain my snort of hilarity. Trust him to jump to *that* conclusion. "I'm not hitting on you!" He pins me with an incredulous look, and I sigh. "Yeah. Let's not go there. All I meant is you're turning into a super-hot guy, Keaton. Girls are going to be crawling all over your ass, but don't forget that you're so much more than that. You have this inner beauty that shines through setting you apart from everyone else. You're one in a million." I get the fright of my life when tears blossom in his eyes. I prop up on one elbow. "Happy or sad tears?"

He sits up, crossing his legs in front of him. "Both. Always both." An anguished expression contorts his face, and I don't think we're talking about the same thing anymore.

I frown, mirroring his position. "Tell me what's bothering you."

His troubled eyes bore into mine, and I spot the conflict warring inside him. "I will. Just not yet."

"Okay. I'm here whenever you want to talk." I envelop him in a quick hug. "I love you, you know that, right?"

He smiles warmly at me. "I know, and I love you, too. Like a sister, not like ..."

I roll my eyes, nudging him in the ribs. "I know that, doofus."

"You still love him, don't you?" he asks quietly.

I scratch the top of my head. "Is it that obvious?"

"Yeah, to be honest, it is. I see how hard you try not to look at him, but when you do, it's all there. You're too genuine a person to hide how you're feeling."

I groan. "Great. Now, I'm a laughingstock as well as everything else."

He shakes his head. "He still loves you, too. I know my brother. He may be better at hiding it, but he's hurting like hell too."

I grind down hard on my teeth. "Could've fooled me. He's hot and heavy with Addison again, and now he doesn't give me the time of day. Ugh!" I grip bunches of my hair as I sigh. "Why can't I love Brad and forget about Ky? It would be so much easier that way." I bury my face in my hands.

"That's what this is about?" Keaton coaxes.

"We kissed and ..." I lock my arms around my knees, struggling to find the right words.

"And it was hot? Or not?" He cocks his head to the side.

"It was good ..."

"Ouch. Poor Brad." He's fighting a smirk.

"Knock it off, dipshit. This is my life I'm making a complete mess of. Have some compassion." I roll my eyes so he knows I'm semi-joking. "It felt good to have someone's arms around me, to feel the warmth of his touch and the taste of his mouth. To know someone cares. And it was a great kiss, but I didn't feel the same spark that I feel when I kiss your brother. Now, all I can think about is how much I miss kissing Ky and what a horrible person I am to give Brad hope where there's none."

"Awks." Keaton sends me a sympathetic look.

"I know, and it's worse, because Ky witnessed the whole thing."

Keaton stuffs a hand in his mouth in a feeble attempt to mask his reaction.

"Glad someone finds it amusing," I snark, as he loses the fight, and his laughter fills the room. "I've fucked everything up! Agh!" I nestle my face in my knees, wishing the ground would open up and swallow me.

"Sorry," Keaton says, sounding in no way apologetic. "You've got to admit it's funny."

I growl at him. "Excuse me if I don't see the funny side. I'm worried that I've ruined our friendship, and Brad probably hates me for making him do that to Ky again." I flop back down on the ground, sighing. "I'm a bleedin' disaster zone."

Keaton lightly chuckles. "You put the rama in drama," he jokes, and I punch him in the arm.

"That's mean. I didn't ask to fall in love with my cousin, and I didn't ask for that kiss. Brad kinda backed me into a corner, and now I have two people to avoid in this house."

"Good luck with that," he says with a wink.

Ugh. It's official.

My life sucks.

Chapter Twenty-Two

I wake abruptly in the early hours of the morning with my salty tongue stuck to the top of my mouth. Thanks to my monster binge-eating session, I'm parched and in dire need of water. I pad quietly in my bare feet toward the kitchen, stifling a yawn as I pass through the lobby. I stop in my tracks when the sound of voices filters out from the living area. I'd recognize Ky's and Brad's husky tones anywhere. I flatten my back to the wall and creep as close to the doorway as I dare.

"I'm sorry I hit you," Ky says, and I roll my eyes.

"I probably deserved it," Brad replies.

"No, you didn't." There's a brief pause. "And you're right. I have no claim over her. Faye's free to kiss whomever she likes." His words batter my fragile heart.

"I swore I'd never do that to you again."

"You haven't done anything wrong, man. If I'm not with her, I'd rather it be you. I know I can trust you to look after her, to treat her right."

My nostrils flare at the insinuation. Like I'm some possession they can swap between them when it suits and that all we need is his approval which he's so graciously giving to us. *Who does he think he is?*

"It doesn't matter, anyway. She doesn't want me." Brad's tone suggests disappointment and acquiescence but no malice.

"That wasn't the way it looked to me," Ky says, confirming he definitely saw the kiss.

"She's in love with you."

"She can't be!" Ky snaps, carving another piece out of my heart. "Hasn't she listened to a word I've said? She needs to move on, and you're the guy to move on with. Do you want me to talk some sense into her?"

That does it.

His patronizing tone combined with his misguided rationale and the implication that I'm the one not thinking clearly summons the beast slumbering inside me. Uncaring that I'm in a flimsy nightie or that I'll be admitting I was eavesdropping, I charge into the room, flipping on the main light so they can both see the extent of my venom.

Seated across from one another on the leather couches, they blink at me in shocked surprise. I stalk toward Ky, pushing him in the chest. "I do not need anyone to talk sense into me, least of all you!" I screech. "How dare you presume to know what I want or what I need. You have no right!"

"Faye." Brad stands up, and I lunge at him, shoving him back down on the couch.

"And you're no better!" I'm shrieking like a hyena, and I'll probably wake the entire house but I don't care. I can't see beyond the red glaze coating my eyes. "You think you can get his permission and I'll fall into your arms?"

"No! It wasn't like that." Brad tries to argue but I shut him up with one of my special death glares.

"I heard enough to know that he was trying to pawn me off on you." I jab my finger in Ky's direction, incensed to see a dark, amused glint in his eyes. "Wipe that smug look off your face, Ky, or I'll do it for you." I glare at him, and his smirk grows wider. "Do you have a death wish?" I snarl.

He stands up, moving carefully but confidently toward me. "Baby, you know I find it hot when you're mad."

I totally lose the plot, shoving him forcefully as I yell in frustration. He makes a grab for me, losing his balance in the process, and we both tumble to the ground. I land unceremoniously on top of him with a groan. I straddle him as I sit upright, prodding my finger repeatedly in his annoyingly perfect chest, furious to see the lustful glaze in his eyes, to feel the telltale bulge hardening under my ass. "You don't get to flirt with me, to call me baby, or hot, or anything!" I climb to my feet. "Save it for your girlfriend!"

I back away, scowling at both of them. "I want nothing to do with either of you. Understood?"

Brad gets up. "Faye, I'm sorry. Come on."

I sway a little, my limbs weakening now that the surge of rage-induced adrenaline is dissipating. "Leave me alone, Brad. Both of you. Stay away from me."

I stomp to the kitchen, yank a couple of bottles of water from the fridge, and storm back to my room, avoiding the penetrating stares of both boys as I walk past the sitting room with my nose held high in the air.

It takes me ages to fall back asleep. Lingering tendrils of frustration occupy my mind, making sleep almost impossible. But, eventually, at some point, I drift off.

I get up Saturday morning, my limbs still seething with anger, and haul ass to the pool for a swim. I vent my frustration in the water, pushing my body for hours until every muscle twinges. Then I spend the rest of the day hiding like a coward in my room. In the cold light of day, I cringe as I recall last night's confrontation, furious that I let either of them get to me like that. Neither of them dares to show his face, and I'm grateful for small mercies.

A heavy thud on my door late afternoon sends my blood pressure into orbit. "Can I come in?" Kal asks, and I emit a relieved sigh.

"It's open." He ambles into the room with his shoulders drooping. "What's happened?" I automatically ask, my stomach plunging to my toes.

"I met with the legal team. They weren't able to get the case dismissed at the pre-hearing, and we've been issued a trial date." He lies sideway on the bed, propping his head up on an elbow. "November fifteenth."

"That's good news, right? It's only a few weeks away."

"It is, and it isn't. Dad pulled some strings to rush the case through, and I'm glad I'm not facing months and months of house arrest, but if it doesn't go my way on that day, I could be in jail this time next month."

"Surely Zoe's testimony will prove you're being set up?"

"It's not that straightforward, according to the attorneys. The prosecution is taking statements from the girls at school, and they're not painting a pretty picture. And Lana produced the condom we used."

"That proves nothing! Only that you had sex which you aren't disputing."

"Her mother is insisting she was a virgin and that she'd never have agreed to sex before marriage."

I raise an eyebrow. "Did we return to the dark ages and I missed the memo somewhere along the way?"

"Greta will make a great character witness, and she's a devout Catholic. Lana has been brought up respecting her faith, so it's pretty much going to come down to my word against hers. You haven't read her statement, Faye. It's vicious— she isn't holding back, and it's primed to tug the heartstrings.

She's going to have the jury eating out of her hand. I'm as good as guilty. She must truly hate me now."

I lie on my belly with my elbows digging into the duvet. "I still can't get over how she's doing this to you. No matter how much her heart hurts, she's no right to screw with your life like this." I lift my legs and cross my ankles, swirling them through the air.

"I wish I could talk to her, discover what's going on in her head, but Keven is drawing a blank." My eyes ask the unspoken question. "Dad has a private investigator on the case, but Ky also asked Keven to run a trace. It's like she's evaporated into thin air."

"People who don't want to be found are usually adept at hiding." My thoughts drift to my mother. While she wasn't physically missing, there's no doubt she was an expert at hiding. "Maybe you can talk to her at the trial?"

He sighs. "I'm not allowed to even look at her."

"This sucks."

He barks out a laugh. "That's the frigging understatement of the year." His laugh withers up and dies. "I don't want to end up in prison." Naked terror is evident on his face, and he looks so young and vulnerable.

"You won't. You didn't do this."

"There are plenty of examples of men who were locked up for years for crimes they didn't commit. Who's to say I'll be any different? It's a very real possibility and one I've got to consider." He flops down on his back, rubbing his hands over his face. "Rape is up to twenty years in state prison. This could ruin my life."

I roll over and lay my head on his shoulder. "No one is going to let you take the rap for something you didn't do. We'll sort something out, or other evidence will come forward. Keven will find something to help."

As the words filter out of my mouth, I detect the desperation in my voice. *How can I expect Kal to believe my reassurances when I barely trust in them myself?*

Rose calls to let me know the diner has reopened and to ask if I can work tonight. If she was here, I'd kiss the heck out of her. This is exactly what I need to keep my mind off tomorrow.

Max pulls up in front of the diner at the same time Theo, Rose's boyfriend, drops her off. I give him a wave as he peels off up the road on his bike. I lean in to give Rose a quick hug, but her concerned frown holds me back. "'Sup?"

She sidesteps me, squinting as she looks behind me. "Is that guy taking photos of you?"

I spin around too fast, making myself dizzy. My jaw slouches when I spot the well-dressed man at the other side of the road, hastily pocketing a camera. "Oh my God!" I turn blazing eyes on Rose. "It's that customer—the guy who asked for me the other week. I knew it! My gut told me he was up to no good." I make a split-second decision and race across the road, shouting at him. "Hey! Mark! Stop!" He is already halfway down the street by now, and he doesn't turn around. I give chase, but by the time I turn the corner at the end of the road, I only see the back of his head as he rounds the next bend. It's time to call it quits—I'll never catch up to him now.

I'm absolutely fuming when I push through the door into the diner. The place is jam-packed and thriving. Either people have genuinely missed the food, or they're here for a gander at David. The thought is abhorrent, but there's a definite element of this community that feeds off gossip and drama, so I can't say I'm surprised.

We are rushed off our feet keeping up with the orders, but I couldn't be happier. I know I'm weird, but I genuinely missed work. I'm the type of person who likes to keep busy, and if I have too much downtime on my hands, I don't know what to do with myself.

Rose and I are sorting out bills at the counter when I feel eyes on me. Slowly, I turn around, my eyes widening when I spot David, standing in the doorway, staring at us. It's the first time he's come out of his office all night. His pants are loose around his paunch, and his wan face looks gaunt. The expression on his face is like he's carrying the weight of the world on his shoulders. A stilled awareness has invaded the diner, and conversation dies out. But David doesn't appear to see anyone. He's in his own little bubble, staring blankly ahead. My heart goes out to him. He's just standing there, staring at us, without moving or speaking.

I move toward him, cautiously placing an arm on his elbow. "David, are you okay? Can I get you anything?"

He turns dull eyes on me, staring at me until a spark of something ignites in his eyes. He pats my hand. "You're a good girl." Leaning in, he kisses my cheek. "Always such a good girl." He pats my hand one final time, giving me a weak smile, before retreating to his office.

"That wasn't weird or anything," Rose deadpans. "He shouldn't be here. He's isn't well enough to return to work."

"I agree. Maybe we should phone his wife?"

"I don't have her number. Provided he stays out back, he's not doing any harm to anyone but himself, I suppose."

I'm completely knackered when I arrive home close to midnight. Rose and I offered to lock up, all but shoving David out the door, insisting he go home. I yawn as I drop my bag in the hall and head into the kitchen. Everywhere is in darkness, and I flip the lights on in the kitchen, cursing under my breath when I see the state of the place. The kitchen is a mess. As usual. My cousins are the biggest slobs on the planet. *Would it kill them to put their dishes in the dishwasher?* Animals. I'd thought that Alex would have gotten herself together by now, but she still's hiding herself away in her bedroom, barely showing her face in the house let alone contemplating going to work. She couldn't be any less like the woman I first met if she was trying. While I am sorry for everything she's going through, she has to snap out of it, and soon.

I start clearing up, yawning as I stack the dishwasher.

"You don't have to do that," Ky says. He's cowering in the shadows of the utility room, leaning against the doorjamb.

I shriek, slapping a hand across my chest, right where my heart is galloping in sheer terror. "Don't frighten me like that. Jeez." I rub the aching spot on my chest. He hobbles into the room, and I gasp. Dried blood is caked on his face and congealed above his lip from an obvious nose injury. His left eyelid is swollen, and the surrounding skin is mottled and discolored. I can already see the beginnings of a black eye forming. Faint bruising dots his right cheekbone. He limps to the table, easing onto the bench. "Who'd you fight this time?" I'm praying he hasn't gone another round with Brad.

"It's nothing you need to worry about." He spits a mouthful of blood into a dirty bowl on the table, and I rummage in the overhead press, retrieving the first aid kit.

"Don't patronize me." I walk toward him, shaking my head. "If you want my help, you'll spill."

He holds my wrist. "I can do it."

"You can barely walk."

"Took a few kicks to the shin, but I'll be fine after a bath and some heat pads."

My fingers lightly probe his jaw and his cheek, and he flinches, wincing. "This is becoming too regular a habit," I chastise, extracting what I need from the kit. "Who was it?"

His shoulders slump in defeat. "Roberts—Jeremy." How he manages to infuse that one word with so much derision is impressive. "And before you ask, he was spouting shit about you that I didn't appreciate."

"You should know better than to rise to the bait. He's probably going to use this now to get me to drop the charges." The police had found the recording on his cell, along with a host of other non-disclosed recordings, and formal charges are being drawn up. While the police are keeping their lips sealed in relation to the other content, Dan has it on good authority that they had tag-teamed a bunch of other girls and recorded them without their knowledge too. Ky was right—they are sick fucks. I move to the sink, returning with a warm bowl of water.

"From what he said tonight, if he's to be believed, and that's a big *if*, neither he or Edwards are going to be charged."

I stall my hand on his face. "What?"

"I'll phone Dad for the deets, but he implied some kind of deal had been struck."

"That's fucking typical. How is he able to buy his way out of this and Kal isn't?"

"I know, it's crap."

I tip his head back, so I can get at his nose. "This will sting." I gently dab at the bloody mess until he's all cleaned up. "Where'd you bump into Jeremy anyway?"

He purses his lips, and I lean back, giving him my best demanding stare. He sighs. "Over at Addison's." That bitter taste is back in my mouth. Serves me right for asking. I unscrew the lid off the arnica and carefully rub it around the bruised skin on his cheek and under his eye. "Don't worry, I won't be returning there any time soon." He grins wickedly. "Her father has banned me from the house."

My eyes narrow to slits. He's smiling like this is the best news ever, and it goes some way toward reaffirming my suspicions, which I hate, because I've zero desire to hop back on that merry-go-round. I'm giving myself whiplash with my altering opinions as it is. "Are you ever going to tell me?"

His smile fades. "Don't."

I fling the contents of the first aid kit back in the bag and stomp over toward the press. I'm leaning up to slide the box into the cupboard when his warm body presses up behind me. I stop, arm extended midair, as his hands snake around my waist. My breath comes out harsh and ragged as intense shivers rip up and down my spine. Brushing my hair to one side, he rests his chin on my shoulder, and I can barely move. His body heat seeps into mine, relaxing me on a bone-deep level. I clamp my lips shut before I whimper.

I shut the press door and reach my hands down to his. Our fingers entwine, and he places the lightest, most delicate kiss against my neck. I shudder and there's no way he doesn't feel my body trembling against his. "Faye." He whispers my name with adoration, and I move to turn around, but he presses me into the counter, holding me securely in position. "Don't turn around, please. I only have so much self-control."

"Ky, please, you need to te—"

"Ssh," he says into my ear, and I moan as his warm breath does funny things to my insides. "I can't deal. Not tonight. Not with what we may be facing tomorrow."

"I'm scared," I admit quietly, leaning back against him and closing my eyes. I want to savor this moment. Cherish the feel of him at my back, his hands locked with mine, his nose nuzzling my neck. We're not kissing or touching intimately or even looking at one another but his presence surrounds me, and my body's wound tight, quivery and jittery and oh so needy. He's affecting me as potently as if we *were* being intimate.

"Me too." He inhales deeply, and the urge to kiss him is riding me hard. I don't know how I'll cope if he's confirmed as my brother.

I don't think I know how to stay away from him.

Nothing seems to matter—his girlfriend, my *whatever* with Brad, the constant push-and-pull of his actions, the knowledge that we could be more closely related. I know they are justifiable reasons to keep my distance, but try telling that to my heart.

My heart doesn't care about that stuff.

The heart wants what the heart wants, and no amount of logic makes a blind difference.

I want him. I'll always want him.

I don't know how long we stay like that, bound in a backward embrace, clinging to each other in the only way we can, but it's more than enough to alleviate the frayed edges of my sanity. Without breaking any rules, Ky has found a way of comforting me like only he can.

After a while, we withdraw, as if by mutual unspoken agreement, going our separate ways without further conversation.

As I lie in bed, worrying about tomorrow and what the results will prove—nervous to the point of vomiting—I close my eyes and remember how good it felt to be held by him, and that's all it takes to coax me to sleep.

Chapter Twenty-Three

Trying to concentrate at school the next day is a bit like riding a bike uphill with no gears. I'm floundering, and for once I'm not on a countdown until the final bell. If I could hit the reverse button, I would.

Brad is a complete sweetheart. He understands how anxious I am, and he babbles away, distracting me with his inane chatter. He seems to have accepted the status quo with us, at least outwardly, and for that I'm grateful. He doesn't appear upset, so I'm figuring I was right, and it was the thought of him plus me that captured his interest and not the actual reality of a relationship.

I intercept a few hostile looks from Peyton, but that's nothing new. She doesn't risk taking it any further, so I can't complain. The fake boyfriend idea was a gem.

Brad drives us home when school ends, and I'm on the verge of puking with nervous adrenaline the instant I step over the threshold. A bunch of luggage rests on the porcelain tiled floor, and I'm assuming it's the trigger for the latest row we're intercepting between Alex and James. They must be in his study, with the door closed, but I can still hear their muted arguing from here.

Brad and I exchange knowing looks as Ky appears in the doorway. "He's moving back in, apparently."

"Oh?" My brows nudge up.

"He got a court order. That's why Mom is blowing a gasket."

The door swings open overhead, and Alex comes hurtling out of the room like a tempest. She's still dressed in her pajamas, and I can't say I blame James for taking such drastic action. Someone needs to at least attempt to take on a parental role, and I, for one, am relieved he's moving back in. Hopefully, he can enforce some form of discipline—not that I'm holding my breath in anticipation—but it'll seem more stable with James around.

Alex rushes past us into the living room, her face red with indignation.

"Faye. Kyler. Can you come up to my study, please," James requests from the top of the stairs.

Mammoth butterflies take up residence in my chest, and I shudder involuntarily. Brad squeezes my hand. "Good luck," he whispers, before disappearing down the corridor.

"After you." Ky gestures me forward with his hand. Our eyes meet and it's the first time we've seen each other since last night. The usual electrifying spark sizzles between us, reeling me in like an invisible force. My heart starts galloping in my chest, and I act without overthinking it, stepping into his warm body and resting my head on his chest. Uncaring if it pisses his dad off, Ky's arms go around me without hesitation. James loudly clears his throat, but Ky doesn't relinquish his hold, and the steady beating of his heart helps calm my fractured nerves. He cups my face affectionately in both his large hands, easing back a little. "It's going to be okay. No matter what, we'll deal." I'm not sure if he's trying to convince himself or me.

James perches on the edge of his desk while we take the two red velvet armchairs. The fire is alight although it does nothing to heat the chill in my bones. "Dr. Stephens is on his way, but I wanted to talk to you first about the situation with Dylan Edwards and Jeremy Roberts."

"I've heard a rumor," Ky admits, crossing a leg over his knee.

"Does that have anything to do with the state of your face?" James asks dryly.

Ky's expression hardens in preparation for the inevitable dressing down. "And what if it does?" he challenges his father.

"I hope you got a good few punches in." James shoots him a sly smirk.

Ky reels back. No doubt he was expecting a lecture instead of a verbal pat on the back. "Don't worry, Dad. I didn't let our side down." He meets James's smirk bang-on with a massive smirk of his own.

I sit up straighter. "If we're finished with all the male bravado, can you tell us what's going on, please?"

James walks behind his desk and retrieves a document from the top drawer. "Unfortunately, the police are dropping the case against them because they don't think they have enough to bring it to full trial. The evidence isn't strong enough to support a conviction, I'm afraid."

"Why the hell not?" I demand.

James grimaces. "It's a minor misdemeanor and it hasn't taken much for Jeremy's father to brush it under the carpet. He has a lot of clout in this town and a top Boston law firm on tap." His face contorts. "Apparently, he's paid off the other girls, and they've retracted their complaints. He's always had it in for this family, so if we pursued this, I've no doubt he'd milk it for all it's worth. I have it on good authority they are planning to run with a drunken, out-of-control party scenario and downplay the recording as a prank. Even if we were to pursue a civil suit, they would annihilate your character and your reputation on the stand. I don't want that happening to you."

"What a crock of shit!" I exclaim, seething as I hop up and start pacing the floor. "So, what?" I turn the full extent of my frustration on James. "They're going to get off scot-free? They can run around recording girls without their knowledge and then blackmail them into threesomes?" I flap my hands in the air in a diva-esque move borrowed from my archnemesis.

James walks to me, placing his hands on my shoulders. "Sit back down, sweetheart, and I'll explain the rest." I plunk into the chair and give him my full attention. "They've signed a confidentiality agreement including confirmation that they have no more copies of the recording they made of you. They agree not to talk publicly about the incident, to stay away from you in the future, and they will submit a sizeable donation to a local charity which supports women who are the victims of abuse." He hands the stapled document to me. "You need to sign this to confirm you will not discuss the matter either and that you'll maintain a reasonable distance from them."

I snatch the papers and pen from his hand, harrumphing. "That won't be a problem, trust me." I sign on the dotted line and hand it back to him.

He kneels down in front of me. "I know this wasn't the outcome you wanted, but at least this won't be hanging over your head anymore. The recording is destroyed. It's gone, and you can chalk it up to experience, and put it behind you."

Ky runs his hand up and down my arm, eliciting a flurry of fiery tingles that extend all the way to my toes. "They won't go near you again. I'll make sure of it."

"Thank you."

"Don't thank me!" His tone is harsh. "Brad is right. This was all my fault." I open my mouth to argue my point, but he places his finger against my mouth, muzzling me. "All that's going through my head since that night is how I pushed you into his arms."

He swallows hard, and I reach out, entwining our hands. "I'm responsible for my own actions. I was locked and being stupid, careless. That's not your fault."

A murderous glint flashes in his eyes. "Jeremy is lucky Addison's father was there last night or I might've killed the son of a bitch." A vein throbs in his neck.

"You have to let it go. Neither of them are worth expending any more energy on."

He angles his body so he's facing me. We are both straining across the gap between our chairs, like two magnets fighting a natural pull. As we stare at one another, he drops his mask, and I see everything he's been trying so hard to keep from me. My heart swells to bursting point, and I grip his hand tighter, wishing I could straddle his hips and kiss the heck out of him. Heat pools low in my stomach, and I want him so bad it's killing me.

"You know I can't allow this to continue once we have the results," James murmurs, ruining the moment. Automatically, we both sit back in our chairs, releasing our hands. "I hope you have at least tried to prepare yourselves, because it's not going to be easy."

"You seem sure of the results," Ky says, and there's a bitter note to his tone. "Do you know already?"

James shakes his head. "No. I'll be hearing at the same time you are." His phone pings on his desk, and he snatches it up. "They are here." He rises. "I'll be back in a few minutes."

My heart is crashing around my ribcage as panic flays me on all sides.

"Come here," Ky whispers, holding his arms out. I need no further invitation. I throw myself onto his lap, clinging to him like a limpet. "I can feel your heart racing," he says, placing his hand on my chest. "Mine too." He takes my hand and places it in the spot where his heart thuds wildly. There is barely any room between us, and it doesn't take much for him to close the gap as he presses his mouth to mine. He kisses me softly and all too briefly. "I needed to kiss you one final time." Moisture glistens in his eyes, startling me. "Dad is right. If the test confirms we're siblings, then we can't act on our feelings again. We can't go there."

"I know," I whisper, and a tear rolls down my cheek. Footsteps on the stairs have me jumping out of his lap like there's a rocket up my ass. I've only reclaimed my chair when James steps into the room with the good doctor.

I shut down internally, as if all my organs are switching off, one life-sustaining body part after another. Nausea swims up my throat, and I clamp a hand over my mouth, fearful I'm actually going to puke.

The doctor greets us by name, passing simple pleasantries, but I don't hear a thing. I can't hear over the roaring in my ears. I'm in a daze when the doctor hands James an envelope and he removes a written report. Ky reaches out, grasping my hand in his, and I cling to him possessively. "Breathe, Faye." He rubs soothing circles on the back of my hand and his touch brings me back to solid ground.

James emits a sharp gasp, and my eyes register the shock on his face. The report slips out of his hands, fluttering to the ground. He sways on his feet, his knees almost giving out, as he clutches the desk in a desperate effort to stay upright.

"Dad?" Ky's tone is laced with concern and fear. "What does it say?"

James blinks successively, struggling to compose himself,

and the doctor presses a finger to the pulse point on his wrist. This somewhat snaps him out of his shocked state. "I'm okay," he reassures the doctor, walking to me on quivering limbs.

He drops to his knees in front of me, and my entire body is one giant ball of stress. My nerves are hanging on by a thread.

Ky's panicked breathing is the only sound in the room.

"It's ..." James croaks, a dart of pain flickering across his face. "I was wrong. I'm not your father. I don't know who is."

Chapter Twenty-Four

My mouth opens and closes like a fish out of water. I'm speechless. I don't know what to say or what to think. Relief is the overriding sentiment, but all manner of other emotions has my head in a tailspin. Some I expected to feel, but disappointment is a weird one. My main thought process these last couple of weeks has been tied to Ky, so much so that I haven't given enough consideration to the "father" aspect of it. Perhaps I was subconsciously deflecting the more serious elements of the revelation on purpose. James is visibly despondent at the news, and whether he wanted it to be true because it was a permanent physical link to my mum or because he liked the idea of being my father, I don't know, and I don't care. He wanted to call me his daughter, and whatever the reason, it feels good to be wanted like that.

I kneel down in front of him, enveloping him in a warm embrace. "I don't know what to say."

He rests his chin atop my head. "I'm sorry, Faye. I truly believed you were mine. I wanted to believe you were mine."

"I told you, Goddammit," Ky snaps, and we jerk apart. He

stands up, glaring at James with hateful eyes. Whatever tentative moment they shared not so long ago is clearly forgotten. "You've put us through hell these last two weeks, and ... ugh!" He scrunches clumps of his hair, kicking at the leg of the chair in frustration. I scramble to my feet and reach for him. "Don't!" He steps back, holding up his hands, not even looking at me. "I'm sorry, I just can't." My chest tightens as I watch him flee the room.

James pulls himself upright, straightening out his clothes. "I don't understand. I thought he'd be pleased?"

I wholeheartedly agree, but I don't admit that out loud. I have a suspicion the situation with that bitch Addison is the root cause of his little outburst, and I fully intend to find out if I'm right.

Dr. Stephens is standing awkwardly in the corner, not knowing where to look. I approach him. "Excuse me, but may I ask a question?"

"Of course, my dear."

I shove my hands in the pockets of my jeans. "Is there any way of confirming who my biological father is?"

"No, not without samples to test, I'm afraid."

James materializes at my side, cautiously circling his arm around my shoulders. I lean into him for strength, peering up at him. "Maybe my dad *is* my dad after all. Perhaps your information wasn't one hundred percent accurate." Hope has the blood thrumming faster in my veins.

"Oh, sweetheart." He kisses the top of my head. "I wish I could tell you that, but I can't. Dr. Stephens obtained a DNA sample from your mom's husband for test purposes, and he was ruled out too."

"The tests were absolutely conclusive, my dear. Neither Mr. Kennedy nor Mr. Donovan is your biological father. I'm very sorry." The doctor pats my hand. "If you procure any other samples, and you require further testing, don't hesitate to let me know, and I'll take care of it for you."

I nod on auto-pilot.

"Thank you, Doctor. That will be all. You can send your final invoice to my wife's assis ... ah, send the paperwork here and mark it for my attention," James explains. The doctor shakes both our hands and leaves.

James pours two whiskeys and hands one to me. I blink up at him. "I know it's unusual, but this is an unusual situation, and I figure if I could use a drink, then so could you."

I swirl the amber-colored liquid in my glass, mulling over everything I've heard. "My mum must have been a right ole slut," I say, taking a large mouthful of my drink. The burning sensation coating my throat matches the searing pain in my gut. It's like playing "who knocked up Faye's mum?" on the roulette wheel. Only problem is, I've no idea what the odds are. I knock back another glug of whiskey, relishing the sharp taste. I expect James to rebuke my statement—to instantly jump to my mum's defense, but he doesn't. "Didn't she even consider how I'd feel?" Tears sting my eyes, but I angrily wipe them away. I've shed enough tears over that woman.

James stares off into space, and I notice his glass is already empty. "Saoirse wasn't a slut. I know that, even if the more I discover, the less I believe I truly knew my sister."

"But someone got her pregnant at seventeen!" I put my glass down on the table. "Please level with me, James. Do you know who my father is, or do you have any ideas on who it could be?"

He places his own glass down beside me. Taking my hands, he looks earnestly into my eyes. "I swear to you, Faye, that I don't know who it could be. I wasn't aware she had a boyfriend, although that's not to say she didn't. I have to accept that fact now."

"Or I'm the product of a one-night stand."

"It's possible, and maybe that's why she ran away." He gets up, taking both our glasses. "We'll never know now." He stares at the ceiling for a minute. "Would you like another?"

Sure, why the heck not? I nod, and he fixes the drinks. He hands mine to me before walking to the bookshelves and removing an album.

He opens the burgundy-colored leather cover and starts flipping through pages and pages of the boys as babies and toddlers. "I like to look at these from time to time. To remind myself why I get up every morning." He points at a family photo. "This is why I'll keep fighting. Family is the only thing worth fighting for."

I can't find my voice to respond; I'm too conflicted and choked with emotion, so I focus on the family photo instead. The triplets are only toddlers in this one, and I can't tell any of them apart. In fact, all the boys look so alike it's hard to tell who is who, even with Kaden and Keven sharing a different birth father. Although, now that the ugly truth has been revealed, I'm noticing subtle differences in my older cousins—like how their eyes are a slightly cooler shade of blue, their hair slightly darker than their younger brothers, the sharper curve of their jawline.

Unnoticeable until you start looking.

No wonder no one suspected anything amiss.

"Wow. He's a bruiser!" I exclaim, pointing to a smiling baby boy with chubby cheeks and a stocky frame. "Which of my cousins is it?"

James smiles nostalgically. "That's Kyler. He was always something of an enigma." His finger sweeps lovingly across the picture. "You'd never have known he was premature. He was always so sturdy and strong." He looks off into space again. "He was such a happy baby. Always smiling and gurgling. Everyone commented on it." James turns his head to me. "His first word was 'dada,' and I thought my heart would burst with joy." His Adam's apple bobs in his throat. "I love Kaden and Keven with all my heart. It was instant, from the first moment I met them. I've always considered them my own, and I never asked Alex anything about her ex, because, as far as I was concerned, I've always been their father."

I cross my feet at the ankles. "I know, initially, they took the news badly, but I'm sure they know that."

"I hope so, because they are my sons in every way that matters. There is no question about that." He smiles as his finger traces across a photo. "But when Kyler came along, and he was my flesh and blood, the *only* flesh and blood I had a connection with in this world, I was overwhelmed by the intensity of my feelings. Bowled over by the amount of love I had in my heart for him. I didn't believe it was possible to love another person that much."

His voice clogs with emotion as he gets lost in the past. "I was obsessed with him. Even when he was asleep, I would stay in his room for hours, staring at him, marveling at how perfect he was, this little part of me." Sheer joy flourishes in his eyes. "I never imagined that seventeen years later he would hate the very sight of me. That I would mess up so spectacularly—twist that perfect moment until there was nothing left of the person I was or the pure, happy child he was."

James has made terrible mistakes in his life, and his actions have hurt the ones he professed to love the most, but I can't hate him. Not when he's as flawed as the rest of us. As flawed as me. Especially when he seems willing to accept responsibility for his mistakes, and he wants to atone for them so badly.

I reach over and hug him. Resting his head on my shoulder, he clings to me, his broad arms clutching my back. "What do I do, Faye? How can I fix it? Please tell me, because I don't know what to do."

"I wish I had the answers, James, but I don't. The only thing you can do is talk to him. Open up like you have with me and hope he'll listen. But don't ever stop trying. Don't give up. Your sons need you to keep fighting for this family even if they don't realize it or appreciate it." I attempt to breathe over the devastating pain. "I would give anything to talk to my parents. To ask them why. To try to understand why they did the things they did. I know they didn't deliberately set out to hurt me, that they thought they were doing the right thing, but I wish they had done things differently."

I release a loud sigh, and James kisses my temple. "I can't rewrite history, and I won't ever get to hear them tell me why, and I'll have to find some way of processing that. But Ky is here, and he needs to hear those things. Even if he refuses to listen, he still needs you to say them, and all you can do is hope that in time he'll understand why you did the things you did. At least you both have that opportunity which is something that isn't available to me."

James is lost in thought, and I decide to give him some privacy to mull things over. I press a quick kiss to his cheek before tiptoeing quietly from the room. I shut the door carefully, leaning back against it as I hold my face in my hands.

There's been so much of the heavy stuff lately, and it's starting to weigh me down. Fingers curl around my wrist, and I gasp, startled. I blink my eyes open, dropping my unfettered hand to my side. Ky stares at me, his cloudy blue eyes probing mine. "How much did you hear?" I whisper.

"Enough." His voice is rough, gravelly, and his eyes pained.

"You should talk to him. He's hurting too."

"He's brought this on all of us. He deserves the pain." His words are laced with anger and bitterness, and I appreciate it's going to take a lot more for Ky to find forgiveness in his heart. If he ever will.

"He's your father. Some day he won't be here, and you'll regret all the wasted moments. All the chances you had to talk to him, really talk to him, to get to know the man behind the parent." A sharp, twisty pain knifes me through the heart. "I know I do. Don't push him away indefinitely. Try to find a way to forgive him."

I turn around and bound down the stairs, racing for my room, desperate to get behind the privacy of my door before I break down.

Chapter Twenty-Five

Brad knocks on my door a couple of hours later, and I update him on everything. After he's gone, I lie in bed for hours listening to music while mulling everything over in my mind.

To know I haven't been illegally cavorting with my own brother is a massive relief. I don't know where I stand with Ky, if there's a chance of resuming our relationship, but at least it's a possibility again. Especially now that Alex and James know how we feel about one another, but Addison is the usual thorn in my side. Considering how Ky's been with me these last couple days, I'm more convinced than ever that what he said to me at the party was a load of horseshit. Addison is holding something over him—I'd bet my last dollar she's the reason Ky has been pushing me away.

The lights are still out in his room, and I hate the thought that he might've gone running to her. I curl up on my side, closing my eyes and trying to block out my confusion, willing sleep to come.

But it's completely futile.

Thoughts turn to my birth father, and I wonder if I'll ever discover who he is or if I even want to. *Does he know about me?* Perhaps he does, and he wanted no involvement, but given my mother's apparent propensity for keeping people in the dark, I'm betting he's as clueless as I am.

The reality is I may never discover who he is, and I'd do well to forget about the whole sorry mess.

A little after three a.m., I decide to get up and fetch a mug of hot chocolate. Maybe some milky, chocolaty goodness will lull me into sleep. The lights are out in the living area as I pass through to the kitchen. I flick on the small row of spotlights over the cooker as I grab some milk from the fridge and a saucepan from the press. I've only put the pan on the hob when warm, familiar hands slide around my waist, and I almost spill milk all over myself and the floor. I open my mouth to scream, but a hand lands over my lips. Ky chuckles while I attempt to control my erratic breathing. "I swear you sneak up on me on purpose!" I hiss.

"You make it so easy," he murmurs. His teasing breath leaks over my neck as he nibbles on my skin. My retort dies on my tongue, along with any lingering irritation.

"What are you doing?" I rasp, not that I'm in any way complaining. His tempting mouth travels lower, kissing that sensitive spot on my collarbone, and I shiver all over.

"I couldn't sleep."

He continues to nuzzle my skin, his tongue darting out to taste me, and I'm quickly losing control of myself. Before it goes any further, I switch off the hob and take a step back. "We need to talk."

He pulls me to him. "Screw talking. I need to kiss you."

With willpower I never knew I possessed, I wriggle out of his arms and walk around the other side of the counter, putting the solid marble unit between us. I don't trust myself one hundred percent not to cave to monkey lust. "No kissing until we have the talk. I won't be your bit on the side, Ky. I'm an all or nothing girl."

He rubs his thumb and forefinger over his stubbly jaw, not removing his eyes from mine. "You could never be that for me. It's always been *you*. Only you."

"I knew it! You better spill your guts. Right. Now." I cross my arms and send him my best stern look.

Propping his elbows on the counter, he shoots me a forlorn look. "It's better if you don't know how badly I've messed up."

"For God's sake, Ky!" I slam my hands down on the counter. "Quit shutting me out! I know you're with her under sufferance." I race around the counter, poking my finger in his chest. "And you're going to tell me how she's doing it this time. I'm not leaving this room until I get the truth."

His opportunistic hands snake around my waist, and he reels me in flush to his body. "You're not helping with the no-kissing rule." He pins me with heated eyes that look close to combustion. "I want to taste your mouth so fucking badly right now. Hell." He reaches down and grabs my ass. "I want to taste every part of you. Right here. Up there on the counter. Spread out for me to feast on."

A wave of red heat spreads up my neck and onto my face. His words send my body into a tailspin, and my core pulses with need. I'm about two seconds away from hauling my ass up onto that counter when the angel on my shoulder knocks some sense into me. I shuck out of his embrace, stepping back. "Stop it. You can't say those things to me."

He stalks up to me, invading my private space again. "I can, and I will." His features soften as he reaches out to me. With great tenderness, he draws me into his chest, burying his face in my hair. "I'll tell you everything, but it's not going to make you feel any better. I was only trying to protect you."

I peer up at him, finding it extremely difficult not to melt under the adoration of his gaze. "Let's talk in the living room." I pry myself out of his embrace. "Go wait for me. I'll make us some hot chocolate."

Ky is sprawled on the long couch when I return. Wordlessly, I hand him his hot chocolate before dropping down onto the couch across from him. He frowns, patting the space alongside him. "I want you beside me."

I shake my head, blowing on the steaming goodness clasped between my hands. "We need to have a serious conversation."

"And you can't do that over here?" He looks incredulous.

"No. You'll only distract me." I take a small sip of my drink.

Grinning smugly, he turns the full strength of his seductive charm on me. "She finally admits it."

I stick out my tongue, and he laughs. "Am *I* not even a little distracting?"

He leans forward, and his molten eyes shimmer with desire. "Oh, you're more than a little distracting, Faye. You're like the most addictive drug. Trying to stay away from you is killing me, and it's getting real old."

I take a large slurp of my drink, more than pleased at his admission. "Technically, there is nothing stopping us now. I'm not your sister."

His expression turns sympathetic. "I'm sorry I left you to deal with the aftermath on your own. How are you feeling about this afternoon?"

I pull my feet up onto the couch, shivering a tad in my sleep shorts and short-sleeved top. I rub my tired eyes. "A bit all over the place."

"I'll bet."

"I mean, I'm glad we're not related like that. That we haven't done anything wrong, but I'm still in the dark in relation to my birth father, and I'm struggling to work out how I feel about that."

"It's a lot to take in. I still can't get my head around the fact that Kaden and Keven have a different dad, and I've had two weeks to process it."

"If everyone kept it in their pants, the world would be a less complex place." I shiver as another blast of cool air raises goose bumps on my arms.

Ky chuckles as he gets up and drops down beside me without invitation. He holds his arm out, and I survey it like he's just asked me to snuggle up to a nuclear weapon. He chuckles again. "You're cold. Stop being silly. Come here."

I chew on my lip as a vicious battle rages internally. Before I can make up my mind, I'm finagled into his side, and his arm wraps around my waist. "You're right. I'm not with Addison by choice. That fucking bitch has me by the balls. Every time I have to touch her, hell, every time I'm in her company, I want to hurl. Everything about her irritates the fuck out of me. I can barely tolerate looking at her."

A sarcastic sneer spreads across my mouth. I can't help it. "Well, you sure fooled me. You put on one hell of a show."

Putting his drink down, he twists me around so I'm facing him. His pained expression speaks volumes. "I'm so sorry you had to see that. It's why I didn't want you there, but you've got to believe me when I say it's only been for show. And I had to put on a good one, because if I don't live up to her expectations, she'll follow through on her threat."

"Which is?"

He claws his hands through his hair. "You remember the night we caught her snooping in my father's study?" I bob my head. "That wasn't all the snooping she was doing."

I gasp as the penny drops. "She was eavesdropping on us?"

He nods. "Worse. She recorded it and she dug up all that

shit that happened in your past. She threatened to expose our relationship and expose what happened in Ireland if I didn't go back to her."

I dig my fingernails into my thigh as a surge of anger sweeps through me. "You should've told me! I thought we were a team? How could you go back to her without at least talking to me about it?"

He stands up, fury bunching his muscles into corded knots. "You think I wanted this?" he hisses. "I didn't want to upset you or worry you especially after Dad had dropped the brother-sister bomb on us."

The blood turns to ice in my veins, and bile floods my mouth. "Please tell me she doesn't know about that?"

He sits back down, visibly calming himself. "No, but that was the main reason why I went along with it. Outing our relationship as cousins is one thing, but revealing we were in a relationship if we were brother and sister is another matter entirely. We could've been arrested, Faye. I couldn't allow that, and I didn't want that hanging over you. That's why I got so mad earlier. If that hadn't been at play, then I would've confided in you when she first approached me. Dad's caused all this crap for no justifiable reason other than he's a fucking idiot."

My anger is slowly fading away. "You still should've told me. I would rather the worry than the hurt." I look away. "You told me you loved her more than me." My anguished eyes lift, meeting his gaze dead-on. "That about killed me. Up until then I'd thought she was playing a game, but when you told me that, that was the moment I stopped believing it was blackmail."

He links our hands. "Babe. I never said I loved her more than you. I would never say that because it isn't true. I remember exactly what I said because I chose my words care-fully." I'm wracking my brain, but I can't summon the exact words he used, although my heart pounds with renewed hurt at the memory.

He caresses my cheek. "I said 'My feelings for you don't compare to how I feel about Addison and I meant it." He scoots in closer and his warm breath fans over my face. "I love you, Faye, and believe me when I say there is no love in my heart for her. There *is* no comparison." He palms my face in his two hands. "I love *you*. Only you. That hasn't changed."

My heart is pounding wildly in anticipation, and an electric undercurrent charges the tiny gap between us. His eyes pierce mine, seeking permission, and I'm damned if I can refuse him any longer.

My hands slide up his firm chest. "I love you, too. So much, Ky."

He gazes at me with a combination of want and need, lust and adoration, and I bridge that final gap, pressing my chest into his, as my hands reach around his neck, and I pull his head down to mine. We both gasp as our lips meet in a frenzied bout of kissing. I'd probably climb into his mouth if I could. I'm devouring him like some sex-crazed floozy, and I'm loving it. His tongue invades my mouth, and he angles my head, strengthening the connection, searing my mouth with passionate kisses. Desire—hot, thick, and heavy—consumes me, and I tingle all over from his taste and his touch. I push him down on the couch with force, straddling him and pressing my hips into his as he rocks up to meet me. We both groan, and I couldn't care less if we woke the whole darn house up. I need him as much as I need oxygen. More, probably.

His hands creep under my top, sending waves of delicious tremors shooting all over my skin. I jump at his touch, rolling my hips into his, while he fluidly lifts my top off. He continues worshipping my mouth with hot, addictive kisses as his hands roughly cup my breasts. I thrust into him, needy and whimpering as I suck on his lower lip. He grabs my hips, pressing me firmly down on his arousal, and we both moan again. "Fuck!" he whispers. "You're so hot like this. If you could only see yourself."

I sit up straighter, tossing my hair over my shoulders as I grind into him, emitting little moans of satisfaction as he pushes against me. His fingers creep up my thighs, moving in a teasing fashion under the flimsy material of my shorts until they hover right where I need them. "Please," I rasp, taken aback at how breathy and needy I sound.

Super-quick, he flips us around so I'm on my back with his powerful body looming over me. "You don't have to beg me, baby. I'm gonna make you feel so good."

Oh, how I've longed to hear those words coming from his mouth again.

His lips collide with mine while he carefully lowers his body on top of me. My legs go around his waist on auto-pilot, and we grind against each other as his mouth moves in a trail down my neck and over my breasts, before stalling at my stomach. His gaze darkens as his fingers play with the band of my shorts. Slowly, he peels them down my legs until I'm bare in front of him. Although it's unlikely anyone will walk in on us at this hour, the chance that we could get caught only adds to the adrenaline rush. Every part of me is coiled tight, and anticipation has me writhing like a snake underneath him.

"You're so beautiful like this." He brushes a feather-soft kiss against one hip, and I moan so loudly it's a wonder the entire neighborhood hasn't heard. He laughs quietly as his fingers caress my other hip, and I'm about ready to scream with frustration when he finally lowers his head. When his mouth brushes against me there, I almost buck off the couch. Keeping a firm hand on my stomach, he nudges my thighs apart and gets to work. I bury my head in a cushion, whimpering into the material as he tastes me, every sweep of his tongue more insistent than the last. When I shatter, he continues to worship me as blissful tremors rock my world, only stopping when he's exhausted every last gasp.

My hair is a mass of knotty strands as I release my face from the cushion and attempt to get my breathing in check. Ky crawls up to me, draping himself around my back as his arms encircle my waist. "Happy, baby?"

I scoot around to face him, slipping my hand between us as I kiss him sweetly. I palm my hand over the bulge in his jeans and he curses. "Lie back, sexy," I demand, shoving his shoulders down. I yank my clothes back on quickly, smirking when I spot his unhappy scowl. "Take your shirt off," I demand, because I'm dying to feast on his chiseled torso. "I want you naked."

"I like you bossing me around," he purrs, tugging the shirt up over his head.

I dip my head and press a firm kiss to his lips. "Good," I whisper. "'Cause you can expect plenty more of that in your future."

He complains briefly when my mouth leaves his, and I start nibbling along his jaw. I pepper his neck and chest with kisses as I travel down his body, marveling at all the defined ridges and curves of his body and the way he jumps under my touch. I flick the button on his jeans and pull them down his legs with force. Propping up on his elbows, he chuckles. "Damn, Faye. You're eager."

Removing his boxers, I lick my lips as I kneel up, surveying the arousal that is all for me. "Oh, baby, you've no idea." I pin him with a sultry look, and I'm rewarded with a lusty growl. "Now lie back down and be a good boy," I tease, wrapping my hand around him as I lower my head.

I return the favor and then some, relishing the way he

moans and moves underneath me. I latch on when it's clear he's at the point of no return, staying with him as each powerful wave rockets through him.

After, I pull his boxers and jeans back up and curl into his side, resting my head on his bare chest.

"I can't get enough of you." His fingers wind through my hair. "And I've missed you so much."

"Me, too."

Silence settles in the room, and though there is other stuff to discuss, neither one of us seems eager to go there. I snuggle in closer to him, swinging my leg over his as he rains kisses on my head.

After a little while, he shifts, and I lift my head up, peering directly into his eyes.

He stares at me. "You feel so perfect wrapped up in my arms. I could stay here with you all day long and never grow tired of it." He kisses my nose.

I beam up at him. "That's sweet."

"It's the truth." He gulps, and I brace myself. "I need to ask you something."

"Okay."

"Do you have feelings for Brad?"

I prop up on an elbow, leaning my hand delicately on his chest. "Do I care about Brad? Yes. He's a great guy, and a great friend, but that's all it is. There's no spark. Not like there is with you."

Air leaks out of his mouth in grateful relief. "Good. At least I won't have to beat his ass again."

I slap his chest. "No more fighting! Especially not with Brad."

He grins, pulling me down for another soul-sucking kiss. We're both panting when we break apart. "Shit, Faye. I've never felt like this with anyone. I don't think I'll ever get enough of you."

"Me either. I want the whole shebang with you, Ky. I want you to be my everything, but I can't do that with the threat of Addison constantly looming over us. I want you to end it with her. For good this time. Let her expose our relationship and my past. I don't care." I press a light kiss to his mouth. "I just want to be with you."

His arms encircle my waist, and he pulls us up into a seated position. I'm sitting in his lap with my legs off to one side. "I want that, too, but it's not that simple."

Yep, figured he might say that. Nothing about Addison is simple. Aggravation starts to well inside me. "What haven't you said?"

"That wasn't her only form of blackmail." His face contorts sourly.

"Out with it."

"She recorded her and Kal having sex that time. If I don't stay with her, she'll release it to Lana and her legal team, and they'll use it to destroy him."

Chapter Twenty-Six

"Oh my God, she's a real piece of work," I exclaim, shaking my head in disbelief. "You know what this means, too?" All the dots are joining in my head. "She has to be behind the recording you were sent." It's the only logical explanation.

"I've come to that same conclusion, and I think Jeremy was in on it too. Those two are thick as thieves and hell-bent on destroying me." He sighs, trailing his fingers up and down my arms.

"I don't get it though." My brow puckers. "Why break you up only to get back together again? It makes no sense."

"Don't even attempt to pick apart her thought process. It's a waste of time. I've never been able to figure out what's going on in her head."

"That reminds me." I turn in his lap. "I need to tell you something." I proceed to tell him about spying on Addison at her house, what Rose and I overheard, and how I asked Keven to dig into her background. Ky throws back his head and laughs. "What's so funny?"

"I asked him the very same thing."

"Huh." I rub my temple. "I'm beginning to doubt your brother's expertise. He's only come up empty-handed so far."

Ky grins. "That's a bit harsh. He's swamped with course work, and we have him searching for Lana too, and he has other stuff he does on the side."

His grin disappears, but I don't go there. I haven't forgotten those dodgy-looking dudes Keven was in the alley with outside the restaurant, and I've a fair idea that whatever he's mixed up in isn't good or legal. "Well, we need to talk to him. To get him to prioritize his Addison investigation because you can't break it off with her otherwise." It kills me to say that, but I don't doubt Addison will follow through on her threat.

"I know. I'm sorry, but I can't risk her releasing that tape of Kal before the trial."

"That's almost a month away." I can't disguise my unhappiness.

He holds me even closer. "I hate it too, but I have to keep pretending until I can kick her to the curb."

A repugnant thought enters my mind, settling in my stomach like rancid milk. I can't ask him this to his face so I bury myself in his neck before opening my mouth. "Are you sleeping with her?" I whisper.

He grips my shoulders and forces me to look at him. "No, and I won't be going there. You have my word." His body shakes with silent laughter. "I told her I'm being treated for herpes and that the doc has said no sex for a few months. Plus, I lied and said Mom had banned her from the house, and now I'm banned from hers, so there's less opportunity for her to pester me for sex."

Even the thought of her pestering him for sex makes me want to gouge her eyeballs out and rip every hair from her head. At least I won't have to stomach them pawing at one another in the house. I slide off his lap, clamping a hand over his mouth to quell his protest. "You need to tell me where you're going with her so I can avoid the same place. I don't want a repeat of the party."

"Why do you think I didn't want you there?" He tucks my hair behind my ears. "I'm hella sorry you had to see that."

"It's okay." And it is. I know now that he was trying to protect me and Kal in the best way he knew how. Doesn't mean he wasn't an idiot for trying to handle it on his own. "But in future, you tell me everything. You have to stop trying to protect me. Either we're a team or we're not. There's no middle ground."

He drapes his arm around my shoulder. "We're a team, and I won't shut you out in future. I promise."

I lean into him, kissing him briefly and pulling back before he can take it any further. "I can't be with you while you're with her." I hold up a finger when he opens his mouth to argue. "I know you're only faking it, but I can't have you kissing and touching me when you've come straight from her. I just ... I can't deal with that."

"Babe." He leans in to kiss me, but I pull back, shaking my head. "I'm hardly with her at all. I've been keeping myself occupied so I have minimal spare time to spend with her. Please." He laces his hands in my hair, pressing his forehead to mine. "I can't bear more separation."

I want to say to hell with it all, but I have some self-respect. I meant what I said before. It's all or nothing. I won't share him. Even if it is a lie. I pull back and stand up. "I can't do it, Ky. I love you, and I want you, but you can't touch me when you're still with her. Let's exert pressure on Keven to dig up some dirt, and when we're ready, we'll get rid of her for good. On our terms."

"Okay." He stands up, pressing his lips fleetingly to mine.

"I'll talk to Keven, and I'll stay away, but only because I love you, and you need this. Don't think for one second that I won't be missing you like crazy, because I will."

The next two weeks crawl by in maddening slow motion. Ky has stayed true to his word, and our paths have barely crossed. I miss him so much, and some days the temptation to say feck it, storm his room, and throw myself at him is so intense that I have to leave the house before I act on it.

There's no denying things have settled down now that James is back. The tension between him and Alex is still unbearable, but at least he's hired a new housekeeper and gardener, and he's involving himself more with his boys. I regularly catch him playing Xbox with Kal and Keaton, and he's insisted that Kaden and Keven show their faces the last two Sundays for dinner.

Alex still hasn't returned to the office, but she's up bright and early every morning, dressed in a business suit, as she heads to her home office. She hides in her room most nights, blatantly avoiding James, and I'm sure there's a glass or two of wine involved, but it's hardly my place to criticize.

Brad has also been keeping his distance. We still travel to and from school together, and we always meet for lunch, but outside of that, he keeps largely to himself, and I hate that there's this blatant tension between us, but I don't know how to fix it. I've noticed him and Ky disappearing together a few times, and I'm happy they are trying to put their differences behind them.

Brad and I are driving home from school on Tuesday when I notice the same black SUV in the line of traffic behind us. "I think we're being followed again."

Brad peers through the mirror and frowns. "You could be right, and I think I know why."

That captures my interest. He veers off the road, pulling into a layby and killing the engine. We both stare at the blacked-out SUV as it glides by. He rummages in the glove box, extracting a wrinkled paper. "Rose gave me this at lunch. I was going to show you back at the house."

I unfold the paper, and my jaw slackens as the front page is revealed. I read the article quickly, my blood boiling at every salacious word. Courtney has been exposed as the woman James was having an affair with, and there are several candid shots of the two of them together in rather compromising poses. But it's the copy of the official Kennedy Apparel memo on page two that incenses me. "I don't believe this." I shake my head.

"It's totally suspect," Brad agrees.

"It's a load of crap." My eyes bounce between Brad and the paper. "There's no way Alex would willingly promote Courtney after what happened. How does someone go from PA to VP literally overnight?" My tone is incredulous. "Ky is going to freak out over this."

"He already is."

"He knows?"

Brad leans back, sighing. "I spoke to him earlier. He's been getting hell at O.C. all day over it." I chew on the inside of my cheek. "I know you asked him to give you space while he's faking it with Addison, but he could probably use your support today. Especially if the newspaper report is correct and a date has been set for the divorce hearing."

I retrieve my phone and tap out a quick message. Ky replies instantly. He's at the house with Keven, and adrenaline courses through my veins. If Keven is over mid-week, then maybe it's because he has some news for us at last. I try to temper my expectation, but I'm as giddy as a goat the rest of the drive.

The lobby is thronged with men and women in crisp suits when we arrive back home. Alex is shaking hands with a tall, gray-haired lady in an elegant red suit as I attempt to sneak past undetected. She latches on to my elbow, smiling as she waves her associates off. Brad shoots me a knowing wink as he slips into the corridor unnoticed. "I need a favor," she murmurs under her breath as she closes the front door.

"Okay," I reply, intrigued and confused as I follow her up the steps to her private suite.

She pulls me into her bathroom, looking circumspectly over her shoulder before shutting the door behind us. She talks in quiet whispers. "I need you to orchestrate a meeting with Courtney, and I'd like you to plant this listening device in her watch." She removes a small brown envelope from her pocket and offers it to me.

Keeping my hands at my sides, I stare at her as if she's gone mad.

Nervously, she smooths one hand down the front of her black skirt. "I know it's a lot to ask, but I can't think of anyone else who can get access to Courtney to do this."

"And you think I can?" I sit down on the lid of the toilet seat, while she perches on the side of the tub.

"James is going to tell the boys tonight that he's officially dating Courtney and that we're going ahead with our divorce. You need to bide your time, and then tell him that you'd like to meet her, to get to know her better. He'll set up something, and then you just need to find a way of installing the chip."

My eyes blink excessively as my mind grapples with this latest information. "What the hell is going on, Alex? Did you really promote her to VP?"

She knots her hands in her lap. "I had no choice, and she'll be our new VP unless she makes some catastrophic error in the period before her promotion takes effect, which I highly doubt, because she's too conniving to make a mistake when she's so close to everything she wants."

"I still don't understand." I frown.

Alex leans forward on her knees. "There's a lot I don't know yet, which is why I need ears on her." She gestures toward the brown envelope in her hand. "She's trying to ruin me, to take everything from me, and she nearly succeeded, but thankfully, I've come to my senses in time. I'm not going down without a fight." Steely resolve glimmers in her eyes, and I'm relieved to see the woman I first met when I moved here. "What she fails to comprehend is that I can be a formidable enemy in my own right. She's going to regret this. If it's the last thing I do, I'll bring that bitch down. She's going to get a taste of her own medicine."

Hell, yeah. There's nothing I'd like to see more. I take the envelope from her hand. "I'll do it. I'll help you."

She exhales gratefully. "Thank you, Faye. I knew I could count on you."

I'm about to head downstairs when she pulls me into an embrace. "You've no idea how much this means to me," she whispers in my ear.

"I want to help, and I've never liked her. You know, when I first met her, I was taken aback at how much she looked like you. That's on purpose, isn't it?"

"I think so. I didn't realize she had issues with me until it was too late. I was too busy to see what was right under my nose."

I pat her arm. "Whatever is going on, I'm sure it isn't your fault."

A strained expression appears on her face. "We're not completely faultless in this. If you give people ammunition, they won't hesitate to use it."

She kisses me on the cheek, smiling. "I'm not going to go

quietly, and she'll soon realize that." I'm delighted she's reclaimed her fighting spirit. Something tells me she's going to need it.

"What was that all about?" Kal asks when I reach the bottom of the stairs. He's lounging against the wall, examining me with inquisitive eyes.

I tweak his nose playfully. "That's for me to know and you to find out!" I tease, preferring to deflect rather than outwardly lie. He pushes off the wall, looping his arm through mine as he smacks a loud kiss on my cheek. "What's that for?"

"That's for putting a smile on Mom's face for the first time in weeks."

Chapter Twenty-Seven

I'm walking to my bedroom when the sounds of girlish giggling piques my curiosity. Bypassing my bedroom, I head on to the games room. A petite girl with a mass of strawberry-blonde corkscrew curls is seated beside Keaton on the sofa, laughing at something he's said.

"Hey." I saunter into the room, smiling at my cousin. "Are you going to introduce me?"

"Melissa, this is Faye. Faye, Melissa."

She gives me a small nervous wave. "Hi." She's softly spoken, and a delicate flush stains her cheeks.

I plunk down on the edge of the couch, beside my cousin. "Nice to meet you. I was beginning to think you were a figment of Keaton's imagination."

Keaton nudges my shoulder. "Funny, ha, ha."

"How did you two meet?" Keaton has been extremely taciturn over his girlfriend, and I know next to nothing about her.

"We go to O.C. together," Melissa confirms. "And we've known each other since sixth grade." Her gray eyes lock on Keaton's, and she beams at him. It's so darn cute.

"Melissa is friends with Brad's sister, Hope," Keaton adds.

"You must miss her."

"I do." She bobs her head. "And I didn't even get a chance to say goodbye."

"You should talk to Brad while you're here. I'm sure he'd love to see you. He misses his family a lot."

"We've spoken a few times. I was hoping he might've had some way of contacting Melissa."

I stand up. "It's a sucky situation," I empathize. "I'd love to stay and chat, but my shift starts soon. Catch you later, dude." Keaton and I high-five. "Nice meeting you, Melissa. Hopefully, I'll see you again soon."

"Faye!" Ky calls out as I stroll past his room. I turn around and my heart thumps excitedly at the sight of him. He's wearing a fitted gray shirt that hugs his muscular chest perfectly and expensive-looking jeans that showcase his toned, long legs. Visions of sliding my hands up under his shirt have me hot and bothered in a millisecond, and I shove my hands in my pockets to fight the urge to run to him and live out my fantasy.

He jerks his head to the side. "Keven is here. He has some news. You need to hear this." He opens his door wide as I step toward him, my heart pounding harder with every step I take. Keven and Brad are in the room, slouched in chairs, talking quietly among themselves. I step into the room, and Ky closes the door behind me. I'm acutely aware of his warm, inviting body at my back. "Hey. You doing okay?" he whispers in my ear.

My entire body trembles, and in a moment of weakness, I lean back, stifling a moan when he presses up against me. The talking in the room stops, and we jump apart but not before Keven sends us a curious stare. Ky reclines against the wall, crossing one ankle over the other while I stand rooted to the spot, uneasy under Keven's scrutiny. "Keven has proof that Addison and Jeremy were behind the email and the recording I was sent," Ky confirms.

I whirl around. "Fantastic. We can use it to get her to back off?" I hate how much hope there is in my voice.

Ky pushes off the wall and walks toward me. "I wish it were that easy." He smooths a hand over my hair. "She recorded it without Brad's consent, but that's all we have to bargain with. It's not enough, and she'll know it if we confront her now."

"We need to keep digging," I surmise, and there's no disguising my disappointment.

Ky reels me into his chest, circling his arms around my waist. I cling onto him as he kisses the top of my head. "I'm afraid so, babe."

"Would someone mind explaining what's going on?" Keven sounds bewildered as he stares at us.

Tucking me into his side, Ky turns us around to face his brother. My mouth opens and closes as I struggle to explain the convoluted mess that is our relationship. Ky has no such qualms. "We love each other, and we'd be together if it wasn't for my manipulative ex."

Keven's eyes dart wide as he folds his arms and stares at us with an indecipherable expression. "Do Mom and Dad know about this?"

"Yep. Kal and Keaton, too." Ky's arms tighten around me, and it's hard to restrain my sigh of contentment.

Keven turns to Brad. "I thought you two had a thing."

A flash of hurt splays over his handsome face before he looks down at his feet. "Nah, man. We're just faking it to keep heat off Faye at school." He gives a lopsided shrug.

"Uh-huh." Keven's gaze bounces between the three of us.

"What the hell does that mean?" Ky's whole demeanor transforms instantly.

"Nothing. Only an observation."

Ky glares at him.

"I hope you two know what you're in for when this gets out."

"I don't care." Ky runs his hand up and down my arm, igniting the usual flame inside me. "Faye is all I want. I can deal with whatever shit people throw at me."

Brad kicks at imaginary dirt on the floor with the toe of his boot.

"You should tell Kaden. He'll be pissed if he's the last to know. You know how he gets."

"Don't say a word. I'll tell him."

"Fine." Keven rises. "I'll keep digging for dirt on Addison, and I'll let you know as soon as I find anything."

"Thanks, man," Ky says. "You sticking around?"

"Yeah. Mom wants me to stay for dinner, and apparently, we have another family meeting later."

"I heard, and it's hardly a coincidence they want to talk to us after today's reports. The press is having a field day."

"Fucking parasites," Keven seethes on his way out. "Catch you later."

Brad is up on his feet, scurrying out after Keven. "Homework," he mumbles, shooting us a weak smile.

"Why is Brad acting all weird?" I frown.

He sighs. "Why'd ya think?"

I don't want to even acknowledge the implication let alone discuss it so I ignore the question, slipping out from under his arm. "I need to get ready for work."

Ky presses his lips to my forehead, and a tiny whimper slips out of my mouth. "I miss you," he whispers. "Please, leave your window unlocked tonight. I need to hold you."

I worry my lip between my teeth. "That'll only make things worse, and you know we won't be able to keep our hands to ourselves if we're in bed together."

A seductive grin lifts the corners of his mouth. "Why do you think I suggested it?"

I smile despite myself. "You're incorrigible." I step around him, smoothing a hand over his delectable butt. "And far too tempting." I jump out of the way before he can drag me back into his arms. A girl only has so much self-control.

I'm at the door when he calls out to me. "So, what about later?"

I spin around and send him a cheeky grin. "I'll think about it."

I'm still thinking about it an hour later as I arrive at work.

"Girl, I know that grin," Rose smirks. "I thought you and loverboy were steering clear of one another until you've dealt with the trash?" I've told Rose the latest with Ky and me so she's completely up to speed. I lean against the counter with my back facing the open floor. It's quiet in here tonight for a change.

"We are, but my willpower is stretched to the limit." I fill her in on Ky's tempting offer.

"The girls in school would parade butt naked through town for the chance to have Kyler Kennedy warming their bed, and here you are considering turning him down." She fake tut-tuts and I bark out a laugh.

"I can't stand the thought that he's coming straight from her to me." My good humor instantly dissipates. "You know that."

"He's not coming straight from her *bed* to yours. Besides,

how is what he's doing all that different from what you're doing with Brad?"

"I'm not kissing Brad or dry humping him against the wall." I shudder as the image of Ky and Addison at the party replays in vivid Technicolor in my mind. Ugh.

"For the record," a familiar voice says behind me. "I've no problem with either of those things. No issue whatsoever."

I spin around, slamming a hand over my chest where my heart is pounding frantically against my ribcage. "Jeez! Brad! You scared the heck out of me. I didn't know you were there."

"Just call me Mr. Invisible," he drawls without any trace of humor. At the last second, he takes stock of himself, offering me a clearly forced smile.

"Faye." A stern voice chastises me, and I mentally curse. I turn around and face my boss. David is standing in the doorway with a strange look on his face. "Stop flirting with your boyfriend and get out on the floor. There are customers that need serving."

My cheeks flare up and I'm too embarrassed to correct him or to argue the point. "Of course, David. I'm sorry."

Rose's brows lift as she shoots me a "What the hell's gotten up his butt?" look.

David has barely had any engagement with us since he returned to work after his hospital stay, preferring to hide out in his office rather than speak with his staff. Most shifts, he comes out at some point and stands wordlessly behind the counter, quietly observing everything, before ducking back into his office for the rest of the night. He's lucky we are conscientious and that we can effectively run this place with our eyes closed. I'm not sure what I've done to annoy him, and it hardly seems fair. Rose flirts with every male that steps foot in this joint, and he doesn't seem to have any issue with her.

David sends Rose home an hour before the diner closes,

and I'm left twiddling my thumbs with nothing to do and no one to talk to. It's like a ghost town in here tonight, and apart from a couple of guys at the counter and one full booth, the place is empty.

I start the cleanup when the chef on duty strolls out the door with a wave, and the last of our customers leave. The empty quietness is a little creepy so I grab a rake of quarters from my purse and line up some tunes on the jukebox. My hips sway to the music as I mop the floors and wipe down the booths. I'm cleaning the hot plated area when David appears in the doorway, crossing his arms as he frowns at me. I stop what I'm doing, glancing up at him with an inquisitive look as I wonder if I've forgotten to do something. David stares at me wordlessly, his frown expanding. His lips turn down, and his eyes narrow as he steps toward me. All the tiny hairs on the back of my neck lift, and I gulp as a sudden uneasy feeling sweeps over me.

"Is something wrong?" I ask, hating that my voice trembles a little.

"I don't know. You tell me?" He glares at me, and instinctively I take a step back toward the counter.

I force a smile on my face. "Nope. Nothing's wrong. Everything's good. I'm almost finished and my ride should be here at any moment."

He takes a step toward me, and I move back again. "Your ride?" His face contorts unpleasantly, and I instinctively step back, my spine hitting the solid edge of the counter.

David moves in, planting his hands on either side of me, effectively caging me in. I jolt back, scared by the ferocious look on his face. I don't know what I've done to set him off, but he's scaring the hell out of me. I know the last few weeks have been very difficult for him, and I sensed he hadn't fully recovered from his breakdown, but this is still way out of line.

Straightening up, I put my hands on his chest and shove. "Please move away from me. This is completely inappropriate and you're scaring me."

He reaches up, yanking my hat off my head and removing the tie from my hair. My hair falls in tousled curls down my back and he rubs a few strands between his fingers. "I know you do it on purpose."

I shove at him again, but he doesn't budge. Adrenaline is coursing through my veins as he pins me with a contemptuous glare. "You're just like your momma."

Wait? What? "I don't understand," I stutter, eyeing my bag on the end of the counter. I need to get to my phone. I don't know what's going on here, but I don't have a good feeling about this.

"I know you're sleeping around, and you have no idea how much it disgusts and disappoints me. You were such a sweet little girl. Where did it all go wrong?" He grabs my wrist and squeezes.

Butterflies are careening around my chest and a line of sweat coasts down my spine. "David. You need to let me go. I want to go home."

He grips my chin, pinching it painfully. "You think I don't know what you'll do when we go home? That I don't know how you sneak out of your window at night? Who is it this time? Who are you whoring with now?"

His eyes glimmer with rage, and terror grips my heart in an ironclad lock. Lifting my leg, I ram my knee into his crotch with force. He drops his hands to his groin, emitting a loud roar. I dart out of his reach, grab my bag, and run out into the corridor toward the emergency exit. My feet slap against the tiled floor as blood rushes to my ears. I race down the corridor toward the exit, glancing over my shoulder as I run. I crash into the door, nudging my shoulder against it, thrusting violently, but it doesn't budge. My heart rate spikes to coronary-inducing proportions as I look up at the large padlock securing the door at the top.

Cursing, I fumble in my bag for my phone.

"You little bitch!" David roars, and I lift my chin, screaming as he hobbles down the corridor toward me. I dash into the nearest room—his office—and shut the door, tugging the leather couch over and pushing it up against the door. A large thud knocks against the door, and David emits a guttural roar. With trembling fingers, I search for my phone. Emptying the contents of my bag on the desk, I snatch up my phone and pull up Ky's details, pressing the call button. The shunting at the door is getting more forceful, and I scream as the door opens a smidgeon and the couch moves back. My eyes flit around the room in panic.

Answer the Goddamned phone, Ky! The shrill ring tone taunts me as I work hard to quell the rising nausea. David yells and the couch moves forward some more. I scream at the top of my lungs, and my heart is beating so fast in my chest it feels like it's about to sprout wings and fly away.

The dial tone rings out, going straight to voicemail as my eyes lock on the rectangular sliding glass frame built into the far wall. David had it installed so he could keep an eye on the diner from his office. I dart toward it as Ky's recorded voice asks me to leave a message. I slide the glass window open but the space is far too narrow to get through. Glancing frantically around the room, I pick up the large dumbbell resting on the floor under David's desk as I leave a message for Ky. "Help me! Call the police! I'm at the diner, and David has lost his mind. He's going to hurt me." I scream hysterically as the couch lurches across the floor and David appears in the doorway with a murderous expression in his gaze. The phone drops out of my hand. Throwing the dumbbell at the window, I hurl myself through it as the glass shatters into pieces. My body is halfway through the frame when David grabs my legs and pulls. A sharp pain rips across my stomach and I scream.

"You're going to pay for this, Emily!" His fingers dig into my flesh as he starts pulling me back into the room. I grip the jagged edge of the frame, ignoring the pain as my fingers curl around broken glass, holding on for dear life as I kick out at him. His mouth curls up in a sneer that sends chills ricocheting all over my body. He leans toward me, and I press my feet together and push with as much strength as I can muster. He stumbles back, losing his hold and his balance, toppling over the desk with a guttural roar. All the hairs on my body lift in utter terror. I scramble out the window, barely feeling the aches and pains, adrenaline fueling my body as I crash land in the diner. My head whacks off the solid floor, and black spots blur my vision. I struggle to my feet, clutching my head in my hand. A sticky substance coats my fingers, and I sway as I inspect my hands. Blood splatters my skin and the nauseated feeling returns. Limping, I stagger toward the front door, whimpering in fright.

I've just passed the counter when I'm slammed into from behind. My terrified screams fill the air as the ground looms before me. A heavy weight pins my body down as I extend my hands in front of me. I crash to the floor, my head landing on my hands as pain explodes in my skull. A metallic taste fills my mouth and my vision blurs. I'm vaguely aware of being turned around.

David sits astride me and his meaty hands lock around my neck. "I don't want to do this, Emily, but I've got to save you from yourself." His hands tighten around my neck, constricting my airflow. I claw at his arms, eyes widening in alarm.

"Daddy loves you, baby girl." Wetness hits my face. "It will all be over soon."

My legs start thrashing about and I try to buck him off, but he's way too heavy. My arms fall slack to my side, and a blanket of darkness creeps slowly into my consciousness.

"Goodbye sweet baby girl." David's anguished voice is the last thing I hear before I black out.

Chapter Twenty-Eight

I emit a sharp gasp as I come to. The pressure on my chest has lifted and I suck in greedy lungsful of air. Twisting on my side, I vomit all over the floor. My eyes flicker open and shut, and fleeting images coast in front of me. Warm hands cup my face. "You're okay, Faye. You're going to be okay. Help is on its way."

I open my mouth to speak, but all that comes out is a hoarse, croaky sound.

"Don't try to talk. He's gone. You're safe. The ambulance will be here any minute." The husky male voice is soothing. A damp cloth moves across my mouth, and my eyes blink open. The man has dark hair and glossy blue eyes, and he looks familiar. I shiver, and my lip wobbles. Tears leak out of my eyes. "Don't cry, honey. You're going to be okay." He rests his forehead against mine. "I won't let anyone hurt you again."

My eyes drift open and shut again. Muffled sounds of multiple voices and footsteps reach my ears. I'm lifted up, and I scream as fiery, hot pain whips across my stomach. The same warm hands cover my cold fingers as my body is placed on a firm surface. A heavy blanket is placed over me, but I can't stop shivering. My head falls to the side, and my eyes open briefly. Flashing lights almost blind me, and my eyes fall shut again.

When I wake up the next time, my body is lulled by a gentle swaying motion and the persistent beep, beep of a machine. Warm hands grip mine, and I fall back asleep.

I don't know how long I'm out of it for, but when I wake again, it's to the sound of voices instantly muting. I stare at the stark white ceiling, and the glare from the bright light has me wincing. "Call the nurse," James says, and I turn toward the sound of his voice.

His concerned face appears in my peripheral vision. "Sweetheart, how are you feeling?"

I move slightly in the hospital bed, instantly conscious of the tightness around my midriff. I wiggle my hands and my toes, relieved to find both in apparent working order. My tongue darts out, moistening my dry lips. "Okay," I croak, recoiling at the sound of my raspy voice. "I think," I add in a whisper.

Ky nudges his father out of the way. His panic-stricken expression brings it all to the forefront of my mind, and I replay the scene in horrific detail. "David!" I croak, shaking and shivering as fear takes a fresh hold of me. Tears roll down my cheeks as my eyes dart around the room in alarm.

Ky grips my hand. "Ssh, baby. It's okay. The cops caught up to him. He's in jail. He can't hurt you anymore." His voice cracks on the last sentence, and my panic attack subsides.

Everything comes back to me, and I look up at Ky with new tears. "I phoned you."

He hunches over the bed, pulling my hand between both of his. "I know you did. I'm sorry, baby. I'm so fucking sorry."

I frown, puzzled. *Why is he apologizing?* He obviously called someone to come rescue me. "I don't understand."

He cringes at my scratchy voice. "I should've answered your call. I'm so sorry, Faye. For as long as I live, I'll never forgive myself for this."

James lands a hand on his shoulder. "Son, she's okay."

"That's not the point!" Ky yells, standing up and glowering at his dad. I flinch from the self-loathing in his tone. "She needed me and I wasn't there for her! She could've died!"

James tentatively pulls Ky into a brief, awkward embrace.

"It's okay," I rush to reassure him.

Ky lifts his head, and the look of self-loathing and vulnerability on his face almost kills me. Dragging a chair over, he sits down beside me. "No, it's not. Not by a long shot, but I'm going to make it up to you. She is not going to keep me from you again."

"What?"

A tormented expression contorts his beautiful face. "I was with Addison when you phoned. She saw it was you and made me ignore it. The first chance I got, I snuck out to the restroom to call you back, and that's when I listened to your message. I called Dad, but he had already been notified, so I came here as quick as I could."

A new pain blends with the existing one. He was with *her*. I nearly died tonight, and he was with *her*. I had one opportunity to reach out for help, and he was the one I reached out to. There was no hesitation, no question. I didn't call James or Brad or the cops. I called the other half of my heart, and he let me down.

He didn't answer my call because she told him not to.

I could've died because he was pandering to her needs. Because he put her first. *Again.*

Something inherent breaks irreparably inside me.

"Faye, baby. Say something." Ky is watching me with panicked eyes.

Tears stream down my face as I wrench my hand from his. "Get out."

"No! Please. I'm sorry. Don't push me away. I can't bear it."

The beeping on the machine accelerates as pain jackknifes my heart until it's a twisted, rotten, corrupted organ in my chest.

My eyes find James's. "I want him to leave." My sobs bounce off the walls. "Make him leave, please."

"Kyler." James' tone is compassionate.

"No!" Ky's voice is laced with pain.

A nurse comes bounding into the room, quickly followed by a man with wavy gray hair wearing an eye-dazzling white lab coat. "Ms. Donovan is in distress. We need everyone to wait out in the corridor," he commands.

"We'll be right outside, Faye," James reassures me, forcing Kyler out the door.

Ky twists around before the door closes, mouthing "I love you. I'm sorry."

I turn away from his anguished face, closing my eyes and praying for darkness to claim me again.

James and Alex are seated by my bed the next time I wake up. "Sweetheart, we were so worried." Alex leans over and kisses my cheek. "I'm so sorry this happened to you."

James reaches over with a cup. "The nurse said you were to drink this." I open my mouth, and he slips the straw in my mouth. The water is cool as it slides down my dry throat.

"What happened?" I croak, my vocal cords still clearly strained. "Who saved me?" That part of my ordeal is so vague.

Alex and James exchange a guarded look. "It's no one you know. A man, a visitor to Wellesley, was out for a late walk, and he saw you being attacked." James's voice quivers. "He fought David until he fled. Then he called an ambulance and waited with you."

"Mark," I whisper, as his face drifts in front of my eyes. "It was Mark."

James and Alex share a startled look. "You know that man, sweetheart?" she asks.

"He came in the diner a couple times," I explain. "I think he's a reporter. I caught him taking photos of me once." None of that matters now. Not when he saved me. James looks like he's just sucked on an entire jar of chilies. "Can I see him? Is he okay?"

Alex pats my hand. "He has a few bruises and a swollen jaw but he's fine. You don't need to worry about him."

"I need to thank him." I try to hoist myself up in the bed, crying out at the dart of pain stretching across my midriff.

"Don't sit up, honey. You've got a lot of stitches in your stomach, and you don't want to tear them." James presses a kiss to my forehead. "And don't worry about ... Mark. We've already thanked him."

"Your cousins are outside," Alex interjects, "and they're very anxious to see you. Brad and Rose too. Are you up for visitors?"

"Sure." A sharp pain pierces my chest cavity, like a dagger straight through my heart. "But not Ky. I don't want to see him."

Alex pats my hand in understanding. Then she gets up and leaves the room.

James leans forward. "I know you're upset with him, Faye, but he feels awful. He's told me what Addison is doing, and I wish he'd come to me about this sooner." He frowns a little. "I know you need some time to deal with it, but don't shut him out. He loves you, and he needs to make it up to you."

"Are you saying this for him or for you?"

The door opens as James bends over, whispering in my ear. "I'm saying it for you."

After three days, I'm discharged from the hospital on condition that I recuperate at home. I'm not allowed to do any kind of physical activity, at least until the stitches are removed in ten days.

My cousins fuss over me like you wouldn't believe. Brad drops in briefly every day after school to update me on the latest, but he doesn't hang about. Kal and Keaton barely leave my side, but all of my cousins take time every day to check in with me, either in person or over the phone, which is super sweet, and it helps me deal with the aftermath of my ordeal more than they realize.

Once the medication is reduced, and I'm more coherent, the reality of what almost happened hits me full force. I'm plagued with horrific nightmares as the terror and fear return in the middle of the night to torture me. I wake up screaming, drenched in sweat, most nights.

The police are still trying to piece together exactly what happened and why David snapped like he did. James has Dan staying close to the investigative team, but every time I ask, I'm told there's no news yet. I've a strong suspicion that he knows more than he's letting on, but I can't fault him for trying to shield me from the truth for a little while longer.

Ky turns up every day begging me to talk to him, but I turn him away. It still hurts too much. One part of me knows I'm being unfair, because I'd agreed he should prolong the farce with Addison for Kal's sake, but the more vulnerable part of my brain latches onto the rejection and the hurt and refuses to let go.

It's just under a week before Kal's trial, and I wake up in the early hours of the morning screaming and crying and gasping for air. This nightmare was the worst one yet. I hold my neck, running my thumbs up and down my skin to reassure myself I'm still here. Still breathing. I'm not in danger anymore. I swear I can almost feel David's thick fingers squeezing the air from my throat. A sob escapes my mouth and I shiver all over. Ky is at my side so fast I wonder if he was actually sleeping in the corridor outside waiting for this to happen. He slides into the bed, cradling me without invitation, but I'm far too upset to push him away. He holds me close while I bawl into his chest, soaking his shirt with my tears. He presses kisses to my hair while I shake in his arms, my entire body trembling and quaking against him. He continues to comfort me without speaking, and I cling to him like a limpet, desperately needing his strength to ground me. Gradually, my weeping subsides, and my heart rate returns to normal. I lift my head, shucking out of his grasp, refusing to look at him. "Thank you." I sniffle. "I'm okay now. You can go back to bed."

I turn on the opposite side, lying down as I pull the covers up over me.

"Faye, I'm sorry I let you down. So unbelievably sorry. Please stop shutting me out. Let me help you now—I'm begging you." Cautiously, he moves behind me, lining his body up against mine outside the duvet. His arms snake around my waist, and I close my eyes, struggling against the urge to melt into his touch. "I love you. I love you so much. I've spoken with Kal, and he knows the score. I'm going to tell Addison to go to hell tomorrow. I'm finished with her. She's not going to come between us again."

I twist around urgently. "No! You can't do that. Not this close to Kal's trial."

"I want you back. I need you. You need me. I'm done with her ruining everything."

His fingers meander in and out of my hair, and I could close the gap between us so easily. His lips look enticingly soft and inviting, and all it would take is one press of my mouth against his, and he'd take this pain away. But I can't forget so easily. It would be a momentary distraction and nothing else.

I shake my head. "You can't let your brother down. He needs you. It's only one more week."

The intense look on his face sends shivers through me. "You're more important."

I push away from him, anger rampaging through me. "Don't say that! It's too bloody late!"

He combs his fingers through his hair. "Then what? What will it take for you to forgive me? Tell me and I'll do it."

He looks so tortured, so distressed, that I take pity on him. Reaching out, I lace my fingers in his. "I've already forgiven you." Shock splatters across his features. "But," I cut in quickly when I see the euphoria in his eyes, "it makes no difference to how I feel. I can understand why you did what you did, and forgive you for it, but I can't forget that you still chose her over me."

"Faye, you know that's not what it was." His eyes beseech me. "I would never willingly choose her over you!"

My anger returns, jumping up and slapping me in the face. "I know no such thing!" I hiss. "I would never have phoned you when you were with her unless it was an emergency." I prod my finger in his chest. "You knew that, and still you chose to ignore my call. You can't tell me you had no other choice when I know you could've made up an excuse later."

"I wasn't thinking clearly in the moment!" he pleads.

"No, you weren't." A bitter taste floods my mouth. "You were too busy making out with her!" I'm yelling at this point, but I'm beyond caring. His face pales as realization dawns. "Yeah, I've seen the pics she posted online. While I was almost strangled to death, you were enjoying a lap dance from that conniving whore. So, tell me, please, how the fuck am I supposed to forget that?!"

The anguish and torment on his face is clear as day, and it's challenging not to react to his primitive reaction, but anger and frustration are still clouding my judgment, and I can't offer him any solace. He's hurt me more than he realizes. His mournful eyes acknowledge my thought process, and he starts retreating into himself. I watch as he shuts down, sheltering himself behind an impassive mask, in the only way he knows. It's not a healthy way to deal with trauma, but it's his usual coping mechanism.

I hate this. Hate that she has come between us again, but I can't change how I feel.

"What are you doing in here?" Kal asks, storming into the room in nothing but a pair of gym shorts. "Get out. You're upsetting her."

Ky ignores him, sticking dark, troubled eyes on me instead. "You think I don't hate myself for that? You think I don't have my own nightmares? You think this is easy for me?" His eyes glisten with unshed tears. "I. Love. You. And I want to make it up to you. I will never let you down again. Please, baby. I am so fucking sorry. You have no idea how much. Please let me in."

Tears cascade down my cheeks as Kal slips into the bed, and I scoot over into his arms. Ky's shoulders droop as all the fight leaves him. "I can't, Ky. I wish I could, but I just can't."

Another five days pass. Ky doesn't come near me, and I'd like to say it eases my heartache, but in all honesty, it makes no difference. My heart still hurts like it's been put through a shredder. My stitches are removed, and I'm left with a long, jagged scar scissoring right across the center of my stomach. Bye-bye bikini-wearing days. Thankfully, there was no permanent damage to my vocal cords and I'm sounding like myself again. The rest of my injuries have fully healed, and I consider it lucky that I survived with so few permanent physical reminders. Mentally, I haven't escaped unscathed, and I don't know how long it's going to take for me to fall asleep at night unafraid.

When the police show up at the house later on—the day before Kal's trial is due to start—I fully expect it to be the reason for their visit, so I'm hugely surprised when James calls me up to his study. Keaton comes with me for moral support. Ky is already in the room, standing sternly in front of the fire, almost challenging me to evict him. I can't look at him for the pain and longing in my heart. Such utter confusion is tearing me apart, and it's a wonder I'm so composed.

"Take a seat, sweetheart," James says, pulling out a chair for me. "The officers want to update us on David's case." I shudder as giant chills swathe me in an icy layer of dread, dropping into the chair as my limbs give out underneath me. "David has confessed to killing his daughter, Emily, and Jessie Higgins, the girl who was murdered last year. He has also coughed up to your attempted murder." I shiver profusely. Ky makes a move to come to me, but I stall him with one look. Keaton sits on the arm of the chair, slinging his arm around me. I lean my head on his shoulder, fisting handfuls of his sweater while the police officer carries on. "However, he has been diagnosed with a psychotic illness and deemed mentally incompetent to stand trial at this time."

"What exactly does that mean?" Ky asks with a growl.

"He has been remanded to a specialist psychiatric facility until such a time as he's deemed fit to stand trial. The court generally doesn't allow more than four months. He'll be assessed again then, and once he's deemed medically competent, a date will be set for his trial. Given his confession, and the evidence against him, we doubt he'll ever see the light of day again." He crouches down in front of me. "I hope this gives you some peace of mind."

"Why?" I whisper. "Why did he do it? Why me?"

The officer straightens up, removing a photograph from his inside jacket pocket. "This was Emily."

He hands it to me, and I spot the resemblance instantly. I hadn't noticed when I saw the photo of Zoe's cousin at the memorial, but there's no denying it now. We all look alike. This photo is clearly a school photo, and Emily is smiling broadly at the camera, her entire face radiant and glowing. Her wide blue eyes are innocent and full of hope, and I choke on a strangled sob. My hand flies to my hair as I scan her thick, long dark hair, falling in smooth sheets down her back exactly like mine. "I look like her." My voice is barely louder than a whisper.

"In his mind, you *were* her. Or at least that's what the psychologists have said. It seems his wife was regularly unfaithful, and their marriage was defined by a history of vicious fights. Combine that scenario with an undiagnosed psychotic disorder, a drug abuse problem, a delusional mindset, and it caused him to snap. By all accounts, Emily was a sweet, innocent child, but he caught her sneaking out to meet her boyfriend one night, and he went berserk. Convinced himself she was going to turn out like her mother so he killed her to maintain her innocence."

I clamp a hand over my mouth.

"God," James says, shaking his head sadly. "That poor child."

"At least he's been stopped before he killed anyone else,

and we can give Jessie's family some closure." The officer plants a gentle hand on my shoulder. "I know what you've been through has been very traumatic, and I understand you've had a difficult year, but you are still very much alive, Ms. Donovan. He tried to take your life, but you fought back. Don't let him succeed after all."

Chapter Twenty-Nine

The officer's words are still reverberating through my mind the next day as I sit in the back of the car en route to the court for Kal's trial. While my brain can process the logic and wisdom of his statement, try telling that to my fragile heart. I've dealt with a lot, and I always get through it. Ultimately, I know this won't be any different. It may not seem like that now, when I'm trapped in this hazy fog, but I know the path will clear.

Sighing to myself, I force all thoughts of my own situation aside to focus on today. My fingers creep along the seat, and I curl my hand in Kal's. His fingers grip mine almost painfully, and we stay like that the entire journey.

The heaving crowd waiting outside the courthouse is intimidating. The second the car door opens, the noise almost deafens me. I keep a firm hold on Kal's hand as we fight our way through the media frenzy. Kal and I are surrounded by his brothers as we slowly make our way forward with James and Alex holding up the rear. Brad refused to come with us. He was afraid the media speculation surrounding his family would bring additional unwarranted attention. Inspecting the baying crowds around us, I don't think Brad's presence would've made any difference. An enlarged team of bodyguards keep the paparazzi at arm's length as we advance toward the courthouse. Questions are thrown at Kal left and right, but he ignores them as his legal team has advised. Cameras are shoved in our faces, and we keep our heads down as we ascend the steps together.

Dan Evans is waiting in the lobby of the courthouse with the criminal attorney representing Kal, when we finally navigate the melee outside. Kal and James go with the legal team for last-minute prep while the rest of us make our way to the courtroom.

We are seated in the front row, directly behind the area reserved for the defense. I scan the room for Lana or her parents, but there's no sign of them yet. My eyes locate Ky, seated at the opposite end of the row, and I can't look away. He returns my sorrowful gaze, and so many unspoken words fill the empty space. I want to end this gulf between us, to get things back on track, but I can't. I can't help how I feel. Sadly, I avert my eyes, knotting my hands in my lap. Keaton slings his arm around my shoulders and kisses my temple. "You still love him," he whispers, and I nod. "But it's not enough," he adds, and I'm seriously impressed at his intuition.

I give him a quick kiss on his cheek. "No, unfortunately not."

"Give it time. He's not going anywhere, and he'll be waiting for you when you're ready."

"When did you get so wise?" I murmur, smiling.

He shrugs. "Guess I was just born perfect."

My smile widens, and I'd laugh if we were in a different environment. Approaching footfalls have us all turning around in our seats. Kal walks into the room, flanked by Alex, James, and his legal team. James has a brief word with the attorney before taking his seat in our row. Kal sits down in front of us alongside the three men and one woman who make up his legal representation.

Time seems to stand still as we sit impatiently, watching the hands move forward on the clock. My eyes roam around the room again, but there's still no sign of Lana. Even though we've all been warned to stay away from her, I'm hoping I might catch her in the restroom and get a chance to ask her what the hell she's playing at.

It's two minutes to show time when she makes her appearance. My breath falters as I watch her step into the room. I can only imagine how Kal must be feeling. Wearing an ill-fitting black skirt suit with a stiff white blouse buttoned tight to her collar and plain black pumps, she's like a walking advertisement for a nunnery. She walks in between her parents with her head stapled to her chest and her gaze fixated on the floor. Greta has a hold on her daughter's elbow as she leads her to the front of the room.

I swing around to look at Kal, noting how he keeps his eyes trained strictly forward. The tense set of his shoulders alerts me to the fact he is aware of her presence. He grips the edge of the desk tautly. Keaton and I share concerned looks.

We all rise as the judge enters the room, and proceedings commence when we reclaim our seats. The charges are read out and a not guilty plea is entered. Lana is called to the witness stand, and a collective gasp arises from the audience.

Her shoulders are slouched as she walks across the floor toward the witness box. When she takes the seat, she straightens her back and sits upright in the chair. There's a defiant stance to her expression as she stares straight ahead, not looking in Kal's direction or at anyone in particular. I knot and unknot my hands in my lap, and my nerves are hanging on by a thread. I take the opportunity to slyly study her while she is swearing on the Bible. Her translucent skin is even paler than usual, and ghastly dark shadows dot the curves under her eyes. Her hair is neat and kept off her face in a severe ponytail. She isn't wearing a scrap of makeup, and she looks about twelve. If the prosecutor wanted to garner sympathy by presenting her in such a light, he's done an admirable job.

Huge concern for my cousin surges to the fore. He can't go down for this. He just can't.

The prosecutor starts asking her questions, most of them simple, to help her relax. She answers in a calm, quiet, confident voice, never once looking in our direction. Gradually, he moves on to the Kennedys, and the courtroom listens avidly as she explains about growing up on the grounds of the Kennedy estate and spending all her free time and most weekends with the Kennedy boys. Very quickly, we fast forward to more recent times, and I inwardly cringe as the questions turn more intimate.

"At this time, Ms. Taylor, what were your feelings toward the defendant, Mr. Kalvin Kennedy?"

Her cheeks flush red as she turns her attention to Kal for the first time. Looking him straight in the eye, she says, "I was in love with him. I'd always been in love with him, but when I was younger, I hadn't been able to put a name to it."

"And how did Mr. Kennedy feel about you?"

Her gaze hasn't strayed from Kal's, and his head is inclined in her direction. "He told me he loved me too."

"So, you two were in a relationship then," the prosecutor surmises, pacing the floor in front of the witness box.

Her face contorts. "Not exactly."

"Can you please elaborate for the court."

"He, ah." She pauses, taking a sip of her water. "He wanted to keep our relationship secret."

The prosecutor spins his head in Kal's direction, slanting him an over-the-top dramatic look. Satisfied with his performance, he turns back around to face Lana. "And why was that?"

She looks away from Kal. "He said it was to protect me, because others wouldn't approve of us being together."

"And you believed him?" The prosecutor quirks a brow, and Lana nods.

"You need to answer the question, Ms. Taylor," the judge instructs.

"Yes," Lana says, staring at Kal again. "I believed him."

"And was this relationship an exclusive one?" The prosecutor asks next.

Her cheeks turn fire engine red. "Not at first, but then he promised me he was finished with other girls. That was when he told me he loved me." She fidgets in her seat, peering down at her lap.

"Other girls?" The prosecutor looks at Kal with shocked surprise, as if this is the first time he's heard mention of this.

Someone give that man an Oscar.

Lana sighs, shifting uneasily in her chair. "Kal was ... is a player. There have been plenty of other girls."

My eyes meet James's and he sends me a worried frown.

"And how did that make you feel?" the prosecutor continues.

Lana turns her head to face Kal again. "Worthless. Invisible. Cheap."

Holy shitballs for dinner. This is awful. Worst of all is how much sympathy I have for Lana right now, and I'm on my cousin's side—it doesn't bode well.

"And was this before or after he promised you exclusivity?"

"Before. When I tried to break things off with him, and I

explained how it was making me feel, he told me he'd stop sleeping around. That he'd commit to me."

"And what happened then?"

"He was more dedicated, and he seemed to be trying to prove he had changed his ways. I was happy." Tears well in her eyes. "He told me he loved me and I was the only girl for him. That he'd always imagined us together. That I was his future." A tear slides down her cheek, and I clamp a hand over my mouth.

Instinctively, I seek out Ky. Feeling eyes on him, he turns and looks at me. My chest heaves as we stare at one another, and all manner of thoughts flit through my mind. "I love you," he mouths, and my emotions skitter all over the place. Keaton nudges me discreetly, and I snap out of it, looking away quickly. Lana has composed herself, and there's no trace of moisture on her cheeks.

"What happened next?" the prosecutor asks, continuing this line of questioning.

She closes her eyes momentarily and her lip wobbles.

"We slept together, and I thought everything was perfect until Addison pulled me aside to tell me something I needed to know."

Everything locks up inside me at the mere mention of her name. Although this isn't news to us—Zoe had already informed us of this—all my cousins have stiffened. Ky's shoulders are corded with tension, and his hands are balled into fists at his side. Kal sits ramrod straight in his chair.

"For the benefit of the jury, can you please explain who Addison is?"

"Addison Sinclair is Kyler Kennedy's girlfriend, or ex-girlfriend. I'm not quite sure on the status of their relationship at this time."

"And what was it this Addison had to tell you?" the prosecutor asks, resting his hands on the witness box. Tears trickle down Lana's face. "Do you need to take a break, Ms. Taylor?"

She vehemently shakes her head. "No. This is very difficult to relive, but I want to keep going."

"Very well. In your own time."

"Addison showed me a recording Kalvin had made a few nights previously. It was a video of him having sex with her, and she thought I needed to know he was messing with me."

I can scarcely hide my shock. I know the recording exists—it's what Addison has been using to blackmail Ky into remaining by her side—but the fact she showed it to Lana and used it to set her on this path sickens me no end. Up to this point, I've viewed Addison as a manipulative pain in my ass. But this changes things. That girl has a downright vicious streak if she's prepared to go to such extremes to destroy someone.

Kal jumps up out of his seat, racing across the floor to Lana before anyone can stop him. "I never filmed that or willingly had sex with her! You've got to believe me. She set me up!" Officers of the court grab Kalvin's arms and pull him back. The crowd is in an uproar, and the judge is slamming her gavel down on the sounding block, demanding order. "She set me up, Lana!" Kal screeches as he's dragged over in front of the judge. Tears are streaming down Lana's face.

The judge's face has turned an unflattering shade of red. She glowers at Kal. "Control yourself, Mr. Kennedy. If you pull a stunt like that again in my courtroom, I'll have you detained. Do you understand?" She slams the gavel down again. "Do you understand?"

"Yes, Your Honor," Kal replies in a suitably chastised manner. "I apologize."

The officers lead him back to his seat, and he purposely avoids making eye contact with any of us. Alex is clinging onto

James, her slim body shaking against him. "Ho. Lee. Shit," Keaton exclaims in my ear. "Ky is going to be arrested for murder if we let him anywhere near Addison after this."

I press my mouth to his ear. "*I'll* be arrested for murder unless someone locks me in my room later," I seethe. If Addison Sinclair is anywhere in the vicinity of this courtroom, I think they'll have to restrain all of us from going for her. "And Ky isn't going anywhere near that bitch again." Not if I have anything to say about it.

The prosecutor clears his throat, approaching the witness box and passing a tissue to Lana. "What happened when you confronted Mr. Kennedy about it?"

Lana draws a shuddering breath, dabbing at her clammy face. "I didn't tell him Addison had come to me or that I had proof he'd slept with her. I told him I'd heard a rumor and asked him if it was true." Her head jerks in his direction. "He denied it."

"And what happened after that?"

Lana pinches the bridge of her nose. "I told him I knew he was lying and that things were over between us. That I'd never forgive him and I never wanted to see him again. Then he left."

The prosecutor frowns, and a look of blatant alarm washes over his face. "What happened before he left, Ms. Taylor?"

She wets her lips. "He begged me to reconsider, not to break up with him. He said it was all a misunderstanding and he could explain. But I didn't want to hear his excuses so I shoved him out of the house."

A glint of fury flashes in the prosecutor's eyes. "Ms. Taylor. I understand it is difficult for you to relive the events of that night, because you have been severely traumatized by the manner in which you were assaulted by Mr. Kennedy, but you need to explain it in detail for the court." He motions to the side. "For the benefit of the jury."

Lana picks up her head and glances in the direction of her parents. "I'm sorry. I'm so sorry." Her chest rises and falls as she steadies herself, peering directly into the prosecutor's eyes. "I lied." There's an audible gasp from the room. "Kalvin Kennedy didn't rape me. He has never physically harmed me."

Chapter Thirty

I offer up silent thanks to whatever entity has been looking out for my cousin. My shoulders sag in relief. Kal's attorney spins around in his seat, sending James a triumphant smile. My heart is thumping wildly in my chest as I face down the row. All my cousins have the same happy shell-shocked look on their faces.

"Ms. Taylor," the judge says in a stern tone of voice. "Do you mean to say you lied about these allegations and they are completely false?"

"Yes, Your Honor," Lana responds in an apologetic yet confident voice. "I'm very sorry for wasting the court's time, and I will accept whatever punishment is necessary, but please don't imprison Kal. He hasn't done anything to deserve it."

Kal stands up in his chair. "Lana! I—"

"Restrain your client!" the judge shrieks at Kal's attorney, and he tugs Kal back down by the elbow, whispering urgently in his ear.

"Before I decide on how to proceed, I would like you to explain to me and the jurors why you lied."

"I was upset and brokenhearted, and I allowed myself to be manipulated by Addison. She suggested I do this. She, ah"—Lana smooths a hand over the top of her head—"she had the condom from when she slept with him, and she told me to give it to the police, that it would help back up my claims."

I clamp a hand over my mouth to cover my visible horror. Kal was right. This was a complete setup. Addison had this all planned out. An intense bout of shivering rips up and down my spine. This is bigger than Ky. It's got to be. There's no way Addison is doing all this purely to trap him in her bed again. She's up to something else.

Ky hops up out of his seat and storms out of the room. I jump up to go after him, but Keaton pulls me back down. Kaden and Keven run out after him, and I try to calm my beating heart.

"I'm sorry, Kal. I'm so sorry." Lana looks directly at him. "You didn't deserve this. I wasn't thinking straight. It just hurt so much in here." She cradles her hand against her chest as more tears trickle down her face.

"It's okay, I und—"

"Mr. Kennedy!" the judge roars, slamming her gavel down violently. "You will not speak in my courtroom unless spoken to! This is your final warning."

"What a fine mess you have brought to my courtroom," she says, sending a menacing glare at the prosecutor and Kal's attorney although her features lose the harsh edge when she faces Lana. "No matter how much he broke your heart, you cannot ever accuse another person of a crime they didn't commit. Especially one like this. Have you any idea, young lady, how much you have cost the state? How much damage you have caused to those who wish to bring legitimate allegations before my courtroom?"

Lana's eyes don't waver as she eyeballs the judge. "More

than I could ever repay, I'm sure, but I'll accept whatever punishment is deemed necessary. It was important that I came here today to put things right. The public needed to hear me say this because I don't want this following Kal around." She swallows noisily. "I don't want this on my conscience for the rest of my life. And the last thing I want is to sway any rape victim from coming forward. I'm truly sorry."

The judge looks angry yet thoughtful. "I'm dismissing all charges against your client," she says, looking at Kal's attorney. "You are free to go, Mr. Kennedy, and this court apologizes to you for any distress. I would like Ms. Taylor and Ms. Sinclair taken in for questioning, and pending sufficient evidence, I expect appropriate charges will be brought."

Kal leans sideways, whispering in his attorney's ear.

"Your Honor, if I may be permitted to approach the bench." Kal's attorney walks up to the judge and there's heated debate, back and forth, before he returns to the desk, updating Kal quickly and quietly.

"I understand Mr. Kennedy would like to say a few words. You have two minutes, Kalvin." The judge gives him a curt nod.

Kal stands, pushing his shoulders back confidently as he starts to speak. "Your Honor, I'd like to appeal for leniency on Lana's behalf." Keaton's eyes go wide as he looks from me to his brothers. "She's a good person with a good heart, and she never would've done anything like this if I hadn't let her down and if Addison hadn't played her." Kal slants his head in Lana's direction. "This is why I spent so long fighting my feelings for you. You don't belong in my world. You're far too good for it. For me. I thought I was ready to be who you needed me to be, but I fell at the first hurdle. I'm so very sorry, Lana. I will never forgive myself for hurting you." I wipe an errant tear from my eye when Lana starts quietly sobbing. Keaton clutches onto my hand.

"Don't blame yourself," Kal continues, in a gentle tone. "I've already forgiven you."

His shoulders tremble as he faces the judge. I'm surprised she tolerated this. "I don't want her charged, Your Honor. It's not right." He looks over his shoulder at his parents. James nods in silent agreement. He turns back around. "My family will cover the legal costs, so, please don't charge Lana with any crime. I don't want this on her record for life. She deserves the opportunity to move on and put all this behind her as much as I do."

Kal sits down, and all the air leaves my lungs. The judge thanks Kal for his heartfelt speech, but she makes no promises. She then draws proceedings to a close, and people start to filter out of the room. I watch as Lana steps out of the witness box on shaky legs. Greta rushes to her daughter's side and pulls her into her arms. Kal stands up, but his attorney places a cautionary hand on his arm.

Lana looks up as they pass our row, catching my eye. Her gaze is full of pain and sorrow, and despite all she's put my cousin through, I can only find compassion in my heart. She's a victim in this as much as Kal.

Out in the corridor, we take our time hugging Kalvin. The relief is evident on all our faces. I look down the passageway, stretching my head, looking for any sign of Ky, but I can't find him, Kaden or Keven.

"I need to speak to her," Kal tells James. "Please, Dad. I can't leave it like this."

James and Alex exchange looks, and Alex surprises me by acquiescing first. "I'll talk to your attorney and see if he can set it up. Hold tight." Her high heels click-click on the polished marble floor as she walks toward the legal team huddled outside a mahogany door at the far side of the corridor.

"Ky is going to kill Addison." Kent chuckles.

"It's hardly funny!" I snap, rummaging in my bag for my new phone.

"Now isn't the time to be making such jokes. The last thing we need is a return visit to this place," James states. "I hope today's been an eye opener, Kent. I don't ever want to see you here."

Kent rolls his eyes. "Chill, Dad. Shoplifting hardly compares to rape."

"Bro!" Keanu elbows him in the ribs. "Don't be so fucking insensitive. Our brother just dodged a bullet, and Faye's right, it's no laughing matter. If Lana hadn't told the truth, Kal may have gone down for this. It's time you wised up before you end up here." Keanu sends Kent a knowing look, and Keaton frowns.

The tappity-tap of Alex's heels announce her return. "I'm sorry, son, but she won't speak to you." She eyeballs me. "However, she has asked to speak with Faye."

Kal is in front of me in a hot snot, beseeching me with his eyes. "Please talk to her."

"I will. Do you want me to pass on a message?"

He leans into my ear. "Tell her I'm so sorry and I'll always love her." His eyes search mine. "That I've always loved her, too."

I bob my head. "I'll tell her."

Lana doesn't look up when I enter the room. The chair scrapes as I sit down. I fold my hands on top of the desk and wait. I'm surprised we are speaking alone—that Greta didn't insist on chaperoning her. Slowly, her head lifts and she faces me. "You must hate me now." Her lip quivers.

I shake my head. "I've never hated you. I was upset and disappointed with you, but I've never hated you."

"Does he hate me?" she whispers.

"No." And I proceed to tell her what he said outside.

Tears flow down her cheeks again, and I pull a tissue from my pocket and hand it to her. "Thanks. I'm such a mess, and I've screwed up so badly. My parents can barely look at me." She blows her nose.

"That's to be expected, but they haven't abandoned you, and they'll help you get through this. Will you come back?"

Her sad eyes meet mine. "No. We won't be returning to Wellesley. I need to move on, and the only way I can do that is if I don't see him anymore. I believe him when he said he didn't intentionally set out to hurt me, but the reality is, he would keep doing it. He's not mature enough to handle this. Maybe, he might've been one day, but there can be no recovering from this." She holds a hand over her mouth as the tears return. "I accused him of rape. I've shamed him and brought the media down on him. I can't believe he talked his parents into covering the costs and they've offered to hire their attorneys to represent me should charges be lodged." She bites down on her lip. "I misjudged them. All of them."

"Why didn't you tell me?"

"Kal asked me to keep our relationship a secret."

"But you told Zoe." Now all Zoe's barbed comments make sense. She knew what was going on, and she was trying to protect Lana.

"She caught us kissing one time, and I had to come clean."

"You still should've told me. Especially after Addison came to you. You knew I didn't like or trust her."

"I couldn't think straight after she showed me that tape." Her cheeks pucker. "Besides, you hadn't exactly confided in me either, had you, Faye?"

Her tone isn't accusatory, more matter of fact. "You knew?"

"I suspected. The way you look at Kyler is the same way I look at Kal."

Tension fills the space between us as we stare at one another. "We were trying to keep our relationship a secret, too, for obvious reasons."

A sad smile crests her lips. "We're so stupid. We had so much in common yet we never thought to support one another."

I lean back in my chair, rolling a finger across my lips. "I never thought of it like that."

"And if we'd confided in one another, then you would've talked sense into me about Addison and we wouldn't be sitting here today." She sighs. "I've fucked up everything, and I'll be paying for that for the rest of my life. Nothing is going to be the same."

"Will you keep in contact with me?"

Her lips curve up at the corner. "You want to?"

I smile. "Yeah. I'd like to know you're okay." I think that would help Kal.

"I'll send you my new deets but only if you promise to keep this between us. Kal can't know, and you can't ever give him my number. I need to let him go, Faye. For both our sakes."

I don't like the thought of lying to my cousin, but I figure he would understand and prefer that at least one of us is keeping in touch with the little girl who claimed his heart when they were kids. "Okay. I promise."

She gets up and walks around the desk. I stand. She pulls a white envelope out of her bag and hands it to me. "Can you give him this?"

I secure it in my bag. "Of course. You mind yourself, Lana." I'm briefly tempted to hug her, but I can't forget what she's put Kal through these last few months, and she'll have to work to earn back my trust. I give her a short wave and walk out of the room, feeling a little lighter than when I entered it.

Kal is on me instantly, and I quickly fill him in on our conversation. I hand him the envelope, and he goes off by himself to read it in private. The rest of us move toward the exit, and we catch up to Keven and Kaden in the lobby. As soon as I spot them, I run toward them. "Where is he? Is he okay?"

Kaden pulls me off to the side as Keven stays to update the rest of the family. "I'm not going to lie, he's in a bad way. He thinks this is all his fault for getting involved with Addison in the first place. He was all set to go over there and give her a piece of his mind, but we talked him off the ledge. He said he needs some time alone so we let him go, but in all honesty, I think he needs you."

"You know."

"He came to me last week and told me everything. He loves you. I've never heard my brother talk about any girl the way he talks about you. I know I've no right to ask you this, but please find it in your heart to forgive him. He needs you. When he was with you, he was happy. I didn't know what was behind his good mood, but I was glad to see him in a better place. When he came to me last week, I could see how lost he was again. He's falling back into that dark space, and I'm very worried about him."

"He hurt me, Kaden, and although I've forgiven him, I don't know if I can forget. I want to, God knows I do, but I'm struggling." It's only as I vocalize the words that I realize I'm already in that place. After hearing how far-reaching Addison's manipulations extend, it's easier to let it go. Continuing to push Ky away serves no purpose except giving Addison what she wants. She has no hold over us anymore, and there is no reason why I need to keep my distance from him. He is a victim too, and instead of supporting him, I've been punishing him. That needs to stop now.

"I understand. He explained." Kaden places his hands lightly on my forearms. "My brother has always had this darkness inside him, and he doesn't let people in easily. But he let you in, and it's more than that, isn't it?"

"We get each other, in a way I've never connected with anyone else. Ever."

"That sounds too precious to throw away."

I level a puzzled look at him. "You're not freaked out over the cousin thing?"

He barks out a laugh. "Seriously? With all the shit this family is dealing with, that's the least of our troubles." His expression grows serious again. "Why does society get to dictate who we can and can't love anyway?" He looks introspective. "Ky needs you. Please be there for him. But if you can't, I understand."

"I'll find him. I'll help him. I want to make things right between us." I gulp nervously. "I love him too."

When we arrive back at the house, Brad is waiting in the lobby. While he has seen updates on TV, and I messaged him a few quick updates from the car, he isn't fully up to speed yet. I explain everything to him as I walk to my bedroom to get changed. "Fuck! Addison is seriously deranged. What the hell is her fixation with Ky and this family? That is not normal behavior."

I head into my closet to get changed. "I don't know, and it's concerning, but she's in some serious shit now. I hope they throw the book at her. It's no less than she deserves," I call out, as I shuck out of my skirt and shirt and pull on my comfy jeans and favorite pale pink sweater. I grab my boots, padding back into my room. I plop down on the bed to pull my socks on. "He hasn't been back here, has he?"

"No," Brad confirms, slouching against my dresser. "And I've tried calling him like a million times since the news broke."

"I think I know where he is." I slip my feet into my boots and lace them up. "Do you know the lake where Ky goes sometimes?" Brad nods. "I'm betting he's there. Can you drive me?"

"Of course. Let me grab my jacket, and I'll meet you out front."

"Today must've been so surreal, huh?" Brad asks, when we are out on the motorway. He's fiddling with the radio station, trying to find something decent to listen to.

"You've no idea. I felt like I was in the middle of an episode of *Keeping Up with the Kardashians* or a cross between that and *Special Victims Unit*."

"I still can't believe Lana got suckered in by Addison. She's a smart girl. It doesn't make sense."

"She was heartbroken and vulnerable, and Addison pounced." I grind down on my teeth. "Addison better hope she's arrested because I will not be responsible for my actions if I see her."

"You can bet she'll be keeping a low profile."

Brad brings the car to a stop at the end of the dirt track. "This is as far as I can go. I'll walk down with you, to make sure he's here." He squints up at the sky. "It's getting dark, and I don't like the idea of you wandering around out here by yourself."

We hop out of the car and Brad retrieves a blanket from the boot, arranging it around my shoulders. "You don't have a jacket, and the air is turning."

"Thanks." We walk in silence toward the lake. As we emerge from the long grass, I sigh in relief when I spot Ky. He's hunched over with his back against a tree, looking like he's carrying the weight of the nation on his shoulders.

"I'll leave you here," Brad whispers, shoving his hands in his pockets.

I frown. "You're not coming, too?"

His nose scrunches up. "Nah. I'll talk to him later. I figure he needs the type of comfort only you can provide."

"Okay. Thanks for the lift." He turns around, and I reach out, holding onto his arm. "You're a good friend." He smiles, but it doesn't quite meet his eyes. "To both of us."

He gives me a lopsided shrug. "I'll see you back at the house."

I watch him walk away, all hunched over and deflated, and I hate how things have altered between us, that he's so guarded around me. I'm too chicken to confront the fact he's still harboring feelings for me, because I don't know what to do about it.

Holding the blanket securely around me, I set out toward Ky.

His head jerks up as my feet crunch on the debris underfoot. His eyes glow a little as he looks around.

"Hey." I maneuver the blanket around my body so it's covering me lengthways and drop down on the ground beside him. "How are you holding up?"

He picks up a stone and flings it out onto the lake. We watch in silence as it skims four times before disappearing under the calm water. "You want the truth?" he asks, a couple minutes later.

I twist my body around so I'm facing him. "Always."

"I'm figuring it would be better for everyone if I took off, because she's not ever going to go away. She's poison and she's trying to destroy everyone I love. She'll give up if I disappear."

I reach out and take his cold hands in mine, squeezing gently. "You can't do that. You can't let her win."

"I only wanted to protect you, to protect Kal, but I've ended up making everything worse."

"I know your motivations were pure and that your heart was in the right place"—I say quietly—"but you can't always protect everyone, all the time, and that responsibility shouldn't fall on your shoulders."

"Maybe it shouldn't, but I will always put myself on the line to protect those I love." There's a faraway look in his eyes, and his Adam's apple jumps in his throat. Picking up another stone, he throws it with the full strength of his pent-up frustration. A dart of pain washes over his face, and there's an undercurrent of something indecipherable in the air.

"Why is it so important to you?" I ask, because I'm sensing there is more to this than a basic protective instinctive.

He goes stock still, and silence bleeds into the space between us. I give him time to gather his thoughts.

He locks his hand around the back of his neck. "Because no one was there to protect me."

All the blood leaches from my face, and tiny goose bumps sprout up and down my arms despite the heavy blanket swathing me. Ky's gaze darkens as he looks out to the lake, lost in clearly difficult thoughts. Tentatively, I touch his arm. "Do you want to talk about it?"

He shakes his head without looking at me. "I can't." He swallows audibly. "Not yet."

I rest my head against his shoulder. "It's okay." I say it, but I don't really mean it. He's hurting much more than I realized, and it goes against the grain to give up without a fight, but I can't push him. I have to let him talk to me about it, whatever it is, when he's good and ready. "Just know that I'm here for you."

His chest heaves as he pins hopeful eyes on mine. "What are you saying exactly?"

I hoist myself onto his lap, circling my arms around his neck. "I can let it go. I *want* to let it go. She's not going to take you from me anymore. No matter what, from now on, I'm yours. I'm here for you now and always. I love you, Ky." I press a kiss to his cheek. "Forever."

Chapter Thirty-One

His heart is beating so fast underneath my palm as he looks deep into my eyes. "You mean it?"

"I do." I weave my fingers through his hair and press a kiss to his forehead. "She's already taken so much from us. I'm not letting her take anything else."

His arms tighten around my waist as he brings my mouth down to his. The instant our lips brush, a calming sensation spreads over my body. Like that feeling you get when you step into your house from the cold and the warmth and comfort of familiarity, of home, envelops you in a welcoming blanket.

Kissing Ky feels like I'm home, and I never want to leave again.

His kisses are soft and gentle and so tender, as if he's savoring each and every one. "I've missed this." His warm breath caresses my mouth as he speaks in between kisses.

"I've felt so empty without you," I whisper, trailing my thumb across his lower lip. "I want this with you. No more looking back."

The look he gives me sets off fireworks inside my chest. He

nips at my bottom lip, and I moan. "I'm sold, baby. I'm all yours."

I mesh my mouth to his, pushing my tongue into his mouth and starting a new tango. Our tongues caress, and our lips move frenetically as our connection sends delicious sparks ripping up and down my body. My heart is hammering in my chest, and liquid lust ignites my veins. I grip his shoulders, moving my lips to his neck, sucking greedily on his skin. His hands sneak under my sweater, inching up my back, and I arch my body, pressing into him as my core pulses with raw need. I move my legs until I'm straddling him, and he lifts his hips, pressing his hard arousal against me. We moan together, before cracking up laughing, and I love how natural it is being with him like this. I run the tips of my fingers over his face, relishing the feel of his skin against mine.

He cups my head in his large hands. "I love you, Faye. So much the strength of it scares the crap out of me sometimes."

I ease off him, lying back down on the blanket. Tugging on his shirt, I yank him toward me. His body covers mine in all the right places, and I grind against him, wet and needy. "I'm the same. That's how I know this is right." My eyes radiate with a combination of love and desire. "I want to feel you moving inside me. Take me here, Ky."

He buries his head in my neck as his hips piston against mine. "You're killing me, babe."

He presses a light kiss to that tender spot on my collarbone, and I squirm underneath him. "Ky." My tone is desperate and breathless. "Please."

Lifting up on his hands, he stares down at me. "You know I want you. You have no idea how many nights I've woken up hard from dreaming about us like that, but I meant what I said in Nantucket. Our first time is going to be special."

"It's beautiful here," I protest. "There couldn't be a more perfect place. And there isn't a sinner around. We're all alone."

He chuckles, tracing circles on my arm with the tip of his finger. I shiver all over, and fire blazes in his eyes. "I can't believe I'm saying this, but we can't do it tonight. Not after the events of today. I don't want anything tarnishing the memory of the first time we make love, and if we do it now, I'll always remember this day for different reasons. I don't want that for you. For us."

Sighing, he sits up, tenderly pulling me up with him. "We've waited this long. We can wait a little while longer." He brings my palm to his mouth and kisses it. I try not to pout, but it's difficult when my body is a writhing mass of hormones. He laughs again. "We're stuck in some warped role reversal. Surely I should be arguing your point and vice versa?"

That raises a smile, and I can't help it. "It's the twenty-first century, babe. Get used to it!" I tease, sliding my hands all over his chest.

"How about this?" He snakes a hand around my waist, pressing his delectable mouth to my ear. "We'll head home and I'll take care of your needs in other ways, and then we can hold each other all night?"

My eyes sparkle as I peer up at him. "That's a worthy compromise."

"Come on then." He climbs to his feet, extending his hand to help me up.

Alex and James make no comment on our conjoined hands when we arrive back in the house. I figure they're just glad to see him home safe and sound. We missed dinner, but they saved us some. Ky plays footsie with me while we eat, situated across the table from one another, and the only thing on my mind is my other hunger—the one in my knickers that's ready to slay me whole.

We sneak into my room when no one is looking, and I swiftly lock the door. Ky closes the curtains and then stalks toward me like a man on a mission. I squeal, flattening my back to the door when he reaches me. His hands cage me in as he dips his head and skims the tip of his nose along my neck. My legs wobble as he audibly inhales. "You smell amazing." His tongue darts out, tasting my flesh, and I whimper. "You taste amazing." I can hear the smile in his voice. One hand moves down my side, brushing against my breast and curving over my hips. "You feel amazing."

"Oh, God." Whimpering again, I'm starting to doubt my legs' ability to hold me upright when they start trembling and quivering beneath me.

His hand welds to my butt, and he squeezes my flesh through my jeans as his mouth descends greedily on mine. His lips are fierce as he kisses me with all the pent-up passion and longing of the last few weeks. I grab handfuls of his hair, angling his head so I can kiss him more passionately. He groans into my mouth, and I grate my hips against his. His arms go around me as he pulls me away from the door, kissing me relentlessly, his mouth devouring mine. My hands grip his shoulders, digging in as a wave of hot desire crashes over me. I have never wanted any boy as much as I want him.

He groans again, holding me flush to his body, and my hands roam over his back and down to his butt. He thrusts me back against the door, and it rattles noisily. Growling, he moves his long, firm body against me as his tongue dips into my ear. Gasping, I lift my legs automatically, wrapping them around his waist. *Oh, hell. This feels so good. More amazing than I ever imagined being with a boy could feel like.* His hands slide under my butt, and he walks us to the bed. Easing me back on the mattress, he dots my face and neck with a slew of drugging kisses. I'm panting and writhing in need as he lowers himself down over my body, grinning up at me. "Do you trust me, baby?"

"I do. I trust you." My raspy tone could be embarrassing with anyone else but not with him. I want him to see, to hear, how much I want him. I've never felt this much with anyone ever before. I never want to feel this with anyone else.

He removes my boots, tossing them flippantly over his shoulder. I push up on my elbows, watching as he removes my socks before pressing feather-light kisses all over my skin. His hands creep up my calves and up over my knees, tracing tiny circles on my inner thighs as I all but die on the bed. He cups me there, and I almost jerk off the bed. "Is this what you need, sweetheart?" His finger moves up and down over my jeans causing an insane friction to build.

I can only nod and moan. He chuckles as he pops the buttons on my jeans and tugs them down my legs, taking my knickers along for the ride. "Take off your sweater and bra. I want you naked."

My bravery deserts me the instant I hear his request. My naked body is no longer unblemished, and although I want this with him, I don't want him to see the horrible disfigurement on my stomach. Because he knows me so well, he already understands the reason for my sudden hesitation. "It doesn't change how I feel about you or how much I want you." I gulp. "Let me see, baby."

Summoning courage, I remove the rest of my clothes with trembling hands. Ky shifts back on his heels, his gaze transfixed on my scar. Instinctively, my hands cover the raised, jagged mark. We lock eyes and his pained expression confuses me. "It's hideous, I know." I squirm in embarrassment as a slight red flush darkens my cheeks. Unable to handle his intense gaze, I look away.

Carefully, he places two fingers under my chin, moving my head so I'm staring him directly in the face. "It's not, and don't be embarrassed." He removes my hands, running his fingers lightly over the length of the scar. "This is a survivor's badge. A constant reminder of how precious life is and how close you came to losing yours." His chest heaves painfully as he dips down, planting a line of delicate kisses against my damaged skin. When he lifts back up, so much emotion is etched across his face. "I see all that when I look at you. I see how strong you are—strong, beautiful, and brave. But I also see my biggest failure. This will always remind me of the time I let you down in the worst possible way." I open my mouth to protest, but he shushes me. "I reckon that's a good thing. It'll only ensure I never let you down again."

Propping up on my elbows, I place a delicate kiss on his mouth. "You have to forgive yourself, and I know you won't fail me again." I palm his face. "If I'm not to get embarrassed over this scar, then you can't get melancholy. That's the deal."

"I'll try," he whispers.

"Good." I kiss him more profoundly this time. "So, where were we?" I tug on his jeans, biting my lip in a deliberate provocative move.

"Right about here," he says, undressing quickly. He crawls over me, completely naked, and his hands roam over every inch of my skin. I shiver all over. "You are so beautiful to me." His fingers move over my breasts, and I mold to his touch. He tweaks my nipple, and I squeak, grabbing his head and forcing his mouth back to mine. My hands explore his ripped chest and abs, snaking lower until I curl my hand around him. He jolts and I smile into our kiss, adoring how much my touch turns him on.

He smooths a hand over my hip and down lower, and his fingers hover exactly where I need them to be. My breath stalls in my chest. He pulls his mouth back as he slips one finger inside me. "I love you."

I start pumping my hand up and down, diving in and grazing my nose along his neck. "And I love you."

Our movements turn more frantic, our kisses more urgent, and things start building to a crescendo inside me. I'm thrusting against his hand and trying to smother my moans while I work him as fast as he works me. We both edge even closer to that heavenly ledge, and our collective breathing is ragged as we kiss like it's the end of the world and we're never going to get to do this again. I shatter, splintering into a million blissful pieces as Ky does the same. Our mouths disguise our moans until we fall back down to Earth.

After a quick cleanup, Ky flops onto the bed on his back, and I join him, giggling for no apparent reason except that I'm happy, euphoric, and on a complete and utter high. He twists his head to face me. "Nothing has ever felt as good as this. I can only imagine how amazing it's going to be when I'm inside you."

I cover my face with my hand as my core pulses with renewed need. I don't know what is happening to me, but I'm like a Duracell bunny on Viagra when I'm with Ky. I've never felt as horny or as sexy before. "Not helping, jerkface," I moan, swatting his shoulder.

He chuckles, lifting my hand away from my face. "Stop covering yourself up. I've gone long enough without seeing your pretty face." He presses a delicate kiss to my lips, and I sigh contentedly. He smiles, a full, wide, genuine smile, the likes I haven't seen on him in weeks, and my heart melts. "What do you want to do now? It's too early to go to sleep."

My mind instantly dredges up all manner of dirty things.

He throws back his head, laughing. "Mind out of the gutter, babe. It's got to be something outside this room. I only have so much self-control."

I force him into watching *Titanic* with me. It's my go-to movie whenever my emotions are heightened. It didn't take much persuasion on my part, even though I can tell this is totally not his thing. Not that he's following the story on the screen anyway. He spends most of the movie touching and kissing me, and we are locked in the midst of a steamy make-out session when Kalvin slips quietly into the room. We don't hear him until he's virtually on top of us. "I hope you're giving her lots of tongue," he purrs, right beside my ear, and I shriek. "Faye looks like she needs a good tonguing."

I almost piss myself laughing. "You are fucking disgusting," Ky says, shoving him back. "And get out of our personal space. You're breathing germs all over us."

Kal smirks, dropping into a seat behind us and propping his feet up. "Just keeping it real, bro."

Ky pauses the movie and turns up the lights. Swiveling in the chair, he nervously eyeballs his brother. "I'm so sorry, Kal. I'm sorry you got dragged into this. It should never have impacted you and Lana. I wish I'd never gotten involved with Addison in the first place." The flash of guilt in his eyes is unmistakable.

Kal drops his feet, straightening up. "It's not your fault. If I hadn't gotten drunk that night at the party, she never would've been able to take advantage of me. And if I hadn't hurt Lana so bad, Addison wouldn't have been able to manipulate her into claiming rape." Leaning over, he slaps Ky on the back. "I've spent weeks going over all the 'what ifs' and it's pointless. It's happened. It's over. Time to move on."

"I'm proud of you." I jump out of my seat, move in beside

him, and pull him into a fierce hug. "And I'm glad you're back to your flirty self. I've missed you."

He presses a kiss to the top of my head. "I don't think I'll ever be the same, but thanks, and for talking to her today."

"I was glad to have the chance to talk to her." I peer into his eyes. "Was the letter what you were hoping it was?"

A sorrowful look fills his eyes, and they lose some of their shine. "Yes and no." He leans his head back, staring at the ceiling. "I know she loves me in the same way I have always loved her. That she wanted the same things for our future, but it's all ruined now. She wants me to keep my distance. Not to try and find her." He gulps, twisting his head to look at me. "I figure if I truly love her, that means I need to let her go. But it hurts, you know."

His eyes grow glassy, and I hug him again. "I'm sorry."

"Me too." He kisses the top of my head, and we are all tongue-tied for a few minutes. "Enough of the heavy." A mischievous glint appears in his eye. "Speaking of moving on." He winks. "Judging by the sounds coming out of your bedroom earlier, is it safe to assume you two are all hot and heavy again?"

My cheeks flare red, and I bury my head in my hands. "Oh my God." Kal splutters out a laugh and I hear the telltale sound of a slap.

"Stop being an ass. You're embarrassing her." Ky immediately jumps to my defense.

"Nothing wrong with a little kissing-cousin action, or more." Kal titters this time, and the slap is louder. "Ow, man. That freaking hurt."

I lift my head up, leaning into Ky. "Stop hitting him." I eyeball Kal. "Did everyone hear?"

"It was only me and Brad in the games room at the time, but he hightailed it out of there pretty fast."

I massage my temples, wondering how the hell things are

going to work out between the three of us now that Ky and I are back together. Brad has been a great friend these last couple of months, and he's like a brother to Ky. Plus, he's got his own shit to deal with, and he needs us, now more than ever. When I think back over the last few weeks, I feel like a piece of crap. All I've been doing is leaning on him, instead of offering support, and I've done nothing constructive to try to bridge the gap between us. That's got to change, but I'm not sure how to pull it off with the weird vibe between us lately.

"I'm going to talk to him," Ky says, as if he can read my mind.

"We need to fix this. He needs us."

He bends down, kissing me softly. "I know. Let me smooth things over. Don't worry, babe, I got this."

Chapter Thirty-Two

The next week passes in a flash. News of Kal's innocence and Addison's game-playing is all everyone is talking about around town. Kal returns to O.C. where he's treated like a king, or so Ky says. There's no word yet on whether charges are being brought against Lana and Addison, and the witch is maintaining a low profile as Brad predicted. She hasn't been in school all week much to Ky's and Kal's relief. Even Peyton is coming in for flack at our school, and she's only her cousin.

The judgmental narrow-mindedness of small town living only fuels my desire to leave it behind someday. Although I've come to look on Wellesley as home, I'd much rather live in a big town or city where I'm merely a number and not fodder for gossip. I hate that everyone knows everyone's business around here.

The diner remains closed, and I figure I'll have to start looking for a new job soon. In the meantime, Ky happily fills all my spare time, and I can't say I'm complaining. His presence is everywhere and I love it. He seems intent on proving himself to me, not that he needs to, but I'm not stopping him. His little thoughtful gestures are slowly mending the broken pieces of my heart. Whether it's the aromatic cup of coffee waiting on my bedside locker every morning when I wake or the bowl of chopped fruit and yogurt waiting in the kitchen, the umbrella left by the front door the day the heavens open up or the towel left on the bench when I go for an early morning swim and forget to bring one—my man is going all out, and I only love him more for it. My throat clogs with emotion at his sweet gestures, and I couldn't love him any more if I tried.

I keep my window unlocked, and he spends every night in my bed. Waking up beside him is my new all-time fave pastime. It's been months since I've been this happy, and I gobble it all up like it's my favorite Belgian chocolate ice cream.

Things are still fraught between James and Alex, but they are making an effort to minimize the public arguments, and any screaming matches tend to take place behind closed doors. There's been no more talk of Courtney or divorce, and Alex even retracted her request in relation to planting the listening device, saying it was "all fixed" whatever that's supposed to mean. Oldies are seriously weird.

"Morning, beautiful." Ky rolls onto his side, tucking me into his body until my back is flush with his chest. Brushing my hair aside, he plants a lingering kiss on my neck, and instant desire sparks to life inside me. Before I can turn around and take advantage, Ky holds me in place at my waist. "Be a good girl now, babe. No tempting me first thing in the morning. You know the drill."

I sigh, and he chuckles. "I want you. Shoot me if there's something wrong with that," I droll.

"I want you too," he whispers. "And I have it all organized." I attempt to wriggle in his arms, but he's having none of it. "Baby, please stop shifting like that. It's not helping."

"Ky." My tone is pleading, and he chuckles again.

"Damn, you're sexy. I can't wait to bury myself deep inside you."

"Ky." My tone is harsher this time, and he takes pity, positioning my head so his mouth fits mine. He kisses me long and hard, keeping me firmly pinned in front of him.

"I could kiss you all day long," he murmurs, breaking away. "I plan to, next weekend, along with other stuff." A devilish glint shimmers in his eye as he sits upright in the bed, pulling me with him.

"I'm about two seconds away from punching you in the nuts, mister."

"Patience is a virtue," he teases. I move my hand around to cup his junk, and he laughs quietly. "Okay, I'll tell you, now cease with the violent threats." I sigh. "So, you know we're helping out next weekend with the re-launch." I nod. May and Rick were hoping to reopen the newly renovated motocross training facility a few weeks ago, but an unforeseen issue with the heating system delayed things. I know Alex wrote them a personal check to help cover the additional cost which they were so grateful for. They are finally reopening next Saturday, and we are all roped into helping. Not that I mind. The track is important to Ky, and that means it's important to me. "Your genius boyfriend talked Mom and Dad into letting us stay overnight at a local hotel," he explains with a smug grin.

He relaxes his hold, and I turn around to face him. "Seriously?"

He winks. "Yes, babe. It's happening." He kisses my cheek before moving his lips to my ear. "Buy something sexy. Actually," he says, moving his mouth along my jaw, "buy lots of sexy stuff. Not that you'll be wearing it for long."

"'Kay." My heart is going ninety to the dozen.

He gets out of bed, smiling. "You nervous?"

I tug my bottom lip between my teeth. "A little, but I'm more excited than anything."

He leans down, taking my lips in his. "We don't have to do it. It's okay if you've changed your mind. I can wait for as long as you need me to."

I lace my hands through his hair. "I haven't changed my mind." This time *I* kiss him. "I want this with you, and I don't know how the hell I'm expected to get through the next week."

He pulls my hand to his mouth, kissing my palm. "I still have some tricks up my sleeve. I'll keep your mind and your body occupied." His seductive tone causes the most intense shiver to whip all over my body. "That is the sexiest thing ever." He growls, throwing himself on top of me outside the covers. Gripping my head, he devours my mouth. When he pulls back, we are both panting. "I love you."

"I love you too." I'll never tire of saying it, and I love how confident he is in expressing himself. When I think back to the person he was when I first came here, I realize how much he's opened up to me, and it fills my heart with joy.

He jumps up. "I'm going to make you breakfast in bed. Stay there. I'll be back in half an hour."

"You're so sweet." I grin up at him. "I love this new you."

He sits on the edge of the bed. "You can't tell anyone. I've a rep to maintain."

He caresses my face, and I love how he can't seem to stop touching me. It's the same for me, and it's so hard having to hide it all the time. "Don't worry. Your secret is safe with me."

He perks up. "About that. I think we should tell the fam today."

My brows lift up. "Yeah?"

"Yeah. I know we can't go public yet, not until the dust has properly settled. We don't want to give the media any more ammunition, and I know Mom needs things to die down, it's been bad for business. But I hate having to hide in our own home. Mom and Dad know, and they don't have an issue with it, and the only ones who aren't aware are Kent and Keanu. It doesn't seem fair. We need to tell them."

"I agree."

He stands up, in only his boxers, and I ogle him like a starving woman eyes up a plate of food. He is one heck of a perfect specimen of man. All toned, ripped muscles and oodles of glistening tanned skin. I could eat him all up.

"Right," he says, clawing his hands through his hair as he scans the room for his clothes. "I'm getting out of here before I jump back in that bed and make a liar of myself."

We spend the day at the track, but I insist on leaving early because I have to bake a cake for the triplets. It's their birthday tomorrow, and I told Alex not to buy a cake. Mum always made me a cake on my birthday, even as I got older and stopped having parties, and it always made my birthdays so special. Anyone can buy a top-of-the-range cake, but there's no substitute for a homemade one created with love. I want to do that for my cousins.

After I've finished baking, James orders takeout, and we spend a rare Saturday night with the whole family at home. Even Kaden and Keven are staying this weekend, and it's so good to have everyone here. My heart skips with potent emotion. As the boys banter, and James and Alex smile at their children, having reached some kind of compromise, I look around the table at my new family, feeling accepted and loved and a part of something I never thought I'd experience again. Ky squeezes my knee under the table as he whispers. "Are you okay?" Concern radiates in his eyes.

"I'm more than okay," I tell him. "I'm happy. I love … our family."

His fingers thread through mine, and I can tell by the look in his eyes that he wants to kiss the face off me, but we haven't relayed our news yet.

Ky asks everyone to come to the living room after dinner so he can make the announcement. It's a tad anticlimactic considering most everyone in the room already knows what he's going to say, but I'm still worried over what Keanu and Kent will think. When everyone is seated, Ky takes my hand and faces his family. "Faye and I have something to tell you." He looks at me, beaming from ear to ear. "We're together. We're in love and we don't want to hide that anymore." He smiles at his parents. "Not here. We understand the need to keep this out of the public domain for now, but we want to be ourselves around the house, if that's okay with you?"

James and Alex nod. Keanu shrugs nonchalantly, and my brows nudge up. "I move in modeling circles," he explains, spotting the questioning look in my eyes. "That's not the most shocking thing I've heard."

Alex opens her mouth to, no doubt, probe him on that leading statement, but Kent hogs the limelight, cracking up laughing as he clutches his stomach like he's in physical pain. "This is priceless!" he snorts, wiping moisture from under his eyes. "You had the nerve to interfere in my life when you two were doing the deed all along!" He hops up, slapping Ky on the back. "She's a hot piece of ass. You're the man, dude!"

Ky grinds his teeth as he snaps at his brother. "Don't you dare talk about Faye so disrespectfully. I'm not opposed to giving you a few slaps. When the hell are you ever going to grow up?"

Kent sneers. "Oh, please. Don't act all high and mighty. I've heard the sounds coming from her room." He tosses me a sleazy look. "I thought she had Brad locked up in there." He folds his arms, eyeballing a petulant Brad. "Unless you are into three-somes after all?" He winks, and Ky jumps up ready to go all Rambo on his brother's ass.

James intervenes before it can turn violent. "Calm down, boys." He pulls Kent to one side and gently bumps Ky back into his seat. My arm winds around his waist, and I lean into him. As if on auto-pilot, his arm goes around my shoulder and he kisses my temple. "Kent. You will apologize to your brother and Faye, and I don't want to hear any more of that kind of talk in this house. We have spoken about this before, and your mother and I will not tolerate it any longer. Effective Monday, you are going to see someone who can help you deal with your issues." Kent opens his mouth to protest, but James holds up one hand. "It's non-negotiable. You will go for a few sessions, and if you don't like it or you feel it isn't helping, then we won't force you to attend after that."

"This is bullshit! He's fucking his cousin and you couldn't give two shits about that, but I use bad language and you want to cart me off to some shrink? I think you need your head examined, Dad. Your priorities are all messed up."

James levels a calm look at his son. "It's about way more than your penchant for cursing, and you know that."

Kent angrily shoves James away. "Aw, whatever. Leave me the fuck alone." With that parting endearment, he storms out of the room.

"Sorry," I look nervously between Alex and James.

"Sweetheart, this is nothing to do with you and Ky. You know Kent has his demons."

"Yes," Kaden says from his position on the corner of the couch. "He does, and I'm glad you are facing up to it and getting him the help he needs."

Alex rises. "I'd like to say something. I know things have

been very stressful around here lately and that I haven't been coping all that well, but that's going to change. I'm going to take more of a backseat with work so I can be here for you all."

James clicks his tongue. "I know the situation between your mother and I has been upsetting you all. We are trying to work through our issues, and, for the time being, the divorce is on hold."

Keaton rushes his dad, hugging him fiercely. "That's the best news ever."

"Honey, we can't guarantee that it won't go ahead." Alex sends James a sharp look. "We have a lot of things to figure out, but for now, we're putting our relationship issues aside to focus on this family. A lot of stuff is out of our hands so time will tell."

"I have some other news," James says with a pained expression. "I heard from Dan this afternoon that neither Lana nor Addison are going to be charged."

"What the fuck?" Ky yells. "I'm glad Lana isn't being charged, but Addison shouldn't be allowed to get away with this."

"I agree, son, but she comes from money and, apparently, a large donation was made to the policemen's retirement fund in exchange for them making this go away. I'm not sure what strings were pulled, but she isn't going to be punished. Dan is going to lodge a restraining order on Monday so she can't come anywhere near any of you in the future, and that's the best we can do."

"I've found something on her," Keven pipes up, and every head swivels in his direction.

"Don't keep us in suspense," Kal says. "Out with it."

"Did you know she was adopted?" Keven speaks directly to Ky. He shakes his head. "Well, she was, and she only discovered it about a year ago."

"Around the time she started acting out," Ky confirms. "Who is her birth mother?"

"That I don't know," Keven admits. "Yet. I'll keep digging."

"About that other matter I asked you to look into," James says. "Do you have a minute to discuss it? In my study?"

"Sure." Keven gets up.

James turns to me. "I need to talk to you in private too. Something has come up. Can you give me a half hour?"

My brow furrows. "Okay."

Everyone goes their separate ways after that. Alex approaches me as I make a move to leave with Ky. "Could I speak to you alone, Faye?"

"I'll be there in a few," I tell Ky, kissing him quickly on the lips. "You two pick a movie and set it up." I gesture between him and Brad and they walk off together.

Alex brings me up to her room and closes the door. "Have a seat." She sits gracefully on her chaise longue, patting the space beside her. "Don't look so worried. I only want to have a little chat. Woman to woman." Oh crap. I think I know where she's going with this. "I know I didn't react well to the news of your relationship with Kyler at first, but I wanted to reassure you that I have no issue with it now. I'd be lying if I said I wasn't concerned about public perception, but we'll cross that bridge when we come to it." She smiles in reassurance, and I am relieved that we have her approval. "You're good for my son, Faye. I've noticed how he is around you. How much his mood has altered. It's been years since I've seen my son happy. Truly happy. You make him happy, and I'd be a terrible mother to deny him that."

"He makes me happy too." I can't help grinning at the truth. "So unbelievably happy."

She hugs me. "I'm delighted for you. You've been through a lot. He's been through a lot." Her smile shrinks. "I'm glad you are there for one another." She takes my hands in hers. "I also have a fairly good idea why he wants to take you to a hotel next weekend." My cheeks erupt in a burst of vibrant color. "Perhaps we should've refused, but then we figure you'll find some other way to be together. You are both nearly eighteen and old enough to make your own decisions. We don't want you sleeping together in this house—sex or no sex—because it sets the wrong example for the others." I want to tell her that ship has sailed, but it won't help our cause, so I bite my tongue.

She sweeps my hair back off my face. "I was having sex at sixteen, so I'm hardly one to throw stones." My eyes expand, and she laughs. "That surprises you?"

"A bit." Alex has always seemed so prim and proper to me, and I wouldn't have pegged her as someone to have sex so young, but they do say you shouldn't judge a book by its cover. I've already worked out that there's a lot more to my aunt than the surface would lead you to believe.

"I remember my first love like it was yesterday." A dreamy look fills her eyes. "He was older, and quite famous in his own right. He had a bad boy rep that was fully deserved." The dreamy look transforms, and that little spark in her eyes dies. "I thought I could change him, but what did I know? I was young and innocent, and I refused to see things that were right in front of my eyes. When I found out I was pregnant, I clung to the hope that he'd change. But he never did. That's when he showed his true colors."

She takes my hands in hers. "Kaden and Keven's father wasn't a good man, but I can't regret those years because he gave me my babies. Kyler is nothing like that—he's a good person. He may be slightly lost, but with you, I believe he has found his way. Which is why I won't stop this. You need each other, and I'm okay with that."

She walks into her bathroom, returning a minute later with

a small cosmetics bag. "I don't know if you're on birth control but you should be. I got my doctor to fill a script for you. There's a six-month supply in there."

"I'm on the pill but I'm down to my last month's supply. I was going to come to you about it." I cross my feet at the ankles. "Mum put me on it when I was fourteen. I never asked, she just did it."

Alex pales. "I'm still struggling to come to terms with that. Your mom and James."

"I know."

There's an awkward silence, and I'm not sure whether I should stay or go.

"I put some condoms in there too," she blurts out. "I'm not sure Kyler would have appreciated his mother or his father handing him those."

I cringe-laugh. "Yeah. It's probably best I don't say where these came from."

"Agreed." She stands up and I rise. "I'm glad we had this talk, and you can come to me anytime you need to. I know he's my son, but we can discuss sex without the need to give me any of the specifics."

Eh, yeah, don't think so. I scratch the back of my head, desperately wanting this convo over and done with. "Thanks," I squeak. "I'll, ah, just get back to him."

She smiles as I practically sprint out of her room.

James's study is slightly ajar as I walk past. His angry tone halts me on the top step. Keven is sitting at his desk with headphones on, his gaze focused on the laptop in front of him. James is on the phone, wearing a line in the carpet as he paces from one end of the room to the next. "I don't give a damn! I told you this last week. It's too soon. She's too fragile. I can't tell her yet." He rolls his eyes to the ceiling. "I didn't say I wouldn't ever tell her. Just not now. You know what she's been through, and I don't want to do anything to upset her any more than she has been." He rubs his hand behind his head. "Fine, fine. You do that. I'll see you in court!"

I flinch as he roars, flinging his phone at the wall in a blatant rage. I tiptoe down the stairs as fast as my legs will carry me.

Chapter Thirty-Three

I find Brad and Ky in the movie room, and I fill them in on what I overheard. "It's Courtney," Ky deduces. "I knew things were too quiet on that front. Girls like her don't go away that easily."

My mobile phone pings with a message from Keven. "Your dad's ready for me. Start the movie. I'll catch up when I'm back."

"No sweat, we'll wait for you," Brad says.

"I've seen all the *Fast and Furious* movies so work away. I'll be able to pick up."

Ky pulls me to him, holding me close as he kisses me hungrily. "Hurry back." He taps my ass as he sends me on my way.

Keven is nowhere to be seen when I open the door to James's study, and the broken phone mess has been cleaned up. James smiles kindly, ushering me into a seat. He fixes two whiskeys and hands one to me. I shake my head, refusing the offer. I don't want to get a taste for that stuff, but it must be serious if he's going there again. "You might need this."

"Hit me with it. I can handle it."

He walks to his desk, retrieving a small cream envelope. When he gives it to me, my hands start to shake. I'd recognize my mum's languid scrawl anywhere. "Where did you get this?" I whisper.

He puts his drink down and kneels in front of me. "Dan received a parcel from Ireland a couple of weeks ago. There were a few letters in it. This is yours. I've already read mine." My eyes widen. "It arrived the day before the attack. I was debating how to tell you when you ended up in the hospital, and I've been waiting for the right time to give it to you. I hope you understand why I held back."

I'm eyeing the envelope like it's a hand grenade. I'm in no doubt whatever it contains has the power to rip me to shreds. *Am I ready for that?*

"Did she explain, in your letter?" I ask.

"Yes."

"You know who my real dad is?" He replies affirmatively again. "Oh." Blood thrums through my veins and my chest tightens.

"You don't have to read it if you aren't up for it. I know it's a lot to take in, but I wasn't happy keeping this from you any longer. Secrets are destroying this family, and that's got to change."

I stand up. "I need to be alone."

"Of course." He pulls me into a gentle hug. "I'll be waiting whenever you're ready to talk about it." I nod on auto-pilot. He places his hands on my shoulder and tilts my head up so I'm looking at him. "Nothing in that letter changes how much we love you and want you here with us. Nothing has to change. We will support you whatever you decide, but I don't want you to worry, sweetheart. Your place is here with us, and it always will be. You're family, Faye."

A myriad of emotions rushes me. "I never thanked you properly." I stare into his confused eyes. "For taking me in. For accepting me."

He kisses my forehead. "Sure, you did, sweetheart. You've shown us in all the things you do. We should be thanking you. Everyone is happier with you here." Not everyone, I think, remembering Kent's blatant hatred from earlier, although I don't take that personally. "I'd hoped when I brought you here that you'd fit in," James continues, "but it's more than that. You bring out the best in us. You don't merely fit in, you *belong*. You belong with us. I love you, sweetheart."

I can't contain it anymore, and I break down, blubbing uncontrollably. He hasn't a clue how much his words mean to me. James holds me as I cry. I'm a little embarrassed when I finally stop. I give him a tentative smile, shucking out of his embrace. "Sorry. I'm all over the place the last couple of weeks."

"It's completely understandable."

"Thanks. I'm going to go back to my room now and ..." My words trail off because I don't know if I'm brave enough to open this letter. It's like a ticking time bomb in my hands.

I stop at the door, turning around to face him. "By the way, I love you too, and I love being a part of this family. I never thought I'd have this again, so, thank you."

I flop down on my bed, staring at the letter for what seems like hours. My finger lovingly traces my name on the envelope, and I hug it to me, closing my eyes and imagining it's my mum. There's a light knock on my door, and Ky sticks his head in the room. "I went looking for you because I was worried. Dad told me. Do you want some company or would you rather be left alone?"

"I don't know," I answer truthfully. "I haven't opened it. I'm not sure I can."

He enters the room, quietly closing the door behind him. Scooting onto the bed beside me, he pulls me into his arms. Instantly, I feel more at ease. I snuggle into his chest, still clutching the envelope in one hand. "You don't have to read it now. You can think about it. Let the idea of it settle in."

"Yeah. I think so. I ... I'm not sure I'm ready to face the truth even though it's all I've wanted since I found out. Guess I'm more of a chicken shit than I thought." I attempt to deflect with humor.

"Bull. You're the strongest person I know." He tilts my head up. "You've been through so much, and this is bound to put you through the wringer again. It's not weak if you need to psych yourself up for that."

I press a brief kiss to his lips. "Thank you. Will you stay or is Brad waiting?"

"I'll stay. Brad understands."

Ky is snoring softly beside me, completely unconscious while I've barely managed to snatch more than twenty-minute naps, at best. My eyes skim over the envelope on my locker as I clock the time. Four twenty a.m. I know I won't get any sleep until I read it. I turn on the bedside lamp and press my mouth to Ky's. "Ky?" I run my hands over his chest and he stirs. I kiss him again, and he opens sleepy eyes, blinking furiously.

"What's wrong?" he croaks.

"I need to read the letter." He forces his eyes wide. "Can you read it with me?"

"Sure. If that's what you want." He reaches out and grasps my wrist.

"I do. I have no secrets from you."

He sits up, draping his arm around my shoulders and pressing a sleepy kiss to my forehead. I take the letter from the locker, and my hands shake as I extract the contents from the envelope. There are six folded pages, all in my mum's messy handwriting. My lower lip wobbles, and I'm fighting tears as I nestle into the crook of Ky's arm. He holds me, pressing kisses into my hair and my face, and gradually I get a grip of myself. I smooth the first page out straight, and my breath quivers as I start reading.

Darling Faye,

Writing this letter is possibly the hardest thing I've ever done. Not only because what I need to share with you is going to be hugely traumatic, but mainly because I don't want to be telling you like this. I hope you never get to read this letter. I hope I am explaining all this in person and that you can find it in your heart to forgive me. To try and understand how difficult it was to do the right thing. To find the right time. To acknowledge that my parenting skills weren't always up to scratch, but I never stopped trying—I wanted to be the best mum because you deserved no less.

You are the singular, most important thing in my life and the one person I love above everyone and everything else. Quite simply, you are the best thing that happened to me, and I am so proud to call you my daughter. I love you, honey.

Tears are flowing down my cheeks as I read.

I've isolated that paragraph and drawn a marker under it on purpose, because I want you to memorise it, to keep it close to your heart, to believe it as you read this letter.

You are my greatest accomplishment, and I don't know what I did right to deserve you, but whatever it was I'm so grateful. Every day, I thank God for bringing you into this world. Every day I thank him for your compassion and your grace and your thoughtfulness and your zest for life. I know there have been challenging times, when you struggled to accept and embrace who you are, but my daughter is the strongest, bravest girl in the whole universe, and she overcame her demons, emerging truer and stronger than ever before. Like I said, I'm so proud of you. For tons of other reasons, too, but if I start down that path, this letter will become a novel and I fear you'd stop reading before I get to the important part.

You are loved. So profoundly. Never forget that.

I can't see over the tears clouding my vision. Large watery drops mark the page where my tears fall. I bury my head in Ky's chest, needing the feel and smell of him to ground me before I can resume reading. He holds me wordlessly, knowing exactly what I need without me having to say it.

> I asked the solicitor to send this letter to you a few months after James's guardianship started, because I wanted to give you some time to settle into your new home before hitting you with all this. By now, I wonder if James has told you the truth about our relationship and why I kept him hidden from you. When I first sat down to write this letter, I omitted any mention of it, focusing on the details of your birth that were relevant. But I was chickening out. You deserve to know the truth—the whole truth, no matter how ugly it is. So, I scrapped that letter and rewrote it from scratch.
>
> So here goes. (Taking a deep breath.)
>
> James and I had an incestuous relationship when we were teens. (Take a minute to let that sink in if you need to, honey.)
>
> It was wrong. I know that now. I knew it at the time, but I couldn't confront him about it because I started it. I set us on that path and that's haunted me my whole life. I spent years thinking I hated him, but I didn't. How could I hate the one person who had always been there

for me? My brother gave up his ambitions to care for me. He became my parents, my brother, my best friend, my confidant, my lover, my shoulder to lean on, and I am the person I am today because of him. So, I can't hate him for that. I never did although there were times where I wanted to.

But it wasn't his fault. It wasn't mine either. It wasn't anyone's fault. It happened because we were thrust together due to circumstance, and we transformed to be what each other needed. It was a fleeting moment in time, one that would've passed. I strongly believe that now.

My biggest regret is running away from him without a word. I can't even imagine what that must have done to James. He didn't deserve that, but I was in a panic, and for the first time in my life, he couldn't be there for me. It was time for me to grow up and face the reality of the situation I found myself in—a situation I had created.

I've thought of him often over the years. Missed him. Longed to play a part in his life again, but it wasn't the appropriate time. I had hoped that when you turned eighteen, after I had explained all this, and when you'd had time to process it, that we could try to reconcile. To form some type of relationship from the ashes of our past. But if you are reading this letter, it means I left it too late to make amends, so, I've included another letter for James. He deserves some closure, and I hope my letter can do that for him. Please, tell him I'm sorry and that he was always in my heart and in my thoughts.

I look up at Ky and his sorrowful expression matches my own. He kisses my cheek, and I cup his face. My mum's words have helped put things in perspective, and I truly hope that her letter offers James some peace.

I'm expecting by now that you've realized why I ran away (my Faye is super smart.) Yes—I was pregnant with you, and I didn't know who the father was. I had only been sleeping with James a few weeks when I met Adam. Adam's family were very well-to-do, and they had a holiday home in Wexford which they used during school holidays and most weekends during spring and summer. We met at a local disco, and it was love at first sight. Even now, after all these years, thoughts of him cause my heart rate to spike unnaturally. We fell hard for one another, and I spent every spare moment with him. James worked a lot of overtime at weekends, and he knew I went to the disco with my friends on Saturday nights, so he never knew. I wanted to tell him.

Tried to tell him so many times, but I worried what it would do to him, so I said nothing.

I've made so many mistakes in my life, Faye, and I look back at how differently things could've been but I have no regrets. How can I when my life's journey brought me you?

When I discovered I was pregnant, I didn't know what to do. I couldn't tell any of my friends. None of them knew about James and me, and they would've automatically assumed the baby was Adam's. I was tempted to tell Adam and hope that you were his. I knew he would look after me, but I couldn't do that to him. I couldn't trick him like that. He was sitting his Leaving Cert in a few months, and he had plans to study business in Trinity, and I couldn't derail his life without proof the baby was his. But therein lay the problem. I had only turned seventeen, and I had no money of my own, and there was no way of organising a paternity test without James finding out. I didn't even know if there was a way of proving it while I was still pregnant, and I was so scared. What if I went about the test and I had to admit my brother could potentially be the father? What if I had the test and it proved you were James's baby? The authorities would've locked both of us up, and you would've been placed into foster care or even put up for adoption. I couldn't contemplate such a scenario. So, I did the only thing I could think of.

I ran away.

I pawned all my mother's jewellery and took whatever cash I could find, and I spent weeks travelling around Ireland, thumbing lifts and staying in hostels, always moving, never stopping in one place long enough for James to find me. Because I knew he was looking for me. That's who my brother was.

After a couple of months, I was running out of money, and I was tired and sick all the time, so I settled in a small village in county Waterford, renting a room with an elderly woman who was all alone. Mary turned out to be my saving grace. It was Mary who introduced me to the local shopkeeper and convinced her to hire me. Gerry and Ann Donovan were getting on in years, and their only son was working away in Belfast. They needed help with the shop but couldn't afford to hire anyone full-time, so the arrangement suited me perfectly. When Mary discovered I was pregnant, she brought me to a doctor in Waterford city and ensured I got the best medical care. She never once judged me which is remarkable because most people her age were not very open-minded at that time.

I met Gerry and Ann's son when he came home for Christmas. Michael was besotted with me from the minute we met. He was seven years older, and I very clearly had a bun in the oven, but that didn't stop your dad. (The fact he wasn't your biological dad doesn't change anything - he IS your father and always will be.) He went on a massive charm offensive, doing his best to woo me, but I insisted we stay as friends. My hormones were all over the place, and I was missing your uncle and pining for Adam, and it didn't feel right to start anything with Michael while I still felt like that. He respected my wishes, and he told me he would wait until I was ready. He was content to be my friend until he could be more.

Michael was in the hospital when you were born, and the third person to see you after me and Mary. He fell in love with you instantly. I was only home from the hospital two days when he proposed. I turned him down flat, but your dad could be very insistent (some would call it stubborn) when he wanted to be (remember the time with the car?) and eventually he wore me down and I agreed.

I smile through my tears, recalling a happier time. "When I was fourteen, my parents took me with them when they were buying a new car. My mum fell in love with this canary yellow

Mini Cooper but my dad insisted it was too small and too bright, and he wanted her to get this Toyota. It was roomier and a more sedate silver with less mileage." A sharp ache twists like a knife in my gut.

"So, you went home with the Toyota?" Ky deduces.

I smile again. "No, we went home with the Mini Cooper, but five days later my mother returned it to the garage and came home with the Toyota. My father kept up a relentless campaign the whole five days, printing off all these reports from the internet showing comparisons between both cars and safety specs and details of resale value. She couldn't take it anymore so she gave in." I rest my head on his chest. "Most men would just give into their wives, and my dad did that a lot too. But our safety was of paramount importance to him. He'd virtually grown up on Mondello Race Track, and he'd seen his fair share of crashes. He was fixated on safety, and that's why he didn't give up. He knew the Toyota would be a better car for my mum."

I sniffle. "Maybe if she'd kept the Mini Cooper, they wouldn't have died as they did. Irony is a bitch."

He holds me tight to him, and his quiet strength gives me the courage to continue. I pick up the letter and resume reading.

Now, listen up carefully because this part is very important. I may not have been in love with your dad when I married him, but I respected and admired him enormously, and I knew I was entrusting my future, and yours, to a good man. I told him the truth, about James and Adam, and he didn't judge me. He was shocked, naturally, but it didn't change how he felt about me, about you. I knew then that I was making the right call, that marrying him was the right thing to do. And I did fall in love with him, and he became everything I hadn't even realised I craved. I hope you saw how much we loved one another and that you believe me when I tell you it was real and genuine. It was different to the love I felt for James, and different to the love I shared with Adam, but I love Michael so completely. I have never regretted the choice I made to marry him, and he has never let me down.

And he loves you so much, Faye. From the minute you were born, he adored you. Worshipped you as if you were his own flesh and blood. His illness means he can't ever father children. That is the real reason why you don't have brothers and sisters. I'm sorry for lying to you about this too, but I worried if I told you that you'd start questioning your existence before you were ready to deal with the truth. He supports my decision regarding your biological dad. He agrees that you have a right to know and a right to decide what you want to do with the knowledge.

Another splinter cracks my heart wide open. I'm not surprised my dad reacted like that—he always had the biggest heart.

James contacted me a few years after I got married, and after I got over my initial panic attack, I agreed to meet with him purely for one reason and one reason only: to find out if he was your dad. By that time, I was in the height of my guilt over what we'd done, and I could barely even glance at James. I look back now and hate myself for how I treated him, but I was so ashamed, and I took it out on him. He deserved better. He seemed happy, and I was grateful for that, and he appeared to truly love his wife and their children. I thought it was ironic that he ended up bringing up another man's children. In a way, it made sense.

I took his cup with me and used the DNA and yours to get some tests done. The tests revealed that he wasn't your father, and I've never felt so conflicted. I cried happy tears. I cried sad tears. My heart ached for Adam, for depriving him of you, but what could I do? I knew he was recently married as I'd seen it in a society magazine, and I didn't feel like I had the right to thrust this knowledge upon him when he had moved on in his life.

Michael begged me to tell Adam, and that

should've made it easier for me, but I was scared Adam might try and gain custody of you. He came from money, and we had very little, and I knew we would lose in any custody battle, so I chose not to tell him. I know now that it was the wrong call. He has missed out on so much of your life, and he can never get that back. You can never get that time back. I'm sorry, Faye. I'm sorry that I failed you, but please believe me when I say I always had your best interests at heart, even if they were misguided at times.

He doesn't know, Faye. To this day, Adam doesn't know he's your dad. I never told him. I misled you on so many things, and I hate myself for it, but it was so hard deciding when to tell you, and how to tell you. There is never a right time to tell someone you love something like this. No matter how or when I tell you, you are going to be devastated. I wish I could save you the pain, but I can't.

I had decided to tell you when you turned thirteen, but you were going through a horrific time after what happened with Daniel and Vera. I spoke to your psychologist, and she advised me to wait. She was concerned it would set back your recovery. Then we moved to Dublin, and you were settling into a new school, and you met Luke and you seemed happy. I didn't want to undo all your progress. So, Dad and I decided we'd tell you when you were eighteen and let you choose whether you wanted to meet Adam or not. We are not passing the responsibility onto you out of selfishness, but I believe, at eighteen, you have the right to choose whether you want to get to know your biological father or not. I've made enough decisions on your behalf. This is the one thing I can let you steer. I've written a letter for Adam too. I've told him he has a daughter, because he has a right to know, and I can't keep it from him any longer, but I've asked him to not contact you until you are ready to meet with him. I don't know if he will respect my wishes. I don't know the man he is today, but James will shelter you if necessary.

The solicitor has Adam's full contact details, and he has been advised to provide same to you should you request them. I haven't supplied them in this letter because I know you will need time to think all of this through.

Writing this letter has been physically draining but strangely cathartic too. There have been tears. Plenty of tears. I imagine you have shed some too. I wonder what you think of me now? I hope you don't despise me, though I wouldn't blame you if you did. But I know my baby girl, and I trust her to make the right decisions, to deal with this with strength and humility and to (hopefully) find a way to forgive me.

Everything I have done has been borne out of love for you.

If I die today, I can say I've had a good life. A great life. Because I had you and Michael in it. Because our little family was everything I would've asked God for if I had known to ask for it. I'm not proud of some of the things I've done, but I don't regret a single thing. You have been the very best part of me and I love you with my whole heart.

I trust my brother with your life in a way I couldn't trust anyone else. I have no doubt James will do right by you which is why I requested him as your guardian. You always longed for an extended family, and now you have one.

Be brave, baby girl. Continue to make me proud (I know you will) but most importantly, BE HAPPY. Love large. When you find the one—the man you can't live without—tell him, show him, love him, every day of your life. Never take it for granted, no matter how many challenges are thrown your way. Don't let anyone dictate the love you have in your life. Be brave to make the right choices for the man you love, and have a great life, Faye, because you deserve it.

No matter what you end up doing, know that I will be looking down from my perch in Heaven, beaming with pride, and so grateful for the years we did have together.

Now, dry your eyes, push your sadness away, and embrace all the wonderful things you have to look forward to.

Never forget how much I loved you. How much we loved you.

Yours, forever,

Mum.

XX

Chapter Thirty-Four

I carefully tuck the letter away and place the envelope in the drawer of my locker. Snuggling back into Ky's chest, I let every emotion I'm feeling run rampant inside me. He holds me securely, running his hand smoothly up and down my back. It's hard to hold onto my anger now that I know the full story. "She must've been so scared," I whisper into Ky's chest. "I can't imagine being pregnant and having to run away and fend for myself."

"I can see where you get your strength from now," he says. "Your mom was an awesome lady. I'm sad I never got to meet her."

"Me too."

More silence descends but it's not uncomfortable.

"She loved your dad," I say, looking up at Ky. "He protected her and cared for her, and she knew he would do the same for me."

"Dad's good at that." His voice is ragged and laced with emotion.

"I have a dad out there somewhere." I lift my head and

twist around so I'm facing him with my hands on his broad chest.

"Do you want to meet him?"

"I don't know. It's a lot to take in." I bite my lip. "What if he doesn't want to meet me?"

"Then he's a fool, and he'll miss out on meeting the most amazing girl to walk the planet."

"You're clearly biased."

He rubs his nose against mine. "I might be, but then so is Brad and my parents and all my brothers. You're amazing, Faye." He grips my chin. "Own it."

I grin as I briefly join our mouths. "I will if you do." He arches a brow. "You're pretty damn amazing yourself."

"Shite," he says, borrowing one of my words. "We've already turned into one of those nausea-inducing couples. I'm gonna get hell for this when we go public."

"Does that bother you?"

He smooths the lines in my forehead with his thumb. "Not at all, and you're worth it." His wide smile lights me up on the inside.

I bite down on my lip as I recall my mother's words. "Do I show you enough? Tell you enough? Love you enough?"

He goes stock-still, staring at me with shell-shocked eyes. Acknowledgment dawns, and even though I wouldn't think it possible, his smile expands even more. "You do, babe." He stares lovingly into my face, leaning forward to plant a cute little kiss on the tip of my nose. My heart is running a marathon in my chest as he holds me close to him. "You're my one and only, Faye. Just thought I'd add that so there's no confusion."

"Really?"

"Really."

I'm knocking on James's bedroom door before the sun has risen in the early morning sky. I can't wait any longer to talk to him. He doesn't object, opening his door and welcoming me with open arms. We spend hours talking about Mum. He reads my letter and I read his. Some of it is difficult to read, but it's as Mum said—it's strangely therapeutic.

Later, the triplets blow out the candles on their cake and open their presents before we head to a restaurant in Boston Harbor to celebrate their birthday. Talk at the table is jovial even when James and I explain in hushed tones about the letters—sans mention of the incest, of course. Alex looks out the window the entire time, and I figure any conversation about my mother is difficult for her now, knowing what she does about the true nature of her relationship with James.

Back at the house, I pull Kaden and Keven aside. It hadn't occurred to me until we were discussing it earlier, how similar our situations are. They also discovered they had a different bio dad when they were eighteen. I'm keen to hear their perspective. "Do you regret it? Meeting your biological dad?"

They share apprehensive looks. "I do." Keven speaks up first. "I wish we'd never tracked him down. I'd rather not have known that pathetic excuse of a man was my father." A sour note crosses over his face.

"I don't regret it," Kaden says. "If we hadn't met him I would've always wondered about him. It's better to face the reality than live a lie or live with some imaginary vision of a perfect dad. I was furious with Mom and Dad for keeping his existence a secret, and I've only recently forgiven them for that, even though I understood why they kept it from me after I met the man. I know why you're asking, and if you want my advice, I'd go meet your dad. Nothing good comes from hiding behind the truth."

"I completely disagree," Keven says. "I wish I'd kept that

imaginary dad in my head instead of meeting that washed-up alco who still thinks he's a worshiped Motocross Champ."

Deep lines crease my brow as a flurry of butterflies swarms my gut. "Wait? He's a Motocross Champion?"

"Not anymore, but he was quite famous in his day."

All the color leaches from my skin as a thought explodes in my mind.

Kaden squeezes my hand, misinterpreting my expression. "I know you've a big decision to make, and we probably haven't helped but it doesn't matter anyway because you're the only one who can make this choice. You and you alone have to make the decision."

"Don't rush into it," Keven proposes. "Take your time to think it through, and you know where we are if you need to discuss it further."

"Thanks a mill," I say, getting up in a bit of a daze, his words not properly registering. An ice-cold grip has seized my heart. "I'm gonna head to my room. I've a lot to think about." My brain is computing all the facts, and I need to find out if my suspicion is correct.

I almost collide with Alex as I leave the living room and enter the lobby. She's tucked in behind the doorframe, just out of sight. Her eyes dart wide when she spots me, but she hurriedly composes herself. "Everything okay, sweetheart?"

"Grand," I lie, forcing a smile. "I've a lot on my mind, and I need some time alone to process things."

"Of course. Let us know if you need anything." She breezes past me up the stairs to her room, and I continue down the corridor toward my bedroom, grateful now that Brad and Ky have headed out on their bikes. What I need to do next requires me to be completely undisturbed.

What did people do for research before Google I wonder as I trawl through numerous articles and skim images on my phone. In less than an hour, I know pretty much all I need to know. It's been niggling at my subconscious since that conversation I had with James in his study, and now I think I know why. This is one occasion where I'm fervently hoping I'm wrong, but I have a strong suspicion I'm right.

Clutching my phone to my chest, I slip out of my room in my socks and tiptoe quietly to the mezzanine level. Lights and the low hum of the TV tell me that Alex hasn't retired to bed yet but her door is closed so I should be able to sneak into James's office without anyone noticing.

I close the door quietly behind me and switch the small desktop lamp on while my eyes scan the room for what I need. A line of leather-bound family albums are stacked in a row on the upper bookshelf, and I make a beeline for them. My eyes skim across the albums until I find the burgundy-colored one James showed me previously. I take it over to one of the velvet-covered chairs, pulling my feet up underneath me. I flip through the pages until I come to the set of baby pictures I need. I compare them, noting the subtle differences that no one would question until they need to. My suspicion is confirmed, and I abhor it.

Resting my head back, I shutter my eyes as agonizing pain shreds my heart into itty-bitty pieces. I want to be wrong about this but I genuinely don't think I am.

I need to confront Alex.

Demand she admit the truth because secrets and lies are destroying this family from the inside out, and the only way they'll be able to pick up the pieces is with a fresh start. That can't happen until all the dirty laundry has been aired. The slate can't be wiped clean until everything is out in the open.

This responsibility shouldn't fall on my shoulders, but Alex has had years to face up to this. Hell, she had the perfect opportunity to do this a few weeks ago, and the fact she didn't volunteer the information then tells me she's not going to willingly do so. It's clear my uncle doesn't know about this either, and I can only imagine what this revelation is going to do to him too. I get up, fierce determination etched across my face. I'll force her to face up to it because this secret can't stay hidden.

Above everything, Ky deserves to know the truth.

And I love him enough to be the one to force it out into the open.

No more bloody lies.

Clasping the album to my chest, I storm out of the study and burst into Alex's bedroom. The door swings open and Alex jumps on the chaise longue, turning startled eyes on me as wine sloshes out of her glass onto her blouse. She's drinking again. That's not a good sign. "Faye," she pants, slapping a hand over her chest. "You frightened me."

I slam the photo album down on the coffee table with a loud thud. "I know."

She frowns, staring at the album with a look of confusion on her face.

Hell. *How many more secrets is she keeping that this one isn't immediately obvious?*

"I don't understand." She starts flipping through the pages as I pace back and forth in front of her, willing myself to calm down. Any sympathy I might've had for her is rapidly diminishing. Her face drops and her eyes stretch wide. I can almost see the little wheels turning in her head.

She stands up, gripping me by the shoulders. "Whatever you think it is, I can explain."

I stare into her piercing green eyes. "Don't even think about bullshitting me. I know I'm right. I can't believe no one else has figured this out! Especially Kaden and Keven!"

Her face turns a sickly shade of pale as she races to the bathroom and throws up. I flop down on the chaise longue, holding my head in my hands. I can't believe this. It's going to devastate him.

"Please don't say anything," she begs returning to the room with a small hand towel pressed to her mouth. She pushes the door closed with her bare foot but it doesn't close all the way.

"I'm sorry, Alex, but I can't agree to that. James doesn't know either, does he?"

She slouches against the wall as her entire frame shakes. "No, and it'll kill him. You can't tell him! You heard what Kaden and Keven said earlier. No good will come from this."

"James has a right to know Ky isn't his biological son! And Ky deserves to know the truth about his father!"

"James loves Ky like he's his own. What harm is there in letting that be? Your own situation is clouding your judgment." Alex stumbles back, dropping inelegantly onto the chaise longue beside me. Her panicked eyes latch onto mine as I sink to my knees in front of her, a dead weight pressing down on my chest.

"How could you do this to them?" I whisper. "How could you live this lie for so long?" I clamp a hand across my mouth as the magnitude of my discovery hits home.

Silence engulfs the room as we stare at one another. Slowly, tears roll down her face, dripping onto her chin. She opens and closes her mouth. "I didn't mean to deceive him," she admits, after a bit. "I swear."

"Did you know all along?" I ask. "Did you trick my uncle into marrying you?"

She shakes her head. "No! My feelings for James were real. And I didn't know, not at first, I swear it."

Maybe I'm gullible, but I believe her.

"I got pregnant the first time I slept with James, or so I thought. We were only back in the States a couple of weeks when I did the test. I was so scared. I thought he'd run out on me, so I didn't tell him straightaway. To be honest, I was in denial. I hadn't gone to the doctor. I kept hoping the test was mistaken, and I was still getting my periods, so I managed to convince myself that it was wrong. But, after a few weeks, my stomach was noticeably larger, and I eventually plucked up the courage to tell James." Tears pump out of her eyes, and her speech comes out in choked, sporadic clumps. "He was so happy. I couldn't believe it, but the genuine joy on his face told me he was sincere. I went to the doctors while he stayed at home to mind the boys."

She breaks down, resting her head on her hands as she cries. Huge wracking sobs rip forth from her chest. I can't get past the horrified lump in my throat. My thoughts are consumed with Ky—this is going to destroy him. I know, because I've been in his shoes. After a couple minutes, she straightens up, sniffling. I grab a few tissues from a box on the table and hand them to her. "I gave the doctor my dates but he said something didn't add up, that the pregnancy was more advanced than I thought. When he calculated the new dates, everything inside me turned to ice." She sways, shaking and crying, as she relives the moment. "Kaden and Keven's biological father had returned a few weeks before I traveled to Ireland, and I'd stupidly let him into my bed, believing him when he said he'd turned over a new leaf, that he wanted me, wanted us. I woke up the next morning to find him gone along with my cash and credit cards and any remnants of my self-esteem."

She cries again, and I fight the urge to console her.

"After I left the doctors, I went to the park and I sat there for hours, cursing God and my own naïveté. I knew my ex wouldn't give a damn about my pregnancy, and there was James, ecstatically happy, waiting at home for me, already loving my two sons as if they were his own and so blissfully happy at the thought of being a father. I cried for hours over the unfairness of it all. I begged God for it somehow to all be a mistake." She sniffs, gripping my hands firmly. "The next day I went to a gynecologist for a second opinion, praying the whole time for a miracle, but he confirmed the doctor's findings, and I knew what I needed to do. I went home that evening to confess it all to James. I hoped he wouldn't leave me because of it, but I knew I had to tell him the truth. That it wasn't fair otherwise." Her lip wobbles as she stares at me through red-rimmed glossy eyes.

"What happened?"

"Before I had a chance to confess, James got down on one knee and proposed to me." The sobs start up in earnest again. "He had even bought replica rings for Kaden and Keven to give to me. As I stood there, looking at the three men in my life, all on one knee, asking me to marry them, I knew what I should do. That I should reveal the truth as I'd intended, but I couldn't do it. I couldn't destroy the family I'd created with James. He was the best thing to happen to me and my boys and I felt it was selfish to take that from them. They needed a father, and James had willingly stepped into that role, and he was such a natural. As I watched him with them, I thought who cares that he isn't their biological father? He was their father in every way that mattered. I knew he would be a better father to Kyler than my asshole ex, so I said nothing. I pushed the truth away. I let James believe he was Ky's father because he was, because he *is*, in all the ways that are important. I have never regretted my decision to marry James. Even with everything that has transpired between us recently, I will never forget what he did for this family. He loves those boys so much, and they couldn't have had a better father. I won't ever regret bringing him into their lives, but I do regret not telling him the truth. And I've had to live with that guilt my entire marriage. It has been on the tip of my tongue so many times, but I was always so scared to admit the truth because I knew what it'd mean. I was selfish and a coward and there's nothing you can say to me about my actions that I haven't already thought."

"You should've come clean when it came out about Kaden and Keven."

"I know, but I couldn't do it. This family is hurting enough already. Ky is hurting enough already. I love him so much and I didn't want to do this to him."

"He deserves to know the truth! And it's because I love him so much that I want him to know the truth. I'm insisting you tell him, Alex, both of them, and if you won't, I will."

Chapter Thirty-Five

The door swings open and I gasp as James steps into the room, a look of sheer horror etched on his face. "Oh my God, no!" Alex wails, scrambling to her feet and ambling toward him. "Did you hear?"

His jaw tenses, a muscle popping in and out as he holds her at arm's length. His lip quivers. "He isn't mine?" His façade crumples, and he sinks to his knees. I'm rooted to the spot, watching in horrid fascination. "I need you to say it to my face." Alex drops down in front of him. "I need you to look me straight in the eye and tell me that boy I love with all my heart isn't mine. Is it true, Alex, is it?" His anguished pleas are ripping my insides to shreds. "Kyler isn't my biological son? Your womanizing asshole ex got you knocked up and you passed the child off as mine? Tell me, Alex." He grips her wrist, shouting now. "Tell me you've lied to me about this for years!" She tears up again, and I wrap my arms around my waist to ward off the bout of shivers attacking me. "Tell me!" James's voice cracks.

"I'm sorry," she whimpers. "I'm so sorry. I thought it was for the best."

"I'm so dense." James slams his palm against his forehead. "I knew he was too big to be premature." His look turns to ice. "How much did you pay the doctor and midwife to lie?"

She hangs her head. "Whatever it took."

"I should've known." James grabs fistfuls of his hair. "Kyler is such a natural at motocross. I never even stopped to think about that fact." My stomach curdles at the stone-cold look that crosses his face. "You can't tell me that Kaden and Keven didn't ask you these questions? Not when they found out who their dad was?"

Her lip wobbles as she pulls herself back up onto the chaise longue. "They only asked me a few weeks ago, after we told the rest of the boys. I didn't realize they had met him."

"What did they ask you, Alex?" James pushes to his feet, extending his hand toward me. He pulls me into his side, and I willingly oblige.

"They asked me if he was Kyler's dad too." She wets her lips nervously. "They put me on the spot, and I panicked. I lied. I told them he was yours because I don't want Kyler mixed up with that man! I already see enough of the same darkness in my son."

James clings to me and his body shakes. I don't know if it's fear or rage or grief or a different emotion altogether. Maybe it's a mix of everything.

Alex starts crying again, but James just stares straight ahead. He clutches me tight, and my heart is breaking for him. "Are any of the others his children?" he asks after a while in a low voice. "Are my other sons mine?"

"They are yours. I swear it."

He goes quiet for a few minutes. "I'm having trouble

believing anything that comes out of your mouth, so I'll be organizing paternity tests to make sure."

"If you do that, they'll all want to know why!" Alex's tone is borderline hysterical.

James lets go of me, crouching down in front of Alex. "If you think I'm staying quiet about this, you can think again. Kyler needs to know first, and then we'll tell Kaden and Keven and the rest of the boys after."

Tears cascade down her cheeks. "I'm sorry, James. I'm so sorry. I thought it was for the best."

"Out of everything that's happened these last few months, this is the worst lie. You know how much I love that boy! When I was in his room, by his cot, singing him to sleep every night when he was a baby, did you feel any guilt? Any remorse? Did you ever consider telling me?"

She swipes her fingers under her eyes. "Guilt and remorse? Yes. I felt those emotions. Did I ever consider telling you?" I spot the resolve returning as her face hardens. "No. I never considered telling you back then. If anything, it strengthened my belief that I'd done the right thing. All I could think about was how Kaden and Keven had missed out on those moments because my ex hadn't been around when they were babies. And I was so glad that you were there for Kyler. You were everything I wanted for my sons. I couldn't have dreamed a more perfect father. You may not have been the perfect husband, but you were the perfect father. I will never take that from you, James."

"I can't forgive you for this, Alex. I don't think I'll ever be able to forgive you."

"Please, honey. Don't say what you're going to say. Not when you're this emotional."

James stands up. He cricks his neck from side to side and closes his eyes. Alex stares forlornly at me, and though she's the orchestrator of this mess, I have sympathy for her. I've never doubted her love for her children, and I believe her when she says she thought she was doing the right thing. It doesn't excuse it, like what my mother did doesn't excuse her behavior, but I have a greater understanding of it.

James opens his eyes and walks toward me. "Would you mind giving Alex and me a few moments alone?" His voice is eerily calm.

My mouth is coated in a layer of bile as I speak. "No problem."

"And would you mind fetching Kyler and bringing him here in about fifteen minutes. Please don't say anything to him yet. He needs to hear this from Alex and me."

"Of course. I'll go see if he's back."

My stomach twists and turns as I step out of the room and fly down the stairs. I pull out my phone and tap out a quick message. *"You home yet?"* Without waiting for a reply, I head to the garage but neither Brad's nor Ky's bikes are there. Returning to the house, I keep checking my phone, but there's no message waiting. I head to my bedroom and flop down on the bed. I'm sick at the thoughts of what is lying in wait for Ky. As if he hasn't been through enough already. I'm beginning to believe there's some truth to this notion of a Kennedy curse. Happiness seems to evade this family, and they appear destined to career from one tragedy to another. He's only just extricated himself from the Addison mess, and we're finally on the same page—and now this. While Ky doesn't have the best relationship with James, he has always known he can rely on him. This is going to destroy him.

It isn't fair.

I check my phone again. Still nothing. I send another message, and this time I copy Brad.

"Where r u?" Brad messages me back straightaway.

"In my room. Where r u?"

There's no immediate reply, and I groan, tossing my phone onto the bed. I peek at the clock. James and Alex will be expecting Ky any second now. I hop up and stride across the room, opening the door with a flourish. I shriek as I, unexpectedly, come face to face with Brad. "Jeez. You startled me!"

"We need to talk."

The solemn expression on his face drains the blood from my face. I look out in the corridor, but it's empty. "Where's Ky?"

Brad takes my elbow and pulls me back into the room, shutting the door with the heel of his boots. "Don't freak out."

"You can't expect me not to freak out when you say something like that! Where is he, Brad? What's going on?"

"Here." He thrusts a folded-up piece of paper in my hand. "He left this for you."

"No!" I clamp a hand over my mouth as it dawns on me. "When did you get back to the house?"

"Right around the time James confronted Alex, screaming at the top of his lungs. We heard everything. Ky heard everything."

Panic and fear almost throttle me. "No, Brad! No! He can't have found out like that. Where is he?" I grip his shoulders firmly. "I need to be with him! You shouldn't have let him leave." I start pacing the floor, and my heart is pounding in my chest. "Shite!" I slam my palm into my forehead. "We have to go after him! He could get killed on that bike!"

"Faye." Brad walks toward me. "Faye. Stop! Calm down. Read the letter."

I'm scared to read it. Terrified of what it might say. "You know what it says?"

He shakes his head. "He told me to only give it to you. I wouldn't invade your privacy like that."

With trembling fingers, I open the page and read.

Faye,

I overheard it all, and I can't believe she lied to me. I can't deal with this, and I can't face either of them so I need to leave. This isn't about you. I LOVE YOU. Nothing about that will ever change, but I need to do this by myself. For myself. Don't come looking for me. I don't want to drag you into this because you are too good to get mixed up in my crap. I need time and space to wrap my head around it, to sort myself out, so I'm properly worthy of you. I will come back for you—I just don't know when.

Don't worry—I'll be fine. This is something I have to do for me. Stay strong. ~~Dad~~ James will need you.

Love you, baby.

Ky.

The page floats to the floor, and I stand rooted to the spot as if my feet were cemented to the ground.

I didn't think my heart could hurt any more, but I was wrong. My heart is rupturing in my chest. Splitting wide open like someone has cleaved it in two.

He's gone.

I've lost the love of my life.

I don't know when he's coming back.

If he's coming back.

If I'll ever see him again.

I don't know where he is going, or if he's okay.

He can't be. Everything he thought he knew about himself has been flipped on its head.

I know all about that. I wish he'd stayed to talk to me, although I understand the urge to flee. Sometimes it's far too tempting to run from the problems, even if you think you're running toward the solution.

He needs me. He just doesn't realize it yet.

With fire in my eyes, I push past a clearly worried Brad, storming out of the room. I know exactly what I need to do and who I need to help me.

He's gone, and he's asked me not to come after him, but he clearly isn't thinking straight if he believes that'll stop me.

Losing Kyler is not an option I'm prepared to accept.

No matter what it takes, I'm going to find him, and I'm not giving up until I do.

Keeping Kyler is the next book in the series. Available now and free to read in Kindle Unlimited.

Nothing or no one will keep them apart...

Kyler Kennedy is in the wind.

Shocked and upset, he has taken off on a solo mission—to track down his mom's ex and demand answers.

Faye understands what it's like to have your world turned upside down. Determined to support her boyfriend, she gives chase, yet nothing could prepare her for the ugly truth. Ky has always been plagued with inner demons, and as he falls apart, Faye finally discovers what he's been hiding from her—from everyone.

When serious accusations arise, Kyler's future hangs in the balance. But Kennedys stick together in times of crisis, and they rally around him now.

At least there is nothing to prevent Faye and Ky from being together. They go public with their relationship, but not everyone is thrilled for them. Bitter enemies reappear, and fresh battle lines are drawn, but Faye is ready to fight back.

No one is taking her new family from her.

Especially not a manipulative ex.

With time running out for Kyler, Faye takes matters into her own hands.

But when you play with fire, you risk getting burned.

Available now in ebook, paperback, and audiobook.

The boy who broke my heart is now the man who wants to mend it.

Jared was my everything until an ocean separated us and he abandoned me when I needed him most.

He forgot the promises he made.

Forgot the love he swore was eternal.

It was over before it began.

Now, he's a hot commodity, universally adored, and I'm the woman no one wants.

Pining for a boy who no longer exists is pathetic. Years pass, men come and go, but I cannot move on.

I didn't believe my fractured heart and broken soul could endure any more pain. Until Jared rocks up to the art gallery where I work, with his fiancée in tow, and I'm drowning again.

Seeing him brings everything to the surface, so I flee. Placing distance between us again, I'm determined to put him behind me once and for all.

Then he reappears at my door, begging me for another chance.

I know I should turn him away.

Try telling that to my heart.

This angsty, new adult romance is a FREE full-length ebook, exclusively available to newsletter subscribers.

Type this link into your browser to claim your free copy: https://bit.ly/TITMHFBB

OR

Scan this code to claim your free copy:

About the Author

Siobhan Davis is a *USA Today, Wall Street Journal,* and Amazon Top 5 bestselling romance author. **Siobhan** writes emotionally intense stories with swoon-worthy romance, complex characters, and tons of unexpected plot twists and turns that will have you flipping the pages beyond bedtime! She has sold over 2 million books, and her titles are translated into several languages.

Prior to becoming a full-time writer, Siobhan forged a successful corporate career in human resource management.

She lives in the Garden County of Ireland with her husband and two sons.

You can connect with Siobhan in the following ways:

Website: www.siobhandavis.com
Facebook: AuthorSiobhanDavis
Instagram: @siobhandavisauthor
Tiktok: @siobhandavisauthor
Email: siobhan@siobhandavis.com

Books by Siobhan Davis

KENNEDY BOYS SERIES
Upper Young Adult/New Adult Contemporary Romance

Finding Kyler
Losing Kyler
Keeping Kyler
The Irish Getaway
Loving Kalvin
Saving Brad
Seducing Kaden
Forgiving Keven
Summer in Nantucket
Releasing Keanu
Adoring Keaton
Reforming Kent
Moonlight in Massachusetts

STAND-ALONES
New Adult Contemporary Romance

Inseparable
Incognito
When Forever Changes
No Feelings Involved
Still Falling for You
Second Chances Box Set

Holding on to Forever
Always Meant to Be
Tell It to My Heart
The One I Want

Reverse Harem Romance
Surviving Amber Springs

Dark Mafia Romance
Vengeance of a Mafia Queen

RYDEVILLE ELITE SERIES
Dark High School Romance

Cruel Intentions
Twisted Betrayal
Sweet Retribution
Charlie
Jackson
Sawyer
*The Hate I Feel^*
*Drew^*

MAZZONE MAFIA SERIES
Dark Mafia Romance

Condemned to Love
Forbidden to Love
Scared to Love
Mazzone Mafia: The Complete Series

THE ACCARDI TWINS
Dark Mafia Romance

CKONY #1 ^
CKONY #2 ^

THE SAINTHOOD (BOYS OF LOWELL HIGH)
Dark HS Reverse Harem Romance

Resurrection
Rebellion
Reign
Revere
The Sainthood: The Complete Series

DIRTY CRAZY BAD DUET
Dark College Reverse Harem Romance

Dirty Crazy Bad - A Prequel Short Story
Dirty Crazy Bad # 1
Dirty Crazy Bad #2

ALL OF ME DUET
Angsty New Adult Romance

Say I'm The One
Let Me Love You
Hold Me Close

*Reeve**
All of Me: The Complete Series

ALINTHIA SERIES
Upper YA/NA Paranormal Romance/Reverse Harem

The Lost Savior
The Secret Heir
The Warrior Princess
The Chosen One
*The Rightful Queen^*

SAVEN SERIES
Young Adult Science Fiction/Paranormal Romance

Saven Deception
Logan
Saven Disclosure
Saven Denial
Saven Defiance
Axton
Saven Deliverance
Saven: The Complete Series

^Release date to be confirmed

* Coming 2023

www.ingramcontent.com/pod-product-compliance
Lightning Source LLC
Chambersburg PA
CBHW032111310726
48972CB00001B/174